PENGUIN BOOKS

THREE TO GET DEADLY

'Janet Evanovich's characters are eccentric and exaggerated, the violence often surreal and the plot dizzily speedy: but she produces as many laughs as anyone writing crime today'
The Times

'Each fast-paced chapter contains another wise-cracking adventure, illustrating a fine sense of the ridiculous. Satirical soap opera with style' *Mail on Sunday*

'Evanovich's series of New Jersey comedy thrillers are among the great joys of contemporary crime fiction . . . *Three to Get Deadly* has all the easy class and wit that you expect to find in the best American TV comedy, but too rarely find in modern fiction' *GQ*

'Stephanie Plum is back in ass-kicking form . . . the pace is car-chase fast, the dialogue sharp and Stephanie – addicted to junk food and red lipstick, and hopeless with men – is utterly delightful' *Cosmopolitan*

'The pace never flags, the humour is grandly surreal, and the dialogue fairly sizzles off the page' *Irish Times*

ABOUT THE AUTHOR

Janet Evanovich now lives in New Hampshire but, like Stephanie Plum, grew up in New Jersey.

She has won many awards for her Stephanie Plum novels, including the Crime Writers' Association John Creasey Award for *One for the Money*, the CWA Last Laugh Award and the Dilys Award for *Two for the Dough* and the CWA Silver Dagger Award for *Three to Get Deadly*. There are now nine novels in the best-selling, chart-topping series.

Janet is also the author of *Visions of Sugar Plums*, the first in her spin-off series of novellas, featuring Stephanie Plum and the enigmatic new character Diesel.

The Stephanie Plum novels

One for the Money

Two for the Dough

Three to get Deadly

Four to Score

High Five

Hot Six

Seven Up

Hard Eight

To the Nines

JANET EVANOVICH

THREE TO GET DEADLY

PENGUIN BOOKS

PENGUIN BOOKS

Published by the Penguin Group
Penguin Books Ltd, 80 Strand, London WC2R 0RL, England
Penguin Putnam Inc., 375 Hudson Street, New York, New York 10014, USA
Penguin Books Australia Ltd, 250 Camberwell Road, Camberwell, Victoria 3124, Australia
Penguin Books Canada Ltd, 10 Alcorn Avenue, Toronto, Ontario, Canada M4V 3B2
Penguin Books India (P) Ltd, 11 Community Centre, Panchsheel Park, New Delhi – 110 017, India
Penguin Books (NZ) Ltd, Cnr Rosedale and Airborne Roads, Albany, Auckland, New Zealand
Penguin Books (South Africa) (Pty) Ltd, 24 Sturdee Avenue, Rosebank 2196, South Africa

Penguin Books Ltd, Registered Offices: 80 Strand, London WC2R 0RL, England

www.penguin.com

First published by in the United States of America by Scribner 1997
First published in Great Britain by Hamish Hamilton 1997
Published in Penguin Books 1997
Reissued in Penguin Books 2004

30

Printed in England by Clays Ltd, St Ives plc

THREE TO GET
DEADLY

CHAPTER

1

It was January in Trenton. The sky was gunmetal gray, and the air sat dead cold on cars and sidewalks. Inside the offices of Vincent Plum, bail bond agent, the atmosphere was no less grim, and I was sweating not from heat but from panic.

"I can't do this," I said to my cousin, Vinnie. "I've never refused a case before, but I can't pick this guy up. Give the paperwork to Ranger. Give it to Barnes."

"I'm not giving this two-bit Failure to Appear to Ranger," Vinnie said. "It's the kind of penny-ante stuff you do. For chrissake, be a professional. You're a bounty hunter. You've been a bounty hunter for five fucking months. What's the big deal?"

"This is Uncle Mo!" I said. "I can't apprehend Uncle Mo. Everyone will hate me. My mother will hate me. My best friend will hate me."

Vinnie slumped his slim, boneless body into the chair behind his desk and rested his head on the padded leather back. "Mo jumped bail. That makes him a slimeball. That's all that counts."

I rolled my eyes so far into the top of my head I almost fell over backward.

Moses Bedemier, better known as Uncle Mo, started selling ice cream and penny candy on June 5, 1958, and has been at it ever since. His store is set on the edge of the burg, a comfy residential chunk of Trenton where houses and minds are proud to be narrow and hearts are generously wide open. I was born and raised in the burg and while my current apartment is approximately a mile outside the burg boundary I'm still tethered by an invisible umbilical. I've been hacking away at the damn thing for years but have never been able to completely sever it.

Moses Bedemier is a solid burg citizen. Over time, Mo and his linoleum have aged, so that both have some pieces chipped at the corners now, and the original colors have blurred from thirty-odd years under fluorescent lights. The yellow brick facade and overhead sheet metal sign advertising the store are dated and weatherbeaten. The chrome and Formica on the stools and countertop have lost their luster. And none of this matters, because in the burg Uncle Mo's is as close as we come to a historic treasure.

And I, Stephanie Plum, 125 pounds, five feet, seven inches, brown-haired, blue-eyed bounty hunter at large, have just been assigned the task of hauling Uncle Mo's revered ass off to jail.

"So what did he do?" I asked Vinnie. "Why was he arrested in the first place?"

"Got caught doing thirty-five in a twenty-five-mile-per-hour zone by Officer Picky . . . better known as Officer Benny Gaspick, fresh out of police academy and so wet behind the ears he doesn't know enough to take Mo's get-out-of-jail-free PBA card and forget the whole thing."

"Bond isn't required on a traffic ticket."

Vinnie planted a pointy-toed patent leather shoe on the corner of his desk. Vinnie was a sexual lunatic, especially enamored with dark-skinned young men wearing nipple rings and pointy-breasted women who owned fourteenth-century torture tools. He was a bail bondsman, which meant he loaned people money to post the bond set by the court. The bond's purpose was to make it economically unpleasant for the suspect to skip town. Once the bond was posted the incarcerated suspect was set free, enabling him to sleep in his own bed while awaiting trial. The price for using Vinnie's service was fifteen percent of the bond and was nonrefundable no matter what the outcome of the charges. If the bailee failed to appear for his court appearance, the court kept Vinnie's money. Not just the fifteen percent profit. The court kept the whole ball of wax, the entire bail bond amount. This never made Vinnie happy.

And that's where I came in. I found the bailee, who was at that point officially a felon, and brought him back into the system. If I found the Failure to Appear, better known as an FTA, in a timely fashion, the court gave Vinnie his cash back. For this fugitive apprehension I received ten percent of the bond amount, and Vinnie was left with a five percent profit.

I'd originally taken the job out of desperation when I'd been laid off (through no fault of my own) as lingerie buyer for E. E. Martin. The alternative to unemployment had been overseeing the boxing machine at the tampon factory. A worthy task, but not something that got me orgasmic.

I wasn't sure why I was still working for Vinnie. I suspected it had something to do with the title. Bounty hunter. It held a certain cachet. Even better, the job didn't require panty hose.

Vinnie smiled his oily smile, enjoying the story he was telling me. "In his misplaced zeal to be Most Hated Cop of the Year, Gaspick delivers a little lecture to Mo on road safety, and while Gaspick is lecturing, Mo squirms in his seat, and Gaspick catches a glimpse of a forty-five stuck in Mo's jacket pocket."

"And Mo got busted for carrying concealed," I said.

"Bingo."

Carrying concealed was frowned upon in Trenton. Permits were issued sparingly to a few jewelers, and judges and couriers. Getting caught carrying concealed illegally was considered unlawful possession of a firearm and was an indictable offense. The weapon was confiscated, bail was set and the bearer of the weapon was shit out of luck.

Of course, this didn't stop a sizable percentage of the population of Jersey from carrying concealed. Guns were bought at Bubba's Gun Shop, inherited from relatives, passed off among neighbors and friends and purchased second-, third- and fourthhand from and by citizens who were fuzzy on the details of gun control. Logic dictated that if the government issued a license to own a gun then it must be okay to put it in your purse. I mean, why else would a person want a gun if not to carry it in her purse. And if it wasn't okay to carry a gun in your purse, then the law was stupid. And no one in Jersey was going to put up with a stupid law.

I was even known, on occasion, to carry concealed. At this very moment I could see Vinnie's ankle holster causing a bulge at the cuff line of his polyester slacks. Not only was he carrying concealed but I'd lay odds his gun wasn't registered.

"This is not a big-time offense," I said to Vinnie. "Not something worth going Failure to Appear."

"Probably Mo forgot he had a court date," Vinnie said. "Probably all you have to do is go remind him."

Hold that thought, I told myself. This might not be such a disaster after all. It was ten o'clock. I could mosey on over to the candy store and talk to Mo. In fact, the more I thought about it, the more I realized my panic had been ungrounded. Mo had no reason to go FTA.

I closed the door on my way out of Vinnie's office, and sidestepped around Connie Rosolli. Connie was the office manager and Vinnie's guard dog. She held Vinnie in the same high esteem one would reserve for slug slime, but she'd worked for Vinnie for a lot of years, and had come to accept that even slug slime was part of God's great scheme.

Connie was wearing fuchsia lipstick, matching nail enamel and a white blouse with big black polka dots. The nail enamel was very cool, but the blouse wasn't a good choice for someone who carried sixty percent of her body weight on her chest. Good thing the fashion police didn't do too many tours of Trenton.

"You aren't going to do it, are you?" she asked. The tone implying that only a dog turd would cause Uncle Mo a moment of grief.

No offense taken. I knew where she lived. We had the same mental zip code. "You mean am I going to talk to Mo? Yeah, I'm going to talk to Mo."

Connie's black eyebrows fused into a straight line of righteous indignation. "That cop had no business arresting Uncle Mo. Everyone knows Uncle Mo would never do anything wrong."

"He was carrying concealed."

"As if that was a crime," Connie said.

"That *is* a crime!"

Lula's head came up from her filing. "What's all the deal about this Uncle Mo, anyway?"

Lula was a former hooker turned file clerk. She'd just recently embarked on a makeover program that included dyeing her hair blond and then straightening it and recurling it into ringlets. The transformation had her looking like a 230-pound black kick-ass Shirley Temple.

"Moses Bedemier," I said. "He runs a candy store on Ferris Street. Very popular person."

"Uh-oh," she said. "I think I know him. He about in his early sixties? Going bald on top? Lotta liver spots? Got a nose looks like a penis?"

"Um, I never really noticed his nose."

Vinnie had given me Uncle Mo's file, which consisted of stapled-together copies of his arrest sheet, his signed bond agreement and a photo. I turned to the photo and stared at Uncle Mo.

Lula stared over my shoulder. "Yup," she said. "That's him all right. That's Old Penis Nose."

Connie was out of her chair. "Are you telling me Uncle Mo was a client? I don't believe that for a second!"

Lula narrowed her eyes and stuck her lip out. "Yo momma."

"Nothing personal," Connie said.

"Hunh," Lula replied, hand on hip.

I zipped my jacket and wrapped my scarf around my neck. "You sure about knowing Uncle Mo?" I asked Lula.

She took one last look at the picture. "Hard to say. You know how all them old white men look alike. Maybe I should come with you to check this dude out in person."

"No!" I shook my head. "Not a good idea."

"You think I can't do this bounty hunter shit?"

Lula hadn't yet embarked on the language makeover.

"Well, of course you can do it," I said. "It's just that this situation is sort of . . . delicate."

"Hell," she said, stuffing herself into her jacket. "I can delicate your ass off."

"Yes, but . . ."

"Anyway, you might need some help here. Suppose he don't want to come peaceful. You might need a big, full-figure woman like me to do some persuading."

Lula and I had crossed paths while I was on my first felon hunt. She'd been a streetwalker, and I'd been street-stupid. I'd unwittingly involved her in the case I was working on, and as a result, one morning I found her battered and bloody on my fire escape.

Lula credited me with saving her life, and I blamed myself

for endangering it. I was in favor of wiping the slate clean, but Lula formed a sort of attachment to me. I wouldn't go so far as to say it was hero worship. It was more like one of those Chinese things where if you save a person's life they belong to you . . . even if you don't want them.

"We're not doing any persuading," I said. "This is Uncle Mo. He sells candy to kids."

Lula had her pocketbook looped over her arm. "I can dig it," she said, following me out the door. "You still driving that old Buick?"

"Yeah. My Lotus is in the shop."

Actually, my Lotus was in my dreams. A couple months ago my Jeep got stolen, and my mother, in a burst of misguided good intentions, strong-armed me into the driver's seat of my uncle Sandor's '53 Buick. Strained finances and lack of backbone had me still peering over the mile-long powder-blue hood, wondering at the terrible acts I must have committed to deserve such a car.

A gust of wind rattled the Fiorello's Deli sign next to Vinnie's office. I pulled my collar up and searched in my pocket for gloves.

"At least the Buick's in good shape," I told Lula. "That's what counts, right?"

"Hunh," Lula said. "Only people who don't have a cool car say things like that. How about the radio. It got a bad radio? It got Dolby?"

"No Dolby."

"Hold on," she said. "You don't expect me to ride around with no Dolby. I need some hot music to get me in the mood to bust ass."

I unlocked the doors to the Buick. "*We are not busting ass*. We're going to *talk* to Uncle Mo."

"Sure," Lula said, settling herself in, giving a disgusted glare to the radio. "I know that."

I drove one block down Hamilton and turned left onto

Rose into the burg. There was little to brighten the neighborhood in January. The blinking twinkle lights and red plastic Santas of Christmas were packed away, and spring was still far in the future. Hydrangea bushes were nothing more than mean brown sticks, lawns were frost-robbed of color and streets were empty of kids, cats, car washers and blaring radios. Windows and doors were shut tight against the cold and gloom.

Even Uncle Mo's felt sterile and unwelcoming as I slowed to a stop in front of the store.

Lula squinted through my side window. "I don't want to rain on your parade," she said, "but I think this sucker's closed."

I parked at the curb. "That's impossible. Uncle Mo never closes. Uncle Mo hasn't been closed a day since he opened in nineteen fifty-eight."

"Well guess what? I'm telling you he's closed now."

I hopped out of Big Blue and walked to Mo's door and looked inside. No lights were on, and Uncle Mo was nowhere to be seen. I tried the door. Locked. I knocked on the door good and loud. Nothing. Damn.

"He must be sick," I said to Lula.

The candy store sat on a corner, facing Ferris Street, with the side of the store running down King. A long line of neat duplexes stretched the length of Ferris, pushing their way to the heart of the burg. King, on the other hand, had fallen on hard times, with most of its duplexes converted to multiple families. The tidy white sheers and starched Martha Washington curtains of the burg weren't in evidence on King. Privacy on King came by way of tacked-up sheets and tattered shades, and from an unpleasant sense that this was no longer a desired community.

"Some scary old lady's looking at us out of the window of that house next door," Lula said.

I looked one house down on Ferris and shivered. "That's

Mrs. Steeger. She was my teacher when I was in the third grade."

"Bet that was fun."

"Longest year of my life."

To this day I got cramps when I had to do long division.

"We should talk to her," I said to Lula.

"Yeah," Lula said. "Nosy old woman like that probably knows lots of stuff."

I hiked my pocketbook higher on my shoulder, and Lula and I marched over and knocked on Mrs. Steeger's door.

The door was opened just far enough for me to see that Mrs. Steeger hadn't changed much over the years. She was still rail thin, with a pinched face and snappy little eyes lying in wait under eyebrows that appeared to have been drawn on with brown marker. She'd been widowed last year. Retired the year before that. She was dressed in a brown dress with little white flowers, stockings and sensible shoes. Her glasses hung from a chain around her neck. Her hair was curled tight, dyed brown. She didn't look like she was adapting to a life of leisure.

I handed her my business card and introduced myself as a fugitive apprehension agent.

"What's that mean?" she wanted to know. "Are you a police officer?"

"Not exactly. I work for Vincent Plum."

"So," she said, considering the information. "You're a bounty hunter."

This was said with the same affection one would have for a drug pusher or child abuser. The tilt of her chin warned of possible disciplinary action, and her attitude implied if I'd mastered long division I might have made something of myself.

"What's this have to do with Moses?" she asked.

"He was arrested on a minor charge and then missed a court appearance. The Plum agency arranged bail, so I need to find Mo and help him set a new date."

"Mo would never do anything wrong," Mrs. Steeger said. God's word.

"Do you know where he is?" I asked.

She drew herself up an extra half inch. "No. And I think it's a shame you can't find anything better to do than to go out harassing good men like Moses Bedemier."

"I'm not harassing him. I'm simply going to help him arrange a new court date."

"Liar, liar, pants on fire," Mrs. Steeger said. "You were a little fibber in the third grade, and you're a little fibber now. Always trying to sneak gum into my classroom."

"Well, thanks anyway," I said to Mrs. Steeger. "Nice seeing you after all these years."

SLAM. Mrs. Steeger closed her door.

"Should of lied," Lula said. "You never learn anything telling the truth like that. Should of told her you worked for the lottery commission, and Mo won a shitload of money."

"Maybe next time."

"Maybe next time we just open the door and start out with some bitch slapping."

I gave Lula a horrified glare.

"Just a suggestion," Lula said.

I stepped over to the next porch and was about to knock when Mrs. Steeger stuck her head out her door again.

"Don't bother," she said. "The Whiteheads are in Florida. Harry always takes his vacation this time of the year. Won't be back for two weeks."

SLAM. She vanished behind the closed door.

"No problem," I said to Lula. "We'll try door number three."

Dorothy Rostowski opened door number three.

"Dorothy?"

"Stephanie?"

"I didn't realize you were living here."

"Almost a year now."

She had a baby on her hip and another in front of the television. She smelled like she'd been knocking back mashed bananas and Chablis.

"I'm looking for Uncle Mo," I said. "I expected he'd be working in the store."

Dorothy shifted the baby. "He hasn't been here for two days. You aren't looking for him for Vinnie, are you?"

"Actually . . ."

"Mo would never do anything wrong."

"Well, sure, but . . ."

"We're just trying to find him on account of he won the lottery," Lula said. "We're gonna lay a whole load of money on his ass."

Dorothy made a disgusted sound and slammed the door closed.

We tried the house next to Dorothy and received the same information. Mo hadn't been at the store for two days. Nothing else was forthcoming, with the exception of some unsolicited advice that I might consider seeking new employment.

Lula and I piled into the Buick and took another look at the bond agreement. Mo listed his address as 605 Ferris. That meant he lived over his store.

Lula and I craned our necks to see into the four second-story windows.

"I think Mo took a hike," Lula said.

Only one way to find out. We got out of the car and walked to the back of the brick building where outdoor stairs led to a second-story porch. We climbed the stairs and knocked on the door. Nothing. We tried the doorknob. Locked. We looked in the windows. Everything was tidy. No sign of Mo. No lights left burning.

"Mo might be dead in there," Lula said. "Or maybe he's sick. Could of had a stroke and be laying on the bathroom floor."

"We are *not* going to break in."

"Would be a humanitarian effort," Lula said.

"And against the law."

"Sometimes these humanitarian efforts go into the gray zone."

I heard footsteps and looked down to see a cop standing at the bottom of the stairs. Steve Olmney. I'd gone to school with him.

"What's going on?" he asked. "We got a complaint from old lady Steeger that someone suspicious was snooping around Uncle Mo's."

"That would be me," I said.

"Where's Mo?"

"We think he might be dead," Lula said. "We think someone better go look to see if he's had a stroke on the bathroom floor."

Olmney came up the stairs and rapped on the door. "Mo?" he yelled. He put his nose to the door. "Doesn't smell dead." He looked in the windows. "Don't see any bodies."

"He's Failure to Appear," I said. "Got picked up on carrying concealed and didn't show in court."

"Mo would never do anything wrong," Olmney said.

I stifled a scream. "Not showing up for a court appearance is wrong."

"Probably he forgot. Maybe he's on vacation. Or maybe his sister in Staten Island got sick. You should check with his sister."

Actually, that sounded like a decent idea.

Lula and I went back to the Buick, and I read through the bond agreement one more time. Sure enough, Mo had listed his sister and given her address.

"We should split up," I said to Lula. "I'll go see the sister, and you can stake out the store."

"I'll stake it out good," Lula said. "I won't miss a thing."

I turned the key in the ignition and pulled away from the curb. "What will you do if you see Mo?"

"I'll snatch the little fucker up by his gonads and squash him into the trunk of my car."

"*No!* You're not authorized to apprehend. If you see Mo, you should get in touch with me right away. Either call me on my cellular phone or else call my pager." I gave her a card with my numbers listed.

"Remember, *no squashing anyone into the trunk of your car!*"

"Sure," Lula said. "I know that."

I dropped Lula at the office and headed for Route 1. It was the middle of the day and traffic was light. I got to Perth Amboy and lined up for the bridge to Staten Island. The roadside leading to the toll booth was littered with mufflers, eaten away from winter salt and rattled loose by the inescapable craters, sinkholes and multilevel strips of macadam patch that composed the bridge.

I slipped into bridge traffic and sat nose to tail with Petrucci's Vegetable Wholesalers and a truck labeled DANGEROUS EXPLOSIVES. I checked a map while I waited. Mo's sister lived toward the middle of the island in a residential area I knew to be similar to the burg.

I paid my toll and inched forward, sucking in a stew of diesel exhaust and other secret ingredients that caught me in the back of the throat. I adjusted to the pollution in less than a quarter of a mile and felt just fine when I reached Mo's sister's house on Crane Street. Adaptation is one of the great advantages to being born and bred in Jersey. We're simply not bested by bad air or tainted water. We're like the catfish with lungs. Take us out of our environment and we can grow whatever body parts we need to survive. After Jersey the rest of the country's a piece of cake. You want to send someone into a fallout zone? Get him from Jersey. He'll be fine.

Mo's sister lived in a pale green duplex with jalousied windows and white-and-yellow aluminum awnings. I parked at the curb and made my way up two flights of cement stairs to the cement stoop. I rang the bell and found myself facing a woman who looked a lot like my relatives on the Mazur side of my family. Good sturdy Hungarian stock. Black hair, black eyebrows and no-nonsense blue eyes. She looked to be in her fifties and didn't seem thrilled to find me on her doorstep.

I gave her my card, introduced myself and told her I was looking for Mo.

Her initial reaction was surprise, then distrust.

"Fugitive apprehension agent," she said. "What's that supposed to mean? What's that got to do with Mo?"

I gave the condensed version by way of explanation. "I'm sure it was just an oversight that Mo didn't appear for his court session, but I need to remind him to reschedule," I told her.

"I don't know anything about this," she said. "I don't see Mo a whole lot. He's always at the store. Why don't you just go to the store."

"He hasn't been at the store for the last two days."

"That doesn't sound like Mo."

None of this sounded like Mo.

I asked if there were other relatives. She said no, not close ones. I asked about a second apartment or vacation house. She said none that she knew of.

I thanked her for her time and returned to my Buick. I looked out at the neighborhood. Not much happening. Mo's ... r was locked up in her house. Probably wondering ... the devil was going on with Mo. Of course there was ... possibility that she was protecting her brother, but my gut instinct said otherwise. She'd seemed genuinely surprised when I'd told her Mo wasn't behind the counter handing out Gummi Bears.

I could watch the house, but that sort of surveillance was tedious and time-consuming, and in this case, I wasn't sure it would be worth the effort.

Besides, I was getting a weird feeling about Mo. Responsible people like Mo didn't forget court dates. Responsible people like Mo worried about that kind of stuff. They lost sleep over it. They consulted attorneys. And responsible people like Mo didn't just up and leave their businesses without so much as a sign in the window.

Maybe Lula was right. Maybe Mo was dead in bed or lying unconscious on his bathroom floor.

I got out of the car and retraced my steps back to the sister's front door.

The door was opened before I had a chance to knock. Two little frown lines had etched themselves into Mo's sister's forehead. "Was there something else?" she asked.

"I'm concerned about Mo. I don't mean to alarm you, but I suppose there's the possibility that he might be sick at home and unable to get to the door."

"I've been standing here thinking the same thing," she said.

"Do you have a key to his apartment?"

"No, and as far as I know no one else does, either. Mo likes his privacy."

"Do you know any of his friends? Did he have a girl-friend?"

"Sorry. We aren't real close like that. Mo is a good brother, but like I said, he's private."

An hour later I was back in the burg. I motored down Ferris and parked behind Lula.

"How's it going?" I asked.

Lula was slouched at the wheel of her red Firebird. "Isn't going at all. Most boring bullshit job I ever had. A person could do this in a coma."

"Anyone stop around to buy candy?"

"A momma and her baby. That's all."

"Did they walk around back?"

"Nope. They just looked in the front door and left."

I glanced at my watch. School would be out soon. There'd be a lot of kids coming by then, but I wasn't interested in kids. I was interested in an adult who might show up to water Mo's plants or retrieve his mail.

"Hang tight here," I said. "I'm going to speak to more neighbors."

"Hang tight, hunh. I'm gonna like freeze to death sitting in this car. This isn't Florida, you know."

"I thought you wanted to be a bounty hunter. This is what bounty hunters do."

"Wouldn't mind doing this if I thought at the end of it all I'd get to shoot someone, but there isn't even any guarantee of that. All I hear's don't do this and don't do that. Can't even stuff the sonovabitch in my trunk if I find him."

I crossed the street and spoke to three more neighbors. Their replies were standard. They had no idea where Mo could be, and they thought I had a lot of nerve implying he was a felon.

A teenager answered in the fourth house. We were dressed almost identically. Doc Martens, jeans, flannel shirt over T-shirt, too much eye makeup, lots of brown curly hair. She was fifteen pounds slimmer and fifteen years younger. I didn't envy her youth, but I did have second thoughts about the dozen doughnuts I'd picked up on my way through the burg, which even as we spoke were calling to me from the backseat of my car.

I gave her my card, and her eyes widened.

"A bounty hunter!" she said. "*Cool!*"

"Do you know Uncle Mo?"

"Sure I know Uncle Mo. Everybody knows Uncle Mo." She leaned forward and lowered her voice. "He do something wrong? Are you after Uncle Mo?"

"He missed a court date on a minor charge. I want to remind him to reschedule."

"That is like amazing. When you find him are you going to rough him up and lock him in the trunk of your car?"

"*No!*" What was with this trunk business? "I just want to talk to him."

"I bet he did something really terrible. I bet you want him for cannibalism."

Cannibalism? The man sold candy. What would he want with fingers and toes? This kid had great taste in shoes, but her mind was a little scary. "Do you know anything about Mo that might be helpful? He have any close friends in the neighborhood? Have you seen him recently?"

"I saw him a couple days ago in the store."

"Maybe you could keep a lookout for me. My numbers are on the card. You see Mo or anyone suspicious you give me a call."

"Like I'd almost be a bounty hunter?"

"Almost."

I jogged back to Lula. "Okay," I told her, "you can return to the office. I found a replacement. The kid across the street is going to spy for us."

"Good thing too. This was getting old."

I followed Lula to the office and called my friend Norma, who worked at the DMV. "Got a name," I told her. "Need a plate and a car."

"What's the name?"

"Moses Bedemier."

"Uncle Mo?"

"That's the one."

"I'm not giving you information on Uncle Mo!"

I gave her the bull about rescheduling, which was sounding very tired.

Computer keys clicked in the background. "If I find out you harmed a single hair on Uncle Mo's head I'll never give you another plate."

"I'm not going to hurt him," I said. "I never hurt anyone."

"What about that guy you killed last August? And what about when you blew up the funeral home?"

"Are you going to give me this information, or what?"

"He owns a ninety-two Honda Civic. Blue. You got a pencil? I'll read off the plate."

"Oh boy," Lula said, peering over my shoulder. "Looks like we got more clues. We gonna look for this car?"

"Yes." And then we'd look for a key to the apartment. Everyone worries about getting locked out. If you don't have someone in the neighborhood you can trust with your key, you hide it nearby. You carefully place it over the doorjamb, put it in a fake rock next to your foundation or slide it under the doormat.

I wasn't about to do forced entry, but if I found a key . . .

"I haven't had any lunch," Lula said. "I can't keep working if I don't have lunch."

I pulled the bag of doughnuts out of my big black leather shoulder bag, and we dug in.

"Things to do. Places to go," I said minutes later, shaking powdered sugar off my shirt, wishing I'd stopped at two doughnuts.

"I'm going with you," Lula said. "Only this time I drive. I got a big motherfucker stereo in my car."

"Just don't drive too fast. I don't want to get picked up by Officer Gaspick."

"Uh-oh," Lula said. "You carrying concealed like Uncle Mo?"

Not at the moment. My .38 Smith & Wesson was at home, sitting on my kitchen counter, in the brown bear cookie jar. Guns scared the hell out of me.

We piled into Lula's red Firebird and headed for Ferris with rap rattling windows in our wake.

"Maybe you should turn it down," I yelled to Lula after a couple blocks. "I'm getting arrhythmia."

Lula punched the air. "Un ha, ha, ha, haa."

"Lula!"

She cut her eyes to me. "You say something?"

I edged the volume back. "You're going to go deaf."

"Hunh," Lula said.

We cruised down Ferris and looked for blue Civics, but there were none parked near the store. We scoped out the cross streets and parallel streets on either side. No blue Civics. We parked at the corner of Ferris and King and walked the alley behind the store, looking into all the garages. No blue Civics. The single-car garage that sat at the edge of the small yard backing off from the candy store was empty.

"He's flown the coop," Lula said. "I bet he's in Mexico laughing his ass off, figuring we're out here doing the two-step through a bunch of bullshit garages."

"What about the dead on the bathroom floor theory?"

Lula was wearing a hot-pink down ski jacket and white fake-fur knee-high boots. She pulled the jacket collar up around her neck and glanced up at Mo's second-story back porch. "We would of found his car. And if he was dead he would of started to smell by now."

That's what I thought, too.

"Course, he could have locked himself in the ice cream freezer," Lula said. "Then he wouldn't smell on account of he'd be frozen. Probably that didn't happen though because Mo would have had to take the ice cream out before he could fit himself in, and we already looked in the store window, and we didn't see a lot of ice cream cartons sitting around melting themselves into next year. Of course, Mo could have eaten all the ice cream first."

Mo's garage was wood and shingle with an old-fashioned double wood door that swung open on hinges and had been left ajar. The garage accessed from the alley, but it had a side door toward the rear that led to a short cement side-walk running to the back of the store.

The interior of the garage was dark and musty, the walls lined with boxes of Tastee Straws, napkins, cleanser, Drygas, Del Monte fruit cup, Hershey's syrup and 10W40 motor oil. Newspapers were stacked in the corner, awaiting recycling.

Mo was a popular person and presumably a trusting soul, but leaving his garage doors open when his garage was filled with store supplies seemed like an excessive burden on human nature. Possibilities were that he left in a hurry and was too distracted to think about the door. Or perhaps he wasn't planning to return. Or maybe he'd been forced to leave, and his abductors had other things on their minds be-sides garage doors.

Of all the possibilities I liked the last one the least.

I pulled a flashlight out of my pocketbook and gave it to Lula with instructions to search the garage for a house key.

"I'm like a bloodhound on a scent when it comes to house keys," Lula said. "Don't you worry about that house key. It's as good as found."

Mrs. Steeger glared at us from the window next door. I smiled and waved, and she stepped back. Most likely en route to the telephone to call the cops on me again.

There was a small yard stuck between the store and the garage, and there were no signs of recreational use of the yard. No swing sets, grills, rusting lawn chairs. Only the sidewalk broke the scrubby grass and hard-packed dirt. I followed the sidewalk to the store's back entry and looked in the trash cans lining the brick wall. All cans were full, garbage neatly bagged in plastic sacks. Some empty card-board cartons had been stacked beside the garbage cans. I toed through the area around the cans and the boxes, look-ing for some sign of a hidden key. I found nothing. I felt over the doorjamb on the back door that led to the candy store. I walked up the stairs and ran my hand under the railing on the small back porch. I knocked on the door one more time and looked in the window.

Lula emerged from the garage and crossed the yard. She climbed the stairs and proudly handed me a key.

"Am I good, or what?" she said.

CHAPTER

2

I plunged the key into the Yale lock on Mo's door, and the door opened.

"Mo?" I yelled.

No answer.

Lula and I looked around. No cops. No kids. No nosy neighbors. Our eyes met, and we silently slid into the apartment. I did a fast walk-through, noting that Mo wasn't dead in the bedroom, bathroom, kitchen or living room. There was food in the refrigerator and clothes in his bedroom closet.

The apartment was clean and tidy. He didn't have an answering machine, so I couldn't snoop on his messages. I riffled through drawers but didn't find an address book. There were no hastily scribbled notes left lying around, detailing plane reservations or hotel accommodations. No brochures advertising Disney World.

I was about to trip downstairs and search the store when Carl Costanza appeared on the back porch. Carl was one of my favorite cops. We'd done communion together, among other things.

"I should have known," Carl said, standing flat-footed, gravity pulling hard on his gun and utility belt. "I should have known when the call came in that it would be you."

"I gotta go," Lula said, easing past Carl, tiptoeing down the stairs. "I can see you two want to have a conversation. Wouldn't want to be an interference."

"Lula," I shouted, "don't you dare leave without me!"

Lula was already rounding the corner of the building. "I might even be coming down with a cold, and I wouldn't want to pass that on to you-all."

"Well," Carl said, "want to tell me about this?"

"You mean about Lula and me being in Uncle Mo's apartment?"

Carl grimaced. "You're going to make up some ridiculous story, aren't you?"

"Mo's FTA. I came here looking for him, and his door was wide open. Must have been the wind."

"Uh-huh."

"And then Lula and I got worried. What if Mo was injured? Like maybe he'd fallen in the bathroom and hit his head and was unconscious."

Carl held his hands up. "Stop. I don't want to hear any more. Are you finished with your search?"

"Yes."

"Did you find Mo unconscious on the bathroom floor?"

"No."

"You're going home now, right?"

"Right." Carl was a good guy, but I thought breaking into Mo's store while Carl was looking over my shoulder might be pressing my luck, so I closed Mo's door and made sure the lock clicked.

When I got out to the street, Lula and the Firebird were nowhere to be seen. I put my head down and walked to my parents' house, where I was pretty sure I could mooch a ride.

My parents lived deep in the burg in a narrow duplex that on a cold day like this would smell like chocolate pudding cooking on the stove. The effect was similar to Lorelei, singing to all those sailors, sucking them in so they'd crash on the rocks.

I walked three blocks down Ferris, and turned onto Green. The raw cold ate through my shoes and gloves and made my ears ache. I was wearing a Gore-Tex shell with a heavy fleece liner, a black turtleneck and a sweatshirt advertising my alma mater, Douglass College. I pulled the jacket hood over my head and tightened the drawstring. Very dorky, but at least my ears wouldn't crack off like icicles.

"What a nice surprise," my mother said when she opened the door to me. "And we're having roast chicken for dinner. Lots of gravy. Just like you like it."

"I can't stay. I have plans."

"What plans? A date?"

"Not a date. These are work plans."

Grandma Mazur peeked around the kitchen door. "Oh boy, you're on a case. Who is it this time?"

"No one you know," I said. "It's something small. Really, I'm doing it as a favor to Vinnie."

"I heard old Tom Gates got arrested for spitting in line at Social Security. Is it Tom Gates you're after?" Grandma asked.

"No. It's not Tom Gates."

"How about that guy they were talking about in the paper today? The one who pulled that motorist through his car window by his necktie."

"That was just a misunderstanding," I said. "They were in dispute over a parking space."

"Well, who then?" Grandma wanted to know.

"Moses Bedemier."

My mother made the sign of the cross. "Holy mother of God, you're hunting down Uncle Mo." She threw her hands into the air. "The man is a saint!"

"He's not a saint. He got arrested for carrying concealed, and then he didn't show up for a court appearance. So now I have to find him and get him rescheduled."

"Carrying concealed," my mother said, rolling her eyes. "What moron would arrest a good man like Mo Bedemier for carrying concealed?"

"Officer Gaspick."

"I don't know any Officer Gaspick," my mother said.

"He's new."

"That's what comes of getting new cops," Grandma said. "No telling what they might do. I bet that gun was planted on Mo. I saw a TV show the other night about how when cops want a promotion they plant drugs on people so they can arrest them. I bet that's what happened here. I bet that Officer Gaspick planted a gun on Mo. Everybody knows Mo would never do anything wrong."

I was getting tired of hearing how Mo would never do anything wrong. In fact, I was beginning to wonder what sort of person this wonderful Uncle Mo really was. It seemed to me everyone knew him, but no one knew him.

My mother had her hands up in supplication. "How will I ever explain this? What will people say?"

"They'll say I'm doing my job," I told my mother.

"Your job! You work for your no-good cousin. If it isn't bad enough you go around shooting people, now you're hunting down Uncle Mo as if he was a common criminal."

"I only shot *one* person! And Uncle Mo *is* a common criminal. He broke the law."

"Course it wasn't one of those laws we care much about," Grandma said, weighing the crime.

"Has Mo ever been married?" I asked. "Does he have a girlfriend?"

"Of course not," my grandmother said.

"What do you mean, of course not? What's wrong with him?"

31

My mother and my grandmother looked at each other. Obviously they'd never thought of it in those terms before.

"I guess he's sort of like a priest," Grandma Mazur finally said. "Like he's married to the store."

Oh boy. Saint Mo, the celibate candyman . . . better known as Old Penis Nose.

"Not that he doesn't know how to have a good time," Grandma said. "I heard him tell one of those lightbulb jokes, once. Nothing blue, though. He would never say anything off-color. He's a real gentleman."

"Do you know anything about him?" I asked. "Does he go to church? Does he belong to the VFW?"

"Well, I don't know," Grandma said. "I just know him from the candy store."

"When was the last time you talked to him?"

"Must have been a couple months ago. We stopped to buy ice cream on the way home from shopping. Remember that, Ellen?"

"It was before Christmas," my mother said.

I made hand gestures for her to elaborate. "And?"

"There's no more," she said. "We went in. We talked about weather. We got ice cream and left."

"Mo looked okay?"

"He looked like he always looks," my mother said. "Maybe a little less hair, a little more of a roll around his middle. He was wearing a white shirt that said UNCLE MO over the pocket, just like always."

"So about the chicken?" my mother wanted to know.

"Rain check," I said. "I need a ride to Vinnie's. Can someone give me a ride?"

"Where's your car?" Grandma asked. "Was your car stolen again?"

"It's parked at Vinnie's. It's sort of a long story."

My mother took her coat out of the hall closet. "I guess I can give you a ride. I need to go to the store anyway."

The phone rang, and Grandma Mazur answered.

"Yep," she said. "Yep. Yep. Yep." Her face wrinkled into a frown. "I hear you," she answered.

"Well, if that isn't something," she said when she got off. "That was Myra Biablocki. She said she was talking to Emma Rodgers and Emma told her she heard Stephanie was on a manhunt to bring down Uncle Mo. Myra said she thought it was a sad day when a person hasn't anything better to do than to make trouble for a good man like Moses Bedemier."

"Your cousin Maureen just got a job at the button factory," my mother said to me. "They're probably still hiring."

"I don't want to work at the button factory. I like my job just fine."

The phone rang again, and we all looked at each other.

"Maybe it's a wrong number," Grandma Mazur offered.

My mother brushed past Grandma and snatched at the phone. "Yes?" Her mouth pinched into a thin line. "Moses Bedemier is *not* above the law," she said. "I suggest you get the facts right before spreading gossip. And for that matter, if I were you, I'd clean my front windows before I took the time to talk on the phone."

"Must be Eleanor, down the street," Grandma said. "I noticed her windows, too."

Life was simple in the burg. Sins were absolved by the Catholic Church, dirty windows were an abomination to the neighborhood, gossip greased the wheel of life and you'd better be damned careful what you said face-to-face to a woman about her daughter. No matter if it was true.

My mother got off the phone, wrapped a scarf around her head and took her pocketbook and keys off the hall table. "Are you coming with us?" she asked Grandma Mazur.

"I got some TV shows I've gotta watch," Grandma said. "And besides, someone's got to take care of the phone calls."

My mother shuddered. "Give me strength."

Five minutes later she dropped me off in front of Vinnie's.

"Think about the button factory," she said. "I hear they pay good. And you'd get benefits. Health insurance."

"I'll think about it," I said. But neither of us was paying much attention to what I said. We were both staring at the man leaning against my car.

"Isn't that Joe Morelli?" my mother asked. "I didn't know things were still friendly between you."

"It isn't, and it never was," I said, which was sort of a fib. Morelli and I had a history that ranged from almost friendly, to frighteningly friendly, to borderline murderous. He'd taken my virginity when I was sixteen, and at eighteen I'd tried to run him down with my father's Buick. Those two incidents pretty much reflected the tone of our ongoing relationship.

"Looks like he's waiting for you."

I blew out some air. "Lucky me."

Morelli was a cop now. Plainclothes. A misnomer for Morelli, because he's lean-hipped and hard-muscled, and there's nothing plain about the way he fits a pair of Levi's. He's two years older than me, five inches taller, has a paper-thin scar slicing through his right eyebrow and an eagle tattooed onto his chest. The eagle is left over from a hitch in the navy. The scar is more recent.

I got out of the car and pasted a big phony smile on my mouth. "Gosh, what a terrific surprise."

Morelli grinned. "Nice lie."

"I can't imagine what you mean by that."

"You've been avoiding me."

The avoiding had been mutual. Morelli had given me the big rush back in November and then all of a sudden . . . nothing.

"I've been busy," I said.

"So I hear."

I gave him a raised eyebrow.

"Two suspicious conduct complaints in one day, plus breaking and entering. You must be going for some sort of personal record," Morelli said.

"Costanza has a big mouth."

"You were lucky it was Costanza. If it had been Gaspick you'd be calling Vinnie for bail right now."

We were caught in a gust of wind, and we hunkered down into our jackets.

"Can I talk to you off the record?" I asked Morelli.

"Shit," Morelli said. "I hate when you start a conversation like this."

"There's something strange about Uncle Mo."

"Oh boy."

"I'm serious!"

"Okay," Morelli said. "So what have you got?"

"A feeling."

"If anyone else said that to me I'd walk away."

"Mo's gone FTA on a carrying charge. It would have gotten him a fine and a slap on the hand. It doesn't make sense."

"Life never makes sense."

"I've been out looking for him. He's nowhere. His car is gone, but his garage door was left open. There are dry goods in the garage. Things he wouldn't want stolen. It doesn't feel right. His store has been closed up for two days. No one knows where he is. His sister doesn't know. His neighbors don't know."

"What did you find in his apartment?"

"Clothes in the closet. Food in the fridge."

"Any sign of struggle?"

"None."

"Maybe he needed to go off to think," Morelli said. "Did he have an attorney?"

"Waived an attorney."

"I think you're jumping to conclusions."

I shrugged. "Maybe, but it still feels strange."

"Out of character for Mo."

"Yeah."

Mrs. Turkevich came out of Fiorello's Deli carrying a grocery bag.

I nodded to her. "Pretty cold today."

"Hmmmph," she said.

"Listen, it's not my fault!" I told her. "I'm just doing my job."

The grin widened on Morelli's face. "Us crime stoppers have a tough life, huh?"

"Are you still working vice?"

"I'm working homicide. Temporarily."

"Is that a promotion?"

"It's more like lateral movement."

I wasn't sure I could see Morelli as a homicide cop. Morelli liked to get out there and make things happen. Homicide was a more cerebral, reactive position.

"Was there a reason for this visit?" I asked.

"I was in the area. Thought I'd see how things were going."

"You mean things like Moses Bedemier?"

"You need to be more careful. Mo has some very protective, very noisy neighbors."

I held my coat collar tight to my neck. "I don't get it. What's so great about this guy?"

Morelli did a palms up. "I guess he's just one of those lovable types. Friends with everyone."

"What I'm finding is that he's friends with no one. He's a very private person. Doesn't even confide in his sister. My grandmother says it's like he's married to the store. Like a priest."

"A lot of people let their work take over their life. It's the American way," Morelli said.

Morelli's pager beeped.

"Christ," Morelli said. "I hope this is something horrible.

A decapitation or maybe a bullet-riddled body found in a Dumpster. Homicide in Trenton is like watching grass grow. We just don't have enough good ones to go around."

I opened the door to my car and slid behind the wheel. "Let me know if it turns out to be Mo."

Morelli had his own keys in hand. His black Toyota 4x4 was parked directly behind me. "Try to stay out of trouble."

I drove off wondering what to do next. I'd covered all of the information given on Mo's bond agreement. I'd canvassed the neighborhood, searched his apartment, spoken to his only sister.

After ten minutes of cruising I found myself in the parking lot of my apartment building. The building and the lot were sterile in January. Brick and macadam unsoftened by summer shrubbery. Leaden Jersey sky, dark enough for the streetlights to blink on.

I got out of the car and walked head down to the building's back entrance, pushed through the double glass doors and was grateful for the sudden warmth.

I stepped into the elevator and punched the button for the second floor, wondering what I'd missed in my search for Bedemier. Usually something popped up in the initial investigation . . . a girlfriend, a hobby, a favorite bakery or liquor store. Nothing had popped up today.

The elevator doors opened, and I walked the short distance down the hall, planning out phone calls. I could check on Mo's bank account to see if there were any recent withdrawals. I could check his credit rating. Sometimes a credit check turned up hidden problems. I could run down utilities accounts on a possible second home. I could call Sue Ann Grebek, who knew everything about everyone.

I unlocked my apartment door, stepped into the quiet foyer and took stock of my apartment. My hamster, Rex, was sleeping in the soup can in his glass cage. There were no lights blinking on my answering machine. There were no sounds of big, hairy, snaggle-toothed guys scrambling to hide under my bed.

I dumped my pocketbook on the kitchen counter and draped my jacket over a chair. I poured some milk into a mug, nuked it for two minutes and dumped a couple spoons of instant hot chocolate mix into the hot milk. I added two marshmallows, and while they were getting gooey I made myself a peanut butter sandwich on mushy, worthless white bread.

I took all this, plus my cordless phone, to the dining room table and dialed Sue Ann.

"Stephanie, Stephanie, Stephanie," Sue Ann said. "My phone's been ringing off the hook. Everybody's talking about how you're out to get Uncle Mo."

"I'm not out to *get* Uncle Mo. He needs to reschedule a court date. It's no big deal."

"So why is everybody in such a snit?"

"You tell me."

"I don't know," Sue Ann said. "Not much to tell. Everybody likes him. He minds his own business. He's nice to the kids."

"There must be something. Haven't you ever heard any rumors?"

"Do you care if they're true?"

"Not at all."

"So, in other words, you're looking for unsubstantiated dirt."

"Exactly."

Silence.

"Well?" I asked.

"My niece says sometimes Mo's store smells like dookey."

"Yuk."

"That's about it," Sue Ann said.

"That's not much."

"He's a saint. What can I say?"

"Saints don't smell like dookey," I told her.

"Maybe old ones do."

After I talked to Sue Ann I ate my sandwich and drank my cocoa and thought about Moses Bedemier. His apartment had been neat, and his furniture had been worn but comfortable. Sort of like mine. The television set was the focal point of the living room. The *TV Guide* on the coffee table had been a week old. The food in the fridge had been simple. Lunch meat, bread, juice, milk.

Mo had been living alone for a lot of years, and I suspected his life relied heavily on routine. No real surprises in his apartment. The one note of whimsy had been the movie magazines. A stack of them in the bedroom. Moses Bedemier must have read himself to sleep with soap opera gossip.

I put in a call to my cousin Bunnie at the credit bureau, and drew another blank. There'd been nothing derogatory or recent under either personal or business files.

I tipped back in my chair and stared aimlessly across the room. The window glass was black and reflective. Occasionally headlights flashed into the parking lot below. Car doors slammed. My neighbors were returning from a hard day at whatever.

Mo was missing, and I hadn't a clue and I didn't know how to go about getting one. I'd run all the usual drills. What was left was to wait. And waiting wasn't my strong suit.

I carted my dishes back to the kitchen and thought some more about Uncle Mo. The problem with finding a missing person is that they could be missing very far away. Here I am looking all around Trenton for Moses Bedemier, and he could be in Guadeloupe wearing thick glasses and a fake nose. Truth is, if he was in Guadeloupe I was out of luck, so best not to think about it. Better to assume Mo is close to home, and then I can feel hopeful.

Most of the time people stay close to home anyway.

They'd be much better off if they ran far away, but far away doesn't feel safe. Home feels safe. Sooner or later most FTAs touch base with their relatives, girlfriends, neighborhood cronies. And usually it's sooner rather than later.

I exchanged my flannel shirt for a Rangers jersey and zapped the television on. Probably I should make more phone calls, but the Rangers were playing and priorities were priorities.

My alarm rang at 7 A.M. I slammed my hand on the off button and peered at the clock, wondering why I had set the thing for such an ungodly hour. There was no sign of the sun anywhere, and rain pinged against my windowpane. Even at the best of times, morning is not my favorite part of day, and this wasn't nearly the best of times.

The next time I awoke it was eight-thirty. Rain still slashed at my window, but at least the sky had lightened from black to gray. I dragged myself out of bed and into the bathroom and stood under the shower for a while. I thought about Mel Gibson and Joe Morelli and tried to decide who had the best butt. Then I thought about Mike Richter, the goalie for the Rangers, because he was no slouch either.

By the time I was towel-drying my hair I'd gone from Richter to Uncle Mo. The conclusion I reached about Uncle Mo was that I'd dead-ended. Intuition told me Uncle Mo hadn't gone far and would eventually surface. Unfortunately, the word "eventually" was not favored in the bounty hunter vocabulary. Eventually did not pay this month's rent.

I gassed my hair with some maximum-hold hair spray, dressed in my usual uniform of jeans and flannel shirt and snapped my bedroom curtains open.

I chanted Rain, rain, go away, come again some other day. But the rain didn't go away, so I revisited my dresser and added thick socks and a sweatshirt to my outfit.

For lack of something better to do, I took myself down to the office. On the way, I cruised past Blue Ribbon Used Cars and wistfully glanced over the lot. Every morning I got up and hoped the car fairy had visited me overnight. Every morning I was disappointed. Maybe it was time to take matters into my own hands.

I parked at the curb and squinted through the rain at the lineup of cars. All very boring . . . except for a little blue Nissan pickup at the end of the lot. The little blue pickup was CUTE. I got out to take a closer look. New paint. Bench seat, slightly worn but not torn. Standard transmission.

A man in a yellow slicker ran over to me. "Want to buy this car?"

"How much?"

"For you? We can make a deal. It's an eighty-four. Runs like a top."

I looked in my checkbook. "I probably can't afford it."

"Hey," he said. "Your credit's good here. We can finance it for you. You'll hardly notice the payments."

"I'd have to take it on a test drive."

"Hold on a minute, and I'll pop some plates on for you."

I did a four-block test drive and I was sold. So I'd give up eating oranges. And I'd cut back on movie rentals. The sacrificing would be worth it. I'd have a truck!

Lula glanced up from the files when I slogged through the door, dripping water on the utility-grade carpet. "Hope you didn't spend a lot of time on your hair this morning," she said.

I took a swipe at the wet mess with my hand. "Beauty is in the eye of the beholder."

"Hah," Lula replied. "If that isn't some load of cocky doody."

"Is the man in?" I asked Connie.

"Not yet."

I slouched back on the brown Naugahyde couch. "I'm not

having any luck with Uncle Mo, and I need money. Don't suppose you'd have any quickies?"

"Only got one Failure to Appear yesterday, and it's strictly chump change. Stuart Baggett." She took a manila folder from her "in" box and flipped the file open. "Age twenty-two. White male Caucasian. Five feet six. Went on a drunken late-night joyride three weeks ago with two of his buddies and shot up fourteen parked cars. Did it with an air rifle. Missed his court date and is now a fugitive . . . not to mention an idiot. Two of the cars he shot up were unoccupied police cars."

I was surprised anyone noticed the damage on the cop cars. Trenton's blue-and-whites had not gone gently into the night. Trenton's blue-and-whites all looked like they'd survived Bosnia.

I took the folder from Connie.

"He lives on Applegate with his parents," she said. "Works at the hot dog place at the mall. Looks like his mother put up the bond."

I dialed his home phone and got his mother. I asked if Stuart was working today and was told he was working until four.

"I could use to go to the mall," Lula said. "I could use to take a break, and then I could watch your bounty huntering technique when you make this apprehension."

"There won't be any technique to watch," I said. "This is just some stupid guy who got drunk and did a stupid stunt. Either he forgot his date, or else he was too embarrassed to show up at court."

"Yeah, but you're gonna finesse him, right? You're gonna pull some bogus shit on him and lure him out to the parking lot where we cuff him and kick his ass into the car."

"I'm going to very nicely inform him of his error and request that he accompany me to the station to reschedule his court date."

"They never gonna make a TV series out of this job," Lula said.

"If you're going near Macy's get me some nail polish. Something real red," Connie said.

I dropped the file into my big black shoulder bag and zipped my jacket. Lula buttoned herself into an ankle-length dark brown oiled canvas duster and settled a matching brown leather cowboy hat on her head.

"Do I look like a bounty hunter or what?" she said.

I just hoped poor Stuart Baggett didn't fall over dead at the sight of her.

The door opened and Ranger stepped in from the rain.

Ranger had been my mentor when I'd started in the business and was one very bad bounty hunter. In this case, bad meaning ultracool. He'd been one of those army guys who went around disguised as the night, eating tree bark and beetles, scaring the bejeezus out of emerging third-world insurgents. He was a civilian now, of sorts, sometimes working for Vinnie as an apprehension agent. He supposedly lived in the 'hood among his Cuban relatives, and he knew things I'd never, ever know.

He wore his black hair slicked back into a ponytail, dressed in black and khaki, had a washboard belly, cast-iron biceps and the reflexes of a rattler.

His mouth twitched into a smile at the sight of Lula in her Wild West garb. He acknowledged my presence with eye contact and an almost imperceptible nod, which was the Ranger equivalent to a double-cheek kiss.

"Congratulations," I said to him. "I heard you captured Jesus Rodrigues." Jesus Rodrigues skipped out on a $500,000 bond and was howling-dog crazy. Ranger always got the biggies. Fine by me. I don't have a death wish.

"Had some luck," Ranger said, pulling a police body receipt from his jacket pocket—the body receipt certifying that Ranger had delivered a wanted body to the authorities.

He brushed past us on his way to Connie's desk, and I thought Lula would keel over on the spot. She clapped a hand to her heart and staggered out the door after me.

"Gives me a fit every time he comes in," she confided. "You get close to that man, and it's like being close to a lightning strike. Like all the little hairs are standing on end all over your body."

"Sounds like you've been watching *X-Files*."

"Hmm," Lula said, eyeing the key chain. "Maybe we should take my car again. That Buick you drive don't say 'Law Enforcement,' you know what I'm saying? It ain't no Starsky and Hutch car. What you need is to work on your image. You need one of these bad-ass coats. You need a car with real wheels. You need to be a blonde. I'm telling you honey, blond is where it's at."

"I have a truck," I said, gesturing to the Nissan. "Bought it this morning." After signing the papers I'd gotten my father to drive back with me, so he could take the Buick home, and I could go with my new pickup. You're making a mistake, he said. Japs don't know how to make cars for Americans. This truck isn't half the car the Buick is.

And that was exactly why I preferred the truck . . . it was half the car the Buick was.

"Isn't this cute as a bug," Lula said. "A baby truck!" She looked in the window. "I don't suppose you'd let me drive. I always wanted to drive one of these itty-bitty trucks."

"Well, sure," I said, handing her the keys. "I guess that'd be okay."

Lula cranked the engine over and pulled away from the curb. The rain had turned sleety and shavings of ice slapped against the windshield. Chunks of slush stuck to the wipers and tracked across the arc of cleared glass.

I looked at the snapshot attached to the bond papers and memorized the face. Didn't want to nab the wrong person. I rooted through my pocketbook and did a fast paraphernalia inventory. I was carrying defense spray, which was a big no-no in a crowded mall. And I carried a stun gun, which on close examination turned out to need a new battery. My two pairs of cuffs were in working order, and I had an almost full can of hair spray. Okay, probably I wasn't the world's best-equipped bounty hunter. But then what did I really need to bring in an old guy with a nose that looked like a penis and a loser hot dog vendor?

"We gotta be professional about this," Lula said, aiming us toward Route 1. "We need a plan."

"How about we get the nail polish first, then we get the guy?"

"Yeah, but how are we going to do this? We can't just stand in line, and when it's our turn we say, 'Two chili dogs to go, and you're under arrest.' "

"It's not that complicated. I simply take him aside, show him my identification and explain the procedure to him."

"You think he's gonna stand still for that? This here's a fugitive we're talking about."

Lula gunned the little truck and hopped over a lane. We spun slush at a few cautious drivers and skipped back into line. The heater was going full blast, and I could feel my eyebrows starting to smoke.

"So what do you think?" I asked Lula. "Drives good, huh? And it's got a great heater."

Brake lights flashed in front of us, red smears beyond the beat of the wipers, and Lula silently stared ahead.

"Lula?"

No response.

"Uh, those cars are stopped ahead," I said, not wanting to offend, but suspecting Lula might be having an out-of-body experience.

She bobbed her head. "Not that I'm afraid of no fugitive . . ."

"CARS!" I yelled. "STOPPED CARS!"

Lula's eyes popped open, and she stomped on the brakes. "Holy shit!"

The Nissan skidded forty feet and careened onto the shoulder, missing a van by half an inch. We did a one-eighty and sat facing traffic.

"Light in the back," Lula said. "You might want to put some weight over the wheels."

My first choice of ballast would be a 230-pound file clerk. "Maybe I should drive."

"I'm okay now," Lula said, easing back into traffic. "It's just I've never been along when you actually apprehended someone."

"It's like picking up laundry. You go to the dry cleaner. You show him your ticket. You take your stuff home. Only in this case, we take the stuff to the police station."

"I know my way around the police station," Lula said.

CHAPTER

3

Lula and I parked at the mall entrance nearest the hot dog stand and hustled, under low gray skies, through the rain and sleet and slush. We marched straight across the mall to Macy's, with people walking into walls, mouths agape at Lula in her duster.

"Uh-oh, look at this," Lula said. "They got pocketbooks on sale here. I'd be fine carrying that little red one with the gold chain."

We paused to look at the red pocketbook and to test-drive it on Lula's shoulder.

"Hard to tell with this big coat on," Lula said.

A salesperson had been hovering. "If you care to take the coat off I'd be happy to hold it for you."

"I sure would like to," Lula said, "but it might not be a good idea. We're bounty hunters after a man, and I got a gun on under this coat."

"Bounty hunters?" the woman said on a gasp. The term synonymous with "lunatic vermin."

I slipped the pocketbook off Lula's shoulder and put it back on the counter. I grabbed Lula by the elbow and yanked her after me, "You don't really have a gun under that coat, do you?"

"A woman's got to protect herself."

I was afraid to ask what sort of gun she was carrying. Probably an assault rifle or a military-issue rocket launcher.

"We need to get nail polish for Connie," I told her. "Something red."

Lula stopped at the fragrance counter and squirted herself with a tester. "What do you think?"

"If it doesn't wear off by the time we get back to the truck, you're taking a bus home."

She tried another one. "This any better?"

"No more perfume! They're making my nose clog up."

"Boy, no pocketbooks, no perfume. You don't know much about shopping, do you?"

"What do you like in nail polish?" I held two colors out for her opinion.

"The one on the left is serious red. Looks like someone opened a vein and bottled it. Dracula'd go ape shit for that red."

I supposed if it was good enough for Dracula, it was good enough for Connie.

I bought the nail enamel, and then we dallied in lipsticks, testing a few on the backs of our hands, not finding any worthy of purchase.

We crossed the mall and took a moment to scope out the hot dog place. Thanks to the weather and the time of day, the mall was relatively empty. That was good. We'd make less of a spectacle of ourselves and Stuart. There were no customers buying hot dogs. One person worked the counter. That one person was Stuart Baggett, right down to his little plastic name tag.

What I needed here was a pimpled skinhead. Or a big

nasty ogre-type guy. I needed an arrest where the lines were clearly drawn. I didn't want another Mo fiasco. I wanted bad man against the good bounty hunter.

What I had was Stuart Baggett, five feet, six inches tall, with freshly cut sandy blond hair and eyes like a cocker spaniel. I did a mental grimace. I was going to look like an idiot arresting this guy.

"Remember," I said to Lula, "I do the talking. And most of all, don't shoot him."

"Not unless he starts something."

"He isn't going to start something, and even if he does there will be *no shooting!*"

"Hunh," Lula said. "No pocketbooks, no perfume, no shooting. You got an awful lot of rules, you know that?"

I put my hands on the counter. "Stuart Baggett?"

"Yes ma'am," he said. "What can I get for you? Chili dog? Frank-n-kraut? Cheese dog?"

I showed him my identification and told him I represented his bond agent.

He blinked. "Bond agent?"

"Yeah," Lula said. "The Italian pervert who sprung your white ass from the tank."

Stuart still looked confused.

"You missed your court date," I said to Stuart.

His face brightened as the lightbulb suddenly snapped on. "Right! My court date. I'm sorry about that, but I had to work. My boss, Eddie Rosenberg, couldn't find anybody to sub for me."

"Did you inform the court of this fact and ask to have your date rescheduled?"

His face returned to nobody home. "Should I have done that?"

"Oh boy," Lula said. "Stupid alert."

"You need to check in with the court," I told Stuart. "I'll give you a ride downtown."

"I can't just walk off," he said. "I'm the only one working today. I have to work until nine."

"Maybe if you called your boss he could find someone to fill in for you."

"Tomorrow's my day off," Stuart said. "I could go tomorrow."

On the surface that sounded like a reasonable idea. My bounty hunting experience, limited as it was, told me otherwise. When tomorrow arrived Stuart would have pressing plans that didn't include a trip to the pokey.

"It would be best if we took care of this today," I said.

"It would be irresponsible," Stuart said, starting to look panicky. "I can't do it now."

Lula grunted. "It isn't like you're doing big business here. We're in the middle of a slush storm, Stuart. Get real."

"Does she work for my bond agent too?" Stuart asked.

"You bet your ass I do," Lula said.

I looked out at the mall, and then I looked at Stuart and his hot dog concession. "She's right, Stuart," I said. "This mall is empty."

"Yeah, but look, I've got all these hot dogs on the grill."

I scrounged in the bottom of my pocketbook and came up with a twenty. "Here's enough money to cover them. Throw the hot dogs in the trash and close up."

"I don't know," Stuart said. "They're really good hot dogs. It doesn't seem right to throw them away."

I did some mental screaming. "Okay, then wrap them up. We'll take them with us."

"I want two chili dogs," Lula said. "And then I want two with sauerkraut and mustard. And do you have any of them curly fries?"

Stuart looked at me. "How about you? How do you want the rest of the hot dogs?"

"Plain."

"Hunh-uh," Lula said. "You better get some chili dogs for

Connie. She's gonna be real disappointed she sees my chili dogs, and she's left with some plain-ass dog."

"Okay, okay! Two more chili dogs," I told Stuart, "and then just put the rest in a bag."

"How about soda?" Lula asked. "I can't eat all these hot dogs without soda."

I ordered three medium fries and three large root beers, and forked over another twenty.

Stuart called his boss and lied his heart out about how he was sick and throwing up all over the place, and that he'd sold all his hot dogs, and no one was in the mall anyway on account of the weather and he was going home.

We pulled the front grate, locked up the concession and left with our bags of food and soda.

The parking lot had some remnants of slush, but the sleet had turned to driving rain. We wedged Stuart and the bags between us and rode in silence back to Trenton. From time to time I checked Stuart's expression. His face was pale, and I suspected he hadn't tried very hard to make his trial date. He looked like a person who'd given his best shot to denial and had lost. I guess being short and cute didn't help all that much when it was time to grow up.

If he hadn't shot up police cars he probably wouldn't even have needed bail. And if he'd played by the rules he probably would have gotten away with probation and fine. New Jersey was up to its armpits in criminals. It didn't have a lot of room in the prison system for amateurs like Stuart.

Lula took a turnoff into center city, stopped for a light and the Nissan stalled out. She started it up again; it ran rough for a few seconds and went into another stall.

"Maybe you're not doing the clutch right," I suggested.

"I guess I know how to do a clutch," Lula said. "Looks to me like you got a lemon car."

"Let me try it," I said, opening my door, running to the driver's side.

Lula stood at roadside and watched. "This car is busted," she said. "You know what I'm telling you?"

I started it up. The car bucked forward a few feet and died.

"Maybe we should look under the hood," Lula said. "Maybe you got a cat in your engine. My neighbor, Midgie, once got a cat in his engine. Cat looked like it had been put through a food processor by the time Midgie figured out to check under the hood."

Stuart made a face that said, *Yuk!*

"Happens all the time," Lula said. "They get cold and they go to the warm engine. Then they fall asleep and when you go to start the car . . . cat stew."

I popped the hood and Lula and I checked for cats.

"Guess that wasn't it," Lula said. "I don't see any cat guts."

We slammed the hood down, and Lula got back behind the wheel. "I can do this," she said. "All I gotta do is race the engine, so it don't stall."

We drove two more blocks and cringed when the light turned red ahead. Lula eased up to the last car in line. "No sweat," she said. "Got this made." She raced the engine. The truck idled rough and started to stall. Lula raced the engine some more and somehow the truck lurched forward and smashed into the car in front.

"Oops," Lula said.

We got out to take a look. The car in front had a nasty crumple in its left rear quarter panel. The Nissan had a chunk torn out of its snoot and a deep gash in its bumper.

The man driving the car in front of us wasn't happy. "Why don't you watch where you're going?" he yelled at Lula. "Why don't you learn how to drive?"

"Don't you yell at me," Lula told him. "I don't take no yelling at. And on top of that I can drive just fine. It happens that my vehicle wasn't working properly."

"You got insurance?" the man wanted to know.

"Damn skippy I got insurance," Lula said. "Not only do I have insurance, but I'm filling out a police report. And on that police report I'm telling them about your brake lights all covered with dirt and ice, which were a contributing factor."

I exchanged information with the man, and Lula and I turned back to the Nissan.

"Uh-oh," Lula said, opening the driver's side door. "I don't see Stuart Baggett in here. Stuart Baggett's done the good-bye thing."

Cars were lined up behind us, straggling around the accident one at a time. I climbed into the truck bed to get some height and looked in all directions, up and down the road, but Stuart was nowhere to be seen. I thunked my head with the heel of my hand. Stupid, stupid, stupid. I hadn't even cuffed him.

"He didn't look smart enough to run off," Lula said.

"Deceptively cute."

"Yeah, that was it. Deceptively cute."

"I suppose we should go to the police station and file an accident report," I said.

"Yeah, and we don't want to forget about the dirty taillights. Insurance companies love that shit."

I piled in next to Lula, and we kept our eyes open for Stuart as we drove, but Stuart was long gone.

Lula looked nervous when we finally chugged into the lot for the municipal building that housed the courts and the police station. "I'd appreciate it if you'd run in and fill out the form," Lula said. "Wouldn't want anybody to get the wrong idea about me being at the police station. Think they see me sitting on the bench they might take away my shoelaces."

I had my hand on the door handle. "You aren't going to leave me stranded again, are you?"

"Who me?"

•   •   •

It took me a half hour to complete the paperwork. When I exited the building there was no blue Nissan parked in the lot and no blue Nissan parked on the street. I wasn't surprised. I went back into the station and called the office.

"I'm stranded again," I said to Connie.

I could hear wrappers rustling, and I could hear Connie swallow.

"What is that?" I demanded. "Are you eating hot dogs? Let me talk to Lula."

" 'Lo," Lula said. "What's up?"

"I'm wet and cold and stranded . . . that's what's up. And I'm hungry. You better not have eaten all those hot dogs."

"We would have waited for you, but didn't seem right to let the food set around."

There was a pause, and I could hear her sipping soda.

"You want a ride?" she finally said. "I could come get you."

"That would be nice."

A half hour later we were back at the office. Lula's hooker friend Jackie was there, and she was eating a hot dog.

"Hey, girlfriend," Lula shouted to Jackie. "You come to see me?"

"Nope," Jackie said. "Came to see Stephanie."

Connie handed me a cold hot dog. "Jackie's got man problems."

"Yeah," Jackie said. "Missing man problems."

Lula leaned forward. "You telling me your old man took off?"

"That's what I'm telling you," Jackie said. "I've been standing out on that corner in the freezing cold, doing my thing, supporting that loser in fine style, and this is the thanks I get. No note. No good-bye. No nothin'. And that isn't even the worst of it. That no good jerk-off took my car."

Lula looked appalled. "He took the Chrysler?"

"That's it, woman. He took the Chrysler. I still have ten payments on that car."

I finished my hot dog and handed the little nail polish bag to Connie. "Vinnie ever show?"

"No. He hasn't come in yet."

"Bet he be doing a nooner somewhere," Lula said. "That man got a 'tosterone problem. He's one of those do it with barnyard animals."

"Anyway, I came to you for help on account of you're good at finding missing shit," Jackie said to me. "I got money. I can pay you."

"She's the best," Lula said. "Stephanie here can find any shit you want. You want her to find your old man, it's a done deal."

"Hell, I don't give a flip about that worthless piece of trash. I want her to find my car," Jackie said. "How am I supposed to get around without a car? I had to take a cab over here today. And how am I supposed to ply my trade in weather like this without no backseat? You think all johns got their own backseat? No way. My business is hurting because of this."

"Have you reported the theft to the police?" I asked.

Jackie shifted her weight, one hand on hip. "Say what?"

"Maybe your car's been impounded," I suggested.

"I already checked impound," Connie said. "They don't have it."

"Was a ninety-two Chrysler LeBaron. Dark blue. Got it used six months ago," Jackie said. She handed me a file card. "Here's the license number. Last I saw it was two days ago."

"Anything else missing? Money? Clothes? This guy pack a bag when he leave?" I asked.

"Only thing missing is his worthless body and my car."

"Maybe he just out drunk somewhere," Lula said. "Maybe he just ho'in' around."

"Nuh-uh. I would of known. He's gone, I'm telling you."

Lula and I exchanged glances, and I suspected Jackie was right about the worthless body part.

"Why don't we take Jackie home," Lula said to me. "And then we could kind of cruise around and see what we can see."

The tone surprised me. Soft and serious. Not the Lula who played bounty hunter at the mall.

"We could do that," I said. "We might find something."

All of us watching Jackie. Jackie not showing much but anger at losing her car. That was Jackie's way.

Lula had her hat on her head and her duster buckled up. "I'll be back later to do the filing," she told Connie.

"Just don't go into any banks in that getup," Connie said.

Jackie rented a two-room apartment three blocks from Uncle Mo's. Since we were in the neighborhood, we made a short detour to Ferris Street and looked things over.

"Nothing new here," Lula said, letting her Firebird idle in the middle of the empty street. "No lights, no nothing."

We drove down King and turned into the alley behind Mo's store. I hopped out and peeked into the garage. No car. No lights on in the back of the upstairs apartment.

"There's something going on here," I said. "It doesn't make sense."

Lula slowly made her way to Jackie's rooming house, taking a street for four blocks and then doubling back one street over, the three of us on the lookout for Jackie's car. We'd covered a sizable chunk of neighborhood by the time we reached Jackie's house, but nothing turned up.

"Don't you worry," Lula said to Jackie. "We'll find your car. You go on in and watch some TV. Only thing good to do on a day like this is watch TV. Go check out the bitches on them daytime shows."

Jackie disappeared behind a screen of rain, into the

maroon-shingled two-story row house. The street was lined with cars. None of them Jackie's Chrysler.

"What's he like?" I asked Lula.

"Jackie's old man? Nothing special. Comes and goes. Sells some."

"What's his name?"

"Cameron Brown. Street name is Maggot. Guess that tell you something."

"Would he take off with Jackie's car?"

"In a heartbeat." Lula pulled away from the curb. "You're the expert finder here. What we do next?"

"Let's do more of the same," I said. "Let's keep driving. Canvass the places Brown would ordinarily hang at."

Two hours later Lula missed a street in the rain, and before we could make a correction we were down by the river, weaving our way through a complex of high-rises.

"This is getting old," Lula said. "Bad enough straining my eyeballs looking for some dumb car, but now I'm lost."

"We're not lost," I told her. "We're in Trenton."

"Yeah, but I've never been in this part of Trenton before. I don't feel comfortable driving around buildings that haven't got gang slogans sprayed on them. Look at this place. No boarded-up windows. No garbage in the gutter. No brothers selling goods on the street. Don't know how people can live like this." She squinted into the gray rain and eased the car into a parking lot. "I'm turning around," she said. "I'm taking us back to the office, and I'm gonna nuke up some of them leftover hot dogs and then I'm gonna do my filing."

It was okay by me because riding around in the pouring rain in slum neighborhoods wasn't my favorite thing to do anyway.

Lula swung down a line of cars and there in front of us was the Chrysler.

We both sat dumbstruck, barely believing our eyes. We'd painstakingly covered every likely street and alley, and here was the car, parked in a most unlikely place.

"Sonovabitch," Lula said.

I studied the building at the edge of the lot. Eight stories high. A big cube of uninspired brick and low-energy window glass. "Looks like apartments."

Lula nodded, and we returned our attention to the Chrysler. Not especially anxious to investigate.

"I guess we should take a look," Lula finally said.

We both heaved a sigh and got out of the Firebird. The rain had tapered to a drizzle, and the temperature was dropping. The cold seeped through my skin, straight to my bones, and the possibility of finding Cameron Brown dead in the trunk of Jackie's car did nothing to warm me from the inside out.

We gingerly looked in the windows and tried the doors. The doors were locked. The interior of the car was empty. No Cameron Brown. No obvious clues . . . like notes detailing Brown's recent life history or maps with a bright orange X to mark the spot. We stood side by side, looking at the trunk.

"Don't see no blood dripping out," Lula said. "That's a good sign." She went to her own trunk and returned with a crowbar. She slipped it under the Chrysler's trunk lid and popped the lid open.

Spare tire, dirty yellow blanket, a couple grimy towels. No Cameron Brown.

Lula and I expelled air in a simultaneous whoosh.

"How long has Jackie been seeing this guy?" I asked.

"About six months. Jackie doesn't have good luck with men. Doesn't want to see what's real."

Lula tossed the crowbar onto her backseat and we both got back into the Firebird.

"So what's real this time around?" I asked.

"This Maggot's a user from the word go. He pimping Jackie and then using her car to deal. He could of got a car of his own, but he uses Jackie's because everybody knows she a ho, and if the cops stop him and there's stuff in the trunk he just say he don't know how it got there. He say he just borrowed the car from his ho girlfriend. And everybody knows Jackie do some drugs. Only reason anybody be a ho is 'cause they do drugs."

"Think Brown was selling drugs here?"

Lula shook her head, no. "He don't sell drugs to this kind of folks. He pushes to the kiddies."

"Then maybe he has a girlfriend upstairs."

Lula rolled the engine over and pulled out of the lot. "Maybe, but it looks kind of high-class for Cameron Brown."

By the time I dragged into my apartment at five o'clock I was thoroughly depressed. I was back to driving the Buick. My pickup was at a Nissan service center awaiting repairs after Blue Ribbon Used Cars refused responsibility, citing a clause on my sales receipt that said I'd bought the car "as is." No returns. No guarantees.

My shoes were soaked through, my nose was running and I couldn't stop thinking about Jackie. Finding her car seemed totally inadequate. I wanted to improve her life. I wanted to get her off drugs, and I wanted to change her profession. Hell, she wasn't so dumb. She could probably be a brain surgeon if she just had a decent haircut.

I left my shoes in the hall and dropped the rest of my clothes on the bathroom floor. I stood in the shower until I was defrosted. I toweled my hair dry and ran my fingers through it by way of styling. I dressed in thick white socks, sweatpants and sweatshirt.

I took a soda from the fridge, snatched a pad and pen

from the kitchen counter and settled myself at the dining table. I wanted to review my ideas on Mo Bedemier, and I wanted to figure out what I was missing.

I awoke at nine o'clock with the spiral binding of the steno pad imprinted on the left side of my face and my notebook pages as blank as my mind. I shoved the hair out of my eyes, punched 4 on my speed dial and ordered a pizza to be delivered—extra cheese, black olives, peppers and onions.

I took hold of the pen and drew a line on the empty page. I drew a happy face. I drew a grumpy face. I drew a heart with my initials in it, but then I didn't have anyone else's initials to write next to mine, so I went back to thinking about Mo.

Where would Mo go? He left most of his clothes behind. His drawers were filled with socks and underwear. His toiletries were intact. Toothbrush, razor, deodorant in the medicine chest over the bathroom sink. That had to mean something, right? The logical conclusion was that he had another apartment where he kept a spare toothbrush. Trouble was . . . life wasn't always logical. The utilities check hadn't turned up anything. Of course that only meant that if Mo had a second house or apartment, it wasn't registered under his name.

The other possibility, that Mo was snatched and most likely was dead somewhere, waiting to be found, was too depressing to ponder. Best to set that one aside for now, I decided.

And what about Mo's mail? I couldn't remember seeing a mailbox. Probably the mailman brought the mail into the store and gave it to Mo. So what was happening to the mail now?

Check the post office, I wrote on the pad.

I smelled pizza get off the elevator, and I hustled to the foyer, flipped the chain, threw the bolts back on the two Yale locks, opened the door and stared out at Joe Morelli.

"Pizza delivery," he said.

I narrowed my eyes.

"I was at Pino's when the order came in."

"So this really is my pizza?"

Morelli pushed past me and set the pizza on the kitchen counter. "Cross my heart and hope to die." He got two beers out of the refrigerator, balanced the pizza box on one hand and carted everything into the living room and set it all on the coffee table. He picked the channel changer off the sofa and punched the Knicks game on.

"Make yourself at home," I said.

Morelli smiled.

I set two plates, a roll of paper towels and a pizza cutter next to the pizza box. Truth is, I wasn't completely unhappy to see Morelli. He radiated body heat, which I seemed to be lacking today, and as a cop he had resources that were useful to a bounty hunter. There might be other reasons as well, having to do with ego and lust, but I didn't feel like admitting to those reasons.

I recut the pizza and slid pieces onto plates. I handed one plate to Morelli. "You know a guy named Cameron Brown?"

"Pimp," Morelli said. "Very oily. Deals some dope." He looked at me over the edge of his pizza. "Why?"

"You remember Jackie? Lula's friend?"

"Jackie the hooker."

"Yeah. Well she came to Vinnie's office today to see if I could find her car. Seems her boyfriend, Cameron Brown, took off with it."

"And?"

"And, Lula and I cruised around awhile and finally found the car parked in the RiverEdge Apartments parking lot."

Morelli stopped eating. "Keep going."

"That's about it. Jackie said she didn't care about finding Cameron. She just wanted her car."

"So what's your problem?"

I chewed some pizza. "I don't know. The whole thing feels . . . nasty. Unfinished."

"Stay out of it."

"Excuse me?"

"It's Jackie's problem," Morelli said. "Mind your own business. You got her car back. Let it rest."

"She's sort of my friend."

"She's a doper. She's nobody's friend."

I knew he was right, but I was still surprised at the harsh comment and at the emphatic tone. A little alarm sounded in my brain. Usually when Morelli felt this strongly about my not getting involved in something it was because he didn't want me muddying waters he'd staked out for himself.

Morelli sank back into the couch with his bottle of beer. "What ever happened to the all-out search for Mo?"

"I'm all out of ideas." I had wolfed down two pieces of pizza and was eyeing a third. "So tell me," I said to Morelli. "What's going on with Jackie and her old man? Why don't you want me getting involved?"

"Like I said, it's none of your business." Morelli leaned forward, raised the lid on Rex's hamster cage and chucked a chunk of pizza crust into Rex's little ceramic food dish.

"Tell me anyway," I said.

"There's not much to tell. I just think there's a funny climate on the streets. The dealers are pulling back, getting cautious. Rumor has it some have disappeared."

His attention was diverted to the television. "Watch this," he said. "Watch the replay of this layup."

"The guys in vice must be ecstatic."

"Yeah," Morelli said. "They're sitting around playing cards and eating jelly doughnuts for lack of crime."

I was still debating the third piece of pizza. My thighs really didn't need it, but life was so short, and physical gratification was hard to come by these days. The hell with it. Eat the damn thing and get it over with, I thought.

I saw a smile twitch at the corners of Morelli's mouth.

"What?" I yelled at him.

He held two hands in the air. "Hey, don't yell at me just because you have no willpower."

"I have plenty of willpower." Man, I *hated* when Morelli was right. "Why are you here anyway?"

"Just being sociable."

"And you want to see if I have anything new on Mo."

"Yeah."

I'd expected him to deny it, and now I was left with nothing accusatory to say.

"Why are you so interested in Mo?" I asked.

Morelli shrugged. "Everyone in the burg is interested in Mo. I spent a lot of time in that store as a kid."

Morning dawned late under a tedious cloud cover that was the color and texture of cement curbing. I finished up the pizza for breakfast and was feeding Rex Cheerios and raisins when the phone rang.

"Man, this is one ugly morning," Lula said. "And it's getting uglier by the minute."

"Are you referring to the weather?" I asked.

"That too. Mostly I'm referring to human nature. We got a situation on our hands. Jackie's got herself staked out in the FancyAss parking lot, looking to catch her old man doin' the deed. I told her to go home, but she don't listen to me. I told her he probably isn't even there. What would he be doing with a woman could afford to live in a place like that? I told her that motherfucker got capped. I told her she be better off checking the Dumpsters, but it go on deaf ears."

"And?"

"And I thought you could talk to her. She's gonna freeze to death. She's been sitting there all night."

"What makes you think she'll listen to me?"

"You could tell her you got some surveillance going on, and she don't need to butt in."

"That would be a lie."

"What, you never lied before?"

"Okay," I said. "I'll see what I can do."

Half an hour later, I turned the Buick into the RiverEdge Apartments parking lot. Jackie was there, all right, parked in her Chrysler. I pulled up behind her, got out, and rapped on her window.

"Yeah?" Jackie said by way of greeting, not sounding all that happy.

"What are you doing here?"

"I'm waiting for that shit-ass car thief to come out, and then I'm going to put a hole in him big enough to drive a truck through."

I don't know a whole lot about guns, but the cannon resting on the seat next to Jackie looked like it could do the job.

"That's a pretty good idea," I said, "but you look cold. Why don't you let me take over the surveillance for a while?"

"Thanks all the same, but you found him, and now I get to kill him."

"Makes perfect sense to me. I just thought it might be better to kill him when it warms up some. After all, there isn't any real rush. No point sitting out here, catching a cold, just to kill a guy."

"Yeah, but I feel like killing him now. I don't feel like waiting. Besides, I'm not gonna do any business today what with this weather. Only crazy men go out to get their oil changed on a day like this, and I don't need any of that lunatic dick shit. Nope, I might as well sit here. Better than standing on my corner."

She could be right.

"Okay," I said. "Be careful."

"Hunh," Jackie said.

I drove over to the office and told Lula that Jackie was hunkered in for the siege.

"Hunh," Lula said.

Vinnie popped out of his office.

"Well?" Vinnie asked.

We all looked at him. Well what?

Vinnie settled on me. "Where's Mo? Why don't we have Mo in custody? How hard could it be to catch an old man who sells candy?"

"Mo's done a disappearing act," I said. "He's temporarily vanished."

"So where have you looked? You check his apartment? You check his sister? You check his boyfriend?"

The office went suddenly silent.

I found my voice first. "Boyfriend?"

Vinnie smiled. His teeth white and even in his olive complexion. "You didn't know?"

"Oh my God," Connie said, doing the sign of the cross. "Oh my God."

My head was reeling. "Are you sure?" I asked Vinnie. As if I'd doubt Vinnie for a nanosecond when it came to expertise in alternative sexual behavior.

"Moses Bedemier is a flaming fruit," Vinnie said, his face wreathed in happiness, his hands jiggling change in the deep pockets of his pleated polyester slacks. "Moses Bedemier wears ladies' panties."

Vincent Plum, bail bonds. Specializing in sensitivity and political correctness.

I turned to Lula. "I thought you said Mo was a customer."

"Unh-uh. I said I knew him. Sometimes when I was on the corner he'd ride by late at night and ask directions of Jackie or me. He'd want to know where to find Freddie the Frog or Little Lionel. I figure he do some drugs."

"Oh my God," Connie said. "A homosexual and a drug user. Oh my God."

"How do you know?" I asked Vinnie.

"I'd heard rumors. And then I saw him and his significant other having dinner in New Hope a couple months ago."

"How do you know it was a significant other and not just a friend?"

"What, you want details?" Vinnie said, smiling wide, enjoying the moment.

I grimaced and shook my head, no.

Connie squeezed her eyes shut tight.

"Yo ass," Lula said.

"Do you have a name?" I asked Vinnie. "What's this guy look like?"

"The guy was Mo's age. Smaller, slimmer. Soft, like Mo. Dark hair, bald on top. I don't have a name, but I can make some phone calls."

I didn't give much credence to the drug buyer theory, but I wouldn't want it to be said I'd left a stone unturned. When Lula was hooking she'd plied her trade on Stark Street, a mile-long strip of bars and crack houses and row houses converted to airless apartments and rooms to let. It'd be a waste of time for me to canvass Stark Street. No one would talk to me. That left me with two alternatives. Lula was one of them. Ranger was the other.

CHAPTER

4

I could ask Ranger to make inquiries on Mo. Or I could ask Lula. This was a dilemma, being that Ranger would be my first choice, but Lula was here in front of me, on the scent, reading my mind.

"Well?" Lula asked. Shifting her weight. Nervous. Belligerent. Rhino mode. Looking like her feelings would be hurt if I didn't ask her to work with me. Looking like at any moment she might narrow her eyes and squash me like a bug.

So I was beginning to see the wisdom of using Lula. No point to hurting her feelings, right? And probably Lula would be cool with this. I mean, what was the big deal? All she had to do was show Mo's picture to a few drug dealers and hookers. So she wasn't subtle. Hey, was that a crime?

"You have a lot of contacts on Stark Street," I said to Lula. "Maybe you could flash Mo's picture. See if someone can give us a lead."

Lula's face brightened. "You bet. I could do that."

"Yeah," Vinnie said. "Get her out of the office for a while. She makes me nervous."

"You should be nervous," Lula told him. "I'm keeping my eye on your sad ass. You better not trifle with me, mister."

Vinnie set his teeth, and I thought I saw wisps of steam curl out of his ears and evaporate off the top of his head. But maybe it was just my imagination.

"I'll make some phone calls. I'll see if I can get a name for Mo's boyfriend," Vinnie said, retreating into his private lair, slamming the door behind him.

Lula had one arm rammed into her coat. "And I'm gonna get right on this. I'm gonna detect the shit out of this case."

With everyone else in motion, there didn't seem to be much for me to do. I retraced my steps back to my Buick and drove home on autopilot. I pulled into the lot to my apartment building and looked up at my window. I'd left the light burning in my bedroom, and it was all cheerful and welcoming now. A rectangle of comfort floating high above the gray miasma of morning ice smog.

Mr. Kleinschmidt was in the lobby when I swung through the double glass doors.

"Ho," Mr. Kleinschmidt said. "It's the early bounty hunter that catches the worm. Tracking down a ruthless murderer today?"

"Nope. No murderers," I said.

"Drug dealer? Rapist?"

"Nope. Nope."

"Who then? What gets you up and out so early?"

"Actually, I'm looking for Moses Bedemier."

"That's not funny," Mr. Kleinschmidt said. "That's not a good joke. I know Moses Bedemier. Mo would never do anything bad. I think you should look for someone else."

I stepped into the elevator and pushed the second-floor button. I gave Mr. Kleinschmidt a little finger-wave good-bye, but he didn't wave back.

"Why me?" I said to the empty elevator. "Why me?"

I let myself into my apartment and looked in at Rex. He

was sleeping in his soup can. Nice and quiet. That's one of the terrific things about having a hamster as a roommate; hamsters keep their thoughts to themselves. If Rex had an opinion about Moses Bedemier, he didn't lay it on me.

I nuked a cup of coffee and settled down to make phone calls.

I started with my cousin Jeanine, who worked at the post office. Jeanine told me Mo's mail was being held, and that Mo hadn't left a forwarding address, nor had he retrieved anything.

I talked to Linda Shantz, Loretta Beeber and Margaret Molinowsky. No one had much to say about Mo, but I found out my archenemy, Joyce Barnhardt, had a drug-resistant yeast infection. That cheered me up some.

At one o'clock I called Vinnie to see if he'd been able to get a name for me. The call was switched to the answering service, and I realized it was Saturday. The office was only open for a half day on Saturday.

I thought about doing something athletic, like going for a run, but when I looked out the living room window it was still January, so I trashed the physical fitness idea.

I returned to the phone and dialed up some more busybodies. I figured it would take me days to go through my list of gossips, and in the meantime I could pretend I was accomplishing something.

By three-thirty my ear felt swollen, and I wasn't sure how much longer I could take being glued to the phone. I was contemplating a nap when someone hammered on my door.

I opened the door and Lula rolled in.

"Outta my way," she said. "I'm so frozen I can't walk straight. My black ass turned blue a half hour ago."

"Do you want hot chocolate?"

"I'm way past hot chocolate. I need alcohol."

I'm not much of a drinker. I'd long ago decided it was best not to muddy the waters of my brain with serious booze. I had a hard enough time making sense when I was sober.

"I haven't got much in the way of alcohol," I told Lula. "Light beer, red wine, mouthwash."

"Pass on that. I just wanted to tell you about Mo, anyway. Carla, the ho on Seventh and Stark, says she saw Mo two days ago. According to Carla, Mo was looking for Shorty O."

I felt my mouth fall open. Mo was on Stark Street two days ago. Holy cow.

"How reliable is Carla?"

"Well she wasn't shaking or nothing today, so I think she could see the picture I showed her," Lula said. "And she wouldn't mess with me."

"What about Shorty O? Do you know him?"

"Everybody knows Shorty O. Shorty's one of those influential people on Stark Street. Middle management. Do some demolition work when there's a need. I would have talked to him, but I couldn't find him."

"Do you think Mo found him?"

"Hard to say."

"Anyone else see Mo?"

"Not that I know of. I asked lots of people, too, but with this weather, people aren't out looking around." Lula stamped her feet and made flapping warm-up motions with her arms. "I gotta go. I'm going home. It's Saturday, and I got a date tonight. I gotta get my hair done. Just because I'm a natural beauty don't mean I don't need extra help sometime."

I thanked Lula and saw her to the elevator. I returned to my apartment and thought about this latest development. Hard to believe Mo was on Stark Street for whatever reason. Still, I wasn't going to totally discount anything . . . no matter how preposterous. Especially since this was my only lead.

I punched the speed-dial number for Ranger and left a

message on his machine. If anyone could find Shorty O, it would be Ranger.

Sunday morning I got up at ten. I made hot chocolate and French toast, carried it into the living room and slid the Winnie the Pooh video into the VCR. When Winnie was done having his adventures in the Hundred Acre Wood it was almost noon, and I thought it was time to go to work. Since I didn't have a social life, and I didn't have an office, work time was any time I wanted.

And what I wanted today was to get stupid, spineless Stuart Baggett. Mo was cooking on the back burner, but Stuart wasn't cooking at all.

I showered and dressed and resurrected Stuart's file. He lived with his parents at 10 Applegate Street in Mercerville. I spread my street map on the dining room table and located Applegate. It looked to be about two miles from the mall where Stuart worked. Very convenient.

I've been told there are places in the country where stores close on Sunday. This would never happen in Jersey. We wouldn't stand for it. In Jersey it's part of our constitutional rights to shop seven days a week.

I parked the Buick in the mall lot and diligently ignored the stares from people with less imaginative cars. Since my bank account was at an all-time low, I went straight to the hot dog stand. Best not to detour through the shoe department at Macy's and succumb to temptation.

Two young women were behind the hot dog counter.

"Yes ma'am," one said. "What would you like?"

"I'm looking for Stuart Baggett."

"He doesn't work here anymore."

Oh boy. Minor guilt trip. I got the poor schnook fired. "Gee, that's a shame," I said. "Do you know what happened? Do you know where I can find him?"

"He quit. Closed up early a couple days ago and never came back. Don't know where he is."

A small setback, but not devastating since I still had his home to visit.

Applegate was a pleasant street of well-kept single-family houses and mature trees. The Baggett house was a white Cape with blue shutters and a dark blue door. There were two cars and a kid's bike in the driveway.

Mrs. Baggett answered the door. Stuart was close enough to my age that we might be friends. I thought I'd go with this approach first, saying very little, letting Mrs. Baggett assume the obvious.

"Hi," I said. "I'm looking for Stuart."

There was a moment's hesitation, which might have been concern, or maybe she was just trying to place me. "I'm sorry," she said. "Stuart's not home. Was he supposed to meet you here?"

"No. I just thought I might catch him."

"He's with one of his friends," Mrs. Baggett said. "Moved out yesterday. Said he had a new job, and he was going to share a place with this friend of his."

"Do you have an address or a phone number?"

"No. I don't even have a name. He had some words with his father and stormed off. Would you like to leave a message?"

I gave her my card. "Stuart failed to appear in court. He needs to reschedule his court date as soon as possible. It's very important."

Mrs. Baggett made a distressed little sound. "I don't know what to do with him. He's just gone wild."

"I'd appreciate it if you'd call me if you hear from him."

She nodded her head. "I will. I'll call you."

I could expend a lot of energy looking for Stuart, or I could wait for him to go home. I decided to go with the latter. Mrs. Baggett looked like a responsible, intelligent woman. I felt pretty confident that she'd get back to me. If not I'd make a return visit later in the week.

Ranger called back a little after seven with news that Shorty O had gone south for the winter. No one had seen him in days, and that probably included Mo.

At eight o'clock I was standing across the street from Uncle Mo's, and I was feeling nervous. Even though I had a key to his apartment, there were some who might regard what I was about to do as breaking and entering. Of course I could always fib, and say Uncle Mo had asked me to look after his things. If it was a judge who was doing the asking I guess my answer might fall into that undesirable area of perjury. Perjury seemed like a good thing to avoid. Although in Jersey, written law often bowed to common sense. Which meant perjury was better than being dispatched to the landfill.

The sky was dark. The moon obscured by cloud cover. Lights were on in houses up and down Mo's street, but Mo's apartment windows were black. A car cruised by and parked three houses away. I was lost in shadow and the driver walked from his car to his house without seeming to notice me. I'd left the Buick on Lindal Street, one block away.

I could see Mrs. Steeger moving in her front room. I was waiting for her to settle before going closer. She peered out her living room window, and my heart stopped dead in my chest. She drew back from the window, and I gasped for air. Little black dots danced in front of my eyes. I clapped a hand to my chest. The woman made my blood run cold.

Headlights swung around the corner, and a car stopped at the Steeger house. The driver beeped, and Mrs. Steeger opened her door and waved. A moment later she was locking up behind herself. I held my breath and willed myself invisible. Mrs. Steeger carefully picked her way along the dark steps and sidewalk to the car. She seated herself next to the driver, slammed the door shut and the car drove off.

My lucky day.

I crossed the street and tried Mo's house key on the candy store door with no success. I walked to the back and tried the same key on the rear entrance. The key didn't work there either.

It had occurred to me while talking to Ranger that due to police interruption, I'd never gotten around to searching Mo's store. I don't know what I expected to find, but it felt like unfinished business.

Since the house keys didn't work on the store doors, I assumed there had to be another set of keys in Mo's apartment. I took the stairs as if I owned the place. When in doubt, always look like you know what you're doing. I pulled a flashlight out of my pocketbook and knocked twice. I called to Uncle Mo. No answer. I unlocked the door, took one step inside and swept a beam of light around the room. Everything seemed to be in order, so I closed the door behind myself and did a fast walk-through of the rest of the apartment. There were no keys lying on open surfaces and no cute little key hooks on any of the walls. There was no evidence that anyone had been in the apartment since my last visit.

The kitchen was small. White metal cupboards over a gray Formica countertop and an old white porcelain sink that had a few black chips showing. The cupboards held a mismatched assortment of glasses, cups, plates and bowls. No keys. I went through the under-the-counter drawers. One dedicated to silverware. One for dish towels. One for plastic wrap, aluminum foil, plastic bags. One for junk. Still no keys.

I took a moment to look at the photos on the wall next to

the fridge. Pictures of children. All from the burg. I recognized almost everyone. I searched until I found mine. Twelve years old, eating an ice cream cone. I remembered Mo taking the picture.

I poked in the refrigerator, checking for cleverly hollowed out heads of cabbage and fake cola cans. Not finding any, I moved on to the bedroom.

The double bed was covered with a quilted bedspread, its yellow and brown flowers faded, the cotton material softened from years of service. The bed and nightstand were inexpensive walnut veneer. Uncle Mo lived modestly. Guess there wasn't all that much profit in ice cream cones.

I started with the top bureau drawer and sure enough, there was the key ring consigned to its own compartment in a removable wooden jewelry tray. I pocketed the key ring, closed the drawer and was about to leave when the stack of movie magazines caught my eye. *Premiere*, *Entertainment Weekly*, *Soap Opera Digest*, *Juggs*. Whoa! *Juggs*? Not the sort of reading material one would expect to find in a gay man's bedroom.

I wedged the flashlight under my armpit, sank to the floor and flipped through the first half of *Juggs*. Appalling. I flipped through the second half. Equally appalling and fascinatingly disgusting. The next magazine in the stack had a naked man on the cover. He was wearing a black mask and black socks and his Mr. Happy hung almost to his knees. He looked like he'd been sired by Thunder the Wonder Horse. I was tempted to look inside, but the pages were stuck together, so I moved on. I found a couple magazines that I'd never heard of that were devoted primarily to amateurish snapshots of people in various stages of undress, in a variety of embarrassing poses labeled "Mary and Frank from Sioux City" and "Rebecca Sue in Her Kitchen." There were some more *Entertainment Weekly*s, and on the bottom of the pile there were a couple photographic catalogues, which reminded me that I'd found a couple unopened boxes of film in the fridge.

And this reminded me that I was supposed to be conducting an illegal search, not comparing anatomical features with women wearing crotchless panties and spiked dog collars.

I neatened everything up and crept out of the room, out of the apartment, thinking that Uncle Mo was a very weird guy.

There were two keys on the ring. I tried one of the keys on the back door to the store and struck out. I tried the second key and had to squelch a nervous giggle when the door clicked open. There'd been a part of me that hadn't wanted the keys to work. Probably it was the smart part. The part that knew I wouldn't look good in prison clothes.

The door opened to a narrow hall. Three doors ran off the hall, and the hall opened to the store. I could look the length of the hall and the length of the store, through the front plate-glass window, and see lights shining in the house across the street. This meant they could also see lights shining in the store, so I would have to be careful how I used my flashlight. I gave the hall and the store a quick flick of the beam to make sure I was alone. I opened the first door to my right and discovered stairs leading to a basement.

I called, "Hello, anybody down there?"

No one answered, so I closed the door. Hollering into the dark was about as brave as I was going to get on the cellar investigation.

The second door was a lavatory. The third door was a broom closet. I cut the light and took a moment to allow my eyes to adjust. It had probably been two or three years since I'd been in the store, but I knew it well, and I knew nothing had changed. Nothing ever changed at Uncle Mo's.

A counter ran front to rear. The back half of the counter was luncheonette style with five stationary stools. Behind this part of the counter Mo had a small cooktop, a plastic cooler of lemonade, a four-spigot soda dispenser, two milkshake shakers, an ice cream cone dispenser and two hotplates for brewing coffee. The front half of the counter consisted of a display case for tubs of ice cream and another display case devoted to candy.

I prowled around, not sure what I was looking for, but pretty sure I hadn't found it. Nothing seemed out of place. Mo had neatened up before he left. There were no dirty dishes or spoons in the sink. No indication that Mo had been disrupted or left in a rush.

I opened the cash drawer. Empty. Not a nickel. I hadn't found any money in the apartment either.

A shadow cut into the ambient light filtering through the front window, and I crouched low behind the counter. The shadow passed, and I wasted no time scuttling to the back of the store. I held up in the hallway, listening.

Footsteps sounded on the cement walkway. I stopped breathing and watched the doorknob turn. The door didn't open. The door was locked. I heard the rasp of a key and stood rooted to the floor in dumbstruck panic. If it was anyone other than Mo I was in very deep shit.

I quietly took two steps back, listening carefully. The key wasn't working. Maybe it wasn't working because it wasn't a key! Maybe someone else was trying to break into Uncle Mo's!

Damn. What were the chances of two people breaking into Mo's at the same time? I shook my head in disgust. Crime was getting out of hand in Trenton.

I slipped into the bathroom, silently closed the door and held my breath. I heard the tumbler click and the back door swing open. Two footsteps. Someone was standing in the hall, getting used to the dark.

Go for the cash drawer and get this over with, I thought. Take all the friggin' ice cream. Have a party.

Shoes scuffed on the wood floor, and a door opened next to me. This would be the door to the cellar. It was held open long enough for someone to look down into the darkness and then was quietly closed. Whoever was in Mo's store was doing the exact same thing I'd done, and I knew with sickening certainty my door would be opened next. There was no way for me to lock the door, and no window to use for escape.

I had my flashlight in one hand and defense spray in the other. I had a gun in my pocketbook, but I knew from past experience I'd be slow to use it. And besides, I wasn't sure I'd remembered to load the gun. Better to go with the defense spray. I was willing to gas almost anyone.

I heard a hand grasp the bathroom doorknob and in the next instant the door to the bathroom was yanked open. I pressed my thumb against the flashlight's switch, catching angry black eyes in my beam. The plan had been to temporarily blind the intruder, make identification and decide how to act.

The error in the plan was in assuming blindness led to paralysis.

Less than a millisecond after hitting the flashlight on button, I felt myself fly through the air and slam against the back wall of the lavatory. There was a red flash, fireworks exploded in my brain and then everything went black.

My next memory was of struggling to regain consciousness, struggling to open my eyes, struggling to place my surroundings.

It was dark. Night. I put my hand to my face. My face was sticky. A black stain spread from under my cheek. I dumbly stared at the stain. Blood, I thought. Car crash. No, that wasn't right. Then I remembered. I was at Mo's. I was on my side in the little lavatory, my body impossibly twisted around the toilet, my head under the small sink.

It was very quiet. I didn't move. I listened to the silence and waited for my head to clear. I ran my tongue over my teeth. No teeth were broken. I gingerly touched my nose. My nose seemed okay.

The blood had to be coming from somewhere. I was lying in a pool of it.

I pushed up to hands and knees and saw the source of the blood. A body lying facedown in the narrow hallway. Light from an alley streetlight carried through the store's open back door, enabling me to recognize the man on the floor.

It was the guy who'd pitched me against the wall.

I crept forward and took a closer look, seeing the hole in the back of the man's shirt where the bullet had entered, and a similar hole in the back of his head. The wall to my right had been sprayed with blood and brain and the left half of the dead man's face. His right eye was intact, wide and unseeing. The mouth was open, as if he'd been mildly surprised.

The sound that carved up from my throat was part scream, part gag as I floundered away from the body, arms windmilling out, searching for a handhold where none existed. I sat down hard on the floor, back to the wall, unable to think, breathing hard, only aware that time was passing. I swallowed back bile and closed my eyes, and a thought snaked into the horror. The thought was of hope . . . that this wasn't so bad, so final. That the man could be saved. That a miracle would happen.

I opened my eyes and all hope vanished. The man on the floor was beyond a medical miracle. I had brain gunk and bone fragments stuck to my jeans. My assailant had been murdered, and I'd missed it. Unconscious in the bathroom. The idea was ludicrous.

And the killer. Dear God, where was the killer? My heart gave a painful contraction. For all I knew he was hidden in shadow, watching me struggle. My shoulder bag was on the floor, under the sink. I reached inside and found my gun. The gun wasn't loaded. Dammit, I was such a screwup.

I rose to a crouch and looked through the open back door. The yard was partially illuminated, as was the hallway. I was cold in a way that had nothing to do with the weather. I was bathed in sweat, shivering with fear. I wiped my hands on my jeans. Go for the door, I thought, then run for Ferris Street.

I clenched my teeth and took off, stumbling over the obstructing body. I burst through the door and sprinted the length of the building and across the street. I ran to shadow and held up, gasping for air, searching the neighborhood for movement or for the glint of a gun or belt buckle.

A siren sounded in the distance, and at the end of the street I caught the flash of cop lights. Someone had called the police. A second blue-and-white turned the corner at Lindal. The two cars angled into the curb in front of the store. The uniforms got out and trained a flashlight beam into Mo's front window. I didn't recognize either of the uniforms.

I had myself backed into a corner between stoop and porch, two houses down. I kept my eye on the road and rummaged in my pocketbook, looking for my cell phone. I found the phone and dialed Morelli. Personal feelings aside, Morelli was a very good cop. I wanted him to be first homicide on the scene.

It was well after midnight when Morelli brought me home. He parked his Toyota in my lot and escorted me into the building. He punched the elevator button and stood silently beside me. Neither of us had spoken a word since we'd left the station. We were both too weary for anything other than the most necessary conversation.

I'd given an on-scene report to Morelli and was ordered to go to St. Francis Hospital to have my head examined, inside and out. I was told I had a concussion and a lump. My scalp was intact. After the hospital, I went home to shower and change my clothes and was brought to the station in a blue-and-white for further questioning. I'd done my best to recall details accurately, with the exception of a small memory lapse concerning the key to Mo's apartment and store and how those two doors happened to swing open for me. No need to burden the police with things that didn't matter. Especially if it might give them the wrong idea about unlawful entry. And then there was the matter of my gun, which happened to no longer be in my pocketbook by the time I got to the police station. Wouldn't want to confuse the issue with that either. Or to be embarrassed by the fact that I'd forgotten to load the miserable thing.

When I closed my eyes I saw the intruder. Heavy-lidded black eyes, dark skin, long dreadlocks, mustache and goatee. A big man. Taller than me. And he'd been strong. And quick. What else? He was dead. Very dead. Shot in the back at close range with a .45.

The motive for the shooting was unknown. Also unknown was why I'd been spared.

Mrs. Bartle, across from Mo's store, had called the police. First, to report seeing a suspicious light through the storefront window, and then a second time when she heard gunshot.

Morelli and I stepped out of the elevator and walked the short distance down the hall to my apartment. I unlocked my door, stepped inside and flipped the light switch. Rex paused on his wheel and blinked at us.

Morelli casually looked into the kitchen. He moved to the living room and lit a table lamp. He sauntered into the bedroom and bath and returned to me. "Just checking," he said.

"What were you checking for?"

"I suppose I was checking for the phantom assailant."

I collapsed into a chair. "I wasn't sure you believed me. I don't exactly have an airtight alibi."

"Honey, you don't have any alibi at all. The only reason I didn't book you for murder is I'm too tired to fill out the paperwork."

I didn't have the energy for indignation. "You know I didn't kill him."

"I don't know anything," Morelli said. "What I have is opinion. And my opinion is that you didn't kill the guy with the dreads. Unfortunately, there are no facts to support that opinion."

Morelli was wearing boots and jeans and a heavy olive drab jacket that looked like army issue. The jacket had lots of pockets and flaps and was slightly worn at the cuffs and collar. By day Morelli looked lean and predatory, but sometimes late at night when his features were softened by exhaustion and eighteen hours of beard growth there were glimpses of a more vulnerable Morelli. I found the vulnerable Morelli to be dangerously endearing. Fortunately, the vulnerable Morelli wasn't showing its face tonight. Tonight Morelli was all tired cop.

Morelli strolled into the kitchen, lifted the lid on my brown bear cookie jar and looked inside. "Where's your thirty-eight? It wasn't on you, and it's not in your cookie jar."

"It's sort of lost." It was lost two houses down and across the street from Mo's store, neatly tucked into an azalea bush. I'd called Ranger when I'd stopped home to shower, and I'd asked him to quietly retrieve the gun for me.

"Sort of lost," Morelli said. "Unh."

I saw him out and locked the door after him. I dragged myself into the bedroom and flopped on the bed. I lay there fully clothed with all the lights blazing and finally fell asleep when I could see the sun shining through my bedroom curtains.

At nine o'clock I opened my eyes to pounding on my apartment door. I lay there for a moment hoping the pounder would go away if I ignored him.

"Open up. It's the police," the pounder yelled.

Eddie Gazarra. My second-best friend all through grade school, now a cop, married to my cousin Shirley.

I rolled out of bed, shuffled to the door and squinted at Gazarra. "What?"

"Jesus," he said. "You look like hell. You look like you slept in those clothes."

My head was throbbing and my eyes felt like they were filled with sand. "It makes it easier in the morning," I said. "Not a lot of fuss."

Gazarra shook his head. "Tsk, tsk, tsk."

I looked down at the white bakery bag hanging from his chunky Polish hand. "Are there doughnuts in that bag?"

"Fuckin' A," Gazarra said.

"Do you have coffee too?"

He held a second bag aloft.

"God bless you," I said. "God bless your children and their children."

Gazarra got a couple plates from the kitchen, grabbed the roll of paper towels and took everything into the dining room. We divided up the doughnuts and coffee and ate in silence until all that was left was a splot of raspberry jelly on the front of Gazarra's uniform.

"So what is this?" I finally asked. "Social call, pity party, show of faith?"

"All of the above," Gazarra said. "Plus a weather report, which you didn't get from me."

"I hope it's warm and sunny."

Gazarra flicked at the mess on his shirtfront with a wad of paper napkin. "There are members of the department who'd like to pin last night's homicide on you."

"That's crazy! I had no motive. I didn't even know that guy."

"Turns out his name is Ronald Anders. Arrested on the eleventh of November for possession and sale of a controlled substance and illegal possession of firearms. Failed to appear in court two weeks later. Recovery never made . . . until last night. Guess who his bondsman is?"

"Vinnie."

"Yes."

Direct hit to the brain. No one had said anything to me about the FTA, including Morelli.

The doughnuts were sitting heavy in my stomach. "How about Morelli? Does Morelli want to charge me?"

Gazarra stuffed the paper coffee cups and napkins into a bag and carted it all off to the kitchen. "I don't know. I'm short on details. What I know is that you might want to get your ducks in a row just in case."

We faced each other at the door.

"You're a good friend," I said to Gazarra.

"Yeah," Gazarra said. "I know."

I closed and locked the door behind him and leaned my forehead against the doorjamb. The backs of my eyeballs hurt and the pain radiated out to the rest of my skull. If ever there was a time for clear thought, this was it, and here I was without a clear thought in my head. I stood a few minutes longer trying to think, but no wondrous revelations, no brilliant deductions burst into my consciousness. After a while I suspected I'd been dozing.

I was debating taking a shower when there was a loud rap on the door. I rolled my eye to the peephole and looked out. Joe Morelli.

Shit.

CHAPTER

5

"Open the door," Morelli said. "I know you're in there. I can hear you breathing."

I figured that was a big fat lie because I'd stopped breathing with the first rap of his knuckles.

Morelli knocked on the door again. "Come on, Stephanie," he said. "Your car's in the lot. I know you're home."

Mr. Wolesky, across the hall, opened his door. "What, you never heard of people in the shower? People sleeping? People going for a walk? I'm trying to watch some TV here. You keep making noise I'm gonna call the cops."

Morelli gave Mr. Wolesky a look that sent Mr. Wolesky scurrying back into his apartment. SLAM, click, click.

Morelli moved out of sight, and I waited with my eye glued to the peephole. I heard the elevator doors open and close, and then everything was quiet. Reprieve. Morelli was leaving.

I didn't know what Morelli wanted, and it seemed prudent not to find out—just in case it involved arresting me. I ran to my bedroom window, looked through the slit between the curtains and peeked down at the parking lot. I watched Morelli leave the building and get into an unmarked car.

I continued to watch, but nothing happened. He wasn't leaving. It looked like he was talking on his car phone. A few minutes went by, and my phone rang. Gosh, I thought, I wonder who that could be? On the odd chance it might be Morelli I let the machine pick it up. No message was left. I looked down into the lot. Morelli wasn't on his phone anymore. He was just sitting there, staking out the building.

I took a fast shower, dressed in clean clothes, fed Rex and went back to the window to check on Morelli. Still there. Rats.

I dialed Ranger's number.

"Yo," Ranger answered.

"It's Stephanie."

"I have something that belongs to you."

"That's a relief," I said, "but that's not my most pressing problem. I've got Joe Morelli sitting out in my parking lot."

"He coming or going?"

"There's a small chance he might want to arrest me."

"Not a good way to start the day, babe."

"I think I can get out the front door without being seen. Can you meet me at Bessie's in half an hour?"

"Be there," Ranger said.

I disconnected, called the office and asked for Lula.

"Your nickel," Lula said.

"It's Stephanie," I told her. "I need a ride."

"Oh boy. Is this more bounty hunter shit?"

"Yeah," I said. "This is bounty hunter shit. I want you to pick me up at my front door in ten minutes. I don't want you to park in the lot. I want you to cruise by the front of the building until you see me standing on the curb."

I blasted my hair with the dryer and did another take-a-look at Morelli. No change. He had to be freezing. Fifteen minutes more, and he'd be back in the building. I zipped myself into my jacket, grabbed my big shoulder bag and took the stairs to the first floor. I quickly crossed the small lobby and exited the front door.

There was no sign of Lula, so I huddled with my back to the building, crunched down inside my coat. Hard to believe Morelli would be here to arrest me, but stranger things have been known to happen. Innocent people were accused of crimes every day. More likely Morelli wanted to do another question session. I couldn't get excited about that either.

I heard Lula before I saw her. To be more specific, I felt the vibrations in the soles of my feet and against my rib cage. The Firebird slid to a stop in front of me, Lula's head bobbing in time to the music, lips moving to the beat. Boombaba boombaba.

I jumped in next to her and motioned to take off. The Firebird sprang to life and rocketed into the stream of traffic.

"Where we going?" Lula shouted.

I adjusted the volume. "Bessie's. I'm meeting Ranger."

"Your Buick on the blink too?"

"The Buick is fine. It's my life that's on the blink. Did you hear about the homicide at Uncle Mo's last night?"

"You mean that you aced Ronald Anders? Sure I heard. Everybody heard."

"I didn't ace him! I was knocked out. Someone killed him while I was unconscious."

"Sure. That's what's going around, but I figured . . . you know, dead or alive, right?"

"Wrong!"

"All right, all right. No cause to go PMS. How come you need a ride to Bessie's?"

"Joe Morelli is camped out in my parking lot, waiting to talk to me, and I don't want to be talked to."

"I guess I could understand that. He got one fine ass, but he's a cop all the same."

Bessie's was a coffee and doughnut shop around the corner from the Social Security offices. It was a scruffy little place with dusty floors and dirty windows, and it was always packed with the chronically unemployed and with worker drones from Social Security. It was the perfect place to get a cheap cup of terrible coffee and to fade away into the huddled masses.

Lula dropped me at the curb, cranked the noise level back to deafening and rumbled off. I elbowed my way to the back of the shop where Ranger was waiting. He had the last stool at the counter with his back to the wall. I never asked how he consistently managed to procure such a position. Sometimes it's best not to know these things.

I took the stool next to him, raising an eyebrow at the coffee and cruller on the counter. "Thought you weren't into internal pollution," I said. Lately Ranger'd been on a health food thing.

"Props," Ranger told me. "Didn't want to look out of place."

I didn't want to burst his fantasy bubble, but the only time Ranger wouldn't look out of place would be standing in a lineup between Rambo and Batman.

"I have a problem," I said to Ranger. "I think I'm in over my head."

"Babe, you've been in over your head since the first day I met you."

I ordered coffee and waited for my cup to arrive. "It's different this time. I might be a suspect in a homicide investigation. The guy on Mo's floor was Ronald Anders. One of Vinnie's skips."

"Tell me about it."

"I went to Uncle Mo's to look around."

"Hold it," Ranger said. "You break into the store?"

"Well, sort of. I had a key. But I guess technically it was an illegal entry."

"That's cool."

"Anyway, I was in the store, and I saw someone pass by the front window, so I went to the back door to leave. Before I could get out I heard footsteps, and then someone trying the lock. I hid in the bathroom. The back door opened and closed. The cellar door opened and closed. And then the door to the bathroom opened, and I was eyeball to eyeball with some big, pissed-off, Rasta-type guy who threw me against the wall and knocked me out. When I came around the guy was dead. What does this mean?"

"It means after you got knocked out someone else arrived and shot Ronald Anders," Ranger said.

"Who? Who would do that?"

We looked at each other, knowing we were both considering the same possibility. Mo.

"Nah," I said. "Impossible."

Ranger shrugged.

"That's a ridiculous idea," I told Ranger. "Mo isn't the sort of man who goes around shooting people."

"Who else could have shot Anders?"

"Anyone."

"That narrows it down." Ranger slid a five onto the counter and stood. "I'll see what I can find."

"My gun?"

He transferred my .38 from his pocket to my shoulder bag. "Not going to do you much good if you don't put bullets in it."

"One more thing," I said. "Could you give me a ride to the office?"

Connie came out of her chair when I blew through the door. "Are you okay? Lula said you actually got knocked out last night."

"Yes, I'm okay. Yes, I got knocked out. No, I didn't kill Ronald Anders."

Vinnie popped out of his office. "Christ, look who's here," he said. "The bounty hunter from hell. I suppose you want your recovery money for whacking Anders."

"I didn't whack Anders!" I shouted.

"Yeah, right," Vinnie said. "Whatever. Just next time try not to shoot your FTA in the back. It doesn't look good."

I gave Vinnie a hand gesture, but he was already back in his office with the door closed.

"Details," Connie said, leaning forward, eyes wide. "I want to know everything."

Truth is, there wasn't much to tell, but I went through the routine one more time.

When I was done Lula gave a disgusted sigh. "That's a pretty lame story," she said. "Cops gonna be after you like flies on a bad bean pie."

"Let me get this straight," Connie said. "You never saw the killer. You didn't smell him or hear him. In fact, you haven't got a teeny-tiny clue who he could be."

"I know the killer came from outside," I said. "And I think Ronald Anders knew the killer. I think Anders let the killer into the store and then turned his back on him."

"A partner?"

"Maybe."

"Maybe it was Old Penis Nose," Lula said. "Maybe Ronald Anders ran a tab and couldn't pay for his Snickers bars, so our man popped him."

"That's disgusting," Connie said. "That's not even funny."

"Hunh," Lula said. "You got a better idea?"

"Yeah," Connie said, "my idea is that you better get to work instead of saying dumb things about Uncle Mo."

"I'd like to get to work," I said, "but I don't know what to do. I'm at a total dead end. I'm a failure as a bounty hunter."

"You're not a failure," Connie said. "You got an apprehension this week. You got Ronald Anders."

"He was dead!"

"Hey, that's the way it goes sometimes." Connie pulled a stack of manila folders from her bottom drawer. "It's just that you're stalled on Mo. You should keep working other cases." She slid a folder from the top of the stack and flipped it open. "Here's a good one. Leroy Watkins. Came in yesterday, and I haven't given it out yet. You could have it if you want."

"He isn't cute, is he?" I asked Connie. "My image is at an all-time low. I'm not taking on any more cases where the FTA is Mr. Popularity."

"I know Leroy," Lula said. "Everybody call him Snake on account of his dick is . . ."

I squinched my eyes closed. "Don't tell me." I looked over at Connie. "What'd Leroy do to get himself arrested?"

"Tried to sell some dope to a narc."

"He ever resist arrest?" I asked.

"Not that I know of," Connie said. "There's nothing on his charge sheet about shooting cops."

I took the file from Connie. If Leroy Watkins was certifiably ugly I might take a crack at it. I flipped to the photo. Yow! He was ugly, all right.

"Okay," I said. "I'll see if I can find him." I glanced over at Connie. "There isn't anything else I should know, is there? Like, was he armed when arrested?"

"Nothing out of the ordinary," Connie said. "A forty-five, a twenty-two and a seven-inch blade."

My voice pitched to incredulity. "Two guns and a knife? Forget it! What do I look like, a suicide waiting to happen?"

We were all quiet for a minute while we considered my chances of success.

"I could go with you," Lula said. "We could be discreet."

Discreet? Lula?

"You think he's dangerous?" Connie asked Lula.

"He ain't no Boy Scout. Don't know if he'd want to shoot us, though. Probably he's just FTA so he could stay on the street and make maximum profit before getting locked down. I know his woman, Shirlene. We could go talk to her."

Talk to his woman. That sounded reasonable. I thought I might be able to handle that. "Okay," I said. "We'll give it a try."

Shirlene lived in a third-floor walk-up at the southern end of Stark Street. The cement stoop was littered with globules of rock salt that had eaten their way through yesterday's ice, leaving a doily of frozen gray slush. The front door to the building was weathered and stood ajar. The small inside hall was steeped in frigid damp.

"Feels like a meat locker in here," I said.

Lula snorted. "That's what it is, all right . . . a meat locker. Plain and simple. That's the trouble with Stark Street. It's all one big meat locker."

We were both panting by the time we got to the third floor.

"I've got to get in better shape," I said to Lula. "I've got to join a gym or something."

"I'm in plenty good shape," Lula said. "It's the altitude that gets me. If it wasn't for the altitude I wouldn't be breathing hard at all." She stared at Shirlene's door. "What are we gonna do if Snake's at home? I figure I should ask, being that you don't like violence except when you're out cold."

"Snake at home? Are you telling me Snake lives here?"

Lula blinked her big duck-egg eyes at me. "You mean you didn't understand that?"

"I thought we were visiting his woman's place."

"Well, yeah," Lula said, "but that happen to be Snake's place too."

"Oh boy."

"Don't worry," Lula said. "That Snake gives us any trouble I'll bust a cap up his ass." She knocked on the door. "I don't take no hard time from no Snake."

No one answered, so Lula knocked louder.

"HEY!" she yelled at the door.

We stood for a moment, listening in utter silence, and then from inside the apartment, inches from the closed door, came the unmistakable ratchet of a pump shotgun.

Lula and I locked eyes for a fraction of a second and shared a simultaneous thought, OH SHIT! We spun on our heels, hurled ourselves down the first flight of stairs and skidded across the second-floor landing.

BOOM! A gun blast blew a two-foot hole in Shirlene's front door, and plaster chunked out of the opposite wall.

"Out of my way!" Lula yelled. "Feet don't fail me!"

I had a head start on the next set of stairs, but Lula missed the first step, slid three steps on her ass and knocked me over like I was a bowling pin. The two of us rolled the rest of the way to the bottom, screaming and swearing until we landed in a heap on the foyer floor.

We scrambled to our feet and almost ripped the front door off its hinges trying to get out. We ran the two and a half blocks to Lula's Firebird, and Lula burned rubber from the curb. Neither of us said anything until we were parked in front of Vinnie's office.

"It wasn't that I was scared," Lula said. "It's just I didn't want to get blood on this here new sweatsuit. You know how hard it is to get blood out of this stuff."

"Yeah," I said, still breathing hard. "Blood is a bitch."

"Okay, so maybe I was a little scared," Lula said. "I mean, hell, that motherfucker would of shot us dead! Shit. What was he thinking of? What's the matter with him?"

"I've got to get a new job," I said to Lula. "I don't like getting shot at."

"I tell you, now that I'm thinking about it, I'm starting to get pissed off. Who the hell does that jerk think he is, anyway? I've got a mind to call him up and tell him what I think."

I handed Lula the file folder. "Be my guest. The phone number's on the first page. And while you're at it, tell him he'd better get his butt over here, because next time someone raps on his door it'll be Ranger."

"Fuckin' A," Lula said. "Ranger'd root that little pecker out. Ranger'd stomp on his miserable ass."

"Boy, I really hate being shot at," I said. "I really *hate* it!"

Lula wrenched her door open. "I'm not taking this shit. I'm not standing still for this kind of treatment."

"Me either," I said, getting caught up in the moment. "That creep needs to be locked up."

"Yeah," Lula said. "And we're just the ones to do it!"

I wasn't sure about that last part, but I let it slide, and Lula and I marched into the office like storm troopers invading Poland.

Connie looked up from her paperwork. "Uh-oh, what's going on?"

"We've just been shot at," Lula said, lower lip protruding a good two inches. "Can you believe it? I mean, I've been caught in drive-bys. I'm used to that shit. This shit was different. This shit was directed at me personally. I didn't like this shit one bit. This shit was offensive, you know what I'm saying?"

Connie raised her eyebrows. "Leroy Watkins?"

"Shot at us through a closed door," I said.

Connie nodded her head. "And?"

"And we ran away," I said. "Lula was worried about bloodstains on her new warm-up suit."

Lula had the file in one hand and Connie's phone in the

other. "That Leroy Watkins isn't getting away with this. I'm gonna call up his ass and tell him what I think. I'm gonna tell him I'm not taking this shit."

Lula punched in some numbers and stood hand on hip.

"I want to talk to Leroy," she said into the phone.

Someone responded at the other end, and Lula leaned forward. "What do you mean I can't talk to him? He just almost dropped a cap in me, and now he's not available to talk to me? I'll available his ass."

The phone was returned to Connie after five more minutes of discussion.

"Snake says he didn't know it was us," Lula said. "He said he'd go down to court with us if we come back."

"Who'd he think he was shooting at?" I asked Lula.

"He said he didn't know who he was shooting at. He said it just pays to be careful these days."

"He destroyed his door!"

"Guess a man in Snake's business got to worry."

I grabbed my bag and hung it on my shoulder. "Okay, let's get this over with."

"The filing is starting to get out of hand," Connie said to Lula. "This won't take you all day, will it?"

"Hell no," Lula said. "We'll be back before lunch."

I pulled on gloves but thought twice about a hat. You wear a hat in the morning and you look like a fool for the rest of the day. Not that I looked all that wonderful this morning. It was more that I didn't want to compound the problem. Especially since Morelli was sitting in my parking lot. Just in case the unthinkable happened, and I got arrested . . . I didn't want to have hat hair for my mug shot.

We rumbled off to Stark Street, each of us lost in our own thoughts. My thoughts ran mostly to warm beaches and half-naked men serving me long, cool drinks. From the stony expression on Lula's face I suspected her thoughts ran a lot darker.

Lula pulled up to the curb in front of Shirlene's apartment building and heaved herself out of the car. We stood on the sidewalk and looked up at the third-floor windows.

"He said he wasn't going to shoot at us, right?" I asked, just to be sure.

"That's what he said."

"You believe him?"

Lula shrugged.

Ranger would go in with gun drawn, but that wasn't my style. I felt stupid with a gun in my hand. After all, what purpose did it serve? Was I going to shoot Leroy Watkins if he refused to get in the car with me? I don't think so.

I grimaced at Lula. She grimaced back. We entered the building and slowly climbed the stairs, listening for the shotgun ratchet.

When we got to the third floor, Shirlene was in the dingy hall, staring at her ruined door. Shirlene was medium height, lean and sinewy. Her age would be somewhere between twenty and fifty. She was wearing pink terry cloth bedroom slippers, faded pink warm-up pants that were a size too small and a matching sweatshirt that was dotted with various-hued food stains, none of which looked recent. Her hair was short and chopped. Her mouth turned down at the corners. Her eyes were expressionless. She held a piece of cardboard box in one hand and a hammer in the other.

"Not gonna be able to hammer anything into that cheapskate door," Lula told her. "You need mollies. Only thing gonna hold that cardboard in place is mollies."

"Haven't got any mollies," Shirlene said.

"Where's Leroy?" Lula asked. "He isn't gonna shoot at us again, is he?"

"Leroy's gone," Shirlene said.

"Gone? What do you mean gone?"

"Gone is gone," Shirlene said.

"Where'd he go?"

"Don't know," Shirlene said.

"When will he be back?"

"Don't know that either."

Lula stuffed her fists onto her hips. "Well, what *do* you know?"

"I know I gotta get this door fixed," Shirlene said. "And you're standing here taking up my time."

Lula walked into the front room. "You don't mind if I look around, do you?"

Shirlene didn't say anything. We both knew nothing short of that twelve-gauge pump was going to stop Lula from looking around.

Lula disappeared into the back room for a moment. "You're right," she said to Shirlene. "He's gone. He take any clothes with him? He look like he gonna be gone a long time?"

"He took his gym bag, and you know what he got in there."

I looked over at Lula, eyebrows raised in silent question.

Lula made her hand into a gun shape and aimed it at me. "Oh," I said.

"My time is valuable," Lula said to Shirlene. "What's the matter with that man, doggin' me like this? He think I haven't got anything better to do than to hike up those stairs?"

I gave Shirlene my card, and Lula and I trudged down the stairs with Lula grumbling the whole way.

"Walk up the stairs, walk down the stairs. Walk up the stairs, walk down the stairs," she said. "Leroy better hope I never catch up with him."

Now that I was back on the street I wasn't all that sad not to have made an apprehension. An apprehension would have meant a trip to the police station. And the police station was the last place I wanted to visit right now.

"I guess we could try some bars," I said with no enthusiasm.

"Snake's not gonna be in a bar at this time of day," Lula said. "Snake's more likely to be hanging around a school-yard, checking up on his sales force."

That gave me some incentive. "Okay. Let's drive by some schools."

An hour later we were out of schools and still hadn't found Snake.

"Any other ideas?" I asked Lula.

"Who's listed on his bail ticket?"

"Shirlene."

"No one else? No mama?"

"Nope. Just Shirlene."

"I don't know," Lula said. "Usually a man like Snake is out on the street. Even in weather like this he could be on the street." She slowly drove down Stark. "Not nobody out here today. Don't even see anybody we can ask on."

We drove by Jackie's corner, and it was empty too.

"Maybe she's with a client," I said.

Lula shook her head. "Nuh-uh, she isn't with no client. She's in that snooty parking lot, waiting for her man. Bet my life on it."

Lula cruised the block around my apartment building while I checked for Morelli. I didn't see his car, or anything that resembled a cop or a copmobile, so I had Lula drop me at the front door. I entered the lobby cautiously, not completely convinced of Morelli's departure. I did a fast survey and crossed to the stairs. So far, so good. I crept up the stairs, cracked the door at the second floor, peeked out to an empty hallway and sighed in relief. No Morelli.

I couldn't avoid Morelli forever, but I figured if I avoided him long enough he'd find other leads, and eventually I'd be off the hook.

I unlocked my door and was met with the sound of Rex running on his wheel. I bolted the door behind myself, hung my bag and jacket on one of the four coat hooks I'd installed in my tiny foyer and took a left into the kitchen.

The light was blinking on my answering machine. Four messages.

The first was from Morelli. "Call me."

I knew it was Morelli because my nipples contracted at the sound of his voice. His tone held a hint of annoyance. No surprise there.

The second message was just as cryptic. "Leave Mo alone. Or else." A man's voice, muffled. Unrecognizable. Great. Just what I needed. Anonymous threatening messages.

The third was from the Nissan service center telling me I had new points and plugs. The timing had been reset. And my car was ready to be picked up.

The fourth was from my mother. "Stephanie! Are you there? Are you all right? What's this I hear about a shooting? Hello? Hello?"

Good news travels fast in the burg. Bad news travels even faster. And if there's scandal attached, life as we know it comes to a halt until every detail of the tawdry event has been retold, examined, exclaimed over and enhanced.

If I allowed myself to consider what was being said about me at this very moment I'd probably fall over in a faint.

I dialed my parents' number and got a busy signal. I briefly considered whether this absolved me from the obligatory explanatory phone call and decided it didn't.

I made myself a tuna fish, potato chip and pickle sandwich and ate it at the kitchen counter.

I tried calling my mother again. Still busy.

I put Rex in the bathtub while I cleaned his cage. Then I cleaned the tub. Then I cleaned the rest of the bathroom. I ran the vacuum. I damp-mopped the kitchen floor. I scoured some of the crud off the top of the stove. Just in case I was arrested, I didn't want my mother coming in to my apartment and finding it dirty.

At three o'clock I gave up with the cleaning and tried another call to my mother. No luck.

I called Sue Ann to get the scoop on myself and to set the record straight. You could always get Sue Ann. Sue Ann had call waiting.

"You ever hear anything about Uncle Mo being . . . odd?" I asked Sue Ann.

"Odd?"

"Romantically."

"You know something!" Sue Ann shouted into the phone. "What is it? What is it? What's the dirt on Uncle Mo? He's having an affair, right?"

"I don't know. I was just wondering. Probably you should forget I said anything."

I disconnected and tried my mother again. Her line was still busy. It was close to four o'clock, and the light was fading. I went to the window and peered down at the parking lot. No sign of Morelli.

"So what do you think?" I asked Rex. "Should I keep trying the phone or should I just take a ride over?"

Rex telepathically suggested that communicating with my mother in person would have the added advantage of being able to scrounge dinner.

I thought this was pretty clever considering Rex had a brain the size of a dried pea.

I grabbed my shoulder bag and my jacket and squinted into the security peephole on my front door. No one in view. I cracked the door and looked out at the hall. Clear. I took the stairs, crossed the small lobby and exited through the rear door to the lot.

The seniors always snapped up all the good slots close to the back entrance, so my Buick was parked at the outer edge, next to the Dumpster.

I could hear a steady drone of cars on St. James, and streetlights had just blinked on. I had almost reached the Buick when a black Jeep Cherokee suddenly wheeled into the lot and rolled to a stop.

The tinted driver's side window slid down and a man wearing a ski mask looked out at me, leveled a .45 and squeezed off two rounds that zinged into the blacktop about six inches from my foot. I stood rooted to the spot, paralyzed by fear and astonishment.

"This is a warning," the man said. "Stop looking for Mo. Next time these bullets will be in your brain." He discharged three rounds into the heavy iron side of the Dumpster. I dove for cover. A fourth round whistled overhead.

The window rolled up, and the car sped out of the lot.

CHAPTER

6

When my heart resumed beating I got to my feet and cautiously looked over the edge of the Dumpster. Mrs. Karwatt was coming toward me, halfway across the lot, picking her way around icy spots on the macadam, clutching a small plastic bag of garbage to her chest.

"Did you see that?" I asked, my voice approaching a level audible only to canines.

"What?"

"That man in the car. He shot at me!"

"No!"

"Didn't you hear it?"

"For goodness' sakes," she said. "Isn't that terrible. I thought it was a backfire. I had my eyes fixed on the ice. Gotta be careful, you know. My sister slipped and broke her hip last winter. Had to put her in a home. Never did recover right. It's not so bad, though. She gets green Jell-O for dessert twice a week at lunchtime."

I ran a shaky finger over the holes in the Dumpster where the bullets had impacted. "This is the second time today someone's shot at me!"

"Getting so a body can't go out of the house," Mrs. Karwatt said. "What with the ice and the shooting. Ever since we put a man on the moon the whole planet's gone to heck in a handbasket."

I was looking for someone to nail for my sorry life, but I didn't think it was fair to lay it all on Neil Armstrong.

Mrs. Karwatt pitched her bag into the Dumpster and headed back to the building. I sort of wanted to go with her, but my knees were shaky, and my feet weren't moving.

I wrenched the door open on the Buick and collapsed onto the seat, hands clutching the wheel. Okay, I said to myself. Get a grip. These were two freak incidents. The first shooting was mistaken identity. And the second shooting was . . . what? A death threat.

SHIT.

I pulled the cell phone out of my shoulder bag and dialed up Morelli.

"Someone just shot at me!" I yelled into the phone at him. "I was getting into my car in my parking lot, and this guy in a ski mask drove up and told me to lay off looking for Mo. And then he shot at me. Warning shots, he said. And then he drove away."

"Are you hurt?"

"No."

"Are you in immediate danger?"

"No."

"Did you make a mess in your pants?"

"Came damn close."

We were silent for a couple beats while we digested all this.

"Did you get his plate number?" Morelli asked. "Can you give me a description of the guy?"

"I was too rattled to think to get the plate. The guy was average build. White. That's all I've got."

"Are you going to be okay?"

"Yeah." I nodded my head in the car. "I feel better now. I just . . . I had to tell somebody."

"While I have you on the phone . . ." Morelli said.

Damn! I forgot I was avoiding Morelli! I snapped the cell phone closed. No sweat, I told myself. No harm done. But probably it's not a good idea to hang out in the lot. That left me with two choices. I could go with my plan to visit my parents, or I could return to my apartment and hide in my coat closet. The coat closet held a lot of appeal short-term, but at some point I'd have to venture out, and by that time I'd most likely have missed dinner.

Go with dinner, I thought. Do the coat closet later.

My mother wasn't smiling when she opened the door.

"Now what?" she said.

"I didn't do it."

"You used to say that when you were a little girl, and it was always a fib."

"Cross my heart," I said. "I didn't shoot anybody. I accidentally got knocked out, and when I came to I was sharing a hallway with a dead guy."

"You got knocked out!" My mother smacked the heel of her hand against her forehead. "I have to have a daughter who goes around getting herself knocked out."

Grandma Mazur was in line behind my mother.

"Are you sure you didn't pop him one? I could keep a secret, you know."

"I didn't pop him!"

"Well that's a big disappointment," she said. "I had a good story all ready to tell the girls at the beauty parlor."

My father was in the living room, hiding in front of the TV. "Unh," he said, never moving a muscle.

I sniffed the air. "Meat loaf."

"Got a new recipe from Betty Szajack," my mother said.

"She puts sliced olives in her meat loaf, and she makes it with soaked bread instead of crackermeal."

The best way to defuse my mother is to talk about food. For thirty years, we've expressed love and anger in terms of gravy and mashed potatoes.

"So are you staying for supper?" my mother wanted to know. "I have spice cake with chocolate mocha icing for dessert."

"Sure," I said. "That would be nice."

I helped Grandma Mazur set the table while my mother finished up in the kitchen. We were about to sit down when the doorbell rang.

"Probably the paperboy trying to juice us out of more money," Grandma said. "I'm wise to his tricks."

I answered the door and found myself looking into Joe Morelli's brown eyes.

He grinned when he saw me. "Surprise."

"What do you want?"

"You asking for the long list or the short list?"

"I don't want any list." I made an attempt to close the door, but he muscled his way into the foyer. "Out!" I said. "This isn't a good time."

He ignored me and strolled into the dining room. "Evening," he said to my mother. He acknowledged my father with a nod of his head, and he winked at my grandmother.

"We're having meat loaf with olives," Grandma Mazur said to Morelli. "You want some? We got plenty."

"I wouldn't want to impose," Morelli said.

This triggered eye rolling on my part.

My mother pulled an extra side chair up next to me and laid out another plate. "We wouldn't think of having you leave without supper," she said to Morelli.

"I'd think of it," I said.

My mother smacked me on the top of my head with a wooden serving spoon. "Miss Fresh Mouth."

Morelli helped himself to two slabs of meat loaf, mashed potatoes, green beans and applesauce. He made polite conversation with my mother and grandmother and discussed sports scores with my father. On the surface Morelli seemed relaxed and smiling, but there were unguarded moments when I caught him watching me with the offhand intensity of a tree toad eyeing a tasty insect.

"So what's going on between you and my granddaughter?" Grandma asked Morelli. "Being that you're here for supper I guess everything's pretty serious."

"Getting more serious by the minute," Morelli said.

"Morelli and I have a working relationship," I said to Grandma. "Nothing more."

Morelli slouched back. "You shouldn't fib to your grandma. You know you're crazy about me."

"Well, listen to that," Grandma said, clearly charmed. "Isn't he the one."

Morelli leaned toward me and lowered his voice. "Speaking of work, I have a matter I'd like to discuss with you in private. I thought maybe we could go for a ride together after the table is cleared."

"Sure," I said. And maybe I'll poke out my eye with the turkey baster.

I gathered the plates together and hauled them off to the kitchen. My mother and Grandma Mazur followed with the serving dishes.

"You go ahead and cut the cake," I told my mother. "I'll get the coffee going."

I waited a moment until I had the kitchen to myself, then I promptly did a quiet exit through the back door. I had no intention of going for a ride that would culminate in a body cavity search. Not that a body cavity search would be a new experience. Morelli had already performed this procedure on me at various ages, with varying degrees of success. The new twist would be that this time the search might be done by a prison matron—and that was even less appealing than falling prey to Morelli.

I was wearing jeans and boots and a flannel shirt over a T-shirt, and my teeth were chattering by the time I'd cut through my parents' backyard and run the two blocks to Mary Lou's house. Mary Lou's been my best friend for as long as I can remember. For six years now she's been more or less happily married to Leonard Stankovic of Stankovic and Sons, Plumbing and Heating. She has two kids and a mortgage and a part-time job as a bookkeeper for an Oldsmobile dealership.

I didn't bother with the formality of knocking on her door. I just barged in and stood there stomping my feet and flapping my arms in her living room, and saying, "D-d-damn it's c-c-cold!"

Mary Lou was on her hands and knees picking up little plastic cars and men that looked like fireplugs. "Maybe it would help if you tried wearing a coat."

"I was at my parents' house and Morelli showed up, and so I had to sneak out the back door."

"I don't buy into that one," Mary Lou said. "If you were with Morelli just now you'd be missing a lot more clothes than your coat."

"This is serious. I'm afraid he might want to arrest me."

Mary Lou's two-year-old, Mikey, toddled in from the kitchen and latched onto Mary Lou's leg dog style.

I thought kids were okay from a distance, but I wasn't all that excited about the way they smelled up close. I suppose when they belong to you it makes a difference.

"You probably should stop shooting guys," Mary Lou said. "You shoot a lot of guys, and eventually the cops get cranky about it."

"I didn't shoot this one. Anyway, I had to sneak out of the house, and I had to leave my coat and everything behind."

Lenny and the four-year-old were sitting in front of the

TV watching a rerun of *The Munsters*. Lenny was an okay person but sort of a mouth breather. Mary Lou had always gone for that type, preferring brawn to brain. Not that Lenny was entirely stupid. It's just that you'd never get him confused with Linus Pauling.

Mary Lou dumped the fireplug people into a plastic laundry basket that was filled with toys, and the two-year-old let out a howl. He cried flat out with his hands clasping and unclasping, reaching for who knows what. Mary Lou, I suppose. Or maybe for his toys that were being put away for the night. He cried with his mouth wide open and his eyes scrunched tight, and in between sobs he shrieked, "No, no, no!"

Mary Lou took a graham cracker from her pocket and gave it to Mikey.

Mikey shoved the cracker into his mouth and continued to blubber, chewing and rubbing his face with his fat baby hands. Cracker mush mixed with tears and baby snot worked its way into his hair and onto his face. Brown drool rolled off his chin and stained his shirt.

Mary Lou gave Mikey a "been there, seen this" look. "Mikey's tired," she said.

Like I said before, kids were okay from a distance, but I didn't think they'd ever replace hamsters.

"I need to use your phone to call home," I said to Mary Lou.

She wiped at the mush with her shirttail. "Help yourself."

I dialed from the kitchen, straining to hear over the racket in Mary Lou's living room. "Is Morelli still there?" I asked my mother.

"He just left."

"Are you sure? He's not hanging around outside, is he?"

"I heard his car drive away."

I borrowed a sweatshirt from Mary Lou and ran back to my parents' house. I cut through the backyard and jogged down the driveway to check the street. The street looked clear. No Morelli. I retraced my steps to the kitchen door and let myself in.

"Well," my mother said, "what gives?"

"Never catch me walking out on a hunk like Joe Morelli," Grandma said. "I guess I'd know what to do with a man like that."

I guessed I knew what to do with him too, but probably it was illegal to neuter a cop. "You didn't give him any spice cake to take home, did you?" I asked my mother.

My mother tipped her chin up a fraction of an inch. "I gave him the whole thing. It was the least I could do after you left him sitting here high and dry."

"The whole thing!" I shouted. "How could you do that? I didn't get a single piece!"

"That's what happens when you walk out. And how was I to know where you were? You could have been kidnapped. You could have had a brain seizure and wandered off with amnesia. How was I to know you'd be back and want spice cake?"

"I had reasons for leaving," I wailed. "Perfectly good reasons."

"What reasons?"

"Morelli was going to arrest me . . . maybe."

My mother took a deep breath. "Arrest you?"

"There's a small possibility that I might be a homicide suspect."

My mother made the sign of the cross.

Grandma didn't look nearly so glum. "There was a woman on TV the other day. On one of them talk shows. She said she'd been arrested for smoking dope. She said when you get arrested the cops lock you up in a little cell and then sit around watching you on closed-circuit TV, waiting for you to go to the bathroom. She said there's this stainless steel commode in one corner of your cell, and it hasn't got a toilet seat or anything, and that's where you have to go. And she said the commode faces the TV camera just so they can all get a good view of the whole thing."

My stomach went hollow and little black dots danced in front of my eyes. I wondered if I had enough money in my bank account to buy a ticket to Brazil.

Grandma's expression got crafty. "The woman on TV said what you needed to do before you got arrested was to drink a lot of Kaopectate. She said you needed to get good and plugged up so you could wait until you got out on bail."

I sat down in a chair and put my head between my knees.

"This is what comes of working for your father's cousin," my mother said. "You're a smart girl. You should have a decent job. You should be a schoolteacher."

I thought of Mary Lou's kid with the graham crackers smeared in his hair, and felt better about being a bounty hunter. You see, it could always be worse, I thought. I could be a schoolteacher.

"I need to go home," I said, retrieving my coat from the hall closet. "Lots of work to do tomorrow. Got to get to bed early."

"Here," my mother said, handing me a grocery bag. "Some meat loaf. Enough for a nice sandwich."

I looked in the bag. Meat loaf. No spice cake.

"Thanks," I said to my mother. "Are you sure there isn't any spice cake left?"

"A homicide suspect," my mother said. "How could such a thing happen?"

I didn't know. I wondered the same thing. In fact, I wondered all the way home. I wasn't such a bad person. I only cheated a little on my taxes, and I paid most of my bills. I didn't cuss at old people (at least not to their face). I didn't do drugs. So why was I having such rotten luck? Okay, so I didn't go to church as often as I should, but my mother went regularly. I thought that should count for something.

I rolled Big Blue into the lot. It was late. All the good

spots were taken, so I was back by the Dumpster again. What's new. At least it afforded me cover from a drive-by. Maybe I'd park here all the time.

I looked up at my apartment and realized my lights were on. That was weird, because I was almost positive I'd shut them off when I left this afternoon. I got out of the car and walked to the middle of the lot. I looked up at my windows again. The lights were still on. What did this mean? It could mean the lights had been on when I left, and I was suffering from early onset of dementia. Probably I could add a touch of paranoia to the dementia.

A shadowy figure appeared briefly toward the far wall of my living room, and my heart skipped a beat. Someone was in my apartment. I was relieved to be able to rule out the dementia, but I still had a problem. I really didn't want to do my own investigating and get shot at for the third time today. Unfortunately, the alternative was to call the police. Since I was low on Kaopectate, I didn't think calling the police was a good alternative.

The figure reappeared. Long enough for me to decide it was a man. He moved closer to the window, and I was able to see his face.

The face belonged to Morelli.

Of all the nerve. Morelli had broken into my apartment. And that wasn't even the worst of it. He was eating something. I suspected it was spice cake.

"PIG!" I yelled. "Creep!"

He didn't seem to hear. Probably the TV was on.

I did a fast walk around the lot and found Morelli's black Toyota 4x4. I gave the back bumper a kick, and the alarm went off.

Faces appeared in the windows above me while the alarm wailed away.

Mrs. Karwatt on the second floor threw her window open and leaned out. "What's going on out there?"

A shotgun barrel poked from Mr. Weinstein's window. "Whose alarm is that? It's not my Cadillac, is it?"

The only window without a face was mine. I figured that was because Morelli was thundering down the stairs.

I ran to my car with my keys in my hand.

"Stay away from that car, or I'll shoot," Mr. Weinstein shouted.

"It's *my* car," I yelled back.

"The hell it is," Mr. Weinstein said, squinting at me through his inch-thick trifocals. BOOM! Mr. Weinstein fired and took out the windshield on the car next to me.

I bolted across the grass median into the street and streaked for the houses on the other side. I stopped and looked back. Morelli was pacing under the rear overhang, shouting at Mr. Weinstein, obviously afraid to venture out into the lot for fear of getting shot.

I slipped into the shadows between two houses, hopped a backyard fence and came out onto Elm Street. I crossed Elm and repeated the pattern, bringing me to Hartland. I jogged a block up Hartland, crossed Hamilton and plastered myself against the brick wall of an all-night convenience store.

The previous owner of the store had been Joe Echo. He'd sold it in November, and the new Asian owner, Sam Pei, had changed the name to The American Store. I thought the name was appropriate. The American Store contained a sampling of everything an American might need at four times the price. A box of Fig Newtons for $7.50. No matter that there were only twelve in a box. I guess when you needed a Fig Newton in the middle of the night, you damn well didn't care what it cost.

I pulled a knit cap out of my pocket and tugged it down over my ears. The battery was low on my cell phone, so I searched in my shoulder bag for a quarter, found one, dropped it into the pay phone and dialed my number.

Morelli answered on the fourth ring.

I unclenched my teeth enough to get a few words out. "What the hell are you doing in my apartment?"

"Waiting for you," Morelli said.

"What were you eating just now?"

"Spice cake. There's still some left, but you'd better hurry."

I neatly clicked the phone back into the receiver. "*Ugh!*"

I bought a Snickers from Mr. Pei and ate it while I walked. Time to be realistic. Morelli was a lot better at this cops-and-robbers stuff than I was. It seemed to me that if he wanted to arrest me, he would have done it by now. For that matter, if he was serious about bringing me in for further questioning he would have done it. Probably there was no immediate need for the Kaopectate.

So why was Morelli harassing me? Because he wanted something. What did he want? Information that I might be withholding? Maybe he thought he could worm some missing details out of me better under more casual circumstances. Or maybe he wanted to threaten me without witnesses. Or maybe he wanted to ask me for a date.

I turned the corner at Hartland and decided I should talk to Morelli. This was no longer a simple recovery. Mo was still missing. A man had been killed. I'd been threatened. And there were some details I'd neglected to tell Morelli when I'd been questioned at the station. Not to mention the spice cake.

Everything looked status quo when I got to my parking lot. Lights were on in my apartment. Morelli's car hadn't been moved. A small gathering of people were clustered around the Chrysler Mr. Weinstein had used for target practice. Mr. Weinstein was there with a big piece of plastic bagging and a roll of duct tape in his hand.

"Another minute and he would have been driving off in this car, I'm telling you," Mr. Weinstein was saying. "Better a broken windshield than a stolen car."

"Isn't that the truth," Arty Boyt said. "Good thing you had that gun handy."

Everyone else nodded. Good thing, they all said.

I slipped into the building and went to the pay phone at the front of the small lobby. I dropped a quarter and called upstairs.

"It's me again," I said when Morelli answered.

"Where are you?"

"Far away."

"Liar." I could hear the smile in his voice. "I saw you cross the parking lot."

"Why are you stalking me?"

"Cops don't stalk. Cops pursue."

"Okay. Why are you pursuing me?"

"We need to talk," Morelli said.

"That's it? Just talk?"

"You had something else in mind?"

"Nope."

We were both silent for a moment, contemplating the something else.

"Well," I said, "what do you want to talk about?"

"I want to talk about Mo, and I don't want to do it on the phone."

"I heard some people might want to arrest me."

"That's true," Morelli said. "But I'm not one of them."

"I have your word?"

"I won't arrest you tonight. I'd rather not make a blanket statement that covers eternity."

He was waiting with the door open when I got off the elevator.

"You look cold and tired," he said.

"Dodging bullets is exhausting. I don't know how you cops do it day after day."

"I assume you're talking about Mr. Weinstein."

I hung my jacket and my shoulder bag on a wall hook.

"I'm talking about everyone. People keep shooting at me." I sliced myself off a big chunk of spice cake and told Morelli about Snake.

"So what do you think?" I asked.

"I think bounty hunters should be tested and licensed. And I think you'd flunk the test."

"I'm learning."

"Yeah," Morelli said. "Let's hope you don't get dead in the process."

Ordinarily I'd consider a remark like that to be an insult, but I'd actually been thinking along the same lines myself. "What's the deal with Uncle Mo?"

"I don't know," Morelli said. "At first I was worried he was dead. Now I don't know what to think."

"What kind of prints did you get from his store?"

"Yours, Mo's and Anders's from the doorknobs in the rear. We didn't bother with the public areas. Two-thirds of the burg would have showed up."

"The neighbors see anything?"

"Only the lady across the street who reported the flash-light." Morelli was slouched against my kitchen counter, arms crossed over his chest. "Any other questions?"

"Do you know who killed Anders?"

"No. Do you?"

I rinsed my plate and put it in the dishwasher. "No." I looked at Morelli. "How did Anders get into the store? I heard him fumbling out there, trying the doorknob. At first I thought he had a key, but the door wouldn't open. So then I decided he must be jimmying the lock."

"There was no sign of forced entry."

"Can we unofficially walk through this?"

"You must be reading my mind," Morelli said.

"I'm not saying any of this to a cop, right?"

"Right."

I poured myself a glass of milk. "This is what I know. The

back door to Mo's store was locked. I opened it with a key I got from his apartment. After I was in the store I pulled the door closed. When Ronald Anders tried to get in, the door was locked. At first it sounded like he had a key, but the door wouldn't open. He fiddled with it for a couple minutes, and the door clicked open. Did you find anything on him that he could have used to pick a lock?"

"No."

"Did you find a key to the store on him?"

"No."

I raised my eyebrows.

Morelli raised his eyebrows.

"Either someone needed a set of picks, or else someone lifted a key that doesn't work especially well," I said. "Or maybe someone opened the door with a sticky key, let Ronald Anders into the store, disappeared for a few minutes, returned and killed Anders."

Morelli and I sighed. The logical person to have a sticky key would be Uncle Mo. And it wasn't so far-fetched that Mo would know Anders in light of the fact that Mo had been seen on Stark Street from time to time. Maybe this was drug related. Maybe Mo was buying. Hell, maybe Mo was selling. After perusing Mo's bedtime books I was willing to believe almost anything about him.

"You have anybody talking to the kids who hang at the store?" I asked Morelli. "When you were working vice did you hear anything about drugs coming out of Mo's?"

"Just the opposite," Morelli said. "Mo's was a safe zone. Mo was militant against dope. Everyone knew."

I had another idea. "How militant?" I asked. "Militant enough to kill a dealer?"

Morelli looked at me with his unreadable cop face.

"That would be strange," I said. "Lovable, out-of-shape ice cream guy turns killer. Revenge of the small businessman."

Anders was shot in the back. He'd been carrying a gun, but

the gun hadn't been touched. The gun had been found when the police rolled the body. The gun had been stuffed into the waistband of Anders's double-pleated rapper slacks. Whoever got nailed for the murder would have a hard time pleading self-defense.

"Is that it?" I asked Morelli.

"For now."

Morelli was wearing jeans, boots and a long-sleeved driver's shirt with the sleeves pushed up. He had his service pistol clipped to his belt. He grabbed his khaki jacket from one of the wall hooks in the entrance hall and shrugged into it.

"I'd appreciate it if you didn't take any vacations in foreign countries for a couple days," he said.

"Gee, and I have tickets to Monaco."

He gave me a chuck under my chin, smiled and left.

I stared at the closed front door for a moment. A chuck under the chin. What was that? In the past, Morelli had tried to stick his tongue down my throat. Or at the very least he'd make a lewd suggestion. I was suspicious of a chuck under the chin. Now that I thought about it, he'd been a perfect gentleman when he'd brought the pizza. And what about last night? He'd left without so much as a handshake.

I checked myself out in the hall mirror. My hair was still squashed under the knit cap. Not real sexy, but that had never slowed Morelli down before. I pulled the cap off and my hair sprang out. Eek. Good thing I'd left the cap on.

I went back to the kitchen and dialed Ranger.

"Yo," Ranger said.

"Anyone bragging about killing Ronald Anders?"

"No one's bragging about anything these days. The streets are quiet."

"Turf war?"

"Don't know. A couple players are missing. A couple dopers are dead. Got some hot shit going around killing people."

"ODs?"

"That's the way the death certificates read."

"You think something different?"

"Feels dark, babe."

I disconnected and a minute later the phone rang.

"We got a situation on our hands," Lula said.

"A situation?"

"Just got a call from Jackie, and I can't make any sense of what she's saying. Something about how her old man jacked her over again."

"Where is she?"

"She's at the FancyAss Apartments. She's been there day and night, and she sounds flipped out. I told her to wait right where she was, and we'd come fast as we could."

Fifteen minutes later I pulled into the RiverEdge lot. The sky was black and dense above evenly spaced pools of artificial light thrown by the overhead halogen lamps. Jackie had parked her Chrysler on the fringe of one of those pools. The river was a block away, and the ice fog swirled around the lamps and settled on the cars.

Jackie stood beside her car, waving her arms while she yelled at Lula, and Lula was yelling back at Jackie.

"Calm down," Lula was saying. "Calm down!"

"He's dead," Jackie shouted. "Dead, dead, dead. Fucking dead. Dead as a goddamn doorknob. What a bitch!"

I looked at Lula, and Lula gave me an I-don't-know shrug.

"I just got here," Lula said. "I can't get her to say anything besides the motherfucker's dead. Maybe she's too coked up. Maybe we need to get something to slow her down."

"I'm not coked up, you dumb ho," Jackie said. "I'm trying to tell you he's dead, and you're not fucking listening."

I looked around the lot. "Is he dead anywhere nearby?"

I really wanted a no on this one. I'd already had my millennium quota of dead.

"You see that big bush by the Dumpster?" Jackie said.

"Yeah."

"You see that ugly-ass foot sticking out of that big bush?"

Oh boy. She was right. There was a foot sticking out of the bush.

"Shit, Jackie," I said. "You didn't kill that foot, did you?"

"No, I didn't kill that foot. That's what I've been trying to tell you. Someone jacked me over. I've been sitting out here, freezing my ass off, waiting to kill that sonovabitch Cameron Brown, and someone beat me to it. It isn't fair!"

Jackie wheeled off for the Dumpster with Lula and me scrambling to keep up.

"I decided to neaten up the car," Jackie said. "So I come over here with a bag of trash, and I'm throwing it in the Dumpster, and I see something sort of reflecting light. And I look a little harder, and I see it's a watch. And then I see it's attached to a wrist. And I say, Goddamn, I know that watch and that wrist. So I dig around some and look what I come up with. Look what I hauled out of the goddamn garbage."

She stopped at the bush, reached down, grabbed hold of the foot and dragged a man's body out into the open. "Just look at this. He's dead. And if that isn't bad enough, he's frozen solid. This motherfucker is one big frosty Popsicle. It's not even like I get to see him rot. Damn."

Jackie dropped the foot and gave Cameron a good solid kick in the ribs.

Lula and I jumped back and sucked in some air.

"Dang," Lula said.

"That ain't the half of it," Jackie said. "I've been sitting here waiting to shoot him, and that's what I'm going to do."

Jackie opened her coat, pulled a 9mm Beretta out of her sweatpants and drilled half a clip into Cameron Brown. Cameron jumped around some from the impact, but mostly the bullets didn't have much effect—except for putting a bunch of extra holes in various body parts.

"Are you nuts?" Lula yelled. "This guy's dead! You're shooting a dead man!"

"Isn't my fault," Jackie said. "I wanted to shoot him while he was alive, but somebody beat me to it. I'm just making the best of a bad situation."

"You've been drinking," Lula said.

"Damn skippy. Would have froze to death if I didn't have a nip once in a while."

Jackie raised the gun, looking to unload a few more rounds into Cameron.

"Hold on," Lula said. "I hear sirens."

We stood still and listened to the whoop, whoop, whoop.

"Coming this way!" Lula said. "Every man for himself!"

We all ran for our cars and took off at the same time, almost crashing into each other trying to get out of the lot.

CHAPTER

7

Jackie and Lula and I rendezvoused at a Dunkin' Donuts parking lot, about a quarter mile from RiverEdge. We parked our cars side by side and got out to have a huddle.

"I need a doughnut," Jackie said. "I want one of those fancy ones with the colored sprinkles on top."

"You need more than a doughnut," Lula told her. "You need your head examined. You just shot up a dead man. What were you thinking?"

Jackie was rummaging in her pockets, looking for doughnut money. "I guess I got a right to shoot someone if I want to."

"Nuh-uh," Lula said. "There's rules. This man was already dead, and you showed disrespect for the deceased."

"The deceased didn't deserve no respect. He stole my car."

"Everybody deserves respect when they're dead," Lula said. "It's a rule."

"Says who?"

"Says God."

"Oh yeah? Well, God don't know jack-shit about rules. I'm telling you, that's a stupid rule."

Lula had her hands on her hips, and her eyes bugged out of her head. "Don't you talk about God like that, you worthless ho. I'm not gonna stand here and let you blaspheme God."

"Hold it!" I shouted. "What about the police?"

"What about them?" Jackie wanted to know.

"We need to call them."

Jackie and Lula looked at me like I was speaking Klingon.

"Someone killed Cameron Brown before Jackie made Swiss cheese out of him. We can't just leave Brown lying there alongside the Dumpster," I told them.

"No need to worry about that," Lula said. "That place is crawling with cops by now. They'll find Cameron. He's right out there in the open."

"Yeah, but shooting dead people is probably a crime. That makes us accessories if we don't report it."

"I'm not going to the police," Jackie said. "Unh-uh. No way."

"It's the right thing to do," I said.

"The hell," Jackie said. "It's the stupid thing to do."

"Stephanie's right," Lula told Jackie. "It's the dope and the liquor that's stopping you from doing the right thing. Just like it's the dope and the liquor that makes you blaspheme God. You gotta do something for yourself," Lula said to Jackie. "You gotta go to detox."

"Don't need detox," Jackie said.

"Uh-huh," Lula told her.

"Unh-uh."

"Uh-huh."

"I know what you're doing," Jackie said. "You've been trying to get me to detox ever since you got straight. This here's just a trick."

"You bet your ass," Lula said. "And either you go to detox, or we turn you in." Lula looked at me. "Isn't that right?"

"Yeah," I said. "That's right." Seemed like that's what the court would do anyway. Probably the clinic on Perry Street would do it better.

It started with polite rapping on my door. And then when I didn't answer, it turned to pounding. I looked through my peephole and saw Morelli pacing and muttering. He turned and gave my door another shot with his fist.

"Come on, Stephanie," he said. "Wake up. Get out of bed and answer your door."

It was eight-thirty, and I'd been awake for an hour. I'd taken a shower, gotten dressed and had breakfast. I wasn't answering my door because I didn't want to talk to Morelli. I suspected he'd just come from RiverEdge.

I heard him fiddling with the lock. The lock clicked open. Thirty seconds later he had the deadbolt. My front door pushed open but caught on the chain.

"I know you're there," Morelli said. "I can smell your shampoo. Open the door, or I'm coming back with a bolt cutter."

I slid the chain and opened the door. "Now what?"

"We found Cameron Brown."

I opened my eyes wider to simulate surprise. "No!"

"Yes. Frozen solid. And extremely dead. Been dead for days is my guess. Found him next to the Dumpster at the RiverEdge condo complex."

"I'll have to tell Jackie."

"Uh-huh. Funny thing about the body. Looked like who-ever killed Brown had him tossed into the Dumpster. And then someone came along last night, dragged the body out of the Dumpster and pumped half a clip into him."

"No!"

"Yes. It gets even funnier. Two of the RiverEdge residents came forward, saying they heard a bunch of women arguing in the lot, late at night, then they heard gunshots. When they looked out their windows what do you suppose they saw?"

"What?"

"Three cars leaving the lot. One of them was an old Buick. They thought it might be powder blue with a white top."

"Did they get a plate? Did they see the women?"

"No."

"Guess that's a tough break for you guys, huh?"

"I thought you might be able to shed some light on the incident."

"Am I talking to you as a cop this morning?"

"Shit," Morelli said. "I don't want to hear this."

"So, is it against the law to shoot someone after he's already dead?"

"Yes, it's against the law."

I made a small grimace. "I thought it would be. Just exactly what law is it against?"

"I don't know," Morelli said. "But I'm sure there's something. I suppose there were extenuating circumstances."

"A woman scorned . . ."

"Is this scorned woman going to come forward?"

"She's going into detox."

"Your job description reads 'bounty hunter,'" Morelli said. "Social worker is a whole different job."

"You want some coffee?"

He shook his head, no. "I've got paperwork. Then I've got an autopsy."

I watched him walk down the hall and disappear into the elevator. Only an idiot would think they could talk to Morelli and not be talking to Morelli the cop. Cops never stopped being cops. It had to be the world's hardest job.

Trenton cops wore more hats than I could name. They were arbitrators, social workers, peacekeepers, baby-sitters and law enforcers. The job was boring, terrifying, disgusting, exhausting and often made no sense at all. The pay was abysmal, the hours were inhuman, the department budget was a joke, the uniforms were short in the crotch. And year after year after year, the Trenton cops held the city together.

Rex was in his soup can, butt side out, half buried under wood shavings, hunkered in for his morning nap. I cracked a walnut and dropped it into his cage. After a moment there was movement under the wood shavings. Rex backed himself out, snatched half of the walnut and carried it into his can. I watched a couple minutes longer, but the show was over.

I checked my pocketbook to make sure I had the essentials . . . beeper, tissues, hair spray, flashlight, cuffs, lipstick, gun with bullets, recharged cell phone, recharged stun gun, hairbrush, gum, pepper spray, nail file. Was I a kick-ass bounty hunter, or what?

I grabbed my keys and stuffed myself into my jacket. First thing on my agenda was a visit to the office. I wanted to make sure Jackie was holding up her part of the bargain.

The sky felt low and forbidding over the parking lot, and the air was as cold as a witch's fadiddy. The lock was frozen on the Buick, and the windshield was coated with ice. I hammered on the lock, but it wouldn't break loose, so I trekked back to my apartment and got some deicer and a plastic scraper. Ten minutes later, I had my door open, the heater going full blast, and I'd chipped a squint hole in the ice on my windshield.

I slid behind the wheel, tested the hole for vision and decided it would do if I didn't drive too fast. By the time I got to Vinnie's I was nice and toasty and could see my entire hood, not to mention the road. Jackie's Chrysler was parked in front of the office. I took the slot behind her and hustled inside.

Jackie was pacing in front of Connie's desk.

"Don't see why I need to do this," Jackie was saying. "It isn't like I can't control myself. It isn't like I couldn't stop if I wanted. I just like to do some once in a while. Don't see what's so wrong about that. Everybody do some once in a while."

"I don't," Connie said.

"Me either," Lula said.

"Me either," I said.

Jackie looked at us one by one. "Hunh."

"You'll be happy when you get straight," Lula said.

"Oh yeah?" Jackie said. "I'm happy now. I'm so goddamn happy I can't hardly stand it. Sometimes I just happy myself into a state."

Connie had her copy of Mo's file on her desk. "We don't get Mo in the next five days and we're going to have to forfeit the bond," she said to me.

I flipped the file open and took another look at the bond agreement and the picture.

Jackie looked over my shoulder. "Hey," she said, "it's Old Penis Nose. You after him? I just saw him."

Everyone turned and stared at Jackie.

"Yep, that's him all right," she said, flicking a false red fingernail against the photo. "Drives a blue Honda. Remember we used to see him on the street sometimes. Saw him coming out of the apartment building on Montgomery. The one next to the mission."

Lula and I looked at each other. Duh.

"He alone?" I asked Jackie.

"I wasn't paying much attention, but I don't remember anyone else."

"I'm gonna drive Jackie over to the clinic on Perry Street," Lula said. "Help her get started."

The problem with the clinic on Perry Street was that it was filled with dopers. Therefore, the street outside was filled with dealers. The dopers came to get their daily dose of methadone, but on the way in and out it was like walking through a controlled-substance supermarket. Easiest place to get dope in any city is always at the meth clinic.

Lula wasn't going along to make sure Jackie got started. Lula was going along to make sure Jackie didn't OD before she even signed the papers.

Lula followed me to my parents' house and waited while I parked the Buick in the driveway. Then she and Jackie dropped me at the Nissan service center.

"Don't let them give you no baloney about that truck," Lula said. "You test-drive it. You tell them you'll bust a cap up their ass if that truck isn't fixed."

"Okay," I said. "Don't worry. Nobody's taking advantage of me."

I waved her off and went in search of the service manager. "So what do you think?" I asked him. "Is the truck in okay shape?"

"We've got it running like a top."

"Excellent," I said, relieved that I didn't have to do any cap busting.

Jackie had seen Mo coming out of an apartment building on the corner of Montgomery and Grant. I wouldn't call it a hot lead, but it was better than nothing, and I thought it deserved a look. Montgomery and Grant were southeast of the burg in an area of Trenton that worked hard at staying prosperous. The apartment building anchored the street, with the rest of the block given over to small businesses. Sal's Café, A&G Appliances, Star Seafood, Montgomery Street Freedom Mission and the Montgomery Street Freedom Church.

I circled the block, looking for a blue Honda. None

turned up. The apartment building had its own underground parking, but a key card was required to get past the gate. No problem. I could park on the street and check the garage on foot.

I did three laps around the block, and finally someone pulled out of a desirable space at the curb. I wanted to be on Montgomery, in view of both the front door and the garage entrance. I thought I'd snoop in the garage, take a look at the mailboxes, and then maybe I'd hang out and see if anything interested me.

There were seventy-two mailboxes. None had the name "Moses Bedemier" printed on it. The garage was only a third full. I found two blue Hondas, but none with the correct plate.

I went back to the truck and sat. I watched the people on the street. I watched the cars. I didn't see anyone I knew. At one o'clock I got a sandwich at Sal's Café. I showed Mo's picture and asked if he'd been seen.

The waitress looked at it.

"Maybe," she said. "Looks sort of familiar, but it's hard to say for sure. We get so many people passing through. A lot of older men come in for coffee before the mission opens its doors for breakfast. It started out being for the homeless, but it's used more by seniors who are lonely and strapped for money."

At four I left the pickup and positioned myself just inside the building entrance where I could flash Mo's picture and question the tenants. By seven I was out of tenants and out of luck. Not a single person had recognized Mo's picture.

I bagged the stakeout at eight. I was cold. I was starved. And I was twitchy with pent-up energy. I drove back to the burg, to Pino's Pizzeria.

Two blocks from Pino's I stopped for a stop sign, and sensed seismic activity under the hood. I sat through a few shakes and some rough idle. KAPOW. The truck backfired and stalled. "Son of a bitch!" I yelled out. "Goddamn Japanese piece-of-shit truck. Goddamn lying, cheating, goat-piss mechanic!"

I rested my forehead on the steering wheel for a second. I sounded like my father. This was probably how it felt to go down on the *Titanic*.

I babied the truck into Pino's lot, swiveled from behind the wheel and bellied up to the bar. I ordered a draft beer, a deluxe fried chicken sandwich, a small pepperoni pizza and fries. Failure makes me hungry.

Pino's was a cop hangout. Partly because half of the force lived in the burg, and Pino's was in a convenient location. Partly because Pino had two sons who were cops, and cops supported cops. And partly because the pizza was top of the line. Lots of cheese and grease, a little tomato sauce and great crust. Nobody cared that the roaches in the kitchen were as big as barn cats.

Morelli was at the other end of the bar. He watched me order, but held his distance. When my food arrived he moved to the stool next to me.

"Let me guess," he said, surveying the plates. "You've had a bad day."

I made a so-so gesture with my hand.

He was six hours over on a five o'clock shadow. Even in the darkened barroom I could see the tiny network of lines that appeared around his eyes when he was tired. He slouched with one elbow on the bar and picked at my fries.

"If you had a decent sex life you wouldn't need to gratify yourself like this," he said, his mouth curved into a grin, his teeth white and even against the dark beard.

"My sex life is okay."

"Yeah," Morelli said. "But sometimes it's fun to have a partner."

I moved my fries out of his reach. "Been to any good autopsies lately?"

"Postponed to tomorrow morning. The doc is hoping Cameron Brown will be thawed out by then."

"Know anything on cause of death? Like what kind of bullet did the job?"

"Won't know until tomorrow. Why the interest?"

I had my mouth full of chicken sandwich. I chewed and swallowed and washed it back with beer. "Just curious." Curious because this was the second dead drug dealer I'd stumbled over since starting the Mo search. It was a stretch to think there might be a connection. Still, my radar was emitting a low-level hum.

Morelli looked pained. "You and your girlfriends didn't do him the first time, did you?"

"No!"

He stood and tugged at my hair. "Be careful driving home."

He snagged a brown leather bomber jacket off a hook on the wall at the far end of the bar and left.

I stared after him, dumbstruck. He'd tugged my hair. First a chuck on the chin, and now a tug at my hair. This was a definite put-off. It was one thing for me to snub Morelli. It was an entirely different matter for him to snub me. This was *not* how the game was played.

I rolled out of Pino's at nine-thirty, feeling sulky and suspicious. I stood staring at my truck for a moment before getting in. More misery. My truck wasn't cute anymore. It looked like it needed orthodontia. I'd gotten new points and plugs, but I didn't have money for the body work. I slipped behind the wheel and shoved the key in the ignition. The truck started and . . . stalled.

"SHIT!"

My parents' house was only three blocks away. I raced the engine all the way and was relieved to finally be able to let the rotten truck die at the curb.

The Buick sat gloating in the driveway. Nothing was ever wrong with the Buick.

•   •   •

The phone woke me out of a dead sleep. The digital display on my bedside clock read 2 A.M. The voice at the other end was girlish.

"Hi ya," the voice said. "It's Gillian!"

Gillian. I didn't know anyone named Gillian. "You have the wrong number," I told her.

"Oops," she said. "Sorreee. I was looking for Stephanie Plum."

I pushed myself up on an elbow. "This is Stephanie Plum."

"This is Gillian Wurtzer. You gave me your card, and you said I should call you if I saw Uncle Mo."

Now I was fully awake. Gillian, the kid across from Mo's!

Gillian giggled. "My boyfriend was over tonight. You know, helping me with my homework. And he just left. And while we were saying good-bye I noticed there was a light on in the candy store. It must have been the hall light in the back. And I saw someone moving around in there. I couldn't tell if it was Uncle Mo or not, but I thought I should call you anyway."

"Is the light still on?"

"Yes."

"I'm ten minutes away. Keep your eye on the store, but don't go out. I'll be right there."

I was wearing a red flannel nightgown and thick white socks. I pulled on a pair of jeans, shoved my feet into my Doc Martens, grabbed my jacket and my pocketbook and flew down the hall, punching Ranger's number into my cell phone while I ran.

By the time I reached the Buick I'd explained it all to Ranger and had the phone back in my pocketbook. It had begun to drizzle with the temperature hovering at freezing so that every car in the lot sat under a shroud of ice. Déjà vu. I used my nail file to chip the ice away from the door handle and counted to ten in an attempt to lower my blood pressure. When the blood stopped pounding in my ears I used the nail file to carve a six-inch hole in the ice on my windshield. I jumped in the car and took off, driving with my nose practically pressed to the glass.

Please, please, please still be there.

I really wanted to catch Uncle Mo. Not so much for the money as for the curiosity. I wanted to know what was going on. I wanted to know who killed Ronald Anders. And I wanted to know why.

The burg was quiet at this time of night. Houses were dark. Streets were empty of traffic. Streetlights were hazy behind misting rain. I slowly rolled by Mo's store. A light was burning in the back hall, just like Gillian had said. There was no sign of Ranger. No blue Honda parked at the curb. No movement anywhere. I took King and turned into the alley leading to Mo's garage. The garage door was open, and deep in shadow, I could see a car parked in the garage. The car was a Honda.

I cut my lights and angled the Buick so that it was blocking the Honda's exit. I sat for a moment with my window cracked, listening, watching. I silently slipped out of the Buick, walked the length of the alley down King to Ferris and crossed the street. I stood in black shade, behind the Wurtzers' oak, and I waited for Ranger, waited for the store light to be extinguished, for a form to appear.

I glanced at my watch. I'd give Ranger three more minutes. If Ranger wasn't here in three minutes I'd cross the street and cover the back door. I had my gun in one pocket and pepper spray in the other.

Car lights appeared a block down King. When the car reached Ferris the lights in the store blinked out. I took off at a sprint just as Ranger's BMW turned the corner and slid to a stop.

Ranger owned two cars. The first was a black Bronco

equipped with a state-of-the-art Bird Dog tracking system. When Ranger was doing a takedown and expected to transport felons he drove the Bronco. When Ranger wasn't responsible for a takedown, he drove a black BMW, limited production 850 Ci. I'd priced the car and found it listed at close to seven figures.

"The lights just went out," I called in a stage whisper. "His car's in the garage. He's going to go out the back door."

Ranger was dressed in black. Black jeans, black shirt, black flak vest with FUGITIVE APPREHENSION AGENT lettered in yellow on the back. His earring shone silver against dark skin. His hair was held back in his usual ponytail. He had his gun in hand when his foot hit the curb. If he'd been after me I'd have wet my pants on the spot.

"I'll take the back," he said, already moving away from me. "You cover the front."

This was fine with me. I was perfectly happy to play second string.

I scooted to one side of the candy shop's front door, pressing myself against the brick front. I had fairly good vision through the window, into the store, and I was in a good position to nab Uncle Mo if he bolted for Ferris Street.

A dog barked in the distance. It was the only sound in the sleeping neighborhood. Ranger was undoubtedly at the back door, but there was no indication of entry or capture. My stomach was clenched in anticipation. I had my lower lip caught between my teeth. Minutes passed. Suddenly the store was flooded with light. I inched to the window and looked inside. I could clearly see Ranger in the back hall. No one else was visible.

Ranger was opening doors just as I had done days ago. He was looking for Mo, and in my gut I knew he wouldn't find him. Mo had slipped away. And it was all my fault. I should have moved sooner. I shouldn't have waited for Ranger.

I turned at the sound of labored breathing and almost

collided with Mo. His face was shadowed, but the shadows did little to hide his annoyance.

"You blocked my car," he said. "And now your cohort is nosing around in my store. You keep this up, and you'll ruin everything!"

"You failed to show for your court appearance. I don't know why you decided to run, but it's not a good idea. You should let me drive you to the police station to reschedule."

"I'm not ready. It's too soon. You'll have to talk to my lawyer."

"You have a lawyer?"

"Yes." His eyes locked onto Ranger's Beemer. The door was open, and the keys dangled from the ignition. "Ohhh," he said. "This will do nicely."

"Oh no. Not a good idea."

His mouth tipped up at the corners into an ironic smile. "It looks like the Batmobile."

"It's not the Batmobile. Batman doesn't drive a BMW. And I can't let you go driving off in it. You're going to have to come with me."

Mo was carrying a plastic bag in one hand and a bear-sized can of pepper spray in the other. He narrowed his eyes and pointed the can at me. "Don't make me use this."

I'd seen people get sprayed. It wasn't fun. "Bond is the one in the BMW," I told him. "Happy driving."

"Bond," he repeated. "Of course."

And then he took off.

Ranger rounded the corner at a run and stopped short in the middle of the sidewalk, watching the Beemer's tail-lights disappear into the night. "Mo?"

I nodded and pulled my collar tight to my neck.

"Probably there's a good reason why you didn't take him down."

"His can of pepper spray was bigger than my can of pepper spray."

We stood there for a few more minutes, squinting into the mist, but Ranger's car didn't reappear.

"I'm going to have to kill him," Ranger said, his voice matter-of-fact.

I thought Ranger might be kidding, but then again . . . maybe not.

I'd once asked Ranger how he could afford such expensive cars, and he said he'd made some good investments. I wasn't sure what he meant by that. A money market account seemed a little tame for Ranger. If I had to venture a guess on the contents of Ranger's portfolio, I'd lean toward running guns to well-connected foreign gunmongers.

"Find anything unusual in the store?" I asked Ranger. Like a dead body.

"Nothing. He must have seen you on the street. Didn't even take the time to make sure the back door was closed. Just cleared out of there."

I filled Ranger in on Cameron Brown and the RiverEdge while we walked back to my car. Then I told him about Jackie seeing Mo on Montgomery Street, coming out of the apartment building. I told Ranger how I'd staked the building out but hadn't come up with anything.

Ranger looked at my bedraggled hair and at the red flannel nightgown hanging under my jacket. "Who are you supposed to be?"

"I was in a hurry."

"You're going to give bounty hunters a bad name you go around looking like that."

I unlocked the passenger door for Ranger, climbed behind the wheel and cranked the engine over. "Where to?"

"Montgomery Street."

That would have been my choice too. I'd listened to the BMW drive away. It had gone southeast, toward Montgomery.

•   •   •

"Nobody home," Ranger said, after walking the underground lot.

"We could wait."

"Babe, I don't know how to break this to you, but we're not exactly inconspicuous. Doing surveillance in this car is like trying to hide a whale in a jelly jar."

Fine by me. I was cold and wet and tired. I wanted to go home and crawl into my nice warm bed and sleep until July.

"Now what?" I asked.

"You can drop me at Twelfth and Major."

No one knew where Ranger lived. I had Norma run a check on him once at the DMV and his address turned out to be an empty lot.

"You aren't really going to kill him, are you?" I asked, nosing the Buick toward Twelfth.

"You steal an eight-fifty Ci, you should be killed."

"It's Uncle Mo."

"Uncle Mo is wacko," Ranger said.

"Yes, but he's my wacko. I'd appreciate it if you didn't kill him until after I log him in and straighten a few things out." Like who killed Ronald Anders.

"Professional courtesy."

"Yeah."

"You have any leads?"

"No."

"We'll work together on this one," Ranger said. "I'll pick you up tomorrow at five."

"Five in the morning?"

"You got a problem with that?"

"Nope. No problem."

Trenton is creepy at three in the morning. Forlorn and subterranean, the pulse of the city checked behind black glass and acid-etched brick. Even the night people, the drunks and the kiddie crews, were tucked away, leaving the occasional fluorescent wash of light to derelict pigeons, walking the sidewalks, pecking at fool's food.

What sort of person would cruise these streets at this hour? Cops, shift workers, evildoers, bounty hunters.

I swung into my lot and cut the engine. Chunks of yellow dotted the big block building in front of me. Mrs. Karwatt, Mrs. Bestler, the DeKune apartment, Mr. Paglionne. Seniors don't waste a lot of time sleeping. Mr. Walesky, across the hall from me, was probably watching TV.

I stepped away from the Buick and heard a car door open and close behind me. My heart did a little tap dance at the sound. I looked to the building entrance and saw two figures move from the shadows. My gun was still in my pocket. I hauled it out and spun around, almost smacking a wiry little guy in the nose with it.

He immediately jumped back a step, hands in the air. "Take it easy," he said.

I had the other two in my peripheral vision. They'd stopped and raised their hands. All three men were wearing ski masks and brown coveralls over their street clothes.

"Who are you?" I asked. "What's going on?"

"We're concerned citizens," the wiry little guy said. "We don't want to hurt you, but if you keep after Mo we're going to have to take action." He reached into his breast pocket and pulled out an envelope. "You're a businesswoman. We understand that. So here's the deal. The money in this envelope represents your fee for bringing Mo in to Vinnie, plus a two-hundred-dollar bonus. Take the money and hop a plane for Barbados."

"Number one, I don't want your money. Number two, I want some answers."

The wiry guy made a come-on signal with his hand, and car lights blinked on behind him. The car rolled forward and the back door opened.

"Get in that car, and I'll shoot," I said.

"I'm unarmed. You wouldn't want to shoot an unarmed man."

He was right there. Not that it mattered. It had been an empty threat to begin with.

I'd set my alarm for four fifty-five and was so startled when it rang that I fell out of bed. I hadn't allowed myself time for a shower, so I brushed my teeth, dressed myself in some clothes I found on the floor from the previous day and staggered downstairs.

Ranger was waiting for me in the lot. He pulled a piece of paper, folded into four sections, from his jacket pocket and gave it to me. "A list of Montgomery Street tenants," he said. "Anything jump out at you?"

I didn't ask how he'd gotten the list. I didn't want to know the details of Ranger's network. I suspected his methods for acquiring information might sometimes involve broken bones and small-caliber bullet holes.

I handed the list back to him. "Don't know any of these people."

"Then we go door-to-door at nine o'clock."

Oh goody.

"In the meantime we'll stake out the lobby and the garage."

The plan was for Ranger to take the lobby and for me to take the garage, to position ourselves at the elevator banks and question the tenants as they left for work. At nine o'clock, after drawing a big zero, we started working the floors.

The first four floors were a washout.

"This doesn't feel hopeful," I said to Ranger. "We've talked to a lot of people, and we haven't even had a nibble."

Ranger shrugged. "People don't notice. Especially in a building like this. No sense of community. And there's another possible reason for no one to have seen him."

"Jackie might have been wrong."

"She's not the most reliable witness."

We walked up a flight and started moving down the hall, knocking on doors, showing Mo's picture. Third door down I got a hit.

The woman was older than most in the building. Sixties, I guessed. Nicely dressed.

"I've seen this man," she said. She studied the photo. "I just don't know . . . Maybe Stanley Larkin. Yes, I think I must have seen him with Stanley."

"Is Larkin's apartment on this floor?" I asked.

"Two doors down on this side. Number five-eleven." Two little frown lines creased her forehead. "You said you were apprehension agents. What does that mean?"

I gave her the minor charge, the missed-a-court-appearance line, and she seemed relieved.

Ranger knocked on Larkin's door, and we both flattened ourselves against the wall so Larkin couldn't see us through the security peephole.

A moment later, Larkin opened the door. "Yes?"

Ranger badged him. "Bond enforcement. May we step inside to ask you a few questions?"

"I don't know," Larkin said. "I don't think so. I mean, what is this all about?"

Larkin was in his late sixties. About five feet, ten inches. Ruddy complexion. Sandy hair, thin on the top.

"It will only take a moment," Ranger said, his hand on Larkin's elbow, gently guiding him back a few steps.

I used the opportunity to step inside and look around. It was a small apartment packed with furniture. Avocado green wall-to-wall carpet. Harvest gold drapes straight from the seventies. I could see the kitchen from where I stood. One juice glass and one cereal bowl in the dish drain. A coffee mug and newspaper on the kitchen table.

Ranger was showing Larkin the picture, asking him about Mo. Larkin was shaking his head.

"No," Larkin said. "I don't know him. Mrs. Greer must have been confused. I have some older men friends. Maybe from a distance one of them might look like this man."

I quietly stepped to the bedroom door. Queen-size bed in the bedroom. Perfectly made with a dark green paisley spread. A few pictures on the dresser in an assortment of silver frames. Night table at bedside with a clock radio.

Ranger handed Stanley Larkin a card. "Just in case," Ranger said. "If you see him, we'd appreciate a call."

"Of course," Stanley said.

"What do you think?" I asked when we were alone in the hall.

"I think we need to finish the building. If no one else places Mo with Larkin, my inclination is to put it on hold. Larkin didn't feel like he had secrets."

CHAPTER

8

Ranger and I went back to the Bronco and stared at the apartment building.

"False alarm," I said. No one else had recognized Mo.

Ranger was silent.

"Sorry about your car."

"It's only a car, babe. I can get a new one."

It occurred to me that it might be significant Ranger had said he could *get* a new Beemer as opposed to *buying* a new Beemer. And it also occurred to me that it might be pointless to suggest filing a police report or informing an insurance company of theft.

"You think we should stake out the building?" I asked.

Ranger looked the length of the street. "We could hang around for a while."

We slouched down, arms crossed over our chests, seat pushed back to give more leg room. Ranger never said anything when we waited like this. Ranger had a conversational potential only slightly greater than Rex's. That was fine by me because I had my own thoughts.

I was bothered that Mo had gone back to the store. Even if the store was the most important thing in my life I'm not sure I'd have risked a visit. Mo was carrying a plastic bag, which could have been filled with anything from underwear to ice cream cones. He also hadn't smelled all that good. He'd smelled musty. And he'd smelled like sweat and dirt. Either he'd been working hard in the garden, or else he was living on the street.

I was still speculating on these possibilities when at twelve o'clock Ranger got us drinks and sandwiches from Sal's.

My sandwich looked like brown bread and grass. "What is this?" I asked.

"Mixed sprouts, shredded carrot, cucumber and raisins."

Raisins! Thank God. I was afraid someone had scooped my sandwich out of the rabbit cage.

"Bedemier has to be staying somewhere," Ranger said. "Did you check out the possibility of a second apartment?"

"Did that first thing. Drew a blank."

"Have you canvassed motels?"

I gave him an openmouthed, goggle-eyed look that said, *Ugh! No!*

"It would pass the time," Ranger said. "Keep us out of trouble."

Ranger's sense of humor.

"Maybe Mo is living on the street. Last time I saw him he smelled like a cave."

"Hard to check on caves," Ranger said. "Easier to check on motels."

"You have any ideas on how you want to do this?"

Ranger pulled a section of the Yellow Pages out of his pocket. "Sal didn't need these," he said. He handed half the pages to me. "You get the first half of the alphabet. Show the picture. Ask about the car. If you find him, don't do anything. Call me."

"What if we zero on this?"

"We enlarge our canvass zone."

I shouldn't have asked.

Half hour later I was behind the wheel of the Buick. I'd rearranged my list according to geography, starting with the closest motels, working my way to Bordentown.

I'd called my father and asked him to please take my pickup back to the Nissan service center. He'd murmured something about throwing good money after bad, and that kids never listened anymore, and then he'd hung up.

By five o'clock I'd gone through two tanks of gas and had struck out from A to J. By five o'clock it had gotten very dark, and I wasn't looking forward to going home. Driving Uncle Sandor's Buick was like rolling along in my own private bomb shelter. Once I parked the bomb shelter in my parking lot, unlocked the door and set foot on the blacktop, I was open season for the Uncle Mo Fan Club.

I didn't feel like being open season on an empty stomach, so I detoured to my parents' house.

My mother was at the door when I pulled up to the curb. "What a nice surprise," she said. "Are you staying for supper? I have a ham in the oven and butterscotch pudding for dessert."

"Did you put pineapple and cloves on the ham?" I asked. "Are there mashed potatoes?"

The pager hooked to my belt started to beep. Ranger's number flashed on the screen.

Grandma came over and took a close look. "Maybe when my Social Security check comes in I'll get one of these gizmos."

From deep in his chair in the living room my father boosted the sound on the TV.

I dialed Ranger's number on the kitchen phone.

"Who are you talking to?" Grandma Mazur wanted to know.

"Ranger."

Grandma's eyes got wide. "The bounty hunter! What does he want?"

"A progress report. Nothing important."

"You should ask him over for dinner."

I put the phone to my chest. "I don't think that's a good idea."

"Tell him we got ham," Grandma said.

"I'm sure he's busy."

My mother looked up from measuring out flour. "Who's busy?"

"Stephanie's boyfriend," Grandma said. "The bounty hunter one. He's on the phone right now."

"And he's too busy to come to dinner?" my mother said. More indignant disbelief than a question. "Whoever heard of such a thing? The man has to eat, doesn't he? Tell him we have plenty of food. Tell him we're setting an extra plate."

"They're setting an extra plate," I told Ranger.

There was a moment of silence at the other end.

"You come from a long line of scary women," Ranger finally said.

Water bubbled up from the boiling potatoes and spattered on the stove. Red cabbage cooked in the two-quart pot. Peas and carrots simmered on the far burner. The kitchen windowpanes were frost-etched on the bottom and steamy on the top. The wall behind the stove had started to sweat.

My mother stabbed at the potatoes. "The potatoes are done," she said.

"I have to go," I told Ranger. "The potatoes are done."

"What'll happen if I don't show up?" Ranger wanted to know.

"Don't ask."

"Shit," Ranger said.

• • •

My father is an equal opportunity bigot. He wouldn't deprive a man of his rights. And he's not a hate-filled man. He simply knows in his heart that Italians are superior, that stereotypes were created by God, and if a person is worth anything at all he drives a Buick.

He was now staring at Ranger with the sort of dumbfounded confusion you'd expect of a man whose home had just been firebombed for no good reason.

Ranger was in his black mode today. Double gold studs in his ears, form-fitting long-sleeved black T pushed up to his elbows, black-banded diver's watch at his wrist, black rapper slacks tucked into black combat boots with enough gold chain around his neck to secure bail for murder one.

"Have some ham," Grandma said to Ranger, passing him the plate. "Are you a Negro?" she asked.

Ranger didn't blink an eye. "Cuban."

Grandma looked disappointed. "Too bad," she said. "It would have been something to tell the girls at the beauty parlor I had dinner with a Negro."

Ranger smiled and spooned out potatoes.

I'd decided at an early age to stop being embarrassed over my family. This is yet another advantage to living in Jersey. In Jersey everyone has the right to embarrass themselves with no reflection on anyone else. In fact, embarrassing yourself periodically is almost required.

I could see my mother going through mental gymnastics, searching for a safe subject. "Ranger is an unusual name," she managed. "Is it a nickname?"

"It's a street name," Ranger said. "I was a Ranger in the army."

"I heard about them Rangers on TV," Grandma said. "I heard they get dogs pregnant."

My father's mouth dropped open and a piece of ham fell out.

My mother froze, her fork poised in midair.

"That's sort of a joke," I told Grandma. "Rangers don't get dogs pregnant in real life."

I looked to Ranger for corroboration and got another smile.

"I'm having a hard time finding Mo," I told my mother. "You hear anything at the supermarket?"

My mother sighed. "People don't talk much about Mo. People mostly talk about you."

Grandma mashed her peas into her potatoes. "Elsie Farnsworth said she saw Mo at the chicken place getting a bucket of extra spicy. And Mavis Rheinhart said she saw him going into Giovachinni's Market. Binney Rice said she saw Mo looking in her bedroom window the night before last. Course, two weeks ago Binney was telling everyone Donald Trump was looking in her window."

Ranger declined the butterscotch pudding, not wanting to disrupt the consistency of his blood sugar level. I had two puddings and coffee, choosing to keep my pancreas at peak performance. Use it or lose it is my philosophy.

I helped clear the table and was seeing Ranger to the door when his cell phone chirped. The conversation was short.

"Got a skip in a bar on Stark Street," Ranger said. "Want to ride shotgun?"

Half an hour later we had the Bronco parked in front of Ed's Place. Ed's was standard fare for Stark Street. One room with a couple chipped Formica tables in the front and a bar across the back. The air was stale and smoke-choked, smelling like beer and dirty hair and cold French fries. The tables were empty. A knot of men stood at the bar, forsaking the three bar stools. Eyes swiveled in the dark when Ranger and I walked through the door.

The bartender gave an almost imperceptible nod. His eyes cut to an alcove at one end of the bar. A dented sheet metal sign on the wall by the alcove said GENTS.

Ranger's voice was low at my ear. "Stay here and cover the door."

Cover the door? Moi? Was he kidding? I gave a little finger wave to the men at the bar. No one waved back. I pulled the .38 five-shot out of my pocket and shoved it into the front of my Levi's. This didn't get any waves either.

Ranger disappeared into the alcove. I heard him knock on a door. He knocked again . . . louder. There was the sound of a doorknob being tried, another knock and then the unmistakable sound of a boot kicking in a door.

Ranger burst from the hallway on a run. "Went out the window into the alley."

I followed Ranger into the street. We stopped for a split second, listening for footfalls, and Ranger took off again, through the alley to the back of the bar. I was skidding on ice, kicking at garbage, and I was breathing hard. I caught my toe on a piece of board and went down to one knee. I pulled myself up and swore while I hopped for a few steps until the pain faded.

Ranger and I came out of the alley and hit the cross street. A dark figure ran for the front door of a row house halfway down the block, and we pounded after him. Ranger charged through the front door, and I took the alley two houses down to secure the rear exit. I was gasping for air and fumbling for my pepper spray as I came up to the back door. I had my hand in my pocket when the door flew open, and Melvin Morley III crashed into me.

Morley was as big as a grizzly. He was accused of armed robbery and assault with a deadly weapon. He was drunk as a skunk and didn't smell much better.

We hit the ground with a solid thud. Him on the bottom. Me on top. My fingers reflexively grabbed at his jacket.

"Hey, big boy," I said. Maybe I could distract him with my female charms.

He gave a grunt and flicked me away like I was lint. I rolled back and grabbed hold of his pants leg.

"Help!" I yelled. "HELLLLLLP!"

Morley hauled me up by my armpits and held me at eye level, my feet at least nine inches off the ground. "Dumb white bitch," he said, giving me a couple vicious shakes that snapped my head back.

"F-f-fugitive apprehension agent," I said. "Y-y-you're under arrest."

"Nobody's arresting Morley," he said. "I'll kill anyone who tries."

I flailed my arms and swung my legs, and my toe mysteriously connected with Morley's knee.

"Ouch," Morley yelled.

His big ham hands released me, and he buckled over. I staggered back a couple feet when I hit the ground, knocking into Ranger.

"Hey, big boy?" Ranger said.

"I thought it might distract him."

Morley was curled into a fetal position doing shallow breathing, holding his knee. "She broke my knee," he said on a gasp. "She broke my fucking knee."

"Think it was your boot that distracted him," Ranger said.

A happy accident.

"So if you were standing there the whole time, why didn't you help me?"

"Didn't look like you needed any help, babe. Why don't you run around and get the car while I baby-sit Mr. Morley. He's going to be slow walking."

It was almost ten when Ranger brought me back to my parents' house on High Street. Poochie, Mrs. Crandle's two-hundred-year-old toy poodle, was sitting on the porch across the street, conjuring up one last tinkle before he called it a night. The lights were off next door in Mrs. Ciak's house. Early to bed, early to rise, made old Mrs. Ciak wise. My mother and grandmother obviously didn't feel like they needed any help from a few extra winks, because they were standing with their noses pressed to the glass pane in the storm door, squinting into the darkness at me.

"Probably been standing there since you left," Ranger said.

"My sister is normal," I said. "Always has been."

Ranger nodded. "Makes it all the more confusing."

I waved good-bye to Ranger and headed for the porch.

"There's still some butterscotch pudding left," my mother said when I opened the door.

"Did you shoot anyone?" Grandma wanted to know. "Was there a big to-do?"

"There was a little to-do," I told her. "And we didn't shoot anyone. We almost never shoot people."

My father leaned forward in his chair in the living room. "What's this about shooting?"

"Stephanie didn't shoot anyone today," my mother said.

My father stared at us all for a moment, looking like he might be contemplating the advantages of a six-month tour on an aircraft carrier, and then he returned his attention to the TV.

"I can't stay," I said to my mother. "I just stopped in so you could see everything was okay."

"Okay?" my mother shouted. "You go out in the middle of the night, chasing criminals! How could that possibly be okay? And look at you! What happened to your pants? Your pants have a big hole in them!"

"I tripped."

My mother pressed her lips together. "So do you want pudding, or not?"

"Of course I want pudding."

I opened my eyes to a perfectly black room, and the skin-crawling feeling that I wasn't alone. I had no basis in fact for the feeling. I'd been dragged from sleep by some deep intuition. Possibly the intuition had been triggered by the rustle of clothing or a sweep of air. My heart knocked against my ribs as I waited for movement, for the scent of another person's sweat, for a sign that my fears were true.

I scanned the room but found only familiar shapes. The digital readout on my clock said five-thirty. My eyes cut to my dresser at the sound of a drawer slamming shut, and finally I picked out the intruder.

A pair of sweats sailed through the air and hit me in the head.

"If we're going to work together, you've got to get into shape," the intruder said.

"Ranger?"

"I made you some tea. It's on your nightstand."

I switched the light on. Sure enough, there was a cup of tea steaming on my nightstand. So much for the illusion of Stephanie Plum, keen-sensed bounty hunter.

"I hate tea," I said, sniffing at the noxious brew. I took a sip. YUK! "What *is* this?"

"Ginseng."

"It's weird. It tastes awful."

"Good for your circulation," Ranger said. "Helps oxygenate."

"What are you doing in my bedroom?" Ordinarily I'd be curious as to the mode of entry. With Ranger it was a pointless question. Ranger had ways.

"I'm trying to get you out of bed," Ranger said. "It's late."

"It's five-thirty!"

"I'll be in the living room warming up."

I watched his back disappear through the bedroom door. Was he serious? Warm up for what? I pulled the sweats on and padded out to him. He was doing one-armed push-ups.

"We'll start out with fifty," he said.

I got down on the floor and made an attempt at a push-up. After about five minutes Ranger was finished, and I'd al-most done one.

"Okay," Ranger said, jogging in place. "Let's hit the streets."

"I want breakfast."

"We'll do a fast five-mile run, and then we'll come back for breakfast."

A five-mile run? Was he nuts? It was five-thirty in the morning. It was dark out. It was cold. I peeked out the win-dow. It was fucking snowing!

"Great," I said. "Piece of cake."

I zipped myself into a down ski jacket, filled the pockets with tissues and lip balm, pulled on a knit cap, wrapped a scarf around my neck, stuffed my hands into big wool mit-tens and followed Ranger down the stairs.

Ranger ran effortlessly for several blocks. His stride was steady and measured. His attention directed inward. I struggled beside him . . . nose running, breathing labored, attention directed to surviving the next moment.

We slipped through the gate to the playing field behind the high school and swung onto the track. I dropped back to a walk and applied some lip balm. Ranger lapped me, and I picked it up to a jog. Ranger lapped me a few more times, and then he nudged me off the track, back through the gate to the street.

The sun wasn't yet on the horizon, but the sky had begun to lighten under the snow and the cloud cover. I could see the sheen on Ranger's face, see the sweat soaking through his shirt. His face still bore the same meditative expression. His breathing was even once again, now that he had slowed his pace to mine.

We ran in silence back to my apartment, entering the front door, jogging through the lobby. He took the stairs, and I took the elevator.

He was waiting for me when the doors opened.

"I thought you were behind me," he said.

"I was. Way behind."

"It's all in the attitude," Ranger said. "You want to be tough, you have to live healthy."

"To begin with, I don't want to be tough. I want to be . . . adequate."

Ranger stripped off his sweatshirt. "Adequate is being able to run five miles. How are you going to catch the bad guys if you can't outrun them?"

"Connie gives the bad guys who can run to you. I get the fat, out-of-shape bad guys."

Ranger took a bag out of my refrigerator and dumped a load of stuff from the bag into my blender. He flipped the blender switch and the stuff in the jar turned pink.

"What are you making?" I wanted to know.

"A smoothie." He poured half the smoothie into a big glass and handed it to me.

I took a sip. Not bad. If it was in a much smaller glass and sitting alongside a huge stack of hotcakes drenched in maple syrup, it would be just about tolerable.

"It needs something," I said. "It needs . . . chocolate."

Ranger drank the remaining smoothie. "I'm going home to take a shower and make some phone calls. I'll be back in an hour."

To celebrate our partnership I dressed up like Ranger. Black boots, black jeans, black turtleneck, small silver hoop earrings.

He gave me the once-over when I opened the door to him.

"Smart ass," he said.

I sent him what I hoped was an enigmatic smile.

He was wearing a black leather jacket with fringe running the length of each sleeve. Little blue and black beads were hooked three-quarters down the fringe.

I didn't have any fringe on my black leather jacket. And I

didn't have any beads. I had more zippers than Ranger, so I guess it all evened out. I slipped the jacket on and clapped a black Metallica ball cap over my freshly washed hair.

"Now what?" I asked.

"Now we look for Mo."

It was still snowing, but it was cozy in Ranger's Bronco. We cruised the streets, looking for the Batmobile in parking lots and middle-class neighborhoods. At my suggestion we visited some photo stores. Two of the merchants said they recognized Mo but hadn't seen him lately. The snow was still coming down, and traffic was crawling around cars that couldn't make grades.

"Mo's not going to be out in this," Ranger said. "We might as well close up shop for the day."

I wasn't going to argue. It was lunchtime. I was starving, and I didn't want to graze on sprouts and bean curd.

Ranger dropped me at the front door to my building and motored off in four-wheel drive. I took the stairs two at a time, practically ran down the hall and unlocked my door. Everything was quiet and peaceful inside. Rex was sleeping. The refrigerator hummed softly. The snow clacked on the windows. I kicked my shoes off, shuffled out of the black jeans and carted an armload of food into my bedroom. I switched the television on and crawled into bed with the channel changer.

Do I know how to have a good time, or what?

At six-thirty I was coming off a two-hour MTV stint and was approaching a vegetative state. I was trying to choose between a Turner classic and the news when a thought straggled into the front of my brain.

Mo had a lawyer.

Since when? The paperwork I'd been given said he'd waived an attorney. The only one I could think to ask was Joe Morelli.

"Yeah?" Morelli said when he answered the phone.

Just yeah. No hello. "You have a bad day?"

"I didn't have a good day."

"Do you know who Mo is using for a lawyer?"

"Mo waived counsel."

"I ran into him, and he said he had a lawyer."

There was a pause at the other end. "You ran into Mo?"

"He was at the candy store."

"And?"

"And he got away."

"I hear they're hiring at the button factory."

"At least I know he has a lawyer. That's more than you know."

"You got me there," Morelli said. "I'll check with the court tomorrow, but to the best of my knowledge, we haven't been informed of counsel."

A new question to add to the list. Why would Mo get a lawyer? Mo would get a lawyer if he was thinking of turning himself in. Probably there were other reasons, too, but I couldn't think of them.

I went to the window and peered outside. It had stopped snowing, and the streets looked cleared. I paced in my bedroom. I paced in my living room. I went to the dining room table and wrote, "Mo gets a lawyer" on the steno pad. Then I wrote, "Three people think they might have seen Mo on Montgomery Street."

I drew a big round head and filled it with question marks. It was my head.

I did some more pacing. Montgomery Street nagged at me. Hell, I thought, I'll take a ride over there. I haven't got anything else to do.

I got dressed and plowed through the night in the Buick. I parked on Montgomery in almost precisely the same spot I'd parked on previous snooping sessions. I saw precisely the same things. Yellow apartment building, mission, church, appliance store. The only difference was that it was dark now, and it had been light then. Technically it had been dark for the first two hours I'd spent here with Ranger, but I'd been in a sleep-deprived stupor, so it hadn't counted.

Just for kicks, I trained my binoculars on the apartment building, peeping into the lit, undraped windows. I didn't see any nudity, or any murders or any Mo. Peeping isn't all it's cracked up to be.

Lights were out in the mission, but the church next to the mission was getting some traffic. The mission and the church occupied two buildings that were two stories each. They'd been shops at one time. An office supply store and a dry cleaner. The Reverend Bill, a fire-and-brimstone preacher, had bought the buildings five years ago and set up his storefront church. He was one of those hooray for people, let's get back to family values preachers. Every now and then his picture would be in the paper for picketing an abortion clinic or for throwing cow's blood on some woman in a fur coat.

The people entering the church looked normal enough. Nobody carried a picket sign or a bucket of blood. Mostly families. A few single men. I counted twenty-six men, women and children in a half-hour period and then the meeting or the service must have started, because the front door remained closed, and no one else showed up. It wasn't an ethnically diverse group, but that wasn't shocking. The surrounding neighborhood was predominantly white, blue-collar. People usually choose a church that's within their community.

The appliance store and Sal's Café closed at nine. A half hour later, the twenty-six people filed out of the church. I scanned the apartment building windows one more time with the binoculars. I had my eyes glued to the third floor when someone rapped on my passenger-side window.

It was Carl Costanza in cop uniform. He looked in at me and shook his head. I unlocked the door, and Carl took a seat.

"You really need to get a social life," Carl said.

"You sound like my mother."

"We got a complaint about some pervert sitting in a Buick, looking in people's windows with binoculars."

"I'm checking out a Mo sighting."

Costanza reached for the binoculars and looked the building over. "Are you going to be checking it out much longer?"

"No. I'm done. I don't know why I even came back here tonight. I just have this feeling, you know?"

"Nobody ever takes their clothes off in this neighborhood," Costanza said, still going window to window. "Have you talked to Reverend Bill?"

"Not yet."

"You should go do that while I keep an eye on things. I've got a second-floor apartment that looks promising."

"You think Mo might be there?"

"No. I think a naked woman might be there. Come on, sweetheart," Carl crooned, watching the woman in the window, "unbutton your shirt for Uncle Carl."

"You're sick."

"I live to serve," Costanza said.

I crossed the street and tried to peek past the curtains covering the two plate-glass windows in the front of the Freedom Church. I didn't get much mileage from that, so I opened the door and looked inside.

The entire downstairs portion was essentially one large room, set up auditorium style with a bunch of folding chairs arranged in rows and a raised platform set against the back wall. The platform had some blue material tacked to it to make a skirt. A lectern stood in the middle of the platform. I assumed this was the pulpit.

A man was stacking books at one end of the platform. He was medium height, medium weight and had a head like a bowling ball. He wore round tortoiseshell glasses, and had pink scrubbed-clean skin, and looked like he should be saying things like, "Okley dokley, neighbor." I recognized him from his press photos. It was Reverend Bill.

He straightened and smiled when he saw me. His voice was soft and pleasantly melodic. Easy to imagine him in a choir robe. Hard to imagine him throwing cow's blood, but I guess when the moment seizes you . . .

"Of course I know Moses Bedemier," he said affably. "Everyone knows Uncle Mo. He packs one heck of an ice cream cone."

"A couple people have reported seeing him here on Montgomery recently."

"You mean since his disappearance?"

"You know about that?"

"Several of our parishioners are from the burg. Everyone has been concerned. This is pretty strange behavior for a man as stable as Mo Bedemier."

I gave Reverend Bill my card. "If you should see him, I'd appreciate a call."

"Of course." He silently stared at the card, lost in thought, serious. "I hope he's okay."

CHAPTER
9

I didn't want Ranger showing up in my bedroom at the crack of dawn again, so I made sure my windows were locked and the bolt thrown on my front door. Then, to be extra sure, I jury-rigged a tower of pots and pans in front of the door, so that if the door was opened the pots would come crashing down and wake me up. I'd done this once before with a tower of glasses. It had worked like a charm except for the broken glass all over the floor and the necessity of drinking from paper cups until my next paycheck arrived.

I reread my scribblings on the steno pad, but no wondrous revelation jumped off the page at me.

At 5 A.M. the pots clattered to the floor, and I rushed out in my flannel nightshirt to find Ranger smiling in my foyer.

"Hey babe," Ranger said.

I picked my way around the pots and examined my door. The two Yale locks were intact, the bolt was thrown, the chain was attached. My conclusion was that Ranger had knocked the pots over when he slid under the doorjamb.

"I don't suppose it would do me any good to ask how you got in," I said.

"Someday when things are slow we'll have a class in advanced B and E."

"You ever hear of a doorbell?"

Ranger just kept smiling.

Okay, so I wouldn't answer the doorbell. I'd look out the peephole, see Ranger standing there and I'd go back to bed.

"I'm not running," I said. "I went running yesterday. I hated it. I'm not doing it again, ever. Been there, done that."

"Exercise improves your sex life," Ranger said.

I wasn't going to share any embarrassing secrets with Ranger, but my sex life was at an all-time low. You can't improve something that doesn't exist.

"Is it snowing?" I asked.

"No."

"Is it raining?"

"No."

"You aren't going to expect me to drink another one of those smoothies, are you?"

Ranger gave me the once-over. "Wouldn't hurt. You look like Smokey the Bear in that nightgown."

"I do *not* look like Smokey the Bear! All right, so I haven't shaved my legs in a couple days . . . that does not make me look like Smokey the Bear. And I certainly am *not* as fat as Smokey the Bear."

Ranger did more of the smile thing.

I stomped off into the bedroom and slammed the door. I stuffed myself into long johns and sweats, laced up my running shoes and marched back to the foyer where Ranger stood, arms crossed.

"Don't expect me to do this every day," I said to Ranger, teeth clenched. "I'm just doing this to humor you."

An hour later I dragged myself into my apartment and collapsed onto the couch. I thought about the gun on my night table and wondered if it was loaded. And then I thought about using it on Ranger. And then I thought about using it on myself. One more early-morning run and I'd be dead anyway. May as well get it over with now.

"I'm ready for a job at the sanitary products factory," I told Rex, who was hiding in his soup can. "You don't have to be in shape to cram tampons into a box. I could probably blow up to three hundred pounds and still do a good job at the sanitary products plant." I wrenched the shoes off my feet and peeled wet socks away. "Why am I knocking myself out over this? I'm teamed up with a madman, and we're both fixated on finding an old guy who sells ice cream."

Rex backed out of his can and looked at me, whiskers whirring.

"Exactly," I said to Rex. "It's dumb. Dumb, dumb, dumb."

I gave a grunt and got to my feet. I padded into the kitchen and started coffee brewing. At least Ranger hadn't come back with me to supervise breakfast.

"He had to go home on account of the accident," I said to Rex. "Honest to God, I didn't mean to trip him. And I certainly hadn't wanted him to tear the knee out of his sweatsuit when he went down. And of course I'd felt very bad about the pulled groin."

Rex gave me one of those looks that said, Yeah, right.

When I was a little girl I wanted to be a reindeer—the flying kind. I spent a couple years galloping around looking for lichen and fantasizing about boy reindeer. Then one day I saw *Peter Pan* and my reindeer phase was over. I didn't understand the allure of not growing up, because every little girl in the burg couldn't wait to grow up and get boobs and go steady. I did understand that a flying Peter Pan was better than a flying reindeer. Mary Lou had seen *Peter Pan* too, but Mary Lou's ambition was to be Wendy, so Mary Lou and I made a good pair. On most any day we could be seen holding hands, running through the neighborhood singing, "I can fly! I can fly!" If we'd been older this probably would have started rumors.

The Peter Pan stage was actually pretty short-lived because a few months into Peter Pan I discovered Wonder Woman. Wonder Woman couldn't fly, but she had big, fat bulging boobs crammed into a sexy Wondersuit. Barbie was firmly entrenched as role model in the burg, but Wonder Woman gave her a good run for her money. Not only did Wonder Woman spill over her Wondercups but she also kicked serious ass. If I had to name the single most influential person in my life it would have to be Wonder Woman.

All during my teens and early twenties I wanted to be a rock star. The fact that I can't play a musical instrument or carry a tune did nothing to diminish the fantasy. During my more realistic moments I wanted to be a rock star's girlfriend.

For a very short time, while I was working as a lingerie buyer for E. E. Martin, my aspirations ran toward corporate America. My fantasies were of an elegantly dressed woman, barking orders at toadying men while her limo waited at curbside. The reality of E. E. Martin was that I worked in Newark and considered it a good day if no one peed on my shoe in the train station.

I was currently having problems coming up with a good fantasy. I had reverted back to wanting to be Wonder Woman, but it was a cruel fact of life that I was going to have a hard time filling Wonder Woman's Wonderbra.

I popped a frozen waffle into the toaster and ate it cookie style when it was done. I drank two cups of coffee and walked my sore muscles into the bathroom to take a shower.

I stood under the steaming water for a long time, reviewing my mental list of things to do. I needed to call about my pickup. I needed to do laundry and pay some bills. I had to return Mary Lou's sweatshirt. And last but not least, I had to find Uncle Mo.

First thing I called about the pickup.

"It's your carburetor," the service manager of the blue team told me. "We could put a new one in or we could try to rebuild the one you've got. It'd be a lot cheaper to rebuild. Of course there's no guarantee with a rebuild."

"What do you mean it's my carburetor? I just got points and plugs."

"Yeah," he said. "It needed them too."

"And now you're sure it needs a carburetor."

"Yeah. Ninety-five percent sure. Sometimes you get problems like this, and you've got faulty EGR valve operation. Sometimes you've got faulty PCV valve airflow or faulty choke vacuum diaphragm. Could be a defective fuel pump . . . but I don't think that's it. I think you need a new carburetor."

"Fine. Good. Wonderful. Give me a carburetor. How long will it take?"

"Not long. We'll call you."

Next on my list was to stop off at the office and see if anything new had turned up. And while I was there, maybe just for the heck of it I'd run a credit history on Andrew Larkin, the Montgomery Street tenant Ranger and I had questioned.

I threw on a bunch of warm clothes, hustled downstairs, chipped the latest layer of ice off the Buick and rumbled on down to the office.

Lula and Connie were already busy at work. Vinnie's door was closed.

"Is he in?" I asked.

"Haven't seen him," Connie said.

"Yeah," Lula added. "Maybe somebody drove a stake in his heart last night, and he won't be in at all."

The phone rang, and Connie handed it over to Lula. "Someone named Shirlene," Connie said.

I raised my eyebrows to Lula. Shirlene, who was Leroy Watkins's woman?

"Yes!" Lula said when she got off the phone. "We're on a roll! We got ourselves another live one. Shirlene says Leroy came home last night. And then they got into a big fight, and Leroy beat up some on Shirlene and kicked her out to the street. So Shirlene says we could have his ugly ass."

I had my keys in my hand and my coat zipped. "Let's go."

"This is gonna be easy," Lula said when we hit Stark Street. "We're just gonna sneak up on ol' Leroy. Probably he think it gonna be Shirlene at the door. I just hope he don't come to the door too happy, you know what I mean?"

I knew exactly what she meant, and I didn't want to think about it. I parked in front of Leroy's building, and we both sat there in silence.

"Well," Lula finally said. "He probably wouldn't want to ruin his door a second time. Probably he caught it from the landlord. Doors don't grow on trees, you know."

I considered that. "Maybe he isn't even in there," I added. "When was the last Shirlene saw him?"

"Last night."

We did some more sitting.

"We could wait out here for him," Lula said. "Do a stake-out."

"Or we could call."

Lula looked up into the third-story windows. "Calling might be a good idea."

A few more minutes passed.

I took a deep breath. "Okay, let's do it."

"Damn skippy," Lula said.

We paused in the foyer and took stock of the building. A television blaring somewhere. A baby crying. We walked the first flight of stairs slowly, listening as we crept step by step. We stopped on the second-floor landing and took a few deep breaths.

"You aren't gonna hyperventilate, are you?" Lula asked. "I'd hate to have you keel over on me from hyperventilating."

"I'm okay," I told her.

"Yeah," she said. "Me too."

When we got to the third-floor landing neither of us was breathing at all.

We stood there staring at the door that had been patched with cardboard and two slats of stained plywood. I motioned to Lula to stand aside of the door. She jumped to attention and plastered herself against the wall. I did the same on the opposite side.

I rapped on the door. "Pizza delivery," I yelled.

There was no response.

I rapped harder and the door swung open. Lula and I still weren't breathing, and I could feel my blood pounding behind my eyeballs. Neither Lula nor I made a move for a full minute. We just pressed into the wall, not making a sound.

I called out again. "Leroy? It's Lula and Stephanie Plum. Are you there, Leroy?"

After a while Lula said, "I don't think he's here."

"Don't move," I said. "I'm going in."

"Help yourself," Lula said. "I'd go in first, but I don't want to be a hog about this searching shit."

I inched my way into the apartment and looked around. Everything was as I'd remembered. There was no sign of occupancy. I peeked into the bedroom. No one there.

"Well?" Lula asked from the hall.

"Looks empty."

Lula poked her head around the doorjamb. "Too bad. I was looking to do another takedown. I was ready to kick some butt."

I approached the closed bathroom door with my pepper spray in hand. I flipped the door open and jumped back. The door crashed against the wall and Lula dove behind the couch.

I looked into the empty bathroom, and then I looked over at Lula.

Lula picked herself up. "Just testing my reflexes," Lula said. "Trying out new techniques."

"Uh-huh."

"Wasn't that I was scared," she said. "Hell, takes more than a man like Leroy to scare a woman like me."

"You were scared," I said.

"Was not."

"Uh-huh."

"Unh-uh, was not. I'll show you who's scared. And it won't be me. Guess I can open doors too."

Lula stomped over to the closet door and wrenched it open. The door swung wide with Lula glaring straight into the jammed-together coats and other clothes.

The clothes parted and Leroy Watkins, buck naked, sporting a bullet hole in the middle of his forehead, fell out onto Lula.

Lula lost her footing, and the two of them went down to the floor—Leroy, arms outstretched, stiff as a board, looking like Frankenstein from the 'hood, on top of Lula.

"Holy cow," I yelled. "Jesus, Mary and Joseph!"

"Eeeeeeeeee," Lula screamed, flat on her back, arms and legs flailing, with Leroy deadweight on her chest.

I was jumping around, hollering, "Get up. Get up."

And Lula was rolling around, hollering, "Get him off. Get him off."

I grabbed an arm and yanked, and Lula sprang to her feet, shaking herself like a dog in a rainstorm. "Ugh. Gross. Yuk."

We squinted down at Leroy.

"Dead," I said. "Definitely dead."

"You better believe it. Wasn't shot with no BB gun, either. Got a hole in his head about the size of Rhode Island."

"Smells bad."

"Think he pooped in the closet," Lula said.

We both gagged and ran to the window and stuck our heads out for air. When the ringing stopped in my ears I went to the phone and dialed Morelli. "Got a customer for you," I told him.

"Another one?"

He sounded incredulous, and I couldn't blame him. This was my third dead body in the space of a week.

"Leroy Watkins fell out of a closet on top of Lula," I said. "All the king's horses and all the king's men aren't going to put Leroy Watkins together again."

I gave him the address, hung up and went out to the hall to wait.

Two uniforms were the first to arrive. Morelli followed them by thirty seconds. I gave Morelli the details and fidgeted while he checked out the crime scene.

Leroy had been naked and not especially bloody. I thought one possibility was that someone had surprised him in the shower. The bathroom hadn't been covered with gore, but then I hadn't felt inclined to peek behind the drawn shower curtain.

Morelli returned after walking through the apartment and securing the scene. He ushered us down to the second-floor landing, away from the activity, and we went through our story one more time.

Two more uniforms trundled up the stairs. I didn't know either of them. They looked to Joe, and he asked them to wait at the door. A television continued to drone on. The muffled sound of young children arguing carried into the hallway. None of the residents opened a door to snoop on the police activity. I suppose curiosity isn't a healthy character trait in this neighborhood.

Morelli drew the zipper up on my jacket. "I don't need anything else from you . . . for now."

Lula was halfway down the stairs before I even turned around.

"I'm out of here," Lula said. "I got filing to do."

"Cops make her nervous," I told Morelli.

"Yeah," he said. "I know the feeling. They make me nervous too."

"Who do you think did Leroy?" I asked Morelli.

"Anybody could have done Leroy. Leroy's mother could have done Leroy."

"Is it unusual for three dealers to get faded in the space of a week?"

"Not if there's some kind of war going on."

"Is there some kind of war going on?"

"Not that I know of."

A couple suits stopped at the landing. Morelli jerked his thumb toward the next flight of stairs; the men grunted acknowledgment and continued on.

"I need to go," Morelli said. "See you around."

See you around? Just like that? All right, so there was a dead guy upstairs, and the building was crawling with cops. I should be happy Morelli was being so professional. I should be happy I didn't have to fight him off, right? Still, "see you around" felt a little bit like "don't call me, I'll call you." Not that I *wanted* Morelli to call me. It was more that I wondered why he didn't want to. What was wrong with me, anyway? Why wasn't he making serious passes?

"Is something bugging you?" I asked Morelli. But Morelli was already gone, disappeared in the knot of cops on the third-floor landing.

Maybe I should drop a few pounds, I thought, slumping down the stairs. Maybe I should have some red highlights put in my hair.

Lula was waiting for me in the car.

"I guess that wasn't so bad," Lula said. "We didn't get shot at."

"What do you think of my hair?" I asked. "You think I should add some red highlights?"

Lula hauled back and looked at me. "Red would be bitchin'."

•   •   •

I dropped Lula at the office and went home to check my messages and my bank account. There were no messages, and I had a few dollars left in checking. I was almost current on my bills. My rent was paid for the month. If I continued to mooch meals from my mother I could afford highlights. I studied myself in the mirror, fluffing my hair, imagining a radiant new color. "Go for it," I said to myself. Especially since the alternative was to dwell on Leroy Watkins.

I locked up and drove to the mall, where I persuaded Mr. Alexander to work me into his schedule. Forty-five minutes later I was under the dryer with my hair soaked in chemical foam, wrapped in fifty-two squares of aluminum foil. Stephanie Plum, space creature. I was trying to read a magazine, but my eyes kept watering from the heat and fumes. I dabbed at my eyes and looked out through the wide-open arch door and plate-glass windows into the mall.

It was Saturday, and the mall was crowded. Passersby glanced my way. Their stares were emotionless. Empty curiosity. Mothers and children. Kids hanging out. Stuart Baggett. *Holy cow!* It was that little twerp Stuart Baggett at the mall!

Our eyes met and held for a moment. Recognition registered. Stuart mouthed my name and took off. I flipped the dryer hood back and came out of the seat like I was shot from a cannon.

We were on the lower level, sprinting toward Sears. Stuart had a good head start and hit the escalator running. He was pushing people out of his way, apologizing profusely, looking charmingly cute.

I jumped onto the escalator and elbowed my way forward, closing ground. A woman with shopping bags belligerently stood in front of me.

"Excuse me," I said. "I need to get through."

"I got a right to be on this escalator," she said. "You think you own this place?"

"I'm after that kid!"

"You're a kook, that's what you are. Help!" she yelled. "This woman is crazy! This is a crazy woman."

Stuart was off the escalator, moving back down the mall. I held my breath and danced in place, keeping him in view. Twenty seconds later I was off the stairs, running full tilt with the foil flapping against my head, the brown beauty parlor smock still tied at the waist.

Suddenly Stuart was gone, lost in the crowd. I slowed to a walk, scanning ahead, checking side stores. I jogged through Macy's. Scarves, sportswear, cosmetics, shoes. I reached the exit and peered out into the parking lot. No sign of Stuart.

I caught myself in a mirror and stopped dead. I looked like Flypaper Woman meets Alcoa Aluminum. Foilhead does Quaker Bridge Mall. If I saw anyone I knew while I looked like this I'd drop dead on the spot.

I had to pass back through Macy's to get to the mall, including a foray through cosmetics where I might encounter Joyce Barnhardt, queen of the makeover. And after Macy's I still had to negotiate the escalator and main corridor of the mall. This was not something I wanted to do in my present condition.

I'd left my shoulder bag at the beauty parlor, so purchasing a scarf was out of the question. I could rip out the little foil squares wrapped around my hair, but I'd paid sixty dollars to have the squares put on.

I took another look in the mirror. Okay, so I was getting my hair done. What's the big deal? I raised my chin a fraction of an inch. Belligerent. I'd seen my mother and grandmother take this stance a million times. There's no better defense than a steely-eyed offense.

I briskly walked the length of the store and turned to the escalator. A few people stared, but most kept their eyes firmly averted.

Mr. Alexander was pacing at the entrance to the salon. He was looking up and down the mall, and he was muttering. He saw me, and he rolled his eyes.

Mr. Alexander always wore black. His long hair was slicked back in a ducktail. His feet were clad in black patent leather loafers. Gold cross earrings dangled from his earlobes. When he rolled his eyes he pinched his lips together.

"Where did you go?" he demanded.

"After a bail jumper," I said. "Unfortunately, I lost him."

Mr. Alexander tugged a foil packet off my head. "Unfortunately, you should have had your head in the rinse bowl ten minutes ago! That's unfortunate." He waved his hand at one of his underlings. "Miss Plum is done," he said. "We need to rinse her immediately." He removed another foil and rolled his eyes. "Unh," he said.

"What?"

"I'm not responsible for this," Mr. Alexander said.

"What? What?"

Mr. Alexander waved his hand again. "It will be fine," he said. "A little more spectacular than we'd originally imagined."

Spectacular was good, right? I held that thought through the rinse and the comb-out.

"This will be wonderful once you get used to it," Mr. Alexander said from behind a cloud of hair spray.

I squinted into the mirror. My hair was orange. Okay, don't panic. It was probably the lights. "It looks orange," I told Mr. Alexander.

"California sun–kissed," Mr. Alexander said.

I got out of the chair and took a closer look. "My hair is orange!" I shouted. "It's freaking ORANGE!"

It was five when I left the mall. Today was Saturday, and my mother expected me for pot roast at six. "Pity roast" was a more accurate term. Unwed daughter, too pathetic to have a date on a Saturday night, is sucked in by four pounds of rolled rump.

I parked the Buick in front of the house and took a quick look at my hair in the rearview mirror. Not much showed in the dark. Mr. Alexander had assured me I looked fine. Everyone in the salon agreed. I looked fine, they all said. Someone suggested I might want to boost my makeup now that my hair had been "lifted." I took that to mean I was pale in comparison to my neon hair.

My mother opened the door with a look of silent resignation.

My grandmother stood on tippytoes behind my mother, trying to get a better look. "Dang!" Grandma said. "You've got orange hair! And it looks like there's more of it. Looks like one of them clown wigs. How'd you grow all that hair?"

I patted my head. "I meant to have some highlights put in, but the solution got left on too long, so my hair got a little frizzy." And orange.

"I've got to try that," Grandma said. "I wouldn't mind having a big bush of orange hair. Brighten things up around here." Grandma stuck her head out the front door and scanned the neighborhood. "Anybody with you? Any new boyfriends? I liked that last one. He was a real looker."

"Sorry," I said. "I'm alone today."

"We could call him," Grandma said. "We got an extra potato in the pot. It's always nice to have a stud-muffin at the table."

My father hunched in the hall, *TV Guide* dangling from his hand. "That's disgusting," he said. "Bad enough I have to hear crap like this on television, now I have to listen to some old bag talking about stud-muffins in my own home."

Grandma narrowed her eyes and glared at my father. "Who you calling an old bag?"

"You!" my father said. "I'm calling *you* an old bag. You wouldn't know what to do with a stud-muffin if you tripped over one."

"I'm old, but I'm not dead," Grandma said. "And I guess I'd know what to do with a stud-muffin. Maybe I need to go out and get one of my own."

My father's upper lip curled back. "Jesus," he said.

"Maybe I'll join one of those dating services," Grandma said. "I might even get married again."

My father perked up at this. He didn't say anything, but his thoughts were transparent. Grandma Mazur remarried and out of his house. Was it possible? Was it too much to hope for?

I hung my coat in the hall closet and followed my mother into the kitchen. A bowl of rice pudding sat cooling on the kitchen table. The potatoes had already been mashed and were warming in a covered pot on the stove.

"I got a tip that Uncle Mo was seen coming out of the apartment building on Montgomery."

My mother wiped her hands on her apron. "The one next to that Freedom Church?"

"Yeah. You know anyone who lives there?"

"No. Margaret Laskey looked at an apartment there once. She said it had no water pressure."

"How about the church? You know anything about the church?"

"Only what I read in the papers."

"I hear that Reverend Bill is a pip," Grandma said. "They were talking about him in the beauty parlor the other day, and they said he made his church up. And then Louise Buzick said her son, Mickey, knew someone who went to that church once and said Reverend Bill was a real snake charmer."

I thought "snake charmer" was a good description for Reverend Bill.

I felt antsy through dinner, not able to get Mo off my mind. I didn't honestly think Andrew Larkin was the contact, but I did think Mo had been on Montgomery. I'd watched men his age go in and out of the mission and thought Mo would fit right in. Maybe Jackie didn't see Mo coming out of the apartment building. Maybe Jackie saw Mo coming out of the mission. Maybe Mo was grabbing a free meal there once in a while.

Halfway through the rice pudding my impatience got the better of me, and I excused myself to check my answering machine.

The first message was from Morelli. He had something interesting to tell me and would stop by to see me later tonight. That was encouraging.

The second message was more mysterious. "Mo's gonna be at the store tonight," the message said. A girl's voice. No name given. Didn't sound like Gillian, but it could have been one of her friends. Or it could have been a snitch. I'd put out a lot of cards.

I called Ranger and left a message for an immediate call-back.

"I have to go," I told my mother.

"So soon? You just got here."

"I have work to do."

"What kind of work? You aren't going out looking for criminals, are you?"

"I got a tip I need to follow up."

"It's nighttime. I don't like you in those bad neighbor-hoods at night."

"I'm not going to a bad neighborhood."

My mother turned to my father. "You should go with her."

"It's not necessary," I said. "I'll be fine."

"You won't be fine," my mother said. "You get knocked out, and people shoot at you. Look at you! You have orange hair!" She put her hand to her chest and closed her eyes. "You're going to give me a heart attack." She opened her eyes. "Wait while I fix some leftovers to take home."

"Not too much," I said. "I'm going on a diet."

My mother slapped her forehead. "A diet. Unh. You're a rail. You don't need to diet. How will you stay healthy if you diet?"

I paced behind her in the kitchen, watching the leftovers bag fill with packets of meat and potatoes, a jar of gravy, half a green-bean casserole, a jar of red cabbage, a pound cake. Okay, so I'd start my diet on Monday.

"There," my mother said, handing me the bag. "Frank, are you ready? Stephanie is going now."

My father appeared in the kitchen door. "What?"

My mother gave him the long-suffering face. "You never listen to me."

"I always listen. What are you talking about?"

"Stephanie is going out looking for criminals. You should go with her."

I grabbed the leftovers bag and ran for the door, snagging my coat from the hall closet. "I swear I'm not doing anything dangerous," I said. "I'll be perfectly safe."

I let myself out and quickly walked to the Buick. I looked back just before sliding behind the wheel. My mother and grandmother were standing in the doorway, hands clasped in front, faces stern. Not convinced of my safety. My father stood behind them, peering over my grandmother's head.

"The car looks pretty good," he said. "How's it running? You giving it high-test? You got any pings?"

"No pings," I called back.

And then I was gone. On my way to Mo's store. Telling myself I was going to be smarter this time. I wasn't going to get knocked out, and I wasn't going to get faked out. I wasn't going to let Mo get the best of me with pepper spray. As soon as I saw him I was going to give him a snootful of the stuff. No questions asked.

I parked across the street from the store and stared into the black plate-glass window. No light. No activity. No light on in the second-floor apartment. I pulled out and circled surrounding blocks, looking for Ranger's BMW. I tried the alley behind the store and checked the garage. No car. I returned to Ferris. Still no sign of life in the store. I parked a block away on King. Maybe I should try Ranger again. I reached over for my pocketbook. No pocketbook. I closed my eyes in disbelief. In my haste to get away without my father, I'd left my pocketbook behind. No big deal. I'd go back and get it.

I put the car into gear and pulled onto Ferris. I glanced into the store windows one last time as I did a slow drive-by. I saw a shadow move to the rear of the store.

Damn!

I angled the Buick into the curb two houses down and jumped out. I'd like the luxury of having a bag full of bounty hunter loot, like pepper spray and handcuffs, but I wasn't willing to risk losing the opportunity for it. I didn't really want to spray Mo anyway. I wanted to talk to him. I wanted to reason with him. Get some answers. Get him to come back into the system without hurting him.

Stephanie Plum, master of rationalization. Believe whatever the moment calls for.

I jogged to a dark spot across from the store and watched for more movement. My heart gave a lurch when a light flickered briefly. Someone had used a penlight and immediately extinguished it. The information on my answering machine had been right. Mo was in the store.

CHAPTER

10

I sprinted across the street and sought cover in the shadows to the side of the store. I hugged the brick wall, creeping back toward the rear exit, thinking I might barricade the door. I'd stand a better chance of capturing Mo if he had just one avenue of escape.

I took a deep breath and peeked around the building corner. The back door to the store was wide open. I didn't think this was a good sign. Mo wouldn't have left the door open if he was in the store. I feared history had repeated itself, and Mo had flown the coop.

I inched my way to the door and stood there listening. Hard to hear over the pounding of my heart but no footfalls carried to me from the neighborhood. No car engines being started. No doors slamming shut.

I did another deep breath and poked my head into the gaping doorway, squinting into the dark hall that led to the counter area.

I heard the scrape of a shoe from deep inside the store

and almost passed out from adrenaline rush. My first instinct was to run away. My second instinct was to shout for help. I didn't follow either of these instincts because the cold barrel of a gun was pressed to my ear.

"Be nice and quiet and walk into the store."

It was the wiry little guy who'd tried to give me money. I couldn't see him, but I recognized the voice. Low and raspy. A smoker's voice. North Jersey accent. Newark, Jersey City, Elizabeth.

"No," I said. "I'm not going into the store."

"I need some help here," the guy with the gun said. "We need to persuade Miss Plum to cooperate."

A second man stepped out of the shadows. He was wearing the requisite ski mask and coveralls. He was taller and heavier. He was shaking a canister of pepper spray. Showing me he knew to make sure the gas is live.

I opened my mouth to scream and was hit with the spray. I felt it suck back to my throat and burn, felt my throat close over. I went down hard to my knees and choked, unable to see, closing my eyes tight to the searing pain, blinded by the spray.

Hands grabbed at me, digging into my jacket, dragging me forward over the doorstep, down the hall. I was thrown to the linoleum at the back of the store, knocking into a teary blur of wall and booth, still unable to catch my breath.

The hands were at me again, wrenching my jacket over my shoulders to form a makeshift straitjacket, binding my arms behind my back and tearing my shirt in the process. I gasped for air and tried to control the fear, tried to ignore the manhandling while I fought the pepper spray. It'll pass, I told myself. You've seen people sprayed before. It passes. Don't panic.

They moved off. Waiting for me to come around. I blinked to see. Three large shapes in the dark. I assumed they were men in ski masks and coveralls.

One of them flashed a penlight in my eyes. "Bet you're not feeling so brave anymore," he said.

I adjusted my jacket and tried to stand but wasn't able to get farther than hands and knees. My nose was running, dripping onto the floor, mixing with drool and tears. My breathing was still shallow, but the earlier panic had passed.

"What's it take?" Jersey City asked me. "We tried to warn you away. We tried to compensate you. Nothing works with you. We're out here trying to do a good deed, and you're being a real pain in the behind."

"Just doing my job," I managed.

"Yeah, well, do your job someplace else."

A match flared in the dark store. It was Jersey City lighting up. He sucked smoke deep into his lungs, let it curl out from his nose. I was still on hands and knees, and the man swooped down and held the glowing tip of the cigarette to the back of my hand. I yelped and jerked my hand away.

"This is just the start," Jersey City said. "We're going to burn you in places that are a lot more painful than the back of your hand. And when we're done you're not going to want to tell anyone about it. And you're not going to want to go chasing after Mo anymore. And if you do . . . we're going to come get you and burn you again. And then maybe we'll kill you."

A door slammed somewhere far off and footsteps sounded on the pavement behind the store. There was an instant of silence while we all listened. And then the back door was opened wide and a shrill voice called into the darkness. "What's going on here?"

It was Mrs. Steeger. Any other time Mrs. Steeger would call the police. Tonight she decided to investigate on her own. Go figure.

"Run!" I yelled to Mrs. Steeger. "Call the police!"

"Stephanie Plum!" Mrs. Steeger said. "I might have known. You come out this instant."

A beam of light played across Mo's backyard. "Who's there?" another voice called. "Mrs. Steeger? Is that you in Mo's backyard?"

Dorothy Rostowski.

A car parked at the curb. Headlights blinked off. The driver's door opened, and a man stepped onto the sidewalk.

"Shit," Jersey City said. "Let's get out of here." He got down on one knee and put his face close to mine. "Get smart," he said. "Because next time we'll make sure nobody saves you."

James Bond would have shown disdain with a clever remark. Indiana Jones would have sneered and said something snotty. The best I could come up with was, "Oh yeah?"

There was scuffling at the back door and some frightened exclamations from Dorothy and Mrs. Steeger.

I dragged myself to my feet and leaned against a booth for support. I was sweating and shivering, and my nose was still running. I wiped my nose on my sleeve and realized my shirt was open and my Levi's were unzipped. I sucked in some air and clenched my teeth. "Damn."

Another deep breath. Come on, Stephanie, get it together. Get yourself dressed and get out there to check on Dorothy and Mrs. Steeger.

I tugged at my jeans, putting a shaking hand to the zipper. My eyes were still watering, and saliva was still pooling in my mouth and I couldn't get the zipper to slide easily. I burst into tears and gave my nose another vicious swipe with my sleeve.

I gathered my shirt together with one hand and lurched toward the back door. Dorothy was standing, arms crossed over her chest. Self-protective. Mrs. Steeger was sitting on the ground. A man squatted in front of her, talking to her. He helped her to her feet and turned to look when I appeared in the doorway. Morelli. Wouldn't you know it.

Morelli raised questioning eyebrows.

"Not now," I said.

I backed up a few paces and sidestepped into the bath-room. I flicked the light on and locked the door. I looked at myself in the rust-rimmed mirror over the sink. Not a pretty sight. I used half a roll of toilet paper to blow my nose. I splashed water on my face and hand and buttoned my shirt. Two of the buttons were missing, but they weren't crucial to modesty.

I did deep breathing, trying to compose myself. I blew my nose some more. I looked at myself again. Not bad except my eyes looked like tomatoes and the cigarette burn was turning into a beauty of a blister.

Morelli had knocked on the door three times, asking if I was okay. My reply each time had been a cranky "Yes! Go away!"

When I finally opened the door, the lights were on in the candy store, and Morelli was behind the counter. I slid onto a stool in front of him, leaned my elbows on the counter and folded my hands.

Morelli set a hot fudge sundae in front of me and gave it a good dose of whipped cream. He handed me a spoon. "Thought this might help."

"Wouldn't hurt," I said, gnawing on my lip, trying hard not to cry. "How's Mrs. Steeger?"

"She's okay. She got shoved out of the way, and it knocked her on her ass."

"Gee, I always wanted to do that."

He gave me the once-over. "Like your hair," he said. "Try-ing something new?"

I flicked a spoonful of whipped cream at him, but I missed, and it went splat on the wall and slimed its way down to the back counter.

Morelli made a sundae for himself and took the stool next to me. We ate in silence, and when we were done we still sat there.

"So," Morelli finally said. "Let's talk."

I told him about the phone call and the assault and about the attempted payoff.

"Tell me about these men," Morelli said.

"They always wear ski masks and coveralls, and it's always been dark, so I've never been able to get a good look. The eerie part is that I think they're regular people. It's like they're from the community, and they're trying to protect Mo but they've turned violent. Like a lynch mob." I looked down at my hand. "They burned me with a cigarette."

A muscle worked in Morelli's jaw. "Anything else?"

"Under the coveralls they look respectable. Wedding bands on their fingers and nice running shoes. This wiry little guy seems to be the leader."

"How little is he?"

"Maybe five-nine. Got a smoker's voice. I've named him Jersey City because he has a Jersey City accent. The other two were bigger and chunkier."

Morelli covered my hand with his, and we sat some more.

"How did you know I was here?" I asked.

"I accessed your answering machine," Morelli said.

"You know my code?"

"Well . . . yeah."

"You do that a lot? Listen in on my messages?"

"Don't worry," Morelli said. "Your messages aren't that interesting."

"You're scum."

"Yeah," Morelli said. "You've told me that before."

I scraped at a little fudge that was left on the side of the sundae dish. "What did you want to see me about?"

"We got ballistics back on Leroy Watkins. Looks like the same gun that killed Cameron Brown and Ronald Anders also killed Leroy Watkins."

I stopped scraping at the fudge and stared at Morelli.

"Oh boy," I said.

Morelli nodded. "My exact thought."

I shifted on my stool. "Is it me, or is it warm in here?"

"It's warm in here," Morelli said. "Mo must have turned the heat up when he came by to visit."

"Doesn't smell all that good either."

"I wasn't going to mention it. I thought it might be you."

I sniffed at myself. "I don't think it's me." I sniffed at Morelli. "It's not you."

Morelli was off the stool, moving through the store. He got to the hall and stopped. "It's pretty strong in the hall." He opened the cellar door. "Uh-oh."

Now I was off my stool. "What's uh-oh?"

"I think I know this smell," Morelli said.

"Is it dookey?"

"Yeah," Morelli said. "It's dookey . . . among other things." He flipped the light at the top of the stairs.

I stood behind Morelli and decided I should be thankful my nose was still partially clogged. "Somebody should go down and investigate."

Morelli had his gun in his hand. "Stay here," he said.

Which was as good as guaranteeing I'd follow him down.

We crept down together, noting at once that the cellar posed no threat. No bad guys lurking in corners. No nasty-breathed, hairy-handed monsters lying in wait.

"Dirt floor," I said.

Morelli holstered his gun. "A lot of these old cellars have dirt floors."

A couple winter overcoats hung on wall pegs. Bags of rock salt, snow shovels, picks and heavy, long-handled spades lined the wall beside the coats. The furnace rumbled, central in the cellar. A jumble of empty cardboard boxes littered a large portion of the room. The smell of damp cardboard mingled with something more foul.

Morelli tossed some of the boxes to one side. The ground beneath the boxes had been recently disturbed. Morelli became more methodical, moving the boxes with the toe of his boot until he uncovered a patch of dirt that showed black garbage bag peeking through.

"Sometimes people get eccentric when they get old," I said. "Don't want to pay for trash pickup."

Morelli took a penknife from his pocket and exposed more of the plastic. He made a slit in the plastic and let out a long breath.

"What is it?" I asked. As if I didn't know.

"It isn't candy." He turned me around and pushed me toward the stairs. "I've seen enough. Let's leave this to the experts. Don't want to contaminate the scene any more than we already have."

We sat in his car while he called in to the station.

"I don't suppose you'd consider going home to your parents' tonight?" he asked.

"Don't suppose I would."

"I'd rather you didn't go back to your apartment alone."

Me too. "I'll be fine," I said.

A blue-and-white cruised to the curb behind Morelli's 4x4. Eddie Gazarra got out of the car and walked our way. We met him on the street, and we all looked to the store.

"Break out the crime tape," Morelli said.

"Shit," Gazarra said. "I'm not going to like this."

Nobody was going to like this. It was not good etiquette to bury bodies in the basement of a candy store. And it would be especially loathsome to accuse Mo of doing the burying.

Another blue-and-white showed up. Some more homicide cops arrived on the scene. The ID detective came with his tool kit and camera. People started appearing on front porches, standing with arms crossed, checking out the traffic jam. The crowds on the porches grew larger. A reporter stood, hands in pockets, behind the crime tape.

Two hours later I was still sitting in Morelli's car when they brought out the first body bag. The media coverage had grown to a handicam and a half dozen reporters and photographers. Three more body bags were trundled out from the cellar. The photographers hustled for shots. Neighbors left the comfort of their living rooms to return to the porches.

I sidled over next to Morelli. "Is this it?"

"This is it," Morelli said. "Four bodies."

"And?"

"And I can't tell you more than that."

"Any forty-five–caliber bullets embedded in bone?"

Morelli stared at me. Answer enough.

"Anything to implicate Mo?" I asked.

Another stare.

Morelli's eyes moved to a spot behind my left shoulder. I followed his eyes and found Ranger standing inches away.

"Yo," Ranger said. "What's the deal here?"

Morelli looked to the store. "Somebody buried four guys in Mo's cellar. The last one was buried shallow."

And he probably hadn't been buried so long ago, I thought. Like maybe the night Mo stole Ranger's car and smelled like sweat and dirt and something worse.

"I've got to move," Morelli said. "I've got paperwork."

I had to go, too. I felt like someone stuck a pin in me and let out the air. I fished car keys and a tissue out of my pocket. I blew my nose one last time and pumped myself back up for the walk to the car.

"How are you feeling?" I asked Ranger.

"Feeling fine."

"Want to run tomorrow morning?"

He raised an eyebrow, but he didn't ask the question. "See you at six."

"Six is good," I said.

I was halfway home before I picked up the headlights in my rearview mirror. I looked again when I turned off Hamilton. The lights belonged to a black Toyota 4x4. Three antennae. Morelli's car. He was following me home to make sure I was safe.

I gave Morelli a wave, and he beeped the horn. Sometimes Morelli could be okay.

I drove two blocks on St. James and hit Dunworth. I turned into my lot and found a place in the middle. Morelli parked next to me.

"Thanks," I said, locking the car, juggling the food bag.

Morelli got out of his car and looked at the bag. "Wish I could come in."

"I know your type," I said. "You're only interested in one thing, Morelli."

"Got my number, do you?"

"Yes. And you can forget it. You're not getting my leftovers."

Morelli curled his fingers around my jacket collar and pulled me close. "Sweetheart, if I wanted your leftovers you wouldn't have a chance in hell of keeping them."

"That's disgusting."

Morelli grinned, his teeth white against swarthy skin and day-old beard. "I'll walk you to the door."

I turned on my heel. "I can take care of myself, thank you." All huffy. In a snit because Morelli was probably right about the leftovers.

He was still watching when I entered the building and the glass door swung closed behind me. I gave him another wave. He waved back and left.

Mrs. Bestler was in the elevator when I got on. "Going up," she said. "Third floor, lingerie and ladies' handbags."

Sometimes Mrs. Bestler played elevator operator to break up the boredom.

"I'm going to the second floor," I told her.

"Ah," she said. "Good choice. Better dresses and designer shoes."

I stepped out of the elevator, shuffled down the hall, unlocked my door and almost fell into my apartment. I was dead-dog tired. I did a cursory walk through my apartment, checking windows and doors to make sure they were secure, checking closets and shadows.

I dropped my clothes in a heap on the floor, plastered a Band-Aid on my burn and stepped into the shower. Out, damn spot. When I was pink and clean I crawled into bed and pretended I was at Disney World. Stephanie Plum, master of denial. Why deal with the trauma of almost being tortured when I could put it off indefinitely? Someday when the memory was fuzzy at the edges I'd dredge it up and give it attention. Stephanie Plum's rule of thumb for mental health—always procrastinate the unpleasant. After all, I could get run over by a truck tomorrow and never have to come to terms with the attack at all.

I was awakened by the phone at five-thirty.

"Yo," Ranger said. "You still want to run?"

"Yes. I'll meet you downstairs at six." Damned if I was going to let a couple loser men get the better of me. Muscle tone wouldn't help a lot when it came to pepper spray, but it'd give me an edge on attitude. Mentally alert, physically fit would be my new motto.

I pulled on long johns and sweats and laced up my running shoes. I gave Rex fresh water and filled his little ceramic food dish with hamster nuggets and raisins. I did fifteen minutes of stretching and went downstairs.

Ranger was jogging in place when I got to the parking lot. I saw his eyes flick to my hair.

"Don't say it," I warned him. "Don't say a single word."

Ranger held his hands up in a backing-off gesture. "None of my business."

The corners of his mouth twitched.

I stuffed my hands on my hips. "You're laughing at me!"

"You look like Ronald McDonald."

"It's not that bad!"

"You want me to take care of your hairdresser?"

"No! It wasn't his fault."

We ran the usual course in silence. We added an extra block on the way home, keeping the pace steady. Easy for Ranger. Hard for me. I bent at the waist to catch my breath when we pulled up at my building's back door. I was happy with the run. Even happier to have it behind me.

A car roared down the street and wheeled into the parking lot. Ranger stepped in front of me, gun drawn. The car slid to a stop, and Lula stuck her head out.

"I saw him!" she yelled. "I saw him! I saw him!"

"Who?"

"Old Penis Nose! I saw Old Penis Nose! I could of got him, but you're always telling me how I'm not supposed to do nothing, how I'm not authorized. So I tried to call you, but you weren't home. So I drove over here. Where the hell you been at six in the morning?"

"Who's Old Penis Nose?" Ranger wanted to know.

"Mo," I said. "Lula thinks his nose looks like a penis."

Ranger smiled. "Where'd you see him?"

"I saw him on Sixth Street right across from my house. I don't usually get up so early, but I had some intestinal problems. Think it was the burrito I had for supper. So anyway I'm in the bathroom, and I look out the window and I see Mo walking into the building across the street."

"You sure it was Mo?" I asked.

"I got a pretty good look," Lula said. "They got a front light they leave on over there. Must own stock in the electric company."

Ranger beeped the security system off on his Bronco. "Let's move."

"Me too!" Lula yelled, backing into a parking space, cutting her engine. "Hold on for me."

We all piled into Ranger's Bronco, and Ranger took off for Sixth Street.

"I bet Old Penis Nose is gonna pop someone," Lula said. "I bet he's got someone all lined up."

I told Lula about the four bodies in Mo's basement.

"When a man's got a nose looks like a penis he's likely to do anything," Lula said. "It's the sort of thing makes serial killers out of otherwise normal people."

I thought chances were pretty good that Mo was involved in the killing of the men in his cellar. I didn't think his nose had anything to do with it. I thought about Cameron Brown and Leroy Watkins and Ronald Anders. All dead drug dealers. And then I wondered if the men buried in Mo's basement would turn out to be dealers, too. "Maybe Mo's a vigilante," I said. More to hear it said out loud than anything else. And I was thinking that maybe he wasn't alone in his vigilantism. Maybe there was a whole pack of them, running around in ski masks and coveralls, threatening and killing whoever they deemed to be a danger to society.

Lula repeated the word. "Vigilante."

"Someone who takes the law into his own hands," I said.

"Hunh. I guess I know what it means. You're telling me Mo is like Zorro and Robin Hood. Only Old Penis Nose don't just slash a big Z in a man's shirt. Old Penis Nose scatters brains halfway across a room in his pursuit of justice." She paused for a moment, thinking it through. "Probably Zorro blew a few heads apart, too. They don't tell you everything in a movie, you know. Probably after Zorro ruined your shirt he cut off your balls. Or maybe he made a Z on your stomach and all your guts fell out. I heard you could cut open a person's stomach, and his guts could all be hanging out onto the floor and he could live for hours like that."

I was riding shotgun beside Ranger. I slid my eyes in his direction, but he was in his zone, doing eighty between cross streets. Foot to the brake, jerk to a stop, giving the

ABS a good test, look both ways. Foot to the floor on the accelerator.

"So what do you think?" Lula asked. "You think Zorro got off on shit like that? Making people look at their guts hanging out?"

My lips parted, but no words came out.

Ranger turned onto Main and then onto Sixth. This was a neighborhood of board and shingle row houses with stoops for porches and sidewalk for front yard. The houses were narrow and dark—sullen patchworks of brown and black and maroon. Originally built for immigrant factory workers, the houses were now predominantly occupied by struggling minorities. Most houses had been converted to rooming houses and apartments.

"Who lives in the house across from you?" Ranger asked Lula.

"A bunch of people," Lula said. "Mostly they come and go. Vanessa Long lives on the first floor, and you never know which of her kids is needing to stay there. Almost always her daughter, Tootie, and Tootie's three kids. Harold sometimes lives there. Old Mrs. Clayton lives on the other side of the hall. There are three rooms on the second floor. Not sure who's in those rooms. They let out weekly. Used to be Earl Bean lived in one, but I haven't seen him lately."

Ranger parked two houses down. "The third floor?"

"Nothing but an attic up there. Crazy Jim Katts lives in it. My guess is Mo was going to see someone on the second floor. It isn't like it's a crack house or anything over there, but when you rent weekly you never know what you get. You probably want to talk to Vanessa. She collects the rent. She knows everything goes on. Her apartment's on the left side when you walk in the door."

Ranger scanned the street. "Mo come in a car?"

"You mean the car he stole from you? Nope. I looked, but I didn't see it. I didn't see any strange cars. Only cars I see were ones that belong."

"You stay here," Ranger said to Lula. He gave an almost imperceptible nod in my direction. "You come with me."

He was wearing black sweatpants and a black hooded sweatshirt. So far as I could tell he'd never broken a sweat during the run. I, on the other hand, started sweating at the quarter-mile mark. My clothes were soaked through, my hair was stuck to my face in ringlets and my legs felt rubbery. I angled out of the car and did a little jig on the sidewalk, trying to keep warm.

"We'll talk to Vanessa," Ranger said. "And we'll look around. You have anything on you?"

I shook my head, no.

"No gun?"

"No gun. Everything's in my pocketbook, and I left my pocketbook at my parents' house."

Ranger looked grim. "Is the gun loaded?"

"I'm not sure."

"Your granny'll be doing target practice, shooting the eyes out of the potatoes."

I tagged after him and made a mental note to get my gun as soon as possible.

The front door to the building was unlocked. The overhead light still on. Inside, the small foyer was dark. Two doors led to the first-floor apartments. Ranger knocked on the left-hand door.

I looked at my watch. Seven forty-five. "It's early," I said.

"It's Sunday," Ranger said. "She'll be getting ready for church. Women need time for their hair."

The door opened the width of the security chain and two inches of face peered out at us.

"Yes?"

"Vanessa?" Ranger asked.

"That's me," she said. "What do you want? If you're looking to rent we're full up."

Ranger badged her. "Bond enforcement," he said. His

voice was soft and polite. Respectful. "I'm looking for a man named Moses Bedemier. He was seen entering this house earlier this morning."

"I don't know anybody named Moses Bedemier."

"White man," Ranger said. "In his sixties. Balding. Wearing a gray overcoat. Probably came here looking to buy drugs."

The door closed and the chain snapped off. "I didn't see no jive junkie coming in here, and if I did I'd kick him out on his bony white ass. I've got kids in this house. I don't put up with that kind coming around. I don't put up with drugs in this house."

"Would you mind if we check the upstairs apartments?" Ranger asked.

"Mind? Hell, I'd insist on it," Vanessa said, disappearing into her living room, returning with a set of keys.

She was as wide as Lula, dressed in a red and yellow flowered cotton housecoat with her hair up in rollers. She had a grown daughter and grandchildren, but she didn't look much over thirty. Maybe thirty-five. She knocked on the first door with a vengeance.

KNOCK, KNOCK, KNOCK!

The door opened and a slim young man squinted out at us. "Yuh?"

"You got anybody in here?" Vanessa asked, poking her head around the doorjamb, seeing for herself. "You doing business in here that you shouldn't be doing?"

"No, ma'am. Not me." He shook his head vigorously.

"Hmmm," Vanessa said and moved on to door number two.

Again KNOCK, KNOCK, KNOCK.

The door was jerked open by a fat man wearing briefs and an undershirt. "Jesus fucking Christ," he yelled. "What's a man got to do to get some sleep around here?" He saw Vanessa and took a step back. "Oh, sorry," he said. "Didn't know it was you."

"I'm looking for some nasty white guy," Vanessa said, arms crossed, chin tucked in outraged authority. "You got one in here?"

"Nobody here but me."

We all stood staring at door number three.

CHAPTER

11

Ranger motioned Vanessa to stand to one side, rapped on the door and waited for a response. After a moment he knocked again.

"Got a lady in here," Vanessa said. "Moved in just last week. Name's Gail." She leaned past Ranger. "Gail? It's Vanessa from downstairs, honey. You open the door."

The bolt slid back and a young woman peeked out at us. She was painfully thin, with sleepy eyes and an open sore at the corner of her mouth.

"You have visitors this morning?" Vanessa asked.

The woman hesitated for a couple beats. Probably wondering what she should say. What new trouble was at her doorstep?

Vanessa looked beyond Gail. "There isn't anybody else in there now, is there?"

Gail gave her head a vehement shake. "Unh-uh. And I didn't invite nobody up here either. He just come of his own accord. Honest. It was some crazy white guy looking for my old man."

Vanessa raised a disapproving eyebrow. "I was led to understand you were living alone."

"My old man split on me. I got out of rehab, and he took off. He said he was worrying about things that been happening." She made a gun with her thumb and forefinger. "Now he's gone. Vanished. Poof."

Ranger was hanging loose behind Vanessa. "Name?" he asked Gail.

Gail looked from Vanessa to Ranger to me. More indecision.

"WELL?" Vanessa demanded, loud enough to make Gail jump six inches.

"Elliot Harp," Gail said, the words tumbling out of her mouth. "Everybody call him Harpoon. But I'm not his woman no more. I swear to it." She licked at the sore on her lip. "Is there more?" she asked.

"No," Ranger told her. "Sorry we had to bother you so early in the morning."

Gail nodded once and closed the door very quietly. Click. She was gone.

Ranger thanked Vanessa. Told her how he appreciated her help. Anytime, Vanessa said. And if he ever needed a room, or for that matter, if he ever needed anything at all . . . *anything*, he should remember about her. Ranger assured Vanessa she was unforgettable, and we left on that note.

"Boy," I said when we were out on the street. "Mr. Charm."

"In sweats, too," he said. "You should see me work my magic in leather."

"Where is he?" Lula wanted to know when we were all settled in Ranger's Bronco. "Where's Old Penis Nose?"

"Don't know," I said. "He came here looking for Elliot Harp, but Elliot wasn't at home."

"Elliot Harp's bad news," Lula said. "Mean. Middle management. Must have at least ten kids running for him."

"About that badge you flash," I said to Ranger.

He pulled away from the curb, flicked me a sideways glance. "You want one?"

"Might come in handy."

Ranger shot Lula a look in the rearview mirror. "You know where Elliot lives?"

"So far as I know he lives on Stark. Has a woman there. Junkie ho."

"Gail?"

"Yep. Gail."

"We just talked to Gail. She said Harp split. Says she doesn't know where he is."

"That could be," Lula said. "Lot of that going around."

"If Mo really wants to find Elliot, where will he look next?" I asked.

Ranger turned at Gainsborough and headed back toward the burg. "He'll go to the street. He'll look for Elliot on the corner. Elliot's running scared, but he still needs to do business."

"Elliot won't be on the street now," Lula said. "Maybe around eleven. The corners are always busy after church. After church is time to pick up a ho and get high."

I returned to my apartment for breakfast and a change of clothes. Lula went shopping for something to settle her stomach. And Ranger went home to the Batcave to eat tofu and tree bark. The plan was to rendezvous again at eleven.

The phone was ringing when I walked in the door, and my message light was blinking. Four new messages.

"Where have you been so early in the morning?" my mother wanted to know when I snatched up the phone. "I called an hour ago and nobody was home."

"I went out to run."

"Have you seen the paper?"

"No."

"They found bodies in Mo's basement! Four bodies. Can you imagine?"

"I have to go," I said. "I have to get a paper. I'll call back later."

"You left your pocketbook here."

"I know. Don't let Grandma play with my gun."

"Your grandmother is out to church. Says she needs more of a social life. Says she's going to find herself a man."

I disconnected and played back my messages. My mother, Mary Lou, Connie, Sue Ann Grebek. They were all reporting on the newspaper article. I called next door to Mrs. Karwatt and asked if she had a paper. Yes, she did, she said. And did I hear about the bodies in Mo's basement.

Three minutes later I was back in my kitchen with Mrs. Karwatt's paper, and my phone was ringing again. Lula this time.

"Did you see it?" she shouted. "Old Penis Nose made the paper! Said how he was picked up for carrying and then disappeared, and how he was under suspicion. Newspaper said a source told them the bodies in Mo's cellar could be drug related. Hah!" she said. "You bet your ass."

I read the article, started coffee brewing, took a shower and unplugged my phone after three more calls. This was the biggest thing to hit the burg since Tony the Vig was found dead in his attic, hanging from a crossbeam with his pants down and his hand wrapped around a record-breaking hard-on. Hell, maybe Mo was even bigger than Tony V's wanger.

And the best part of all of this was that I was finally the good guy. No more bullshit about how Uncle Mo would never do anything wrong. The man had a maggot farm in his cellar.

"Looking good," I said to Rex.

I laced up my boots, wrapped a scarf around my neck

and went with the black leather jacket. I hopped into the Buick and drove over to my parents' house. Grandma Mazur was taking her coat off in the foyer when I arrived.

"Did you hear about the bodies?" she asked.

"Morelli and I made the discovery," I said.

Grandma's eyes opened wide. "No kidding! Were you there when they dug them up? Are you going to be on TV?"

I retrieved my pocketbook from the hall closet and did a fast check of the contents. "I don't think I'll be on TV."

"Boy," Grandma said, "I sure would have liked to have been there."

"How was church?" I asked.

"Boring," she said. "A big waste of time. We got a bunch of duds in that congregation. Nobody hot to trot. I'm gonna try the bingo hall tonight. I hear they got some live lookers coming to bingo."

Ranger was already parked when I swung into the municipal lot on Woodley. He was dressed in army fatigues and a khaki flight jacket.

"What's up?" I said by way of greeting.

"I got word on one of my FTAs. Earl Forster. Robbed a liquor store and shot the clerk in the foot. Jumped on a three-hundred-thousand-dollar bond. Just got a phone call saying Forster's stopped by to see his girlfriend in New Brunswick. I have a man in place, but I need to be there for the takedown. Can you handle the search for Harp by yourself?"

"No problem. Lula knows what he looks like. She knows his corners."

"Don't get close to him," Ranger said. "Only use him to get to Mo. If Mo and Harp go off together, let Mo put Harp away before you go in. We think Mo might be killing drug dealers. We *know* Harp will kill anybody . . . even female bounty hunters."

Cheery thought for the day.

"If it looks like you can do a takedown, but you need extra help, get me on the cell phone or the pager," Ranger said.

"Be careful," I said to the back of his car as he drove away. No point saying it to his face.

Lula barreled into the lot ten minutes later. "Sorry I'm late," she said. "I got this intestinal problem, you know." She looked around. "Where's Ranger?"

"Had business elsewhere. We're on our own."

If I was doing a serious stakeout with another person, I'd use two cars or have one person on foot with a second car in backup. I suspected this would be more of a ride around and look for a man who didn't show up. And since I had no idea what Harp looked like, I elected to ride with Lula.

It was another gray day with a light rain beginning to fall. Temperatures were in the forties, so nothing was freezing. Lula motored the Firebird out of the lot and headed for Stark Street. We kept our eyes open for the Batmobile, Elliot Harp and bad guys in general. We worked our way down Stark, hit the end of the business district, turned and retraced our route. Lula wove her way through the projects, cruised center city and crossed over to King. When she reached Ferris she drove by Mo's. The store was padlocked and sealed with crime scene tape. We did this circuit two more times. It was raining. Not many people out on the street.

"I'm starving to death," Lula said. "I need a burger. I need fries."

I could see the glow of a fast-food drive-through shining red and yellow through the misting rain. I could feel the force field sucking us forward to the speaker box.

"I want a triple-decker burger," Lula yelled at the box. "I want bacon and cheese and special sauce. I want a large fries, and I want lots of them little ketchup packets. And I want a large chocolate milkshake." She turned to me. "You want something?"

"I'll have the same."

"Double that order," Lula shouted. "And don't forget about the ketchup."

We took the bags of food and parked on Stark Street where we could watch the action. Trouble was, there wasn't much action to watch.

"You ever wonder about him?" Lula asked.

"Who?"

"Ranger."

"What's to wonder?"

"I bet you don't know anything about him," Lula said. "Nobody knows anything about him. I bet you don't even know where he lives."

"I know his address."

"Hah! That vacant lot."

I sipped at my milkshake, and Lula finished up her fries.

"I think we should do some detecting on Ranger," Lula said. "I think someday we should follow his ass."

"Hmm," I said, not feeling especially qualified to follow Ranger's ass.

"In fact, I might follow it tomorrow morning. You run with him every day?"

"Not if I can help it."

"Well if you run with him tomorrow, you call me. I could use some exercise."

After an hour of sitting, I was ready to move on. "This isn't working," I said to Lula. "Just for fun, let's drive over to Montgomery."

Lula drove the length of Stark, looped through the projects one last time and cut across town. We drove back and forth on Montgomery and parked two doors down from Sal's Café.

"Bet they've got doughnuts in there," Lula said.

"What about your intestinal problem? Maybe you want to wait and see how it goes with the burger and fries."

"I suppose you're right, but I sure would like to have some doughnuts."

I had to admit, doughnuts seemed like a pretty good idea on a drizzly day.

"Course there's some advantage to having an intestinal disturbance," Lula said. "Those doughnuts probably wouldn't stay with me long enough to find a home on my ass."

"Better take advantage of the opportunity."

Lula had her purse in her hand. "That's exactly what I'm thinking."

I stayed in the car and watched through the window as Lula picked out a dozen doughnuts.

She handed the doughnuts and the coffees off to me and settled behind the wheel. I chose a Bavarian cream and took a chomp. Lula did the same. She took a second doughnut.

"Have you seen Jackie?" I asked Lula. "Is she still with the program?"

"She's going to the clinic. Problem is, you can make a person do the program, but you can't make them take it serious. Jackie don't believe in herself enough to take the program serious."

"Maybe that will change."

"I sure hope so. I'm lucky because I was born with a positive personality. Even when things aren't looking too good, I don't let myself get beaten down. I just start pushing and shoving. Pretty soon I'm so loud and full of bullshit I just forget about being scared. Jackie wasn't born with such a positive personality. Jackie's more a negative person. She pulls all inside herself."

"Not always," I said. "She was pretty extroverted when it came to drilling holes in Cameron Brown."

Lula gazed into the doughnut box, thinking ahead to

doughnut number three. "Yeah. She had a good time on that one. I know it wasn't right what she did to the dead, but I gotta admit, I sort of liked seeing her make old Cameron jump around. She's gotta learn to take charge more like that.

"See, Jackie and me, we've both been beat on a lot. That's the way it is when you haven't got a daddy, and your mama's a crackhead. There's always lots of uncles coming and going and getting high. And when they get high they beat on you.

"Trouble now is that Jackie's still letting people beat on her. She doesn't know she can make it stop. I try to tell her. I tell her to look at me. Nobody's gonna beat on me ever again. I've got self-respect. I'm gonna do something with my life. I might even go to college someday."

"You could do it. Lots of people return to school."

"Fuckin' A," Lula said.

I drank my coffee and looked out the rain-streaked window. Cars drove by in abstract motion. Blurry images and smeary flashes of bright red taillights.

A car pulled out of the underground parking garage across the street. It was a tan sedan with something long and black strapped to the roof. I cracked my window for a better look. Rug, I thought. All rolled up and covered with a plastic tarp.

The driver reached a hand out, checking to see if his cargo was secure. The door opened, and the driver stepped out to make an adjustment.

Suddenly I was at the edge of my seat. "Look at that car with the rug on top!" I hollered, grabbing Lula by the jacket sleeve to get her attention.

"The car at the parking garage?" She put the wipers on and leaned forward to see better. "Holy cow! It's him! It's Old Penis Nose!"

Lula jumped out of the car and took off across the street

after Mo. She had a half-eaten Boston creme in her hand, and she was getting pelted with rain and she was yelling, "Stop! Stop in the name of the law!"

Mo's mouth dropped open. A mixture of disbelief and horror registered on his face. He snapped his mouth shut, jumped into his car and took off, burning rubber.

"Get back here!" I hollered at Lula. "He's getting away!"

Lula pulled up and ran back to the Firebird. "Did you see that? He didn't pay no attention to me! I should of shot him. I should of dropped a cap in that old coot."

Hard to do when you're packing a doughnut.

She threw the car into gear, put her foot to the floor and rocketed off after Mo . . . through the intersection, through a red light.

"I see him!" she shouted, giving the wheel a thump with the heel of her hand. "And that isn't no rug on the top of the car. That's something lumpy wrapped in garbage bags. I'm not even gonna tell you what I think is on top of that car."

I'd had the same thought, and the possibility that Elliot Harp was going for his last ride evoked a desire to drive in the opposite direction. I didn't want to find any more dead people. My emotional stability was approaching meltdown. I was doing a pretty good job of denying the attack in the candy store. I was having less success with flashbacks of murdered men.

Mo turned at Slater, and Lula took the corner with two tires touching pavement.

I had my foot braced against the dash. "Slow down! You're going to kill us."

"Don't worry," Lula said. "I know what I'm doing. I've got perfect reflexes. I'm like a cat."

Mo was coming up to Wells Avenue, and I knew where he was going. He was heading for Route 1. No problem, I thought. He can't outrun us with whatever he has on top of his car. Although probably he didn't care much about his cargo by now.

Lula followed Mo onto the ramp, momentarily fell behind when Mo merged into traffic. We caught him easily enough and stuck to his tail.

The dark green plastic was furiously flapping in the wind. Mo had bound the package to the roof of the car by lacing what looked like clothesline through the windows. He changed lanes and the long lumpy object swung side to side under the ropes.

"He don't watch out, he's gonna lose that sucker," Lula said. She beeped her horn at him. "Pull over, Peckernose!" She gave the Firebird some gas and tapped Mo's rear bumper.

I was braced against the dash, and I'd begun chanting under my breath. Holy Mary, mother of God . . . please don't let me die on Route 1 with my hair looking like this.

Lula gave Mo's back bumper another whack. The impact snapped my head and caused Mo to fishtail out of control. He swerved in front of us, a cord snapped loose and a garbage bag whipped off and sailed over our car.

Lula moved in one more time, but before she could make contact the second cord broke, another garbage bag flew away and a body catapulted off Mo's roof and onto the hood of Lula's Firebird, landing with a loud WUMP!

"EEEEEeeeeeh!" Lula and I screamed in unison.

The body bounced once on the hood, and then smacked into the windshield and stuck like a squashed bug, staring in at us, mouth agape, eyes unseeing.

"I got a body stuck to my windshield!" Lula yelled. "I can't drive like this! I can't get my wipers to work. How am I supposed to drive with a dead guy on my wipers?"

The car rocked from lane to lane; the body vaulted off the hood, did a half flip and landed faceup at the side of the road. Lula stomped on the brake and skidded to a stop on the shoulder. We sat there for a moment, hands to our hearts, unable to talk. We turned and looked out the back window.

"Dang," Lula said.

I thought that summed it up.

We looked at each other and did a double grimace. Lula put the Firebird in reverse and cautiously inched back, staying to the shoulder, out of the traffic lane. She stopped and parked a couple feet from the body. We got out of the car and crept closer.

"At least he's got clothes on," Lula said.

"Is it Harp?"

"That would be my guess. Hard to tell with that big hole where his nose used to be."

The drizzle had turned to a driving rain. I pushed wet hair out of my eyes and blinked at Lula. "We should call the police."

"Yeah," Lula said. "That's a good idea. You call the police, and I'll cover the body. I got a blanket in the back."

I ran back to the car and retrieved my pocketbook. I rummaged around some, found my cell phone, flipped it open and punched the on button. A dim light flashed a low-battery message and cut off.

"No juice," I said to Lula. "I must have left the phone on all last night. We'll have to flag someone down."

A dozen cars zoomed past us, spraying water.

"Plan two?" Lula asked.

"We drive to the nearest exit and call the police."

"You gonna leave the body all by itself?"

"I suppose one of us should stay."

"That would be you," Lula said.

An eighteen-wheeler roared by, almost sideswiping us.

"Ditch staying," I told her.

Lula cut her eyes back to Harp. "We could take him with us. We could ram him into the trunk. And then we could drive him to a funeral parlor or something. You know, do a drop-off."

"That would be altering the crime scene."

"Altering, hell. This dead motherfucker fell out of the sky onto the hood of my car! And anyway, he could get run over by a truck if he stays here."

She had a point. Elliot Harp had been in transit when he bounced off the Firebird. And he wouldn't look good with tire tracks across his chest.

"Okay," I said. "We'll take him with us."

We looked down at Elliot. Both of us swallowing hard.

"Guess you should put him in the trunk," Lula said.

"Me?"

"You don't expect *me* to do it, do you? I'm not touching no dead man. I've still got the creeps from Leroy Watkins."

"He's big. I can't get him in the trunk all by myself."

"This whole thing is giving me the runs," Lula said. "I vote we pretend this never happened, and we get our butts out of here."

"It won't be so bad," I said to her, making an effort at convincing myself. "How about your blanket? We could wrap him in the blanket. Then we could pick him up without actually touching him."

"I suppose that'd be all right," Lula said. "We could give it a try."

I spread the blanket on the ground beside Elliot Harp, took a deep breath, hooked my fingers around his belt and rolled him onto the blanket. I jumped back, squeezed my eyes closed tight and exhaled. No matter how much violent death I saw, I would never get used to it.

"I'm gonna definitely have the runs," Lula said. "I can feel it coming on."

"Forget about the runs and help me with this body!"

Lula grabbed hold of the head end of the blanket, and I grabbed hold of the foot end. Harp had full rigor and wouldn't bend, so we put him in the trunk headfirst with his legs sticking out. We carefully closed the lid on Harp's knees and secured the lid with a piece of rope Lula had in her trunk.

"Hold on," Lula said, pulling a red flowered scarf from her coat pocket, tying the scarf on Harp's foot like a flag. "Don't want to get a ticket. I hear the police are real picky about having things sticking out of your trunk."

Especially dead guys.

We pulled into traffic and had gone about a half mile, looking for a place to turn, when I got to worrying about Harp. I wasn't sure how it would go over with the Trenton police if we drove up to the station with a dead drug dealer hanging out of Lula's trunk. They might not understand the decision-making process that led to moving him off the side of the road.

Lula took a jug handle off Route 1 and stopped for a light. "Where're we going?" she wanted to know.

"To the burg. I need to talk to Eddie Gazarra."

Gazarra was a friend first, cop second. Gazarra could be trusted to give me honest advice on the best method of dead body transfer.

A car pulled up behind us at the light. Almost immediately the car went into reverse, backing away from us at high speed. Lula and I stopped watching the rearview mirror and exchanged glances.

"Maybe we should have done a better job of wrapping the blanket around old Elliot's feet," Lula said.

The light changed, and Lula headed south on Route 1. She cut off at Masters Street, preferring to drive a few blocks out of the way rather than chance crossing center city with Elliot. By the time we hit Hamilton Avenue the sky was dark under cloud cover, and the streetlights had blinked on.

Eddie Gazarra lived in a three-bedroom ranch on the fringe of the burg. The house had been built in the sixties. Red brick and white aluminum siding. Postage stamp fenced-in yard. Bugs the Rabbit lived in a wooden hutch at the rear of the yard, banished from the house after eating through the TV cable.

Lula parked in front of the house, and we stared in silence at the black windows.

"Doesn't look like anyone's home," Lula said.

I agreed, but I went to the door anyway. I pressed the doorbell and waited a few seconds. I pressed the doorbell again. I waded into the azaleas, cupped my hands against the living room window and looked inside. Nobody home.

Gus Balog, Eddie's next-door neighbor, stuck his head out his front door. "What's going on? Is that Stephanie Plum?"

"Yes. I'm looking for Eddie."

"Nobody's home. They took the kids out to that new chicken place. Is that your car . . . that red one?"

"It belongs to an associate."

"What's sticking out the trunk? Looks like legs."

"It's just a dummy. You know, like from a department store."

"Don't look like a dummy," Gus said. "Looks like a dead guy. I heard you were looking for Mo. Those aren't Mo's legs, are they?"

I backed out of the azaleas and retreated to the car. "No. They're not Mo's legs." I jumped into the car and slammed the door shut. "Time to leave," I said to Lula.

Lula cruised around a couple blocks. "Well?" she asked.

"I'm thinking. I'm thinking." The problem was that I could only come up with one other person who might be able to help me out. Joe Morelli. Not someone I wanted to see in my present bedraggled condition. And not someone I wanted to owe an additional favor. And not someone I totally trusted to choose me over the Trenton Police Department.

"I'm cold, and I'm wet and I'm sure as anything gonna have the runs any minute now," Lula said. "You better decide what to do pretty soon, or there could be a big mess in the car."

Morelli had recently moved out of his apartment and into

a row house on Slater Street. I didn't know any of the details, but the move seemed out of character for Morelli. His previous apartment had been sparsely furnished. Comfortable in a utilitarian sort of way. Minimum maintenance. An entire house for Morelli felt much too domestic. Who would clean it? And what about curtains? Who would pick out curtains?

"Take Chambers and turn left when you get to Slater," I said.

Slater was outside the boundaries of the burg by about a half mile. It was an ethnically mixed neighborhood of modest homes and people scraping to maintain them.

I couldn't remember the number, but I'd know the house. I'd given in to morbid curiosity about a month ago and driven by to check things out. It was brown shingle in the middle of the block. Two stories, small cement front porch. A handyman's special.

We drove two blocks down Slater, and I could see Morelli's car parked at the curb half a block ahead. My stomach gave a nervous little twitch, and I did a panicky review of my options.

"What are you doing making those whimpering sounds?" Lula asked.

"I'm reviewing my options."

"And?"

"I don't have any."

Lula idled at Morelli's back bumper. "Looks like a cop car. Smells like a cop car. . . ."

"Joe Morelli."

"Is this his house?"

"Yeah," I said. "Pull over. I'll only be a minute."

I could see lights shining downstairs, to the rear. Probably coming from the kitchen. I knocked on the door and waited, wondering what sort of reception I'd get, praying Morelli was alone. If he had a woman with him I'd be so embarrassed I'd have to move to Florida.

I heard footsteps to the other side of the door, and the door was opened. Morelli wore thick wool socks and jeans, a black T-shirt and a flannel shirt that was unbuttoned and rolled to his elbows. His eyebrows lifted in surprise. He took in my wet hair and mud-splattered Levi's. His gaze shifted to the red Firebird, which Lula had parked under a streetlight. He shook his head.

"Tell me you don't have legs sticking out of that car."

"Uh, well, actually . . ."

"Christ, Stephanie, this makes four! Four dead bodies. Eight if you count the ones in the cellar."

"It's not my fault!" I stuffed my fists onto my hips. "You think I want to keep finding dead bodies? This is no picnic for me either, you know."

"Who is it?"

"We think it's Elliot Harp. He's got a big hole in the middle of his face, so it's hard to tell for sure."

I told him the story about spotting Mo and following him down Route 1, and how we came to have Elliot Harp rammed into Lula's trunk.

"And?" Morelli said.

"And I brought him here. I thought you might want to have first crack at him." And I thought you might write up the report in a favorable manner that didn't cite me for body snatching. And I thought if I dragged you into this I wouldn't be the brunt of bad cop jokes having to do with tailgate delivery of corpses.

I took a fast peek inside Morelli's house, seeing a wood floor in the small foyer and an old-fashioned wood banister on stairs leading up to the second floor.

Morelli made a one-minute sign to Lula, pulled me inside and shut the door. "You should have left the body on the side of the road. You should have flagged someone down. You should have found a phone and called the police."

"Hello," I said. "Are you listening? I just went through all of that. No one would stop, and I decided it was dangerous to stay at roadside."

Morelli cracked the door and looked out at the Firebird. He closed the door and shook his head again. He looked down at his feet and tried to hide the smile.

"It isn't funny!" I said.

"Whose idea was the flag?"

"Lula's. She didn't want to get a ticket."

The smile widened. "You gotta love her."

"So what should I do with this guy?"

"I'll call the ME's office and have someone meet us at the station. You've driven Harp this far . . . a few more miles won't make much difference."

"I didn't do anything illegal, did I?"

Morelli headed off to the back of the house. "You don't want to know the answer to that."

I followed him down the hall to the kitchen, catching a glimpse of the living room, dining room. The rooms were small, but the ceilings were high with elaborate crown molding. Boxes still sat in all the rooms, waiting to be un-packed. A rug was rolled to one side in the dining room.

Morelli retrieved cross trainers from under the kitchen table and sat down to lace them.

"Nice kitchen," I said. "Reminds me a lot of my parents' house." What about shelf paper, I was thinking. I couldn't imagine Morelli picking out shelf paper.

Morelli looked around like he was seeing the kitchen for the first time. "It needs some work."

"Why did you decide to buy a house?"

"I didn't buy it. I inherited it. My aunt Rose left it to me. She and my uncle Sallie bought this house when they were first married. Sallie died ten years ago, and Aunt Rose stayed on. She died in October. She was eighty-three. They didn't have any kids, and I was a favorite nephew, so I got the house. My sister, Mary, got the furniture." Morelli stood at the table and snagged a jacket that had been draped over a kitchen chair.

"You could sell it."

He shrugged into the jacket. "I thought of that, but I decided to give this a try first. See how it felt."

A horn beeped from outside.

"That's Lula," I said. "She's got the runs."

CHAPTER
12

I directed Lula to the rear of the station so we could unload Elliot in as much privacy as possible. We pulled into the drop-off zone and cut the engine. Morelli parked to the side of the lot. The drop-off is covered by closed-circuit TV, so I knew it was only a matter of minutes before the curious spilled out of the back security door.

Lula and I stood to the front of the Firebird, not wanting to get any closer to Elliot than was absolutely necessary. I was soaked to the skin, and without the car's heater blasting away at me I was cold clear to the bone.

"Funny how life works," Lula said. "All this came about because I ate a bad burrito. It's like God knew what he was doing when he gave me the runs."

I hugged my arms tight to my chest and clenched my teeth to keep them from chattering. "The Lord moves in mysterious ways."

"Exactly my thoughts. Now we know Jackie was right about Old Penis Nose being on Montgomery Street. We even did something good for Elliot. Not that he deserves it, but if it wasn't for us he'd be dumped in the river by now."

The rear door to the building opened and two uniforms stepped out. I didn't know their names, but I'd seen them around. Morelli told them he was going to tie up the drop zone for a few minutes. Told them he'd appreciate it if they kept the traffic down.

The Medical Examiner's pickup arrived and backed in close to the Firebird. It was a dark blue Ford Ranger with a white cap divided into compartments that reminded me of kennels.

The ID detective said a few words to Morelli and then went to work.

Arnie Rupp, the supervisor of the violent crimes squad, came out and stood hands in pockets, watching the action. A man in jeans, black Trenton PD ball cap and red and black plaid wool jacket stood next to him. Rupp asked the man if he'd completed the paperwork on the Runion job. The man said, not yet. He'd finish it up first thing in the morning.

I stared at the man and little alarms went off in my brain.

The man stared back at me. Noncommittal. Cop face. Unyielding.

Morelli moved into my line of vision. "I'm sending you and Lula home. You both look half drowned, and this will take some time."

"I appreciate it," Lula said, "because I've got an intestinal disturbance."

Morelli lifted my chin a fraction of an inch with his index finger and studied my face. "Are you going to be okay?"

"Sure. I'm f-f-fine."

"You don't look fine. You look like you're down a couple quarts."

"Who's the guy standing next to Arnie Rupp? The guy in the jeans and cop hat and red and black plaid jacket."

"Mickey Maglio. Major Crimes. Robbery detective."

"Remember when I was telling you about the men in the ski masks and coveralls? The leader, the one who burned my hand and offered me money, had a smoker's voice. Jersey City accent. I know you don't want to hear this, but I swear, Maglio sounds just like him. And he's the right height and the right build."

"You never saw his face?"

I shook my head. "No."

"Maglio's a good cop," Morelli said. "He's got three kids and a pregnant wife."

"I don't know," I said. "I could be wrong. I'm c-c-cold. Maybe I'm not thinking right."

Morelli wrapped his arm around me and dragged me toward a waiting squad car. "I'll look into it. In the meantime let's keep it to ourselves."

Lula got dropped off first due to her pressing needs. I rode in silence for the rest of the trip, shivering in the backseat, unable to sort through my thoughts, afraid I'd burst into tears and look like an idiot in front of my cop chauffeur.

I thanked the officer when he pulled up at my door. I scrambled out of the car, ran into the building and took the stairs. The second-floor hall was empty of people but filled with dinner smells. Fried fish from Mrs. Karwatt. Stew from Mr. Walesky.

My teeth had stopped chattering, but my hands were still shaking, and I had to two-fist the key to get it into the keyhole. I pushed the door open, switched the light on, closed and bolted my door and did a fast security check.

Rex backed out of his soup can and gave me the once-over. He looked startled at my appearance, so I explained my day. When I got to the part about driving Elliot around in Lula's trunk, I burst out laughing. My God, what had I been thinking! It was an absurd thing to do. I laughed until I cried, and then I realized I was no longer laughing. Tears were streaming down my cheeks, and I was sobbing. After a while my nose was running, and my mouth was open but the sobs were soundless.

"Shit," I said to Rex. "This is exhausting."

I blew my nose, dragged myself into the bathroom, stripped and stood under the shower until my skin was scorched and my mind was empty. I got dressed in sweats and cotton socks and cooked my hair into ten inches of red frizz with the hair dryer. I looked like I'd taken a bath with the toaster, but I was way beyond caring. I collapsed onto the bed and instantly fell asleep.

I came awake slowly, my eyes swollen from crying, my mind gauzy and stupid. The clock at bedside said nine-thirty. Someone was knocking. I shuffled into the hall and opened the door without ceremony.

It was Morelli, holding a pizza box and a six-pack.

"You should always look before you open the door," he said.

"I did look."

"You're lying again."

He was right. I hadn't looked. And he was right about being careful.

My eyes locked on the pizza box. "You sure know how to get a person's attention."

Morelli smiled. "Hungry?"

"Are you coming in, or what?"

Morelli dumped the pizza and beer on the coffee table and shrugged out of his jacket. "I'd like to go over the day's events."

I brought plates and a roll of paper towels to the coffee table and sat beside Morelli on the couch. I wolfed down a piece of pizza and told him everything.

By the time I was done, Morelli was on his second beer. "You have any additional thoughts?"

"Only that Gail probably lied to us, so she wouldn't get in trouble with her landlady. Elliot had full rigor when we found him, so he'd been dead awhile. My guess is either Gail told Mo where to find Elliot, or else Elliot was in Gail's room when Mo showed up."

Morelli nodded affirmation. "You're watching the right TV shows," he said. "We ran the plates on the tan car. The car belonged to Elliot Harp."

"Did you find Mo's connection to Montgomery Street?"

"Not yet, but we have men in the neighborhood. The garage was used by a lot of people. It's possible to buy a key card on a monthly basis. No ID necessary. Freedom Church members use the garage. Local merchants use it."

I ate another slice of pizza. I wanted to bring up the topic of Mickey Maglio, but I didn't feel secure about the accusation. Besides, I'd mentioned it once. Morelli was too good a cop to let it slide by and be forgotten.

"So now what?" I asked. "You want to watch some TV?"

Morelli looked at his watch. "Think I'll pass. I should be getting home." He stood and stretched. "Been a long day."

I followed him to the door. "Thanks for helping me dispose of Elliot."

"Hey," Morelli said, punching me lightly on the arm. "What are friends for?"

I blinked. Friends? Morelli and me? "Okay, what's going on?"

"Nothing's going on."

Boy, was that ever the truth. No flirting. No grabbing. Sexist remarks held to a minimum. I narrowed my eyes as I watched him walk to the elevator. There was only one possible explanation. Morelli had a girlfriend. Morelli was enamored with someone else, and I was off the hook.

He disappeared behind the elevator doors, and I retreated into my apartment.

Hooray, I told myself. But I didn't actually feel like

hooray. I felt like someone had thrown a party, and I hadn't been included on the guest list. I puzzled on this, trying to determine the cause for my discomfort. The obvious reason, of course, was that I was jealous. I didn't like the obvious reason, so I kept working for another. Finally I gave up in defeat. Truth is, there was unfinished business between Morelli and me. A couple months ago we'd had Buick inter-ruptus, and as much as I hated to admit it, I'd been thinking of him in torrid terms ever since.

And then there was the house move, which seemed so out of character for Morelli the bachelor. But suppose Morelli was thinking of cohabitating? My God, suppose Morelli was thinking of marriage?

I didn't at all like the idea of Morelli getting married. It would wreck my fantasy life, and it would put added pressure on me. My mother would be saying to me . . . Look! Even Joe Morelli is married!

I dropped onto the couch and punched up the television, but there wasn't anything worth seeing. I cleaned the beer cans and pizza off the coffee table. I plugged the telephone back into the wall and reset the answering machine. I tried the television again.

I had a third beer, and when that was done I felt slightly buzzed. Damn Morelli, I thought. He has a lot of nerve getting involved with some other woman.

The more I thought about it, the more annoyed I became. Who was this woman, anyway?

I called Sue Ann Grebek and discreetly asked who the hell Morelli was boffing, but Sue Ann didn't know. I called Mary Lou and my cousin Jeanine, but they didn't know either.

Well, that settles it, I decided. I'll find out for myself. After all, I'm some sort of investigator. I'll simply investigate.

Trouble was, the events of the last two days had me pretty much freaked out. I wasn't afraid of the dark, but I wasn't in love with it either. Well, okay, I was afraid of the dark. So I called Mary Lou back and asked her if she wanted to spy on Morelli with me.

"Sure," Mary Lou said. "Last time we spied on Morelli we were twelve years old. We're due."

I laced up my running shoes, pulled a hooded sweatshirt over the sweatshirt I was wearing and shoved my hair under a black knit cap. I trucked down the hall, down the stairs, and ran into Dillon Ruddick in the lobby. Dillon was the building super and an all-around nice guy.

"I'll give you five dollars if you'll walk me to my car," I said to Dillon.

"I'll walk you for free," Dillon said. "I was just taking the garbage out."

Another advantage to parking by the Dumpster.

Dillon paused at the Buick. "This is a humdinger of a car," he said.

I couldn't argue with that.

Mary Lou was waiting at the curb when I pulled up to her house. She was wearing tight black jeans, a black leather motorcycle jacket, black high-heeled ankle boots and big gold hoop earrings. Evening wear for the well-dressed burg peeper.

"You ever tell anybody I did this, and I'll deny it. And then I'll hire Manny Russo to shoot you in the knee," Mary Lou said.

"I just want to see if he has a woman with him."

"Why?"

I looked over at her.

"Okay," she said. "I know why."

Morelli's car was parked in front. The living room lights were out in his house, but the kitchen light was on, just as it had been earlier in the evening.

A figure moved through the house, up the stairs. A light blinked on in one of the upstairs rooms. The figure returned to the kitchen.

Mary Lou giggled. And then I giggled. Then we slapped ourselves so we'd stop giggling.

"I'm a mother," Mary Lou said. "I'm not supposed to be doing stuff like this. I'm too old."

"A woman's never too old to make an idiot of herself. It goes along with equality of the sexes and potty parity."

"Suppose we find him in the kitchen with a sock on his dick?"

"In your dreams."

This drew more giggles.

I drove around the corner to the paved alley road that intersected the block. I slowly rolled down the single lane, cut my lights and paused at Morelli's backyard. Morelli moved into view through a rear window. At least he was home. He hadn't gone from my house to some hot babe. I continued to the end of the lane and parked the Buick around the corner, on Arlington Avenue.

"Come on," I said to Mary Lou. "Let's take a closer look."

We crept back to Morelli's yard and stood outside the weathered picket fence, hidden in shadow.

After a few moments Morelli once again crossed in front of the window. This time he had the phone to his ear, and he was smiling.

"Look at that!" Mary Lou said. "He's smiling. I bet he's talking to *her*!"

We slipped inside the gate and tippytoed to the house. I flattened myself against the siding and held my breath. I inched closer to the window. I could hear him talking, but I couldn't make out the words. Blah, blah, blah, blah, blah.

A door opened two houses down, and a big black dog bounded into the small yard. He stopped and stood with ears pricked in our direction.

"WOOF!" the dog said.

"Omigod," Mary Lou whispered. "Jesus fucking Christ."

Mary Lou wasn't an animal person.

"WOOF!"

Suddenly this didn't seem like such a good idea. I didn't like the prospect of getting torn to shreds by the hound from hell. And even worse, I didn't want to get caught by Morelli. Mary Lou and I executed a panic-inspired crab scuttle to the back gate and held up just outside Morelli's broken-down fence. We watched the neighbor's dog slowly move to the edge of his yard. He didn't stop. His yard wasn't fenced. He was on the road now, and he was looking directly at us.

Nice dog, I thought. Probably wanted to play. But just in case . . . it might be smart to head for the car. I backed up a few paces, and the dog charged. "YIPES!"

We had two house widths on Rover, and we ran flat out for all we were worth. We were twenty feet from Arlington when I felt paws impact on my back, knocking me off my feet. My hands hit first, then my knees. I belly-whopped onto the blacktop and felt the air whoosh from my lungs.

I braced for the kill, but the dog just stood over me, tongue lolling, tail wagging.

"Good dog," I said.

He licked my face.

I rolled onto my back and assessed the damage. Torn sweats, scraped hands and knees. Large loss of self-esteem. I got to my feet, shooed the dog back home and limped to the car where Mary Lou was waiting.

"You deserted me," I said to Mary Lou.

"It looked like it might turn into one of those sexual things. I didn't want to interfere."

Fifteen minutes later I was in my apartment, dressed in my nightgown, dabbing antiseptic cream on my skinned knees. And I was feeling much better. Nothing like a totally infantile act to put things into perspective.

I stopped dabbing when the phone rang. Not Morelli, I prayed. I didn't want to hear that he'd seen me running from his yard.

I answered with a tentative hello.

Pause on the other end.

"Hello," I repeated.

"I hope that little discussion we had last time meant something to you," the man said. "Because if I find out you've opened your mouth about any of this, I'm going to come get you. And it's not going to be nice."

"Maglio?"

The caller hung up.

I checked all my locks, plugged the battery on my cell phone into the recharger, made sure my gun was loaded and at bedside along with the pepper spray. I cringed at the possibility that Maglio might be involved. It wasn't good to have a cop for an enemy. Cops could be very dangerous people.

The phone rang again. This time I let the machine get it. The call was from Ranger. Just reporting in, he said. Running tomorrow at seven.

I called Lula as promised and registered her for the program.

I was downstairs at seven, but I wasn't in the finest form. I hadn't slept well, and I was feeling tapped out.

"How'd it go yesterday?" Ranger asked.

I gave him the unabridged version, excluding my juvenile visit to Morelli's backyard.

Ranger's mouth tipped at the corners. "You're making this up, right?"

"Wrong. That's what happened. You asked what happened. I told you what happened."

"Okay, let me get this straight. Elliot Harp flew off Mo's

car, bounced off the Firebird onto the shoulder of Route 1. You picked Elliot up, and put him in the trunk and drove him to the police station."

"More or less."

Ranger gave a bark of laughter. "Bet that went over big with the boys in blue."

A taxi pulled into the lot, not far from where we were standing, and Lula got out. She was dressed in a pink polar fleece sweatsuit and pink furry earmuffs. She looked like the Energizer rabbit on steroids.

"Lula's going running with us," I told Ranger. "She wants to get in better shape."

Ranger gave Lula the once-over. "You don't keep up, you get left behind."

"Your ass," Lula said.

We took off at a pretty good clip. I figured Ranger was testing Lula. She was breathing hard, but she was close on his heels. She managed until we got to the track, and then she found a seat on the sidelines.

"I don't run in circles," she said.

I sat beside her. "Works for me."

Ranger did a lap and jogged by us without acknowledgment of our presence or lack of.

"So why are you really here?" I asked Lula.

Lula's eyes never left Ranger. "I'm here 'cause he's the shit."

"The shit?"

"Yeah, you know . . . the shit. The king. The cool."

"Do we know anyone else who's the shit?"

"John Travolta. He's the shit, too."

We watched Ranger some, and I could see her point about Ranger being the shit.

"I've been thinking," Lula said. "Suppose there really were superheroes?"

"Like Batman?"

222

"That's it. That's what I'm saying. It'd be someone who was the shit."

"Are you telling me you think Ranger's a superhero?"

"Think about it. We don't know where he lives. We don't know anything about him."

"Superheroes are make-believe."

"Oh yeah?" Lula said. "What about God?"

"Hmmmm."

Ranger did a couple more laps and veered from the track. Lula and I jumped off the bench and followed in his footsteps. We collapsed in a heap two miles later, in front of my building.

"Bet you could run forever," Lula said to Ranger, gasping and wheezing. "Bet you got muscles that feel like iron."

"Man of steel," Ranger said.

Lula sent me a knowing look.

"Well, this has been fun," I said to everybody. "But I'm out of here."

"I could use a ride," Lula said to Ranger. "The police still have my car. Maybe you could give me a ride on your way home. Of course I don't want to inconvenience you. I wouldn't want you to go out of your way." She took a momentary pause. "Just exactly where do you live?" she asked Ranger.

Ranger pressed his security remote and the doors clicked open on the Bronco. He motioned to Lula. "Get in."

Ricardo Carlos Manoso. Master of the two-syllable sentence. Superhero at large.

I hooked Lula by the crook of her arm before she took off. "What's your schedule like today?"

"Like any other day."

"If you get a chance maybe you could check some fast-food restaurants for me. I don't want you to spend all day at it, but if you go out for coffee break or lunch keep your eyes open for Stuart Baggett. He has to be working somewhere in the area. My guess is he'll go to what feels familiar."

• • •

An hour later I was on the road, canvassing eateries, doing my part. I figured Lula would stay close to the office, so I took Hamilton Township. I was on Route 33 when my cell phone chirped.

"I found him!" Lula shouted at me. "I took early lunch, and I went to a couple places on account of everyone in the office wanted something different, and I found him! Mr. Cute-as-a-button is serving up chicken now."

"Where?"

"The Cluck in a Bucket on Hamilton."

"You still there?"

"Hell yes," Lula said. "And I didn't let him see me either. I'm holed up in a phone booth."

"Don't move!"

I make lots of mistakes. I try hard not to make the same mistake more than three or four times. This time around, Stuart Baggett would be trussed up like a Christmas goose for his trip to the lockup.

I floored the Buick and roared off for Hamilton Avenue. The money involved in Baggett's capture was now low on my motivating factors list. Baggett had made me look and feel like an idiot. I didn't want revenge. Revenge isn't a productive emotion. I simply wanted to succeed. I wanted to regain some professional pride. Of course, after I restored my professional pride I'd be happy to take the recovery money.

Cluck in a Bucket was a couple blocks past Vinnie's office. It was a brand-new link in a minichain and still in its grand opening stage. I'd driven by and gawked at the big chicken sign but hadn't yet indulged in a bucket of cluck.

I could see the glow from the franchise a block away. The one-story blocky little building had been painted yellow inside and out. At night light spilled from the big plate-glass windows, and a spot played on the seven-foot-tall plastic chicken that was impaled on a rotating pole in the parking lot.

I parked at the back of the Cluck in a Bucket lot and decked myself out in my bounty hunter gear. Cuffs stuffed into one jacket pocket; defense spray in the other. Stun gun clipped to the waistband of my sweats. Smith & Wesson forgotten in the rush, left lying on my bedside table.

Lula was waiting for me just outside the front entrance. "There he is," she said. "He's the one handing out paper chicken hats to the kiddies."

It was Stuart Baggett all right . . . dressed up in a big fat chicken suit, wearing a chicken hat. He did a chicken dance for a family, flapping his elbows, wagging his big chicken butt. He made some squawking sounds and gave each of the kids a yellow-and-red cardboard hat.

"You gotta admit, he makes a cute chicken," Lula said, watching Stuart strut around on his big yellow chicken feet. "Too bad we gotta bust his ass."

Easy for her to say. She didn't have orange hair. I pushed through the front door and crossed the room. I was about ten feet away when Stuart turned and our eyes locked.

"Hello, Stuart," I said.

There was a young woman standing next to Stuart. She was wearing a red-and-yellow Cluck in a Bucket uniform, and she was holding a stack of Cluck in a Bucket giveaway hats. She gave me her best "don't ruin the fun" look and wagged her finger. "His name isn't Stuart," she said. "Today his name is Mr. Cluck."

"Oh yeah?" Lula said. "Well we're gonna haul Mr. Cluck's cute little chicken tushy off to jail. What do you think of that?"

"They're crazy," Stuart said to the Cluck in a Bucket woman. "They're stalkers. They won't leave me alone. They got me fired from my last job because they kept harassing me."

"That's a load of horse pucky," Lula said. "If we were gonna stalk someone it wouldn't be no chicken impersonator working for minimum wage."

"Excuse me," I said, elbowing Lula away from Stuart, turning the force of my most professional smile on the young woman with the hats. "Mr. Baggett is in violation of a bond agreement and needs to reinstate himself with the court."

"Harry," the young woman yelled, waving to a man behind the service counter. "Call the police. We've got a situation here."

"Damn," Lula said. "I hate when people call the police."

"You're ruining everything," Stuart said to me. "Why can't you leave me alone? Who's going to be Mr. Cluck if you take me in?"

I pulled the cuffs out of my pocket. "Don't give me a hard time, Stuart."

"You can't put cuffs on Mr. Cluck!" Stuart said. "What will all these kids think?"

"Wouldn't get my hopes up that they'd give a hello," Lula said. "Isn't like you're Santa Claus. Truth is, you're just some whiny little guy dressed up in a bad suit."

"This isn't a big deal," I said to Stuart as calmly as possible. "I'm going to cuff you and walk you out the door, and if we do it quickly and quietly no one will notice."

I reached out to snap the cuffs on Stuart, and he batted me away with his chicken wing. "Leave me alone," Stuart said, knocking the cuffs out of my hand, sending them sailing across the room. "I'm not going to jail!" He grabbed the mustard and the special-sauce squirters off the condiments counter. "Stand back!" he said.

I had pepper spray and a stun gun, but it seemed like excessive force to use them against a chicken armed with special sauce.

"I haven't got all day," Lula said to Stuart. "I want to get some chicken and go back to work, and you're holding me up. Put those stupid squirters down."

"Don't underestimate these squirters," Stuart said. "I could do a lot of damage with these squirters." He held the red squirter up. "See this? This isn't just any old special sauce. This is extra spicy."

"Oh boy," Lula said. "Think he's been sniffing aerosol from the roach spray."

Lula took a step toward Stuart, and SQUISH, Stuart gave Lula a blast of mustard to the chest.

Lula stopped in her tracks. "What the . . ."

SPLOT! Special sauce on top of the mustard.

"Did you see that?" Lula said, her voice pitched so high she sounded like Minnie Mouse. "He squirted me with special sauce! I'm gonna have to get this jacket dry-cleaned."

"It was your own fault, Fatty," Stuart said. "You made me do it."

"That's it," Lula said. "Out of my way. I'm gonna kill him." She lunged forward, hands reaching for Stuart's chicken neck, slipped on some mustard that had leaked out of Stuart's squirter and went down on her ass.

Stuart took off, shoving his way around tables and customers. I took off after him and caught him with a flying tackle. We both crashed to the floor in a flurry of chicken feathers, Stuart squirting his squirters, and me swearing and grabbing. We rolled around like this for what seemed like an eternity, until I finally got hold of something that wasn't a fake chicken part.

I was breast to breast, on top of Mr. Cluck, twisting his nose in a damn good impression of Moe and Curly, when I felt hands forcefully lifting me off, disengaging my nose hold.

One set of hands belonged to Carl Costanza. The other set of hands belonged to a cop I'd seen around but didn't know on a first-name basis. Both cops were smiling, rocking back on their heels, thumbs stuck into their gun belts.

"I heard about your cousin Vinnie and what he did to that duck," Carl said to me. "Still, I'm surprised to find you on top of a chicken. I always thought you were more like the Mazur side of the family."

I swiped at the gunk on my face. I was covered with mustard, and I had special sauce in my hair. "Very funny. This guy is FTA."

"You got papers?" Carl asked.

I scrounged in my shoulder bag and came up with the bond agreement and the contract to pursue that Vinnie had issued.

"Good enough," Carl said. "Congratulations, you caught yourself a chicken."

I could see the other cop was trying hard not to laugh out loud.

"So what's your problem?" I asked him, feeling sort of aggravated that maybe he was laughing at me.

He held up two hands. "Hey lady, I haven't got a problem. Good bust. Not everyone could have taken that chicken down."

I rolled my eyes and looked at Costanza, but Costanza wasn't entirely successful at controlling his amusement either.

"Good thing we got here before the animal rights people," Costanza said to me. "They wouldn't have been as understanding as us."

I retrieved my cuffs from the other side of the room and clicked them onto Baggett's wrists. Lula had disappeared, of course. I'd resigned myself to the fact that I couldn't expect Lula to share airspace with cops.

"Do you need any help?" Costanza wanted to know.

I shook my head, no. "I can manage. Thanks."

Half an hour later I left the station with my body receipt, happy to escape the cracks about smelling like a barbecue. Not to mention the abuse I took for bringing in a chicken.

A person can take only so much cop humor.

Rex was nosing around in his food cup when I got home, so I gave him a grape and told him about Stuart Baggett. How

Stuart had been dressed up in a chicken suit, and how I'd bravely captured him and brought him to justice. Rex listened while he ate the grape, and I think Rex might have smiled when I got to the part about tackling Mr. Cluck, but it's hard to tell about these things with a hamster.

I love Rex a lot, and he has a lot of redeeming qualities, like cheap food and small poop, but the truth is sometimes I pretend he's a golden retriever. I'd never tell this to Rex, of course. Rex has very sensitive feelings. Still, sometimes I long for a big floppy-eared dog.

I fell asleep on the couch, watching Rex run on the wheel. I was awakened by the phone ringing.

"Got a call about my car," Ranger said. "Want to ride along?"

"Sure."

There was a moment of silence. "Were you sleeping?" he asked.

"Nope. Not me. I was just going out the door to look for Mo." Okay, so it was a fib. Better than looking like a slug. Or even worse, better than admitting to the truth, because the truth was that I was becoming emotionally dysfunctional. I was unable to fall asleep in the dark. And if I did fall asleep, it would be only to doze and to wake up to bad dreams. So I was starting to sleep during daytime hours when I had the chance.

My incentive for finding Mo had changed in the last couple of days. I wanted to find Mo so the killing would stop. I couldn't stand seeing any more blown-apart bodies.

I rolled off the couch and into the shower. While in the shower I noticed blisters on my heels as big as quarters. Thank God. I finally had a legitimate excuse to stop running. Eight minutes later, I was dressed and in the hall, with my apartment locked up behind me.

As soon as I climbed into the Bronco I knew this was serious because Ranger was wearing no-nonsense army fatigues and gold post earrings. Also the tear gas gun and the smoke grenades in the backseat were a tip-off.

"What's the deal?" I asked.

"Very straightforward. I got a call from Moses Bedemier. He apologized for borrowing my car. Said it was parked in his garage, and that his neighbor, Mrs. Steeger, had the keys."

I shuddered at the mention of Mrs. Steeger.

"What's that about?" Ranger asked.

"Mrs. Steeger is the Antichrist."

"Damn," Ranger said. "I left my Antichrist gun at home."

"Looks like you brought everything else."

"Never know when you'll need some tear gas."

"If we have to gas Mrs. Steeger, it'll probably ruin my chances of being Miss Burg in the Mayflower Parade."

Ranger turned into the alley from King and stopped at Mo's garage. He got out and tried the door. The door was locked. He walked to the side window and peered in.

"Well?" I asked.

"It's there."

A back curtain was whisked aside and Mrs. Steeger glared out at us from her house.

"Is that her?" Ranger wanted to know.

"Yup."

"One of us should talk to her."

"That would be you," I said.

"Okay, Tex. I don't think Mo's here, but you cover the back just in case. I'll have a word with Mrs. Steeger."

After ten minutes I was stomping my feet to keep warm and beginning to worry about Ranger. I hadn't heard any shots, so that was a good sign. There'd been no screams, no police sirens, no glass breaking.

Ranger appeared at the back door, smiling. He crossed the yard to me. "Did you really tell fibs when you were a kid?"

"Only when it involved matters of life or death."

"Proud of you, babe."

"Has she got the key?"

"Yeah. She's getting her coat on. Taking this key thing very seriously. Says it's the least she could do for Mo."

"The least she could do?"

"Have you read the paper today?"

I shook my head. "No."

"It turns out that all these murders are having a significant impact on crime. Drug sales are way down. Pharmaceutical representatives are booking flights for obscure southern towns."

"Are you telling me Mo is a hero?"

"Let's just say, he isn't despised."

Mrs. Steeger materialized at the back door wearing a coat and hat. She huffed down the porch stairs and across her yard. "Hmmph," she said to me. "Still snooping, I see."

My left eye started to twitch. I put my finger to my eyelid and sank my teeth into my lower lip.

Ranger grinned.

The superhero wasn't afraid of the Antichrist. The superhero thought an eye twitch was funny.

Mrs. Steeger opened the door and stepped back, arms folded over her chest. "I'll lock up when you get your car out," she said to Ranger.

Guess she was worried we'd snitch some jugs of used motor oil.

Ranger handed me the keys to the Bronco. "I'll drive the BMW, and you can follow."

Normally a person would take his cars home. Since Ranger wasn't normal I wasn't sure where we were headed.

I held the tail through center city. Traffic was heavy and people walked head down into the wind on the sidewalks. Ranger turned off State onto Cameron and pulled into a small, attended parking lot. We were behind the state buildings, two blocks from Stark, in an area of quasi-government office buildings. Definitely not residential.

Ranger got out of his car and spoke to the attendant. The attendant smiled and nodded. Friendly. They knew each other.

I parked behind the Beemer and walked over to Ranger. "Are we leaving the cars here?"

"Benny will take care of them while I pick up my mail."

I looked around. "You live here?"

"Office," Ranger said, gesturing to a four-story brick building next to the lot.

"You have an office?"

"Nothing fancy. It helps to keep the businesses straight."

I followed Ranger through the double glass doors into the vestibule. There were two elevators to our left. A tenant directory hung on the wall beside the elevators. I scanned the directory and could find no mention of Ranger.

"You're not listed," I said.

Ranger moved past the elevators to the stairs. "Don't need to be."

I trotted after him. "What businesses are we talking about?"

"Mostly security related. Bodyguard, debris removal, security consultation. Fugitive apprehension, of course."

We rounded the first floor and were working our way up to two. "What's debris removal?"

"Sometimes a landlord wants to clean up his property. I can put together a team to do the job."

"You mean like throwing crack dealers out the window?"

Ranger passed the second floor and kept going. He shook his head. "Only on the lower floors. You throw them out the upper-story windows and it makes too much of a mess on the sidewalk."

He opened the fire door to the third floor, and I followed him down the hall to number 311. He slid a key card into the magnetic slot, pushed the door open and switched the light on.

It was a one-room office with two windows and a small powder room. Beige carpet, cream-colored walls, mini-blinds at the windows. Furniture consisted of a large cherry desk with a black leather executive chair behind the desk and two client chairs to the front of the desk. No gun turrets at the windows. No government-issue rockets stacked in the corners. A Mac laptop with a separate Bernoulli drive was plugged in on the desk. Its modem was hooked to the phone line. There was also a multiline phone and answering machine on the desk. Everything was neat. No dust. No empty soda cans. No empty pizza boxes. Thankfully, no dead bodies.

Ranger stooped to pick up the mail that had been delivered through the mail slot. He came up with a handful of envelopes and a couple flyers. He divided the mail into two stacks: garbage and later. He threw the garbage into the wastebasket. The later could wait until later. I guess there hadn't been any *now!* mail.

The red light on the answering machine was going ballistic with blinking. Ranger lifted the lid and popped the incoming tape. He put it in his shirt pocket and replaced the tape with a new one from the top drawer of the desk. No *now!* messages there either, I suppose.

I took a peek at the lavatory. Very clean. Soap. Paper towels. Box of tissues. Nothing personal. "You spend much time here?" I asked Ranger.

"No more than is necessary."

I waited for some elaboration but none was forthcoming. I wondered if Ranger was still interested in Mo now that he had his BMW back.

"Are you feeling vengeful?" I asked Ranger. "Does justice need to be served?"

"He's back on your slate, if that's what you're asking." He killed the light and opened the door to leave.

"Did Mrs. Steeger say anything that might be helpful?"

"She said Mo showed up around nine. Mo told her he'd borrowed a car from someone, and that he'd left the car in his garage for safekeeping until the owner came to retrieve it. Then he gave her the key."

"That's it?"

"That's it."

"Maybe I should have a chat with Mrs. Steeger." I knew it was a long shot, but Mo might come back for his key. Or at least call to see if everything worked out. I wasn't looking forward to spending time with Mrs. Steeger, but if I could get her to arrange a meeting or a phone call between Mo and me it would be worth it.

Ranger checked his door to make sure it was locked. "Gonna explain to her how Mo's crime career is in the toilet, and she should pass him your personal number? The one that guarantees him safe passage to the state spa?"

"Thought it was worth a shot."

"Absolutely," Ranger said. "He didn't want to talk to me about it, but you might have more luck. Are you running tomorrow morning?"

"Gee, I'd love to, but I have blisters."

Ranger looked relieved.

CHAPTER

13

I thought it wouldn't hurt to look professional when I went to see Mrs. Steeger, so I'd dressed in a tailored black suit, white silk shirt, leopard print silk scarf, taupe stockings and heels. I wasn't a master at long division, but I could accessorize with the best of them.

I'd called ahead to tell Mrs. Steeger I was stopping by. Then I'd spent a few moments lecturing myself about attitude. I was an adult. I was a professional. And I looked pretty damn good in my black suit. It was unacceptable that I should be intimidated by Mrs. Steeger. As a final precaution against insecurity, I made sure my .38 was loaded and tucked into my shoulder bag. Nothing like packing a pistol to put spring in a girl's step.

I parked on Ferris Street, got out of the car and sashayed up the sidewalk to Steeger's front porch. I gave the door a couple authoritative knocks and stood back.

Mrs. Steeger opened the door and looked me over. "Are you carrying a gun? I don't want you in my house if you're carrying a gun."

"I'm not carrying a gun," I said. Lie number one. I told

myself it was all right to lie since Mrs. Steeger expected it. In fact, she'd probably be disappointed if I told the truth. And hell, I wouldn't want to disappoint Mrs. Steeger.

She led the way into the living room, seated herself in a club chair and motioned me to a corresponding chair on the other side of the coffee table.

The room was compulsively neat, and it occurred to me that Mrs. Steeger had retired while still vital and now had nothing better to do than to polish the polish. Windows were trimmed with white sheers and heavy flowered drapes. Furniture was boxy. Fabric and rug were sensible browns and tans. Mahogany end tables, a dark cherry rocker. Two white Lenox swan nut dishes sat side by side on the coffee table. Nut dishes without nuts. I had a feeling Mrs. Steeger didn't get a lot of company.

She sat there for a moment, poised on the edge of her seat, probably wondering if she was required by burg etiquette to offer me refreshments. I saved her the decision by immediately going into my spiel. I emphasized the fact that Mo was in danger now. He'd put a dent in the pharmaceutical profit margin and not everyone was pleased. Relatives of dead people were unhappy. The pharmaceutical management was bound to be unhappy. Users and abusers were unhappy.

"And Mo isn't good at this," I added. "He isn't a professional hit man." Even as I said it a little voice was whispering . . . eight bodies. How many does it take to make a professional?

I rose and handed Mrs. Steeger my card before she could quiz me on state capitals or ask me to write a book report on John Quincy Adams, biography of a statesman.

Mrs. Steeger held my card between two fingers. The way you do when you're afraid of cootie contamination. "Just exactly what is it you want me to do?"

"I'd like to talk to Mo. See if I can work something out. Get him back into the system before he gets hurt."

"You want him to call you."

"Yes."

"If I hear from him again I'll pass the message."

I extended my hand. "Thank you."

End of visit.

Neither of us had mentioned the incident in the store. This subject was way beyond our comfort zone. Mrs. Steeger hadn't discovered I was lying about the gun and hadn't threatened to send me to the principal's office, so I considered the entire session a rousing success.

I thought it wouldn't hurt to revisit some neighboring houses. Hopefully the climate would be more receptive now that bodies had been discovered in Mo's basement.

Dorothy Rostowski seemed a good place to start. I knocked on her door and waited while kids shouted inside.

Dorothy appeared with a spoon in her hand. "Making supper," she said. "You want to come in?"

"Thanks, but I've only got a minute. I just wanted to let you know I'm still looking for Mo Bedemier."

I felt the climate shift, and Dorothy's husband came to stand at her side.

"There are a lot of people in this community who'd prefer Mo wasn't found," Rostowski said.

My stomach clenched and for a chilling moment I thought he might pull out a gun or a knife or light up a cigarette and threaten me. My mind raced back to the phone call that had lured me to the candy store. Would I have recognized Dorothy's voice on the phone? Would I have recognized Mrs. Molinowsky's niece, Joyce, or Loretta Beeber, or my cousin Marjorie? And who were those men who were prepared to burn me and possibly kill me? Fathers of kids like these? Neighbors? Schoolmates? Maybe one of them had been Dorothy's husband.

"What we'd really like is for all this to be over, so Mo could come back and reopen the store," Dorothy said. "The kids miss him."

I had a hard time hiding my astonishment. "Mo's suspected of killing eight men!"

"Drug dealers," Dorothy said.

"That doesn't make it okay."

"It makes it better than okay. Mo should get a medal."

"Killing people is wrong."

Dorothy looked down at the floor, studying a spot just in front of her toe. Her voice dropped. "Theoretically I know that's true, but I'm fed up with the drugs and the crime. If Mo wants to take matters in his own hands, I'm not going to rain on his parade."

"I don't suppose you'd call me if you saw Mo in the neighborhood?"

"Don't suppose I would," Dorothy said, still avoiding my eyes.

I crossed the street to talk to Mrs. Bartle.

She met me at the door with her arms crossed over her chest. Not good body language, I thought, taking a mental step backward.

"Is this about Mo?" she asked. "Because I'm going to tell you up front if he was running for president I'd be right there with my vote. It's about time somebody did something about the drug problem in this country."

"He's suspected of killing eight men!"

"Too bad it isn't more. Get rid of every last one of them dope pushers."

On the way home I stopped in to see Connie and Lula. Connie was at her desk. Lula was out like a light on the couch.

"She had a tough morning," I said to Connie. "Went running with Ranger and me. Then she got drilled with special sauce by a chicken."

"So I hear."

Lula opened an eye. "Hmmph." She opened the other eye and took in the suit. "What are you all dressed up for?"

"Business. It's a disguise."

"How's the Mo hunt going?" Connie wanted to know.

"Picking up. Ranger got his car back."

This got Lula to her feet. "Say what?"

I told them about the two visits to Mrs. Steeger. Then I told them about Ranger's office.

"You see," Lula said. "Just like Bruce Wayne. Bruce Wayne had an office."

Connie gave Lula one of her "what the hell are you talking about" looks, so Lula explained her Ranger is a superhero theory.

"First off," Connie said. "Bruce Wayne is Batman, and Batman isn't actually a superhero. Batman's just some neurotic guy in a rubber suit. You have to get nuked or come from another planet to be a real superhero."

"Batman's got his own comic book," Lula said.

Connie wasn't impressed with this logic. "Donald Duck has his own comic book. You think Donald Duck is a superhero?"

"What's the office like?" Lula asked. "Does he have a secretary?"

"No secretary," I said. "It's a one-person office with a desk and a couple chairs."

"We should go over there and snoop around," Lula said. "See what we can find."

Anyone snooping around Ranger's private space would have to have a death wish. "Not a good idea," I told Lula. "Not only would he kill us, but it's also not a nice thing to do. He's not the enemy."

Lula didn't look convinced. "That's all true, but I'd still like to snoop."

"You don't really think he's a superhero," Connie said to Lula. "You think he's hot."

"Damn skippy I do," Lula said. "But that doesn't mean he isn't hiding something. The man has secrets, I'm telling you."

Connie leaned forward. "Secrets could mean lots of

things. He could be wanted for murder in twelve states and have assumed a new identity. Even better . . . he could be gay."

"I don't want to think about him being gay," Lula said. "Seems like anymore, all the buff bodies are gay, and all the bad-smelling, rangy men are straight. I find out Ranger's gay and I'm going straight to the freezer section at Shop & Bag. Only men you can count on these days is Ben and Jerry."

Connie and I nodded sympathetically. Used to be I worried about losing my boyfriends to Joyce Barnhardt. Now I had to worry about losing them to her brother, Kevin.

I was curious about Ranger, but I wasn't nearly as curious as Lula. I had bigger fish to fry. I had to find Mo. I had to get my pickup. I had to nail down Joe Morelli's sudden disinterest in me. I was pretty sure it didn't have to do with a shortage of Y chromosomes.

I backtracked to my parents' house, recruited my father to drive the Buick home and zipped off to the garage.

My father didn't say anything on the trip over, but his thoughts were vibrating off the top of his head.

"I know," I said, testily. "I wouldn't be having this trouble if I'd bought a Buick."

The Nissan was parked in a numbered slot in the lot. My father and I cut our eyes to it in silent suspicion.

"You want me to wait?" my father asked.

"Not necessary."

My father cruised off. We'd done this routine before.

Ernie, the service manager, was in the little office attached to the warehouse of bays. He saw me on line and stepped from behind the counter, took my keys from a hook on the wall and pulled my bill. "You talked to Slick about the carburetor?"

"Yes."

Ernie smiled. "We like to keep our customers happy. Don't want you going away without a full explanation."

I was so happy I was practically suicidal. If I had to spend any more time talking to Slick, I was going to slit my throat.

"I'm in sort of a hurry," I said, passing Ernie my credit card. Another lie. I had absolutely nothing to do. I was all dressed up with nowhere to go.

If I was a hotshot detective I'd park myself in a van a couple houses down from the candy store, and I'd watch Mrs. Steeger. Unfortunately, I wasn't a hotshot detective. I didn't have a van. I couldn't afford to buy one. I couldn't afford to rent one. And since everyone in the burg was so nosy, a van probably wouldn't work anyway.

Just for kicks I drove by Morelli's house. Sort of test-driving the pickup. Morelli's car was parked at the curb, and lights were on inside the house. I eased up behind the 4x4 and cut the engine. I checked myself out in the rearview mirror. When a person has orange hair it's best to appraise it in the dark.

"Well, what the hell," I said.

By the time I knocked on Morelli's front door my heart was doing little flutter things in my chest.

Morelli opened the door and grimaced. "If you have another dead guy in your car I don't want to hear about it."

"This is a social call."

"Even worse."

The chest flutterings stopped. "What kind of a crack is that?"

"It's nothing. Forget it. You look frozen. Where's your coat?"

I stepped into the foyer. "I didn't wear a coat. It was warmer when I started out this afternoon."

I followed Morelli back to the kitchen and watched while he filled a cordial glass with amber liquid.

"Here," he said, handing the glass over. "Fastest way to get warm."

I took a sniff. "What is it?"

"Schnapps. My uncle Lou makes it in his cellar."

I tried a teeny taste and my tongue went numb. "I don't know . . ."

Morelli raised eyebrows. "Chicken?"

"I don't see you drinking this stuff."

Morelli took the glass from my hand and tossed the contents down his throat. He refilled the glass and gave it back to me. "Your turn, cupcake."

"To the pope," I said and drained the glass.

"Well?" Morelli asked. "What do you think?"

I did some coughing and openmouthed wheezing. My throat burned, and liquid fire roiled in my stomach and shot through to every extremity. My scalp started to sweat, and my vagina went into spasm. "Pretty good," I finally said to Morelli.

"Want another?"

I shook my finger in a no motion. "Maybe later."

"What's with the suit?"

I told him about Ranger's car, and about my second trip to speak to Mrs. Steeger. I told him about Dorothy Rostowski and Mrs. Bartle.

"People are nuts," Morelli said. "Freaking nuts."

"So why don't you want this to be a social visit?"

"Forget it."

"It's the hair, isn't it?"

"It's not the hair."

"You're secretly married?"

"I'm not secretly anything."

"Well then, what? What?"

"It's you. You're a walking disaster. A man would have to be a total masochist to be interested in you."

"Okay," I said. "Maybe I will have another schnapps."

He poured two out, and we both threw them back. It was easier this time. Less fire. More glow.

"I'm not a walking disaster," I said. "I can't imagine why you think that."

"Every time I get social with you I end up all by myself, naked, in the middle of the street."

I rolled my eyes. "That only happened once . . . and you weren't naked. You were wearing socks and a shirt."

"I was speaking figuratively. If you want to get specific, what about the time you locked me in a freezer truck with three corpses? What about the time you ran over me with the Buick?"

I threw my hands into the air. "Oh sure, bring up the Buick."

He shook his head, disgusted like. "You're impossible. You're not worth the effort."

I curled my fingers into the front of his T-shirt and hauled him closer. "Not even in your dreams could you imagine how impossible I can be."

We were toe to toe with my breasts skimming his chest, our eyes locked.

"I'll drink to that," Morelli said.

The third schnapps went down smooth as silk. I gave the empty glass to Morelli and licked my lips.

Morelli watched the lip licking, and his eyes darkened and his breathing slowed.

Aha! I thought. This was more like it. Got him interested with the old lip-licking routine.

"Shit," Morelli said. "You did that on purpose."

I smiled. Then he smiled.

It looked to me like his "gotcha" smile. Like the cat that just caught the canary. Like I'd been had . . . again.

Then he closed the space between us, took my face in his hands and kissed me.

The kisses got hotter, and I got hotter and Morelli got hotter. And pretty soon we were all so hot that we needed to get rid of some clothes.

We were half undressed when Morelli suggested we go upstairs.

"Hmmm," I said with lowered eyelids. "What sort of a girl do you think I am?"

Morelli murmured his thoughts on the subject and removed my bra. His hand covered my bare breast, and his fingers played with the tip. "Do you like this?" he asked, gently rolling the nipple between thumb and forefinger.

I pressed my lips together to keep from sinking my teeth into his shoulder.

He tried another variation of the nipple roll. "How about this?"

Oh yeah. That too.

Morelli kissed me again, and next thing we were down on the linoleum floor fumbling with zippers and panty hose.

His finger traced a tiny circle on my silk-and-lace panties, directly over ground zero. My brain went numb, and my body said, YES!

Morelli moved lower and performed the same maneuver with the tip of his tongue, once again finding the perfect spot without benefit of treasure map or detailed instructions.

Now *this* was a superhero.

I was on the verge of singing the Hallelujah Chorus when something crashed outside the kitchen window. Morelli picked his head up and listened. There were some scuffling sounds, and Morelli was on his feet, pulling his jeans on. He had his gun in his hand when he opened the back door.

I was right behind him, my shirt held together by a single button, my panty hose draped over a kitchen chair, my gun drawn. "What is it?" I asked.

He shook his head. "I don't see anything."

"Cats?"

"Maybe. The garbage is tipped over. Maybe it was my neighbor's dog."

I put a hand to the wall to steady myself. "Uh-oh," I said.

"What uh-oh?"

"I don't know how to break this to you, but the floor is moving. Either we're having an earthquake, or else I'm drunk."

"You only had three schnapps!"

"I'm not much of a drinker. And I didn't have supper."

My voice sounded like it was resonating from a tin can, far far away.

"Oh boy," Morelli said. "How drunk are you?"

I blinked and squinted at him. He had four eyes. I hated when that happened. "You have four eyes."

"That's not a good sign."

"Maybe I should go home now," I said. Then I threw up.

I woke up with a blinding headache and my tongue stuck to the roof of my mouth. I was wearing a flannel nightshirt, which I dimly remembered crawling into. I was pretty sure I was alone at the time, although the evening was fuzzy from the third schnapps on.

What I clearly remembered was that a Morelli-induced orgasm had once again eluded me. And I was fairly certain Morelli hadn't fared any better.

He'd done the responsible thing and had insisted I sober up some before I went home. We'd logged a couple miles in the cold air. He'd poured coffee into me, force-fed me scrambled eggs and toast, and then he'd driven me to my apartment building. He'd delivered me to my door, and I think he said good night before the nightshirt crawling-into.

I shuffled into the kitchen, got some coffee going and used it to wash down aspirin. I took a shower, drank a glass of orange juice, brushed my teeth three times. I took a peek at myself in the mirror and groaned. Black circles under bloodshot eyes, pasty hungover skin. Not a nice picture. "Stephanie," I said, "you're no good at drinking."

The headache disappeared at midmorning. By noon I was feeling almost human. I took myself into the kitchen and was standing in front of the refrigerator, staring at the crisper drawer, contemplating the creation of the universe, when the phone rang.

My first thought was that it might be Morelli. My second thought was that I definitely didn't want to talk to him. Let the machine take the message, I decided.

"I know you're there," Morelli said. "You might as well answer. You're going to have to talk to me sooner or later."

Better later.

"I have news on Mo's lawyer."

I snatched at the phone. "Hello?"

"You're going to love this one," Morelli said.

I closed my eyes. I was having a bad premonition on the identity of the lawyer. "Don't tell me."

I could feel Morelli smiling at the other end of the line. "Dickie Orr."

Dickie Orr. My ex-husband. The horse's ass. This was a harpoon to the brain on a day when there was already impaired activity.

Dickie was a graduate of Newark Law. He was with the firm Kreiner and Kreiner in the old Shuman Building, and what he lacked in talent, he compensated for in creative overbilling. He was acquiring a reputation for being a hotshot attorney. I was convinced this was due to his inflated pay schedule rather than his court record. People wanted to believe they got what they paid for.

"When did you learn this?"

"About ten minutes ago."

"Is Mo turning himself in?"

"Thinking about it. Guess he's hired himself a dealmaker."

"He's suspected of murdering eight men. What kind of a deal does he want? Lobster every Friday while he's on death row?"

I got a box of Frosted Flakes from the kitchen cupboard and shoved some into my mouth.

"What are you eating?" Morelli wanted to know.

"Frosted Flakes."

"That's kid cereal."

"So what does Mo want?"

"I don't know. I'm going over to talk to Dickie. Maybe you'd like to tag along."

I ate another fistful of cereal. "Is there a price?"

"There's always a price. Meet you at the coffee shop in the Shuman Building in half an hour."

I considered the state of my hair. "I might be a few minutes late."

"I'll wait," Morelli said.

I could make the Shuman Building in ten minutes if I got all the lights right. It would take at least twenty minutes to do hair and makeup. If I wore a hat I could forgo hair, and that would cut the time in half. I decided the hat was the way to go.

I hit the back door running with a few minutes to spare. I'd gone with taupe eyeliner, a bronze-tone blusher, natural lip gloss and lots of black mascara. The key ingredient to hangover makeup is green concealer for the under-eye bags, covered over with quality liquid foundation. I was wearing my Rangers ball cap, and a fringe of orange frizz framed my face. Orphan Annie, eat your heart out.

I paused for a light at Hamilton and Twelfth and noticed the Nissan was running rough at idle. Two blocks later it backfired and stalled. I coaxed it into the center of the city. Ffft, ffft, ffft, KAPOW! Ffft, ffft, ffft, KAPOW!

A Trans Am pulled up next to me at a light. The Trans Am was filled with high school kids. One of them stuck his head out the passenger-side window.

"Hey lady," he said. "Sounds like you got a fartmobile."

I flipped him an Italian goodwill gesture and pulled the

ball cap low on my forehead. When I found a parking space in front of the Shuman Building, I revved the engine, popped the clutch and backed into the parking slot at close to warp speed. The Nissan jumped the curb and rammed a meter. I gnashed my teeth together. Stephanie Plum, rabid woman. I got out and took a look. The meter was fine. The truck had a big dent in the rear bumper. Good. Now the back matched the front. The truck looked like someone had taken a giant pincers to it.

I stormed into the coffee shop, spotted Morelli and stomped over to him. I must have still looked rabid, because Morelli stiffened when he saw me and made one of those unconscious security gestures cops often acquire, surreptitiously feeling to see if their gun is in place.

I tossed my shoulder bag onto the floor and threw myself into the chair across from him.

"I swear I didn't intentionally try to get you drunk," Morelli said.

I squeezed my eyes shut. "Unh."

"Well, okay, so I did," he admitted. "But I didn't mean to get you *that* drunk."

"Take a number."

He smiled. "You have other problems?"

"My car is possessed by the devil."

"You should try my mechanic."

"You have a good mechanic?"

"The best. Bucky Seidler. You remember him from high school?"

"He got suspended for letting a bunch of rats loose in the girls' locker room."

"Yeah. That's Bucky."

"He calm down any?"

"No. But he's a hell of a mechanic."

"I'll think about it."

Morelli thumbed through a stack of cards he kept in his

wallet. "Here it is," he said, passing the card over to me. "Mr. Fix It. You can keep the card."

"Bucky Seidler, proprietor."

"Yeah," Morelli said. "And resident crazy man."

I ordered a Coke and French fries. Morelli ordered a Coke and a cheeseburger.

When the waitress left I leaned my elbows on the table. "Do you think Mo could actually have something to bargain?"

"The rumor going around is that Mo is claiming he didn't kill anybody."

"Being an accomplice to murder is the same as pulling the trigger in Jersey."

"If he was cooperative and had something vital to give us . . ." He made a palms-up "who knows" gesture with his hands.

The waitress set the plates on the Formica-topped table and returned with the drinks.

Morelli snitched one of my French fries. "What did you ever see in Dickie Orr?"

I'd asked myself that same question many times and never found a satisfactory answer. "He had a nice car," I said.

Morelli's mouth curved. "Seems like a sound basis for marriage."

I poured ketchup on the fries and started working my way through them. "You ever think about getting married?"

"Sure."

"Well?"

"It's been my sad observation that cops don't make wonderful husbands. In all good conscience, I'd have to marry someone I didn't especially like, so I wouldn't feel crummy about ruining her life."

"So you'd marry someone like me?"

Morelli's face creased into a broad smile. "I hate to admit this, but I actually like you. You're out of the race."

"Jeez," I said. "What a relief."

"Tell me about Dickie."

I drank half the Coke. "Is this the price?"

He nodded. "I've seen Orr in court. Don't know him personally."

"And what's your opinion?"

"Gets a good haircut. Has lousy taste in ties. Big ego. Little dick."

"You're wrong about the dick."

This earned me another smile.

"He cheats on everything from his taxes to his clients to his girlfriends," I told Morelli.

"Anything else?"

"Probably doesn't pay his parking tickets. Used to do some recreational coke. Not sure if he's still into that. Did the deed with Mallory's wife."

Mallory was a uniform who was known for having a higher-than-normal incidence of accidental injuries on his arrest sheets. Uncooperative arrests had a habit of falling down entire flights of stairs while in Mallory's care.

"You sure about Mallory's wife?" Morelli asked.

"Heard it from Mary Lou, who heard it at the beauty parlor."

"Then it must be true."

"I suppose that's the sort of stuff you were looking for?"

"It'll do."

Morelli finished his cheeseburger and Coke and threw a ten onto the table. "Order yourself a piece of pie. I'll come back when I'm done with Dickie."

I jumped from my seat. "You said you'd take me with you!"

"I lied."

"Creep."

"Sticks and stones . . ."

CHAPTER
14

My indignation at being left behind had been mostly show. I hadn't really expected to drag after Morelli when he talked to Dickie. Dickie wouldn't have said anything in front of me.

I ordered coconut cake and decaf coffee. The room was emptying out from the lunch trade. I nursed the cake and the coffee for twenty minutes and paid the bill. There was no sign of Morelli, and I couldn't imagine the confrontation with Dickie as being lengthy, so I thought Morelli might have left me hanging. Wouldn't be the first time. I shrugged into my jacket, hitched my shoulder bag onto my shoulder and was going out the door to the coffee shop when Morelli rounded the corner.

"Thought maybe I got stood up," I said to Morelli.

"Had to wait for Dickie to get off a conference call."

Wind gusted down the street, and we both ducked our heads against it.

"Learn anything?"

"Not much. No address or phone number for Mo. Says Mo calls him."

"You find out what Mo has to trade?"

"Information."

I raised my eyebrows.

"That's all I can tell you," Morelli said.

Morelli was screwing me over again. "Thanks for nothing."

"It's the best I can do."

"Your best isn't very good, is it?"

"Depends." His eyes darkened. Bedroom eyes. "You thought I was pretty hot last night."

"I was drunk."

Morelli curled his fingers into my jacket collar and dragged me closer. "You wanted me bad."

"It was a low point in my life."

His lips skimmed mine. "How about now? Are you at a low point now?"

"I will never again be that low," I said haughtily.

Morelli kissed me like he meant it and released my collar. "Got to get back to work," he said. He crossed the street, angled into his 4x4 and drove off without looking back.

After a moment I realized my mouth was hanging open. I snapped my mouth shut, whipped out my cell phone and called Connie. I told her about Mo and Dickie, and I asked to talk to Lula.

"Hey girlfriend," Lula said.

"Hey yourself. How's it going?"

"It's a little slow. It's more than halfway through the day, and the body count is zip."

"Got a job for you."

"Oh boy. Here it comes."

"Not to worry. It's very tame. I want you to meet me at the entrance to the Shuman Building."

"Now?"

"Now."

Twenty minutes later we were in the elevator.

"What's going on?" Lula wanted to know. "What are we doing here?"

I pushed the button for the third floor. "Mo's hired himself an attorney. The attorney's name is Dickie Orr, and we're on our way to talk to him."

"Okay, but why do you need me? Is this guy dangerous?"

"No. Dickie Orr isn't dangerous. I'm the one who's dangerous. Dickie Orr is my ex-husband, and your job is to keep me from strangling him."

Lula made a low whistle. "This day's just getting better and better."

The offices of Kreiner and Kreiner were at the end of the hall. There were four names lettered in gold on the office door: Harvey Kreiner, Harvey Kreiner Jr., Steven Owen, Richard Orr.

"So why'd you part ways with this Dickie Orr person?" Lula asked.

"He's a jerk."

"Good enough for me," she said. "I hate him already."

When I was married to Dickie he worked for the district attorney. His career with them was only slightly longer than his career with me. Not enough money came out of either of us, I guess. And after I found him on the dining room table with Joyce Barnhardt I made enough noise to ruin whatever political aspirations he might have had. Our divorce was everything a divorce should be . . . reeking of outrage, filled with loud and lurid accusations. The marriage had lasted less than a year, but the divorce would live on as legend in the burg. After the divorce, when lips loosened in my presence, I learned Dickie's infidelity had stretched far beyond Joyce Barnhardt. During the short tenure of our marriage Dickie had managed to boff half the women in my high school yearbook.

The door with the names opened to a mini lobby with two couches and a coffee table and a modern receptionist desk, all done in pastels. California meets Trenton. The woman behind the desk was upscale help. Very sleek. Pastel dress. Ann Taylor from head to toe.

"Yes," she said. "Can I help you?"

"I'd like to speak to Richard Orr." Just in case the office was too swanky for a guy named Dickie. "Tell him Stephanie is here."

The woman relayed the message and directed me to Dickie's office. The door was open and Dickie stood at his desk when Lula and I appeared on his threshold.

His expression was mildly quizzical . . . which I knew as being expression number seven. Dickie used to practice expressions in front of the mirror. How's this? he'd ask me. Do I look sincere? Do I look appalled? Do I look surprised?

The office was a respectable size with a double window. A realtor would say it was "nicely appointed." Which meant that Dickie had gone with baronial rather than *L.A. Law*. The carpet was a red Oriental. The desk was heavy mahogany antique. The two client chairs were burgundy leather with brass studs. Ultra masculine. The only thing missing was a wolfhound and some hunting trophies. The perfect office for a guy with a big stupid dick.

"This is Lula," I said by way of introduction, approaching the desk. "Lula and I work together."

Dickie inclined his head. "Lula."

"Hunh," Lula said.

"I have a few questions about Mo," I said to Dickie. "For instance, when is he going to turn himself in?"

"That hasn't been determined."

"When it has been determined, I'd like to be informed. I'm working for Vinnie now, and Mo is in violation of his bond agreement."

"Of course," Dickie said. Which meant when cows fly.

I sat in one of his chairs and slouched back. "I understand Mo is talking to the police. I'd like to know what he's got to trade."

"That would be privileged information," Dickie said.

From the corner of my eye I could see Lula morphing into Rhino Woman.

"I hate secrets," Lula said.

Dickie looked over at Lula, and then he looked back at me. "You're kidding, right?"

I smiled. "About Mo's deal . . ."

"I'm not talking about Mo's deal. And you're going to have to excuse me. I have a meeting in five minutes, and I need to prepare."

"How about if I shoot him?" Lula said. "Bet if I shoot him in the foot he tells us everything."

"Not here," I said. "Too many people."

Lula stuck her lower lip out in a pout. "You probably don't want me to beat the crap out of him either."

"Maybe later," I said.

Lula leaned a hand on Dickie's desk. "There's things I can do to a man. You'd probably throw up if I told you about them."

Dickie recoiled from Lula. "This is a joke, right?" He turned to me. "You hire her from Rent-a-thug?"

"Rent-a-thug?" Lula said, eyes big and round. "Excuse me, you little dog turd. I'm a bounty hunter in training. I'm not no rent-a-thug. And I'm not no joke either. You're the joke. You know the saying . . . go fuck yourself? I could make that a possibility for you."

I was back on my feet, and I was smiling because Dickie had gone pale under his tanning-salon tan. "I guess we should go now," I said. "This probably isn't a good place to discuss business. Maybe we can get together another time and share information," I said to Dickie.

Dickie's expression was tight. Not one I'd seen him practice. "Are you threatening me?"

"Hell no," Lula said. "Do we look like the kind of women who'd threaten a man? I don't think so. I don't think I'm the sort of woman looks like she'd threaten some pimple-ass motherfucker like you."

I'm not sure what I'd expected to accomplish by meeting with Dickie, but I felt like I'd gotten my money's worth.

When we were alone in the elevator I turned to Lula. "I think that went well."

"Felt good to me," she said. "We got any more parties to go to?"

"Nope."

"Good deal. I got plans for the rest of the afternoon."

I scooped my car keys out of my pocket. "Have fun. And thanks for riding shotgun."

"See you later," she said.

I drove one block and stopped for a light. The Nissan went into the backfire and stall routine. Stay calm, I told myself. Elevated blood pressure can lead to stroke. My aunt Eleanor'd had a stroke, and it wasn't fun. She called everybody Tootsie and colored her hair with her lipstick.

I restarted the pickup and raced the engine. When the light changed I leaped forward on another backfire. KAPOW! I pulled Morelli's card from my pocket and read the address. Mr. Fix It was on Eighteenth Street, just past the button factory.

"I'm giving you one last chance," I said to the pickup. "Either you shape up, or I'm taking you to Bucky Seidler."

A half a block later it stalled out again. I took it as a sign and made a U-turn. Morelli regularly lied to me, but never about a mechanic. Morelli took his mechanics seriously. I'd give Bucky one shot. If that didn't work, I was going to drive the car off a bridge.

Fifteen minutes later I was chugging down Eighteenth Street, in a part of industrial Trenton that had left prosperity behind. Bucky's garage was a two-bay cinder block structure that sat like an island in a sea of cars. New cars, old cars, smashed cars, rusted cars, cars that had signed on for the vital organ donor program. The bay doors were open. A man in jeans and thermal undershirt stood under a car on the lift in the first bay. He looked out at me as I gasped to a stop on the macadam apron. He wiped his hands on a rag and walked over. He had a butch haircut and a keg of beer hanging over his belt. I hadn't seen him in a while, but I was pretty sure it was Bucky. He looked like the sort of person who'd set rats loose on a bunch of women.

He peered in the window at me. "Stephanie Plum," he said, smiling. "Haven't seen you since high school."

"I'm surprised you recognized me."

"The orange hair threw me for a minute, but then I remembered you from the picture in the paper from when you burned down the funeral home."

"I didn't burn down the funeral home. It was a misprint."

"Too bad," Bucky said. "I thought it was cool. Sounds like you got a car problem."

"It keeps stalling. Joe Morelli suggested I come here. He said you're a good mechanic."

"He gave you a pretty good recommendation, too. Read it on the bathroom wall of Mario's Sub Shop over ten years ago, and I can still remember every word of it."

"I have Mace in my shoulder bag."

"Mostly what I care about is MasterCard."

I sighed. "I've got that too."

"Well," Bucky said, "then let's do business."

I gave him the Nissan's medical history.

Bucky had me run the engine while he looked under the hood.

"Okay," he said. "Been here, done this."

"Can you fix it?"

"Sure."

"How long? How much?"

"Depends on parts."

I'd heard this before.

He jerked his thumb at a bunch of junks lined up against a chain-link fence. "You could pick out one of those to use as a loaner if you want. I got a classic Buick that's a beauty. A fifty-three."

"NO!"

Rex was running on his wheel when I walked through the door. I'd stopped at the supermarket and gotten healthy food for Rex and me. Fruit, low-fat cottage cheese, potatoes and some of those already washed and peeled thumb-sized carrots in a bag. I said howdy to Rex and gave him a grape. My message light was blinking, so I hit the button and listened while I unpacked the groceries.

Ranger called to say he'd heard about Mo and the lawyer, and that it didn't change my job. It's simple, Ranger said. You get hired to find a man and that's what you do.

Message number two was from Bucky Seidler. "I was able to get the part I needed," Bucky said into the machine. "I'll put it in first thing in the morning. You can pick your car up anytime after ten."

I bit into my lower lip. Lord, I hoped it wasn't another carburetor.

The last call started out with a lot of noise. People talking, and the sort of clatter you hear at an arcade. Then a man came on the line. "I'm watching you, Stephanie," the man said. "I'm watching you have lunch with your cop boyfriend. I was watching you last night, too. Watching you diddle on the kitchen floor. Good to see you decided to do something else besides harassing upstanding citizens. You keep concentrating on banging Morelli and maybe you'll live to be an old lady."

I stared at the machine, unable to breathe. My chest was impossibly tight, and my ears were ringing. I leaned against the refrigerator and closed my eyes. Imagine you're at the ocean, I thought. Hear the surf. Breathe with the surf, Stephanie.

When I got my heart rate under control, I rewound the tape and popped it out of the recorder. I took a blank from the junk drawer next to the refrigerator and slid it into the machine. It was a few minutes after five. I called Morelli to make sure he was home.

" 'Lo," Morelli said.

"You going to be there for a while?"

"Yeah. I just got in."

"Don't go away. I have something you need to hear. I'll be right over."

I dropped the tape into my shoulder bag, grabbed my jacket and locked up behind myself. I got down to the first floor and froze at the door. What if they were out there? Waiting for me. Spying on me. I took a few steps back and exhaled. This wasn't good. It was okay to be afraid, but not okay to let it restrict my life. I moved away from the glass panes and checked my shoulder bag. I had the .38, and it was loaded. My cell phone was charged. My stun gun was charged. I transferred the pepper spray to my jacket pocket. Not good enough. I took the spray out of my pocket and held it in my left hand. Car keys in my right.

I paced in the lobby for a few beats to get the fear under control. When I felt strong, I turned and walked out the door and across the lot to my car. I never broke stride. Never turned my head right or left. But I was listening. I was on the balls of my feet, and I was ready to act if I had to.

I'd chosen a green Mazda as a loaner. It was rusted and dented and reeked of cigarettes, but its performance couldn't be faulted. I checked the interior, stuck the key in the lock, opened the door and slid behind the wheel. I locked the door, immediately cranked the engine over and rolled out of the lot.

No one followed that I could tell, and once I got onto St. James there were too many headlights to distinguish a tail. I had my shoulder bag on the seat alongside me and my pepper spray in my lap. To keep my spirits up I sang "Who's Afraid of the Big Bad Wolf?" all the way to Morelli's house. I parked at the curb and checked the street. No cars. No one on foot. I locked the Mazda, marched to Morelli's front door and knocked. I guess I was still nervous because the knock came out like BAM BAM BAM instead of knock, knock, knock.

"Must have had your Wheaties today," Morelli said when he answered the door.

I pushed past him. "You keep your doors locked?"

"Sometimes."

"They locked now?"

Morelli reached behind him and flipped the Yale lock. "Yep."

I went to the living room window and drew the drapes. "Pull the curtains in the dining room and kitchen."

"What's going on?"

"Just humor me."

I followed him into the kitchen and waited while he adjusted Venetian blinds. When he was done I took the tape out of my shoulder bag. "You have a recorder?"

There was a briefcase sitting on the kitchen table. Morelli opened the briefcase and took out a recorder. He slipped the tape into the recorder and pressed the play button.

Ranger came up first.

"Bad advice," Morelli said.

"That's not what I want you to hear."

The noise blasted out and then the man's voice. Morelli's face showed no expression while he listened to the message. Cop face, I thought. He ran the tape through a second time before shutting the machine off.

"Not Mickey Maglio," he said.

"No." A cop would know better than to have his voice recorded.

"You have any clue you were being followed?"

I shook my head. "No."

"Did you pick up a tail tonight?"

"No."

"There's a record store, grunge shop across from the Shuman Building. It's got some video machines in it. It's a kid hangout. The call probably originated from there. I'll send someone over to ask a few questions."

"Guess the crashing and scuffling we heard didn't come from your neighbor's dog."

"Whoever was out there must have knocked the garbage can over trying to get a better look."

"You don't seem very upset by this."

There were dishes drying in a drainer on the sink. A dinner plate, a cereal bowl, a couple glasses. Morelli grabbed the dinner plate and threw it hard against the opposite wall, where it smashed into a million pieces.

"Okay," I said. "So I was wrong."

"You want to stay for dinner?"

"I don't think that's a good idea."

Morelli made chicken sounds.

"Very adult," I said. "Very attractive."

Morelli grinned.

I paused with my hand on the door handle. "I don't suppose you want to tell me more about your conversation with Dickie."

"No more to tell," Morelli said.

Yeah, right.

"And don't follow me home," I said. "I don't need a bodyguard."

"Who said I was going to follow you home?"

"You have your car keys in your hand, and I know the body language. You look like my mother."

The grin widened. "You sure you don't want an escort?"

"Yes, I'm sure." The only thing worse than being scared out of my wits was having Morelli know it.

Morelli opened the door and glanced at the Mazda. "Looks like you've got one of Bucky's loaners."

"Bucky remembered me from high school. Said you gave me quite a recommendation on the men's room wall at Mario's."

"That was during my reckless youth," Morelli said. "These days I'm the soul of discretion."

It was still early, and I couldn't get excited about going home and fixing dinner for one. The alternatives were Cluck in a Bucket or mooching a meal from my parents. I was afraid I might be recognized and remembered at Cluck in a Bucket, so I opted for family.

My mother looked flustered when she came to the door. "Whose car is that?" she asked.

"It's a loaner from a garage. My car is broken again."

"Hah!" my father said from the dining room.

"We were just sitting down," my mother said. "Roast leg of lamb with mashed potatoes and asparagus."

"Is that Stephanie?" Grandma Mazur hollered from the table. "Have you got your gun? I want to show it around."

"I've got my gun, but you can't see it," I said.

There was a man sitting next to Grandma Mazur.

"This here's Fred," Grandma said. "He's my boyfriend."

Fred nodded to me. "Howdy-do."

Fred looked to be about three hundred years old. Gravity had pulled the skin from the top of his head down to his neck, and Fred had tucked it into his shirt collar.

I took my seat across from Grandma and noticed a set of false teeth neatly placed beside Fred's salad fork.

"Those are my choppers," Fred said. "Got them for free from the VA, but they don't fit right. Can't eat with them in."

"Had to put his lamb through the meat grinder," Grandma said. "That's what the lump of gray stuff is on his plate."

"So," my father said to Fred. "You pretty well fixed?"

"I do okay. I get disability from the army." He tapped a finger against his right eye. "Glass," he said. "World War Two."

"Were you overseas?" my father asked.

"Nope. Lost my eye at Camp Kilmer. I was inspecting my bayonet, and then next thing you know I'd poked my eye out with it."

"The fact he's only got one eye don't slow him down none," Grandma said. "I've seen him handle ten bingo cards and never miss a single call. And he's an artist, too. He hooks rugs. You should see the beautiful rugs he makes. He made one with a picture of a tiger on it."

"I imagine you got a house of your own?" my father asked him.

Fred gummed some of the gray glop. "Nope. I just got a room at Senior Citizens. I sure would like to have a house though. I'd like to marry someone like Sweetie here, and I'd be happy to move right in. I'd be quiet too. You wouldn't hardly know I was here."

"Over my dead body," my father said. "You can take your teeth and get the hell out of here. You're nothing but a goddamn gold digger."

Fred opened his eyes wide in alarm. "I can't get out of here. I haven't had dessert yet. Sweetie promised me dessert. And besides, I don't have a ride back to the Seniors."

"Call him a cab," my father ordered. "Stephanie, go call him a cab. Ellen, wrap up his dessert."

Ten minutes later Fred was on his way.

Grandma Mazur helped herself to a cookie and a second cup of coffee. "There's plenty more where he came from," she said. "Tell you the truth he was kind of old for me anyway. And he was creeping me out with that glass eye . . . the way he'd tap on it all the time. It was okay that he took his teeth out, but I didn't want to see that eye rolling around next to his soup spoon."

The Rangers were playing Montreal, so I stayed to see the game. Watching the game also involved eating a lot of junk food since my father is an even worse junk food addict than I am. By the time the third period rolled around we'd gone through a jar of cocktail wieners, a bag of Chee•tos and a can of cashews and were working on a two-pound bag of M&M's.

When I finally waved good-bye I was considering bulimia.

The upside to lacking self-control was that the threat of masked men paled in comparison to worry over the Chee•tos working their way to my thighs. By the time I remembered to be afraid I was inserting the key in my front door.

My apartment felt relatively safe. Only one phone message, and no cocktail wieners tempting me from cupboard shelves. I punched up the message.

It was from Ranger. "Call me."

I dialed his home number and received a single-word answer. "Go."

"Is this a message?" I asked. "Am I talking to a machine?"

"This is very weird, babe, but I could swear your friend Lula is trying to tail me."

"She thinks you're a superhero."

"Lot of people think that."

"You know how you give everybody that vacant lot as your home address? She thinks that's a little odd. She wants to find out where you live. And by the way, where *do* you live?"

I waited for an answer, but all I heard was a disconnect.

I woke up feeling guilty about the junk food binge, so for penance I cleaned the hamster cage, rearranged the jars in the refrigerator and scrubbed the toilet. I looked for ironing, but there was none. When something needs to be ironed I put it in the ironing basket. If a year goes by and the item is still in the basket I throw the item away. This is a good system since eventually I end up only with clothes that don't need ironing.

Bucky had said my car would be ready at ten. Not that I doubted Morelli or Bucky, but I'd come to regard car repairs with the same sort of cynicism I'd previously reserved for Elvis sightings.

I parked the green Mazda against the garage fence and saw that my pickup was waiting for me in front of one of the open bays. It had been freshly washed and was sparkly clean. It would have been slick if only it didn't have a big crumple in its hood and a big dent in its back bumper.

Bucky sauntered out from the other bay.

I looked at the pickup skeptically. "Is it fixed?"

"Emission control valve needed a doohickey," Bucky said. "Two hundred and thirty dollars."

"Doohickey?"

"That's the technical term," Bucky said.

"Two hundred and thirty dollars sounds high for a doohickey."

"Mr. Fix It don't come cheap."

I drove back to my apartment building without a hitch. No stalls. No backfires. And no confidence that this would last. The honeymoon period, I thought skeptically.

I returned to my building and parked in my usual Dumpster spot. I cautiously got out of the truck and looked for possible assailants. Finding none, I crossed the lot and swung through the door into the lobby.

Mr. Wexler was in the lobby, waiting for the senior citizens' minibus to pick him up. "You hear about Mo Bedemier?" Mr. Wexler asked. "Isn't he a pip? I tell you, the man's got a lot of jewels. It's about time somebody did something about the drug problem."

"He's suspected of killing a whole bunch of men!"

"Yep. He's on a roll, all right."

The elevator doors opened, and I got in, but I didn't feel like going to my apartment. I felt like striking out at someone.

I got out of the elevator and confronted Mr. Wexler. "Killing is wrong."

"We kill chickens," Mr. Wexler said. "We kill cows. We kill trees. So big deal, we kill some drug dealers."

It was hard to argue with that kind of logic because I like cows and chickens and trees much better than drug dealers.

I got back into the elevator and rode to the second floor. I stood there for a few minutes, trying to talk myself into a relaxing afternoon of doing nothing, but I couldn't sell the idea. I returned to the lobby, stomped over to my truck and wedged myself behind the steering wheel. As long as I was already in a fairly vicious mood I thought I might as well visit Dickie, the little crumb. I wanted to know what he told Morelli.

I parked in a lot a block from Dickie's office, barreled through the lobby and gave his receptionist my power smile.

"I need to have a few words with Dickie," I said. And before she could answer I turned on my heel and stalked off to Dickie's office.

CHAPTER
15

Dickie didn't look happy to see me. In fact, Dickie didn't look happy at all. He was sitting at his desk with his head in his hands and his hair rumpled. This was serious stuff, because Dickie's hair was always perfect. Dickie woke up in the morning with every hair neatly in place. That he was having a bad day did nothing to dampen my spirits.

He jumped in his seat when he saw me. "You! Are you nuts? Are you wacko?" He shook his head. "This is too much. This time you've gone too far."

"What are you talking about?"

"You know what I'm talking about. I'm talking about restraining orders. Harassment charges. Attempts at intimidating an attorney."

"Are you putting that funny white powder in your coffee again?"

"Okay, so I fooled around a little while we were married. Okay, our divorce didn't go smooth as silk. Okay, I know you have some hostile feelings for me." He unconsciously ran his hand through his hair, causing it to stand on end. "That's no reason to turn into the Terminator. Christ, you need help. Have you ever thought of getting some counseling?"

"I get the feeling you're trying to tell me something."

"I'm talking about sending your goon to attack me in my parking lot this morning!"

"Lula attacked you?"

"Not Lula. The other one."

"I don't have another one."

"The big guy," Dickie said. "In the ski mask and coveralls."

"Hold the phone. I've got the picture. That wasn't my goon. And there's more than one. There's a whole pack of them, and they've been threatening me, too. Just exactly what did he say to you?"

"He said Mo didn't need a lawyer, and I was off the case. I said Mo would have to tell that to me personally. And then the guy pulled a gun on me and said that for a lawyer I wasn't very smart at reading between the lines. I told him I was getting smarter with each passing minute. He put the gun away and left."

"He drive away? You get a plate number?"

Dickie's face flushed. "I didn't think."

"Mo's got a fan club," I said. "Concerned citizens."

"This is too weird."

"What was the deal with Mo? What's your contribution here?"

"You're wasting your time. I'm not discussing this with you."

"I know a lot of stuff about you that you probably wouldn't want to get around. I know about your coke habit."

"That's history."

"I know about Mallory's wife."

Dickie was out of his seat. "You were the one who told Morelli!"

"That Mallory is a mean son of a gun. No telling what he'd do if he found out someone was fooling around with his wife. He could plant drugs in your car, Dickie. Then you'd get arrested, and just think what fun that'd be . . . the strip search, the beating you got when you resisted arrest."

Dickie's eyes shrunk into hard, glittery little marbles. I figured his gonads were undergoing a similar transformation.

"How do I know you won't go to Mallory even if I tell you about Mo?" Dickie asked.

"And lose my edge? I might want to blackmail you again."

"Shit," Dickie said. He pushed back in his chair. He stood and paced and returned to his seat. "There's client confidentiality involved here."

"As if you ever cared about client confidentiality." I looked at my watch. "I haven't got a lot of time. I have other things to do. I need to get in touch with the dispatcher before Mallory goes off shift."

"Bitch," Dickie said.

"Dickhead."

His eyes narrowed. "Slut."

"Asshole."

"Fat cow."

"Listen," I said. "I don't have to take this. I got a divorce."

"If I tell you about Mo, you've got to promise to keep your mouth shut."

"My lips are sealed."

He rested his elbows on his desk, laced his fingers together and leaned forward. If it had been a normal-sized desk we would have been nose to nose. Fortunately, the desk was as big as a football field so we still had some space between us.

"First off, Mo didn't do any of the killing. He got mixed up with some bad guys . . ."

"Bad guys? Could you be more specific than that?"

"I don't know any more than that. I'm working as an intermediary. All I'm doing right now is setting up a line of communication."

"And it's these bad guys who did the killing?"

"Mo was fed up with the gangs and the drugs inching closer to his store, and Mo didn't think the cops could do much. He figured the cops were bound up by laws and plea bargaining.

"But Mo knew a lot from listening to the kids. He knew the dealers' names. He knew who specialized in kiddie sales. So Mo started his own little sting. He'd go to the dealer and suggest a partnership."

"Let the dealer work from Mo's store."

"Yes. He'd set up a meeting, usually in his store or garage, someplace else if the dealer was jumpy. Then Mo would give the meeting information to a friend of his. Mo would disappear from the scene and the dealer would be taken care of by this friend. In the beginning, Mo didn't know the dealers were being killed. I guess he thought they'd get roughed up or threatened and that would be the end of it. By the time he figured it out it was late in the game."

"Why'd Mo jump bail?"

"Mo freaked. The gun he was carrying when Gaspick pulled him over was a murder weapon. It had been used to kill a dealer who subsequently floated in on the tide. I guess Mo had bought into some of it by then. Got caught up in the righteousness of being a vigilante. Mo said he never used the gun. In fact, it was empty when he was pulled over. Mo probably felt like John Wayne or something carrying it around. Don't forget we're talking about a shy, nerdy sort of guy who spent his entire life behind the counter of a candy store in the burg."

I felt a painful stab in the midsection. Morelli had withheld that information from me. He'd never told me about the gun connection and the floater. Now it made sense. Now I realized why Morelli was interested in Mo from the very beginning. And why Mo had jumped bail.

"Why has Mo suddenly decided to turn himself in?"

"Just came to his senses, I suppose," Dickie said. "Realized he was getting more and more involved and started to get scared."

"So what's the deal? Mo sells out his friend for a reduced sentence?"

"I suppose, but it hasn't actually gotten to that yet. Like I said, I'm just setting up a line of communication. And I advised Mo of his rights and the consequences of his participation."

"So maybe these ski mask guys aren't protecting Mo anymore. Maybe sentiments have changed and now they're trying to find Mo before I do. . . . Very noble of you to remain as counsel after being threatened."

"Fuck noble," Dickie said. "I'm off this gig."

I dropped a card on Dickie's desk. "Call me if you hear from anyone."

I found myself smiling in the elevator, comforted by the fact that Dickie had been harassed and threatened. I decided to continue the celebration by paying another visit to Mr. Alexander. If Mr. Alexander could make my hair orange, surely he could make it brown again.

"Impossible!" Mr. Alexander said. "I'm totally booked. I would love to help you out, lovey. I really would, but just look at my schedule. I haven't a free moment."

I held some orange frizz between thumb and forefinger. "I can't live like this. Isn't there *anyone* here who can help me?"

"Maybe tomorrow."

"I've got a gun in my pocketbook. I've got pepper spray

and an electric gizmo that could turn you into a reading lamp. I'm a dangerous woman, and this orange hair is making me crazy. There's no telling what I might do if I don't get my hair fixed."

The receptionist hastily thumbed down the day page. "Cleo has a cancellation at two o'clock. It was only for a cut, but she might be able to squeeze a color in."

"Cleo is a marvel at color," Mr. Alexander said. "If anyone can help you, it's Cleo."

Three hours later, I was back in my apartment building, and I still had orange hair. Cleo had given it her best shot, but the orange had resisted change. It was a shade darker and perhaps not quite so bright, but it was still basically orange.

Okay, fuck it. So I have orange hair. Big deal. It could be worse. It could be ebola. It could be dengue fever. Orange hair wasn't permanent. The hair would grow out. It wasn't as if I'd wrecked my life.

I was alone in the lobby. The elevator doors opened, and I stepped in, my thoughts turning to Mo. Speaking of someone who'd wrecked his life. If Dickie could be believed, here was a man who'd lived his entire life selling candy to kids and then had snapped in frustration and made some bad choices. Now he was stuck in a labyrinth of judgment errors and terrible crimes.

I considered my own life and the choices I'd made. Until recently those choices had been relatively safe and predictable. College, marriage, divorce, work. Then, through no fault of my own, I didn't have a job. Next thing, I was a bounty hunter, and I'd killed a man. It had been self-defense, but it was still a regrettable act that came creeping back to me late at night. I knew things about myself now, and about human nature, that nice girls from the burg weren't supposed to know.

I traveled the length of the hall, searched for my key and opened my front door. I stepped inside, relieved to be home. Before I had a chance to turn and close the door, I was sent sprawling onto the foyer floor with a hard shove from behind.

There were two of them. Both in masks and coveralls. Both too tall to be Maglio. One of them pointed a gun at me. The other held a lunch bag. It was the sort of soft-sided insulated bag an office worker might use. Big enough for a sandwich, an apple and a soda.

"You make a sound, and I'll shoot you," the guy with the gun said, closing and locking the door. "Shooting you isn't what I want to do, but I'll do it if I have to."

"This isn't going to work," I told him. "Mo is talking to the police. He's telling them all about you. He's naming names."

"Mo should have stuck to selling candy. We'll take care of Mo. What we're doing is for the good of the community . . . for the good of America. We're not going to stop just because an old man got squeamish."

"Killing people is for the good of America?"

"Eliminating the drug scourge."

Oh boy. Scourge removers.

The man carrying the lunch bag jerked me to my feet and shoved me toward the living room. I thought about screaming or simply walking away, but I wasn't sure how these lunatics would act. The one seemed comfortable with his gun. It was possible that he'd killed before, and I suspected killing was like anything else . . . the more you did it, the easier it got.

I was still wearing my jacket, still carrying my shoulder bag, the warning of retaliation ringing in my ears. I still had the blister from my last meeting with Mo's vigilantes, and the thought of being burned again sickened my stomach. "I'm going to give you a chance to leave, before you do something really stupid," I said, working to keep the panic out of my voice.

The guy carrying the lunch bag set it on my coffee table.

"You're the stupid one. We keep reasoning with you and warning you, and you refuse to listen. You're still sticking your nose in where it doesn't belong. You and that lawyer you keep visiting. So we figured we'd give you a product demo. Show you the threat firsthand." He removed a small glassine packet from the lunch bag and held it up for me to see. "High-quality boy." The next item to be removed from the carrier was a small bottle of spring water. Then a bottle cap with a wire handle fashioned around it. "The best cooker comes from a wine bottle. Nice and deep. The dopers like this better than a spoon or a soda bottle cap. Do you know what boy is?"

Boy was heroin. Coke was girl. "Yeah, I know what it is."

The man filled the cap with water and mixed in some of the powder from the packet. He pulled a lighter out of his pocket and held it under the cap. Then he produced a syringe from the carrier and filled the syringe with the liquid.

I still had my pocketbook on my shoulder. I ran a shaky hand over the outside, feeling for my .38.

The gunman stepped forward and ripped the bag off my shoulder. "Forget it."

Rex was in his cage on the coffee table. He'd been running on his wheel when we'd come into the room. When the lights flashed on, Rex had paused, whiskers whirring, eyes wide with the expectation of food and attention. After a few moments he'd resumed his running.

The man with the syringe flipped the lid off Rex's cage, reached in and scooped Rex up in his free hand. "Now we get to begin the demonstration."

My heart gave a painful contraction. "Put him back," I said. "He doesn't like strangers."

"We know a lot about you," the man said. "We know you like this hamster. We figure he's like family to you. Now suppose this hamster was a kid. And suppose you thought you were doing all the right things, like feeding that kid good food and helping with his homework and raising him in a neighborhood with a good school. And then somehow, in spite of everything you did, that kid got started experimenting with drugs. How would you feel? Wouldn't you feel like going after the people who were giving him the drugs? And suppose your kid was sold some bad stuff. And your kid died of an overdose. Wouldn't you want to go out there and kill the drug dealer who killed your kid?"

"I'd want him brought to justice."

"The hell you would. You'd want to kill him."

"Are you speaking from personal experience?"

The man with the syringe paused and stared at me. I could see his eyes behind the ski mask, and I guessed my question had hit home.

"I'm sorry," I said.

"Then you understand why we have to do this. It's essential that our work isn't jeopardized. And it's essential that you understand our commitment. We'd prefer not to kill you. We're fair and reasonable people. We have ethics. So, pay attention. This is the last warning. This time we kill the hamster. Next time we kill you."

I felt tears starting behind my eyes. "How can you justify killing an innocent animal?"

"It's a lesson. You ever see anyone die from an overdose? It's not a nice way to go. And it's what's going to happen to you if you don't take a vacation."

Rex's eyes were black and shiny, his whiskers a blur of motion, his little feet treading air, his body squirmy. Not enjoying his confinement.

"Say good-bye," the man with the syringe said. "I'm going to shoot this directly into his heart."

There's a limit to how far a woman can be pushed. I'd been gassed, attacked, stalked by masked men, lied to by Morelli and I'd been swindled by my mechanic. And I'd stayed pretty damn calm through it all. Threatening my hamster brought out a whole new set of rules. Threatening my hamster made me Godzilla. I had no intention of saying good-bye to my hamster.

I blinked back the threat of tears, swiped at my nose and narrowed my eyes. "Listen to me, you two bags of monkey shit," I yelled. "I am not in a good mood. My car keeps stalling. The day before yesterday I threw up on Joe Morelli. I was called a fat cow by my ex-husband. And if that isn't enough . . . my hair is *ORANGE! ORANGE, FOR CHRIS-SAKE!* And now you have the gall to force yourself into my home and threaten my hamster. Well, you have gone too far. You have crossed the line."

I was shouting and waving my arms, totally out of control. And while I was out of control I was watching Rex, because I knew what would happen if he was held long enough. And when it happened I was going to act.

"So if you want to scare someone, you picked the wrong person," I shrieked. "And don't think I'm going to allow you to harm one hair on that hamster's head!"

And then Rex did what any sensible pissed-off hamster would do. He sank his fangs into his captor's thumb.

The man gave a yelp and opened his fist. Rex dropped onto the floor with a thunk and scurried under the couch. And the guy with the gun swung his weapon in Rex's direction and fired off several rounds reflexively.

I grabbed the table lamp to my right and, keeping the momentum going, smashed the lamp against the gunman's head. The man went down like a bag of sand, and I took off for the door.

I had one foot in the hall when I was grabbed from behind and yanked back into the apartment by the man wielding the syringe. I kicked and clawed at him, the two of us wrestling for our lives in front of the door. My foot connected with his crotch and there was a heart-stopping moment of immobility where I saw his eyes widen in pain, and

I thought he might shoot me, or stick me or smack me senseless. But then he doubled over and tried to suck air, inadvertently backing out the door, into the hall.

The elevator door opened, and Mrs. Bestler jumped out with her walker. Clomp, clomp, clomp with lightning speed, she stomped down the hall and rammed the man, knocking him to his knees.

Mrs. Karwatt's door crashed open, and Mrs. Karwatt trained her .45 on the man on the floor. "What's going on? What did I miss?"

Mr. Kleinschmidt came shuffling down the hall carrying an M-16. "I heard a gunshot."

Mrs. Delgado was right behind Mr. Kleinschmidt. Mrs. Delgado had a cleaver and a blue steel Glock with "sidekick" rubber grips.

Mrs. Karwatt looked at Mrs. Delgado's gun. "Loretta," she said, "you got a new gun."

"Birthday present," Mrs. Delgado said proudly. "My daughter Jean Ann gave it to me. Forty caliber, just like the cops use. More stopping power."

"I've been thinking of getting a new gun," Mrs. Karwatt said. "What kind of kick do you get with that Glock?"

I brought Rex into the bedroom with me for the night. He seemed okay after the evening's trauma. I wasn't sure if the same could be said for me. The police had arrived and unmasked the two men. The man with the needle was a stranger to me. The man who'd held the gun had been a schoolmate. He was married now and had two kids. I'd run into him at the food store a couple weeks ago and had said hello.

I slept through most of the morning and felt pretty decent when I got up. I might not be the most patient woman in the world, or the most glamorous, or the most athletic, but

I'm right up there at the top of the line when it comes to re-siliency.

I was pouring a second cup of coffee when the phone rang.

It was Sue Ann Grebek. "Stephanie!" she shouted into the phone. "I've got something good!"

"On Mo?"

"Yeah. High-quality vicious rumor. Only one person re-moved. It might even be true."

"Give it to me!"

"I was just at Fiorello's, and I ran into Myra Balog. You remember Myra? Went steady with that dork Larry Skolnik all through high school. I never knew what she saw in him. He made weird noises with his nose, and he used to write secret messages on his hands. Like 'S.D.O.B.G.' And then he wouldn't tell anyone what it meant.

"Anyway, I got to talking to Myra, and one thing led to an-other and we got to talking about Mo. And Myra said that one day Larry told her this really off-the-wall story about Mo. Said Larry swore it was true. Course we don't know what that means, because Larry probably thought he got beamed up a couple times, too."

"So what was the story?"

I sat and stared at the phone for a few minutes after talking to Sue Ann. I didn't like what I had heard, but it made some sense. I thought about what I'd seen in Mo's apartment and pieces of the puzzle started to fit together.

What I needed to do now was to visit Larry Skolnik. So I double-timed down to the lot, stuck the key in the ignition and held my breath. The engine caught and went into a quiet idle. I slowly exhaled, feeling my cynicism giving way to cautious optimism.

Larry Skolnik worked in his father's dry cleaning store

on lower Hamilton. Larry was behind the counter when I walked into the store. He'd blimped up by about a hundred pounds since high school, but it wasn't all bad news—his hands were message free. He was an okay person, but if I'd have to take a winger on his social life, I'd say he probably talked to his tie a lot.

He smiled when he saw me. "Hey."

"Hey," I said back.

"You got laundry here?"

"Nope. I came to see you. I wanted to ask you about Uncle Mo."

"Moses Bedemier?" A flush crept into his cheeks. "What about him?"

Larry and I were alone in the store. No one else behind the counter. No one else in front of the counter. Just me and Larry and three hundred shirts.

I repeated the story Sue Ann had told me.

Larry fidgeted with a box of homeless shirt buttons that had been placed by the register. "I tried to tell people, but nobody believed me."

"It's true?"

More fidgeting. He chose a white pearl button and examined it more closely. He made a honking sound in his nose. His face flushed some more. "Sorry," he said. "I didn't mean to honk."

"That's okay. A little stress-related honking never hurt anybody."

"Well, I did it. The story is true," Larry said. "And I'm proud of it. So there."

If he said nah, nah, nah, nah, nah, I was going to smack him.

"I hung around the store a lot," Larry said, looking down into the button box when he talked, poking at the buttons with his finger, making canals in the button collection. "And then when I was seventeen Mo gave me a job sweeping up and polishing the glass in the showcase. It was great. I mean, I was working for Uncle Mo. All the kids wanted a job working for Uncle Mo.

"The thing is, that's how we got to sort of be buddies. And then one day he asked me to . . . um, you know. And I'd never done anything like that before, but I thought what the heck."

He stopped talking and stared aimlessly at the buttons. I waited awhile but Larry just keep quietly looking at the buttons. And it occurred to me that maybe Larry wasn't just weird. Maybe Larry wasn't very smart.

"This is important to me," I finally said. "I need to find Mo. I thought maybe you had some idea where he might be. I thought you might still be in touch."

"Do you really think he killed all those people?"

"I'm not sure. I think he must have been involved."

"I think so too," Larry said. "And I have a theory. I don't have it all put together. But maybe you can make something of it." He forgot about the buttons and leaned forward on the counter. "One time I was paired up with a guy named Desmond, and we got to talking. Sort of one pro to another, if you know what I mean. And Desmond told me how Mo found him.

"See, it's important that Mo can always be finding young guys, because that's what Mo likes."

By the time Larry finished telling me his theory I was just about dancing with excitement. I had a totally off-the-wall connection between Mo and the drug dealers. And I had renewed interest in the second-house idea. Mo had driven Larry to a house in the woods when he'd wanted Larry to do his thing.

There was no guarantee that Mo was still using the same house, but it was a place to start looking. Unfortunately, Larry had always gone to the house during evening hours, and even on a good day, Larry's memory wasn't top of the line. What he remembered was going south and then turning into a rural area.

I thanked Larry for his help and promised to come back with dry cleaning. I hopped into the truck and started it up.

I wanted to talk to Vinnie, but Vinnie wouldn't be in the office this early. That was okay. I'd visit the weak link in Mo's chain while I waited for Vinnie.

I parked on the street, across from Lula's apartment. All the row houses looked alike on this block, but Gail's was easy to find. It was the one with the light on over the front stoop.

I went straight to the second floor and knocked on Gail's door. She answered after the second series of knocks. Sleepy-eyed again. A doper.

"Yuh?" she said.

I introduced myself and asked if I could come in.

"Sure," she said. Like who would care.

She sat on the edge of her bed. Hands folded in her lap, fingers occasionally escaping to pick at her skirt. The room was sparsely furnished. Clothes lay in heaps on the floor. A small wood table held a cache of groceries. A box of cereal, half a loaf of bread, peanut butter, a six-pack of Pepsi with two cans missing. A straight-backed chair had been pulled up to the table.

I took the chair for myself and edged it closer to Gail, so we could be friendly. "I need to talk to you about Harp."

Gail grabbed a whole handful of skirt. "I don't know nothin'."

"I'm not a cop. This isn't going to get you into trouble. This is just something I've got to know."

"I already told you."

It wouldn't take much to wear Gail down. Life had already worn her down about as far as she could go. And if that wasn't enough, she'd obviously gotten up early to do some pharmacological experimentation.

"What was the deal with Mo and Elliot? They did business together, didn't they?"

"Yuh. But I didn't have nothin' to do with it. I wouldn't be a party."

• • •

It was almost noon when I got to the office.

Lula was shaking a chicken leg at Connie. "I'm telling you, you don't know nothing about fried chicken. You Italians don't have the right genes. You Italians only know about stuff with tomato paste on it."

"You know what you are?" Connie said, pawing through chicken bucket, settling on a breast. "You're a racist bigot."

Lula chewed off some of the leg meat. "I got a right to be. I'm a minority."

"What? You think Italians aren't minorities?"

"Not anymore. Italians were last year's minorities. Time to move over, baby."

I helped myself to a napkin and a mystery part. "Is Vinnie in?"

"Hey Vinnie," Connie yelled. "Are you in? Stephanie's here."

Vinnie was immediately at the door. "This better be good news."

"I want to know about Mo's boyfriend. The one you saw in New Hope."

"What about him?"

"How do you know they were lovers? Were they kissing? Were they holding hands?"

"No. They were excited. I don't mean like they had a hard-on. I mean like they were charged. And they were looking at pictures of each other. And this other guy was as queer as a three-dollar bill."

"Did you see the pictures?"

"No. I was across the room."

"How do you know they were of Mo and his friend?"

"I guess I don't, but I know they were dirty."

"Must have been one of those psychic things," Lula said. "Like the Great Carnac."

"Hey," Vinnie said. "I know dirty."

No one would argue with that.

"Were you ever able to get a name?" I asked.

"No," Vinnie said. "Nobody knows nothing about Mo. He must not go through the regular channels."

"I need to talk to you in private," I said to Vinnie, motioning him into his office, closing the door behind me. "I have a new network I want you to tap."

Vinnie practically got drooly when I told him where I wanted him to look.

"That Mo!" he said. "Who would have thought?"

I left Vinnie to his task, and I borrowed Connie's phone and dialed Morelli.

"What do you know from my two assailants?" I asked Morelli.

There was a pregnant pause. "We didn't get anything from either of them. They got a lawyer, and they walked."

I sensed there was more. "But?"

"But we did some background checks and came up with an interesting association. If I tell you, you have to promise not to act on it."

"Sure. I promise."

"I don't believe you."

"This must be excellent."

"I'm not telling you over the phone," Morelli said. "Meet me at the luncheonette across from St. Francis."

Morelli ordered a coffee and sandwich at the counter and carried it to the booth. "Been waiting long?"

"A couple minutes."

Morelli ate some of his sandwich. "When I give you this information, you have to promise not to jump out of your seat and act on it. We have men in place. You barge in, and you'll screw everything up."

"If I stay away from the site will you promise to bring me in when Mo comes forward?"

"Yes."

We locked eyes. We both knew he was lying. It wasn't the sort of promise a cop could keep.

"If I'm not present when Mo is captured there's no guarantee Vinnie will get his bond returned."

"I'll make every effort," Morelli said. "I swear, I'll do what I can."

"Just so we have everything straight . . . I know this isn't a gift. You wouldn't be telling me this if I wasn't already in line to get the information from another source." Like Eddie Gazarra or the local paper.

"So I guess you're not treating for dessert."

"What have you got?"

"Both men belonged to the Montgomery Street Freedom Church."

My first reaction was stunned silence. My second was a hoot of laughter. I clapped my hands. "The Montgomery Street Freedom Church! That's perfect."

Morelli ate the rest of his sandwich. "I knew you'd like it."

"It's a natural alliance. Mo wants to get rid of drug dealers, so he goes to the extremist Reverend Bill, and the two of them take vigilantism to a new level. Then, for reasons we aren't sure of, Mo decides to bail out and turn evidence against the good reverend."

Morelli finished his coffee and wiped his mouth with his napkin. "This is all speculation."

And I could speculate one further. I could speculate that this wasn't just about drug dealers.

"Well," I said, "this has been nice, but I need to run. Places to go. People to see."

Morelli wrapped his hand around my wrist and held my palm flat to the table, bringing us nose to nose. "Are you sure there isn't something you want to tell me?"

"I heard Biggie Zaremba had a vasectomy."

"I'm serious, Stephanie. I don't want you messing with this."

"Jesus, Joe, don't you ever stop being a cop?"

"This has nothing to do with being a cop."

I raised an eyebrow. "Oh?"

Another sigh, which sounded a lot like self-disgust. "I don't know why I worry about you. God knows, you can take care of yourself."

"It's because you're Italian. It's chromosomal."

"There's no doubt in my mind," Morelli said, releasing my wrist. "Be careful. Call me if you need help."

"I'm going to go home and wash my hair." I held my hand up. "I swear. Scout's honor. Maybe I'll go shopping."

Morelli stood. "You're hopeless. You were like this as a kid, too."

"What's that supposed to mean?"

"You were nuts. You'd do anything. You used to jump off your father's garage, trying to fly."

"Didn't you ever try to fly?"

"No. Never. I knew I couldn't fly."

"That's because from the day you were born, you had a one-track mind."

Morelli grinned. "It's true. My interests were narrow."

"All you ever thought about was S-E-X. You tricked innocent little girls into your father's garage, so you could look in their underpants."

"Life was a lot simpler back then. Now I have to get them drunk. And, let's be truthful, you were hardly tricked. You practically knocked me over trying to get to the garage."

"You said you were going to teach me to play choo-choo."

The grin widened. "And I kept my word."

The coffee shop door opened, and Vinnie cha-chaed in. Our eyes met, and Vinnie laughed his nasty little laugh and I knew he had something good for me.

CHAPTER
16

I left Morelli and pulled Vinnie outside the coffee shop, so we couldn't be overheard.

"I got an address," Vinnie said, still smiling, knowing his bond was close at hand, pleased to report on a fellow sexual deviant.

A rush of excitement shot from the soles of my feet clear to the roots of my hair. "Tell me!"

"I hit pay dirt with the first phone call. You were right. Moses Bedemier, everyone's favorite uncle, makes dirty movies. Not the kind you can rent in a video store either. These are the real thing! Genuine underground, quality porn.

"He goes under the name M. Bed. And he specializes in discipline. According to my source, you want a good spanking flick, you look for an M. Bed movie." Vinnie shook his head, grinning ear to ear. "I'm telling you the man is famous. He's done a whole series of fraternity initiation films. He did *Tits and Paddles, Gang Spank, Spanky Goes to College.* Real collectors' items. No holds barred. Lots of close-ups. Never fakes anything. That's the difference between the commercial junk and the underground. The underground stuff is real."

"Hold it down, Vinnie," I said. "People are staring."

Vinnie didn't pay any attention. He was waving his hands, and spittle was forming in the corners of his mouth. "The guy is a genius. And his masterpiece is *Bad Boy Bobby and the Schoolmarm*. It's a historical, done in period costume. It's a classic. The best ruler-spanking scene recorded on film."

I thought of Larry Skolnik with dropped drawers and a dunce cap and almost passed out.

"Once you set me in the right direction it was easy," Vinnie said. "I got a friend in the business. Only he does stuff with dogs. He's got a Great Dane that's hung like a bull. And he's got this dog trained to . . ."

I slapped my hands over my ears. *"Ugh! Gross!"*

"Well anyway," Vinnie said. "I was able to find out where Mo makes his movies. This friend of mine uses some of the same actors and actresses as Mo. So he gave me this woman's name. Bebe LaTouch. Heh, heh, heh. Says she's the Dane's favorite."

I felt my upper lip involuntarily curl back and my sphincter muscle tighten.

Vinnie handed me a piece of paper with directions. "I called her up, and according to Bebe, Mo has a house south of here. Off in the woods. She didn't know the address, but she knew how to get there."

This corresponded with the information I'd received from Gail and Larry. Gail told me that Harp had done business with Mo at a location other than the store. She remembered the place because she'd ridden along once when Harp had delivered a "virgin actress."

I took the directions and looked in at Morelli. He was picking at his potato chips and watching me through the door window. I gave him a finger wave and got into the pickup. I rolled the engine over and listened to the idle. Nice and even. No embarrassing backfires. No stalling.

"Thank you, Bucky," I said. And thank God for doohickeys.

I took 206 South for several miles and cut off at White Horse, leading toward Yardville, dropping south again to Crosswicks. At Crosswicks I followed a winding two-lane road to an unmarked cross street where I stopped and checked my map. Everything seemed okay, so I continued on and after about five minutes hit Doyne. I turned right onto Doyne and checked my odometer. After two miles I started looking for a rusty black mailbox at the end of a dirt driveway. I'd passed one house when I'd first made my turn, but nothing now. It was wooded on either side of the road. If Mo was out here, he was well isolated.

At three and a half miles I saw the mailbox. I stopped and squinted through the bare trees at the clapboard bungalow at the end of the driveway. In the summer the bungalow wouldn't be visible. This was the winter, and I could clearly see the carport, and the house. There was a car in the carport, but I had no way of knowing if it belonged to Mo.

I eased down the road about a quarter mile and dialed Ranger's cell phone.

Ranger answered on the fourth ring. "Yo."

"Yo yourself," I said. "I think I have a line on Mo. I'm staking out a bungalow south of Yardville. I need a backup for the takedown."

"Give me directions."

I gave the directions, tapped off on the cell phone and opened the small duffel bag I had on the seat beside me. I was wearing jeans and a turtleneck under my black leather jacket. I took the jacket off, zipped myself into a flak vest and put the jacket back on over the vest. The next item I took out of the duffel was a black nylon webbed gun belt with pouches to hold pepper spray and bludgeoning batons, not to mention my Smith & Wesson. I got out of the truck and strapped on the gun belt, filling the pouches, buckling in my gun. I adjusted the Velcro straps that held my .38 secure to my leg, tucked cuffs into the back of the belt and stuffed two spare nylon cuffs into my jacket pockets.

Now that I knew what Mo was up to I sort of wished I had rubber gloves, too.

I got back into the truck and cracked my knuckles, feeling nervous and stupid, all decked out like SWAT Princess.

I sat there until Ranger rolled to a stop behind me in the Bronco. I walked back to him and saw him smile.

"Looks like you're serious."

"People keep shooting at me."

"That's about as serious as it gets," Ranger said.

He was already wearing his vest. He strapped on his gun belt while I explained the situation.

"This is your takedown," he said. "Do you have a plan?"

"Drive in. Knock on the door. Arrest him."

"You want the front or the back?"

"I want the front."

"I'll leave the Bronco here and circle around through the woods. Give me a couple minutes to get in place, then you do your thing."

It was a long shot that Mo would be in the house. If I'd had more time I'd have set up surveillance. As it was, either we'd scare some poor soul half to death, or we'd risk getting drilled at the door. Then again, maybe Mo really didn't do any of the killing and wasn't all that dangerous.

I gave Ranger a lead and then drove down the driveway, parked behind the car in the carport and walked directly to the bungalow's front door. Shades were drawn in all the windows. I was poised to knock on the door when the door opened, and Mo peered out at me.

"Well," he said, "I guess this is it."

"You don't seem surprised to see me."

"Actually, the sound of a vehicle on my driveway gave me

quite a start. But then I realized it was you, and to tell you the truth, I was relieved."

"Afraid it was Reverend Bill?"

"So, you know about Bill." He shook his head. "I'll be happy when this is all cleared up. I don't feel safe here anymore. I don't feel safe anywhere."

I stood just inside the front door and looked around. Two bedrooms, one bath, living room, eat-in kitchen with a back door. The rug was threadbare but clean. The furniture was shabby. Not a lot of clutter. Colors were faded into a blur of neutral nothing. A couch, an overstuffed club chair, a TV and VCR. No dust on the coffee table.

"I imagine you're not safe either," Mo said. "You've been making Bill real nervous."

I did a mental head shake. I'd unwittingly camped out in front of the Freedom Church. Mo and Bill must have been panicked, thinking I was on to them. Sometimes I amazed even myself. How could a person's instincts be so wrong and at the same time so right?

Mo pulled a shade aside and peeked out the front window. "How did you find me?"

"I took a sort of roundabout route through the burg grapevine."

Mo turned back to me, horror etched onto his face. I looked into his eyes and saw his mind racing a million miles an hour.

"That's impossible," he said, anxiety pinching his lips, turning them white. "Nobody in the burg knows about this house."

"Larry Skolnik knows. You remember Larry? The kid who wrote secret messages on his arm. Works in his father's dry cleaning shop now."

I walked to the open bedroom door and looked in. Bed, neatly made. Throw rug on the floor. Bedside table with lamp and clock. The second bedroom was empty. Tracks on the rug from a recent vacuuming. A few indentations in the rug from furniture or whatever. Clearly the room had recently been cleaned out. I checked the bathroom. There was a heavy drape on the small single window. Darkroom, I thought. Mo probably did some stills of his stars. I walked back to the front door.

"I know about the movies," I said to Mo.

He gaped at me. Panicky. Still not believing. I rattled off his list of credits. Asserting my dominance. Letting Mo know that the game was over.

Mo pulled himself together and raised his chin a fraction of an inch. A defensive posture. "Well, what of it? I make art films involving consenting adults."

"Consenting, maybe. Adults is questionable. Does Reverend Bill know about your hobby?"

"Reverend Bill is one of my most devoted fans. Has been for years. Reverend Bill is a firm believer in corporal punishment for bad behavior."

"Then he knows about this house."

"Not the location. And it's not a hobby. I'm a professional filmmaker. I make good money off my films."

"I bet."

"You don't expect me to retire on the money I make selling ice cream cones, do you?" Mo snapped. "You know what the profit is on penny candy? The profit is nothing."

I hoped he didn't expect me to be sympathetic. I was having a hard time not grimacing every time I thought about my picture on his kitchen wall.

He shook his head, the spark of indignant fire sputtering out. Mo collapsing in on himself. "I can't believe this is happening to me. I was making a good living. Putting money away for retirement. I was providing entertainment to a select group of adults. I was employing deserving young people."

I did some mental eye rolling. Moses Bedemier paid street dealers to recruit fresh blood for his porno movies.

The street dealers knew the runaways and street kids. They knew the teenagers who still looked healthy and would do most anything to get a new high.

"I made one mistake," Mo said. "One mistake and everything started to unravel. It was all because of that awful Jamal Brousse." He paced to the window, clearly agitated, peeking around the shade, clasping and unclasping his hands.

"I hope you were careful not to be followed," he said. "Bill is looking for me."

"I wasn't followed." Probably.

Mo kept going, wanting to share his story, I guess, looking slightly dazed that it had all come to this, talking while he continued to pace. Probably he'd been talking and pacing for hours before I arrived, trying to talk himself into calling the police.

"All because of Brousse," he said. "A drug dealer and a purveyor. I made a single unfortunate transaction with him for a young man to model for me. I just wanted some photographs."

He held up and listened. "Bill will kill us both if he finds us here."

There was no doubt in my mind. As soon as Ranger showed up we were moving out. "What about Brousse?" I asked, more to distract myself from thoughts of Reverend Bill arriving before Ranger, than raw curiosity.

"I honored my agreement with Brousse, but he kept coming back at me, making more and more demands. Blackmailing me. I was desperate. I didn't know what to do. I might not make much money from my store, but I have a certain position in the community that I enjoy. Brousse could have ruined everything.

"And then one day Bill stopped in at the store, and I got an idea. Suppose I told Bill about this guy, Jamal Brousse, who was selling drugs to kids. I figured Bill would put a scare into him. Maybe punch him in the nose or something. Maybe scare him enough so he'd go away. Trouble was Bill liked the idea of community justice so much he killed Brousse.

"But Bill made a mistake on Brousse. Dumped him in the river, and Brousse bobbed in to shore two hours later. Bill didn't like that. Said it was messy. I wanted to stop there, but Bill pressed me to give him another name. I finally caved in, and next thing, Bill had killed another dealer and buried him in my cellar. Before I knew it my cellar was full of dead drug dealers. Even after I got arrested, Bill kept up the killing. Only now it was harder to get to the cellar, so we just hid the bodies as best we could. Cameron Brown, Leroy Watkins." Mo shook his head. "Bill was obsessed with the killing. He organized a death squad. And that was so successful Bill started killing not just dealers but hard-core drug users. The death squad learned how to kill the addicts with ODs, so it'd look more natural.

"That's why I hired an attorney. I couldn't be part of all that craziness anymore. They were even talking about killing you. And you wouldn't believe who was taking part in this. Cops, shoe salesmen, grandmothers and school-teachers. It was insanity. It was like one of those cult things. Like those militia people you see on the television out in Idaho. I even got caught up in it for a while. Carrying a gun. And then that police officer discovered it, and I panicked. It was the gun that had killed Brousse. What was I thinking?"

"Why did you hire a lawyer? Why didn't you just turn yourself in?"

"I'm an old man. I don't want to spend the rest of my life in jail. I guess I hoped if I was cooperative and had a good lawyer I might get off easier. I didn't kill anyone, you know. I just gave Bill some names and set up some meetings."

"You were still participating after you'd gotten a lawyer. You set up Elliot Harp."

"I couldn't get out. I was afraid. I didn't want anyone to know I was talking to the police. As it is, every time I hear a car on the road out there I break into a sweat, thinking it's Bill, and he's found out and come to get me.

"I just wish I'd had some other choice right from the beginning. I feel like I started this in motion. This nightmare."

"There always are choices," Ranger said, laying the barrel of his .44 magnum alongside Mo's head.

Mo rolled his eyes to look at Ranger. "Where'd you come from? I didn't hear you come in!"

"I come in like the fog on little cat feet."

I looked at Ranger. "Very nice."

"Carl Sandburg," Ranger said. "More or less."

Gravel crunched under tire treads outside, and Mo jumped beside me. "It's him!"

I pulled the shade and looked out. "It's not Reverend Bill."

Ranger and Mo raised their eyebrows at me in silent question.

"You're not going to believe this," I said.

I answered the knock at the door and revealed Lula standing on the stoop, beaming, looking pleased.

"Hey girlfriend," she said. "Vinnie told me all about this hideaway house, and I came out to give you a hand."

Mo's voice cracked. "It's the lunatic in the red Firebird!"

"Hunh," Lula said.

I got Mo's jacket from the hall closet and bundled him into it, at the same time checking him for weapons. I ushered him out the front door and was standing with him on the stoop when I caught the far-off sound of a car on the road. We all paused. The car drew closer. We caught a flash of blue through the trees, and then the vehicle turned into the drive. It was a Ford Econoline van with FREEDOM CHURCH lettered on the side. It stopped halfway to the house, its forward progress halted by Lula's Firebird. The side door to the van slid open and a man in mask and coveralls got out. We stared at each other for a moment, and then he hefted a rocket launcher to his shoulder. There was a flash of fire and a *pfnufff!* And my truck blew up, its doors shooting off into space like Frisbees.

"That's a warning shot," the man yelled. "We want Mo."

I was speechless. They'd blown up my truck! They'd turned it into a big yellow fireball.

"Look on the bright side," Lula said to me. "You're not going to have to worry about that puppy stalling no more."

"It was fixed!"

Two more men got out of the van. They sighted assault rifles, and we all stumbled back into the house and slammed the door shut.

"If they can blow up a truck, they can blow up a house," Ranger said, pulling car keys from his pocket, handing them to me. "Take Mo out the back door while I pin these guys down. Cut through the woods to my Bronco and get the hell out of here."

"What about you? I'm not going to leave you here!"

The house was peppered with gunshot, and we all hit the deck.

Ranger knocked out window glass and opened fire. "I'll be fine. I'll give you a good start, and then I'll lose myself in the woods." He glanced over at me. "I've done this before."

I grabbed Mo and shoved him toward the back door. Lula ran after us. All of us scuttled in a crouch across the small backyard to the woods while gunfire once again erupted from the driveway. Mo was struggling to run, and Lula was shouting, "Oh shit! Oh shit!"

We slid on our asses down a small embankment, scrambled to our feet and kept going, crashing through dry, viny undergrowth. Not what you'd call a quiet retreat, but quiet didn't matter with World War III going on behind us.

When I thought we'd gone far enough I began curving back toward the road. There was another explosion, and I turned to see a fireball rise to the sky.

"Has to be the bungalow," Lula said.

Her tone was somber. Ominous. Both of us thinking of Ranger.

Mo went down to his knees, his face chalk white, his hand holding his side where a dark stain had begun to spread on his gray coat. A drop of blood hit dry leaves.

"He must have caught one in the house," Lula said.

I tried to hoist Mo back to his feet. "You can make it," I said. "It's not that much farther."

Sirens sounded on the road, and I saw the red flash of police light bars flicker through the trees to my left.

Mo made an effort to stand and collapsed altogether, facedown on the forest floor.

"Run to the road and get help," I told Lula. "I'll stay here."

"You got a gun?"

"Yeah."

"It loaded?"

"Yes. Go!"

She hesitated. "I don't like leaving you."

"Go!"

She swiped at her eyes. "Shit. I'm scared."

She turned and ran. Looked back once and disappeared from view.

I dragged Mo behind a tree, putting the tree trunk between us and the house. I drew my gun and hunkered down.

I really needed to find another job.

It was dark when Lula dropped me off in my parking lot.

"Good thing Morelli and a bunch of cops were following that Freedom Church van," Lula said. "We would have been toast."

"The cops were following the Freedom van. Morelli was following me."

"Lucky you," Lula said.

Mickey's hands were pointing to seven o'clock, but it felt much later. I was tired to the bone, and I had the beginnings of a headache. I shuffled to the elevator and leaned on the button. Thank goodness for elevators, I thought. I'd sleep in the lobby before I'd be able to muster the energy to walk up the stairs.

Lula, Ranger and I had answered questions at police headquarters for what seemed like hours.

Dickie had popped in while I was talking to yet another detective and offered to represent me. I told him I wasn't being charged with anything, but thanks anyway. He seemed disappointed. Probably was hoping he could plea-bargain me into the license plate factory. Keep me away from Mallory. Or maybe he was hoping I'd done something heinous. I could see the headlines: EX-WIFE OF PROMINENT TRENTON ATTORNEY COMMITS HEINOUS CRIME. ATTORNEY SAYS HE ISN'T SURPRISED.

Just before I left the station word came down that Mo was out of surgery and looked pretty good. There'd been a lot of blood lost, but the bullet had entered and exited clean, missing all vital organs. The news had brought a sense of relief and closure. I'd been psyched to that point, hyped on adrenaline. When I finally signed my name to the printed statement of the day's events and realized Mo would make it, the last dregs of energy dribbled out of me.

Rex and I checked out the feast on the coffee table. Rex from his cage. Me from the couch. Bucket of extra-spicy fried chicken, tray of biscuits, container of cole slaw, baked beans. Plus half a chocolate cake, left over from Saturday dinner with my parents.

The Rangers were playing Boston at the Garden, which meant I was wearing my home team white jersey. It was the end of the first period and the Rangers were ahead by a goal.

"This is the life," I said to Rex. "Doesn't get much better than this."

I reached for a piece of chicken and was startled by a knock on my door.

"Don't worry," I said to Rex. "It's probably just Mrs. Bestler."

But I knew it wasn't Mrs. Bestler. Mrs. Bestler never knocked on my door this late at night. No one knocked on my door this late at night. No one who wasn't trouble. It had been a couple weeks since the two masked men had pushed their way into my apartment, but the experience had left me cautious. I'd enrolled in a self-defense class and was careful not to get so tired that my guard was down. Not that the men in the masks were still threatening.

Reverend Bill and the death squad were living rent free, courtesy of the federal government. And that didn't include Mickey Maglio. There'd been cops involved, but he hadn't been one of them. The man who'd burned me had been Reverend Bill's brother-in-law, imported from Jersey City. At least I'd been right about the accent.

Undoubtedly there were some closet vigilantes still at large, but they were keeping a low profile. Some of the wind had gone out of the movement's sails when Mo's secret life was made public information. And whatever vigilante momentum had been left had died a natural death without Reverend Bill acting as catalyst.

I quietly walked to the door and looked out through my peephole. Joe Morelli looked back at me. I should have guessed.

I opened the door to him. "You must have smelled the chicken."

Morelli grinned and rocked back on his heels. "I wouldn't want to impose."

Yeah, right. I got him a beer from the fridge. "Haven't seen you in a while."

"Not since we closed the case on Mo. You never returned my phone calls."

I flopped onto the couch. "Nothing to say."

Morelli took a pull at his beer. "You still pissed off at me for withholding information?"

"Yes. I helped you out with Dickie, and you gave me nothing in return."

"That's not true. I gave you Reverend Bill."

"Only because you knew I'd get it from other sources. I'm glad I ralphed on you that night in your kitchen."

"I suppose that was my fault too?"

"Damn skippy it was." I actually accepted full responsibility, but I had no intention of conveying this to Morelli.

Morelli took a piece of chicken. "Everyone at headquarters is very impressed with you. You were the only one to pick up on the movie angle."

"Thanks to Sue Ann Grebek and her motor mouth. When she told me about Larry Skolnik I thought about Cameron Brown. The Cameron Brown murder never felt right to me. He sold some drugs, but he wasn't a major player. His primary source of income was prostitution. Then Larry and Gail confirmed it. In fact, Larry had already figured most of it out."

The Rangers scored another goal, and we leaned forward to watch the replay.

I'd been reading the papers and talking to Eddie Gazarra, so I knew some of the details on Mo and Reverend Bill. I knew that both of them were coming up to trial. I wasn't sure what would happen to Mo, but Bill was up on seven counts of murder one. Plus, in a late-afternoon raid, the Alcohol, Tobacco and Firearms people hauled enough weapons out of the two Freedom houses on Montgomery Street to fill a five-ton U-Haul. That was way over the limit for anarchist stockpiling.

"I hear you're back to working vice."

Morelli nodded. "I didn't have the wardrobe for homicide. And they actually expected me to shave every day."

"You still living in the house?"

"Yeah. I like it. It's got more space. Lots of closets. Bigger kitchen. Cellar." He leaned close. "It's even got a back door."

I slid him a sideways glance.

He drew a little circle at my temple with his fingertip, and the pitch dropped on his voice. "It's got a backyard, too."

"Backyards are nice."

The fingertip traced down to my collarbone. "Good for summer activities . . . like barbecues."

I hauled back and looked at him. Morelli barbecuing?

"Play your cards right and I might invite you over for a hamburger," Morelli said.

"Just a hamburger?"

"More than a hamburger."

This brought to mind the old adage—be careful what you wish for because you might get it.

Morelli let some smile creep into his voice. "After the hamburger I could show you my garage. Did I mention that I had a garage?"

"Not until now."

"Well, I have a garage, and I know a game . . ."

Oh boy. "I think I know this game."

The smile spread to his eyes. "Yeah?"

"It has to do with . . . transportation. Trains and such."

"I've learned some new routes since the last time we played," he said.

And then his lips brushed the nape of my neck, sending a jolt of fire straight to my doodah.

Read on for a taste of

VISIONS OF SUGAR PLUMS

By Janet Evanovich

Available from Penguin at £5.99

1

My name is Stephanie Plum and I've got a strange man in my kitchen. He appeared out of nowhere. One minute I was sipping coffee, mentally planning out my day. And then the next minute . . . *poof*, there he was.

He was over six feet, with wavy blond hair pulled into a ponytail, deep-set brown eyes, and an athlete's body. He looked to be late twenties, maybe thirty. He was dressed in jeans, boots, a grungy white thermal shirt hanging loose over the jeans, and a beat-up black leather jacket hanging on broad shoulders. He was sporting two days of beard growth, and he didn't look happy.

"Well, isn't this perfect," he said, clearly disgusted, hands on hips, taking me in.

My heart was tap-dancing in my chest. I was at a total loss. I didn't know what to think or what to say. I didn't know who he was or how he got into my kitchen. He was frightening, but even more than that he had me flustered. It was like going to a birthday party and arriving a day early. It was like . . . what the heck's going on?

"How?" I asked. "What?"

"Hey, don't ask me, lady," he said. "I'm as surprised as you are."

"How'd you get into my apartment?"

"Sweet cakes, you wouldn't believe me if I told you." He moved to the refrigerator, opened the door, and helped himself to a beer. He cracked the beer open, took a long pull, and wiped his mouth with the back of his hand. "You know how people get beamed down on *Star Trek*? It's sort of like that."

Okay, so I've got a big slob of a guy drinking beer in my kitchen, and I think he might be crazy. The only other possibility I can come up with is that I'm hallucinating and he isn't real. I smoked some pot in college but that was about it. Don't think I'd get a flashback from wacky tobacky. There were mushrooms on the pizza last night. Could that be it?

Fortunately, I work in bail bond enforcement, and I'm sort of used to scary guys showing up in closets and under beds. I inched my way across the kitchen, stuck my hand into my brown bear cookie jar, and pulled out my .38 five-shot Smith & Wesson.

"Cripes," he said, "what are you gonna do, shoot me? Like that would change anything." He looked more closely at the gun and shook his head in another wave of disgust. "Honey, there aren't any bullets in that gun."

"There might be one," I said. "I might have one chambered."

"Yeah, right." He finished the beer and sauntered out of the kitchen, into the living room. He looked around and moved to the bedroom.

"Hey," I yelled. "Where do you think you're going?"

He didn't stop.

"That's it," I told him. "I'm calling the police."

"Give me a break," he said. "I'm having a really shitty day." He kicked his boots off and flopped onto my bed, scoping out the room from his prone position. "Where's the television?"

"In the living room."

"Oh man, you don't even have a television in your bedroom. How crapola is this?"

I cautiously moved closer to the bed, and I reached out and touched him.

"Yeah, I'm real," he said. "Sort of. And all my equipment works." He smiled for the first time. It was a knock-your-socks-off smile. Dazzling white teeth and good-humored eyes that crinkled at the corners. "In case you're interested."

The smile was good. The news was bad. I didn't know what *sort of real* meant. And I wasn't sure I liked the idea that his equipment worked. All in all, it didn't do a lot to help my heart rate. Truth is, I'm pretty much a chicken-shit bounty hunter. Still, while I'm not the world's bravest person, I can bluff with the best of them, so I did an eye roll. "Get a grip."

"You'll come around," he said. "They always do."

"They?"

"Women. Women love me," he said.

Good thing I didn't have a bullet chambered as threatened because I'd definitely shoot this guy. "Do you have a name?"

"Diesel."

"Is that your first name or your last name?"

"That's my whole name. Who are *you*?"

"Stephanie Plum."

"You live here alone?"

"No."

"That's a big fib," he said. "You have *living alone* written all over you."

I narrowed my eyes. "Excuse me?"

"You're not exactly a sex goddess," he said. "Hair from hell. Baggy sweatpants. No makeup. Lousy personality. Not that there isn't some potential. You have an okay shape. What are you, 34B? And you've got a good mouth. Nice pouty lips." He threw me another smile. "A guy could get ideas looking at those lips."

Great. The nutcase who somehow got into my apartment was getting ideas about my lips. Thoughts of serial rapists and sex killings went racing through my mind. My mother's warnings echoed in my ears. *Watch out for strangers. Keep your door locked.* Yes, but it's not my fault, I reasoned. My door *was* locked. What's with that?

I took his boots, carried them to the front door, and threw them into the hall. "Your boots are in the hall," I yelled. "If you don't come get them, I'm pitching them down the trash chute."

My neighbor, Mr. Wolesky, stepped out of the elevator. He was holding a small white bakery bag in his hand. "Look at this," he said, "I'm starting the day with a doughnut. That's what Christmas does to me. It makes me crazy and then I need a doughnut. Four days to Christmas and the stores are picked clean," he said. "And they all say everything's on sale but I know they jack up the prices. They always gotta gouge you at Christmas. There should be a law. Somebody should look into it."

Mr. Wolesky unlocked his door, lurched inside, and slammed the door after himself. The door lock clicked into place, and I heard Mr. Wolesky's television go on.

Diesel elbowed me aside, went into the hall, and retrieved his boots. "You know, you have a real attitude problem," he said.

"Attitude this," I told him, closing my door, locking him out of the apartment.

The bolt shot back, the lock tumbled, and Diesel opened the door, walked to the couch, and sat down to put his boots on.

Hard to pick an emotion here. Confused and astounded would be high on the list. Scared bonkers wasn't far behind. "How'd you do that?" I said, squeaky-voiced and breathless. "How'd you unlock my door?"

"I don't know. It's just one of those things we can do."

Goosebumps prickled on my forearms. "Now I'm really creeped out."

"Relax. I'm not going to hurt you. Hell, I'm supposed to

make your life better." He gave a snort and another bark of laughter at that. "Yeah, right," he said.

Deep breath, Stephanie. Not a terrific time to hyperventilate. If I passed out from lack of oxygen God knows what would happen. Suppose he was from outer space, and he conducted an anal probe while I was unconscious? A shiver ripped through me. Yuk! "What are we looking at here?" I asked him. "Ghost? Vampire? Space alien?"

He slouched back into the couch and zapped the television on. "You're in the ball park."

I was at a loss. How do you get rid of someone who can unlock locks? You can't even have him arrested by the police. And even if I decided to call the police, what would I say? I have a sort-of-real guy in my apartment?

"Suppose I cuffed you and chained you to something. What then?"

He was channel surfing, concentrating on the television. "I could get loose."

"Suppose I shot you?"

"I'd be pissed off. And it's not smart to piss me off."

"But could I kill you? Could I hurt you?"

"What is this, twenty questions? I'm looking for a game here. What time is it, anyway? And where am I?"

"You're in Trenton, New Jersey. It's eight o'clock in the morning. And you didn't answer my question."

He flipped the television off. "Crud. Trenton. I should have guessed. Eight in the morning. I have a whole day to look forward to. Wonderful. And the answer to your question is . . . a qualified no. It wouldn't be easy to kill me, but I suppose if you put your mind to it you could come up with something."

read more ⓟ

JANET EVANOVICH

ONE FOR THE MONEY   JANET EVANOVICH

Stephanie Plum is down on her luck. She's lost her job, her car's on the brink of repossession, and her apartment is fast becoming furniture-free.

Enter Cousin Vinnie, a low-life who runs a bail-bond company. If Stephanie can bring in vice cop turned outlaw Joe Morelli, she stands to pick up $10,000. But tracking down a cop wanted for murder isn't easy. And when Benito Ramirez, a prize-fighter with more menace than mentality, wants to be her friend Stephanie soon knows what it's like to be pursued. Unfortunately the best person to protect her just happens to be on the run ...

Winner of the Crime Writer's Association John Creasy Memorial Dagger

JANET EVANOVICH

TWO FOR THE DOUGH   JANET EVANOVICH

Kenny Mancuso shot his childhood buddy Moogey Bues in the knee and then jumped bail. Now bounty hunter extraordinaire Stephanie Plum is on the case to track Kenny down.

Then someone finished Moogey off, Kenny can't be found, twenty-four coffins are missing, and there's some ex-army heavy artillery roaming the streets. And

Joe Morelli – the cop with more than a professional interest in her every move – is tailing Stephanie.

With a healthy disregard for the law, and an unhealthy dependence on marshmallow hot chocolate, Stephanie's a match for anyone – even Morelli. That is, until her eccentric grandmother goes AWOL and little pieces of corpses start to disappear . . .

Winner of the Crime Writers' Association Last Laugh Dagger

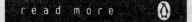

JANET EVANOVICH

VISIONS OF SUGARPLUMS   JANET EVANOVICH

It's five days before christmas, and Stephanie Plum's problems are mounting by the minute. The season of goodwill is not so much passing her by as whizzing past her ears. In her role as bounty hunter, she's been assigned to bring in an elusive seventy-four-year-old toy maker called Sandy Claws. Oh, and that strange man in her apartment *just won't leave*.

Visions of Sugarplums takes Stephanie Plum on a Christmas adventure and introduces a new character that readers will adore. He's as mysterious as Ranger, as sexy as Morelli and ... well, we won't say any more!

refresh yourself at penguin.co.uk

Visit penguin.co.uk for exclusive information and interviews with
bestselling authors, fantastic give-aways and the
inside track on all our books, from the Penguin Classics
to the latest bestsellers.

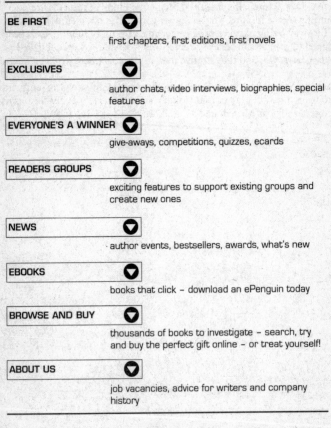

BE FIRST ▼

first chapters, first editions, first novels

EXCLUSIVES ▼

author chats, video interviews, biographies, special
features

EVERYONE'S A WINNER ▼

give-aways, competitions, quizzes, ecards

READERS GROUPS ▼

exciting features to support existing groups and
create new ones

NEWS ▼

author events, bestsellers, awards, what's new

EBOOKS ▼

books that click – download an ePenguin today

BROWSE AND BUY ▼

thousands of books to investigate – search, try
and buy the perfect gift online – or treat yourself!

ABOUT US ▼

job vacancies, advice for writers and company
history

Get Closer To Penguin . . . www.penguin.co.uk